HAVE
I GOT A
STORY
FOR YOU

HAVE
I GOT A
STORY
FOR YOU

MORE THAN A CENTURY OF
FICTION FROM THE *Forward*

EDITED BY EZRA GLINTER

INTRODUCTION BY DARA HORN

W. W. Norton & Company

INDEPENDENT PUBLISHERS SINCE 1923

NEW YORK · LONDON

This book was made possible with the generous support of Edward
Blank and is dedicated to the memory of his mother, May Cohn.

The Story "Zeydes un eyneklekh" ("Grandfathers and
Grandchildren") was published in *Di Kloyz un di gas: dertseylungen*.
Copyright © 1974 by Chaim Grade. Permission granted by YIVO
and its agent, Robin Straus Agency, Inc.

The story "Ekskursye af tsurik" ("A Journey Back in Time") was
published in *Balade fun a kholem*. Copyright © 1986 by Blume Lempel.
Permission granted by Paul Lempel.

The translation of "Mona Bubbe" by Yente Mash was supported in
part by the Yiddish Book Center's translation fellowship program.

Manufacturing by RR Donnelley, North Harrisonburg
Book design by Brooke Koven
Production manager: Louise Mattarelliano

ISBN 978-0-393-06270-0

W. W. Norton & Company, Inc.
500 Fifth Avenue, New York, N.Y. 10110
www.wwnorton.com

W. W. Norton & Company Ltd.
15 Carlisle Street, London W1D 3BS

1 2 3 4 5 6 7 8 9 0

CONTENTS

PREFACE

by Ezra Glinter

O N A SPRING day in 1902, Abraham Cahan was walking along East Broadway towards Division Street, where the *Forward* offices were then located, when he was stopped by William Lief and Albert Feller, the advertising managers of the newspaper. At that time, Cahan was not the editor. Although he had helped found the socialist Yiddish newspaper almost five years earlier, he had quit shortly afterwards and had gone to work for New York's English-language press.

Now the *Forward* had fallen on hard times, and its business managers wanted Cahan back. They believed that his populist sensibilities would save the newspaper from a premature decline, and they would later be proven right. But at that moment, Cahan was unenthusiastic. He had worked for New York's biggest news outlets and had a promising literary career, with short stories in magazines likes *Cosmopolitan* and the *Atlantic Monthly*. Going back to the Yiddish press was not an enticing prospect.

And yet, Cahan went back. Perhaps he agreed to return to the *Forward* because this time he was promised the editorial control he had demanded in the first place. And perhaps he made the choice because he was struggling creatively and thought that the rough-and-tumble of Yiddish journalism would reinspire his writing. But Cahan also took the reins of the *Forward* because he believed the newspaper itself to be a vital creative outlet. It was, as he conceived it, not just a place to report the news, but a kind of "living novel." It told the story of its time and place from the front cover to the back page, through every news report, opinion column, cartoon, poem, recipe, essay, political polemic, and theater review. The *Forward*, in the end, would be his greatest work of literature.

Like other newspapers of its time, the *Forward* published literature in a more conventional sense as well. In its early days this consisted mostly of translations—Tolstoy was a favorite—but the *Forward* soon became associated with the most talented Yiddish writers of the day, from Sholem Asch and Avrom Reyzen in its early decades to Isaac Bashevis Singer and Chaim Grade in later ones. Under the leadership of Cahan and his successors, the newspaper became home to serialized novels and novellas, humor sketches and one-act plays, "high literature" and sensational potboilers. Often the paper would be running two or three novels at once, in addition to short fiction, belles-lettres, and poetry. For more than a century the *Forward* produced an immense trove of literature, most of which remained untapped—until now.

When I began work on this project, I started with a fairly basic research method—to learn from secondary sources which were considered the best as-yet-untranslated pieces the *Forward* had published and go through the microfilm archive to find them. This turned out to be a laborious process. Aside from a few famous authors, bibliographic resources for Yiddish writers are sparse. Often the best I could do was determine the year—or the decade—when a certain writer was appearing in the paper and hope to hit on the story I had in mind. Sometimes I would find the piece I was looking for quickly; at other times I would despair that it ever existed at all.

But the many hours I spent hunched over the microfilm reader had unexpected benefits. While I might have gone in looking for a particular item, I often came out bearing other treasures, some of which made their way into the final selection. Looking at the newspaper's presentation allowed me to see what role each writer played in its overall structure and the value editors placed on particular pieces. Most important, while scrolling through months and years of the *Forward* I had the opportunity to see these stories in the larger context of the newspaper—in other words, to see them as readers first did.

A newspaper, after all, is a diverse entity. The stories now in this book were nestled amid world news, the *Bintel Briv* advice column, reports on labor and union politics, comics, recipes, movie reviews, and advertisements for everything from Ex-Lax to grand pianos. Sometimes the fiction was connected directly to the news, as with B. Kovner's "How Pinnie Celebrated Election Day," which appeared next to an editorial about the defeat of Tammany Hall. Often the connections were less direct, but no less meaningful. When Roshelle Weprinsky's story "By a Far Shore" was published in March of 1942, the front page of the newspaper was full of news of the war and its atrocities. The same issue carried two pseudonymous pieces by Isaac Bashevis Singer on the subjects of pop psychology and war rationing, and a serialized novel by the *Forward*'s future Middle East correspondent, Shlomo Ben-Israel, titled *His 41st Wife*. High literature, that was not.

These cultural-historical associations—the totality of this "living novel"—bound together the contents of the newspaper and gave these works a layer of meaning that is difficult to extract from the whole. While the historical context of these pieces is often still evident— Sholem Asch's novella *The Jewish Soldier* appeared in the very first months of the First World War, for example—inevitably much is lost. And this is only one of the present volume's inevitable limitations.

One of the great joys of putting together this collection was the opportunity to unearth writing that may never have been read by anyone ever again, and to give it new life in a new language. Yet for all of the writers included in this book, many more were excluded, including many who were essential contributors to the *Forward* for decades. And the *Forward* was not the only Yiddish newspaper to publish literature, or even the best. It was simply the biggest, the wealthiest, and now the longest-lasting. Thus, the writers in these pages turned out to be the winners of a kind of posthumous lottery. But their peers, whose work languishes in newspapers like the *Tog* (*Day*) or the *Frayhayt* (*Freedom*) are no less worthy.

In style and theme the stories collected here are extraordinarily diverse, representing the breadth of material that the *Forward* published. But this book excludes the serialized novels that constituted much of the *Forward*'s literary output, not to mention the immense amount of poetry, memoir, belles-letters, travelogue, literary criticism, and other genres that filled its pages. And of course it leaves out the sheer journalism that the newspaper produced over the decades: a 1934 front-page story by Israel Joshua Singer describing a rally of some 20,000 American Nazi supporters at Madison Square Garden; a 1967 profile of David Ben-Gurion by Elie Wiesel; pieces by Isaac Bashevis Singer on everything from the Lubavitcher Rebbe to experiments in hypnotism and extrasensory perception.

Yet the stories and novellas contained in this volume still have a collective meaning that goes beyond their individual merits. The fiction in this book offers a picture not only of the writers who contributed to the newspaper, but also of millions of readers for whom they were writing. Through these stories we are granted a glimpse into their imaginative worlds, from the immigrants newly arrived on American shores to contemporary readers of Yiddish who read and contribute to and translate from the *Forward* to this day, both in print and online. It is their world that Cahan tried to get down on newsprint, and to create from it his living novel. Through this collection, it lives on.

ACKNOWLEDGMENTS

ALTHOUGH I HAD the unique pleasure of assembling this collection and of editing its translations, none of this would have been possible without the assistance and contributions of many people. I owe a special gratitude to all of my colleagues at the *Forward* who made up for my weekly absences while I worked on this book, and especially to Adam Langer, Bob Goldfarb, Chana Pollack, and Jordan Kutzik, whose help, advice, and support were critical throughout the process. Equally important were the talented staff at W. W. Norton, including my editor, Amy Cherry, her assistant Remy Cawley, and rights manager Jillian Brall, whose advice was indispensable to this project. Most of all I owe an immense debt to all of the translators who worked with me on this volume and who greatly exceeded their duties by helping me with research and recommendations, and who contributed their talents for a fraction of what they are worth.

A research-intensive project such as this could never exist without the organizations, staff, and facilities that make such work possible. My thanks go to the YIVO Institute for Jewish Research and the Center for Jewish History for providing me and many other researchers with their beautiful facilities at no charge, and to Zachary Loeb and his colleagues for patiently assisting with countless microfilm and book requests. I also thank Jan Shwarz, Amanda Siegel, David Stromberg, and Amir Shomroni for sharing their research and recommendations, and Eddy Portnoy for being my first guide to the vast world of newspaper microfilm. And I am immensely grateful to the family members of the writers included in these pages, who graciously shared their own family histories and memories with me.

On behalf of the *Forward*, I'd also like to express my appreciation to Edward Blank, whose generous financial sponsorship made this book possible. This book is dedicated to the memory of his mother, May Cohn, who came to the United States for the opportunity to be free and whose love, sacrifice, and counsel helped him achieve his potential.

For writers, an editor is usually their sounding board, encouraging good instincts and curbing weaker ones. But to whom does an editor turn for such advice? For me that person was most often Esther Goodman, my Yiddish teacher of many years, who was the first person with whom I read most of these stories and who never failed to offer her unvarnished opinion of their merits. Last but not least, I owe everything to my parents, Nancy and Harry Glinter, without whom nothing I do would be possible, and to my grandmothers, Clara Cohen and Mania Epstein, who lived in a world of Yiddish long before I ever had the privilege of entering it. These stories are for them.

INTRODUCTION

by Dara Horn

W HAT DOES IT mean to be the "newspaper of record"? The question seems simple, but it goes to the heart of everything it means to be part of a culture, a civilization, and more fundamentally, to be a human being.

For the better part of a hundred years, the *Forward* was the newspaper of record for American Jews—and not merely for American Jews, but for Ashkenazi Jewish culture as a whole. While many other Yiddish-language publications thrived in the Americas, in pre-Holocaust Europe, and elsewhere in the world, none came close to the *Forward*'s reach. At its peak, the *Forward*'s daily circulation exceeded 250,000 copies, a number that all but a handful of English-language publications today would envy. With size came stature and influence. This marquee publication had the power to attract the most talented writers of the time both domestically and overseas, and even in some cases to sponsor them for American immigration.

The *Forward*'s journalistic mission went deeper than just reporting current events. The paper's most influential editor, Abraham Cahan, used it to change the Yiddish language itself, teaching immigrant readers English while they were still reading in Yiddish. The appearance of such Anglicized expressions as *makhn a lebn* (to make a living), which did not exist in European Yiddish, were not merely descriptions of how readers spoke, but prescriptions for how they *should* speak. A *Forward* reader was expected to become an American as quickly as possible, with help from the *Forward*.

With its foreign correspondents, coverage of matters ignored by the English-language press, advice columns for new Americans, even the adjustments to the Yiddish language—all this would suffice to make the *Forward* the "paper of record" of the Ashkenazi world.

But what does it mean to record human experience? If this question matters to every person on the planet, imagine how much more it might mean for those people whose entire world has disappeared while they still live and breathe. This outlandish scenario, the equivalent of surviving a zombie apocalypse, was the normal daily life of the vast majority of *Forward* readers from 1897 to the present. In a sense, it has been the Jewish reality since the destruction of the Second Temple in 70 C.E. But this cycle of destruction and displacement accelerated exponentially in the years since the *Forward*'s founding. Its earliest generation of readers abandoned a Europe their families had inhabited for over a thousand years. Its subsequent readers survived the physical destruction of that world. Even the Yiddish *Forward*'s readers and contributors today are often survivors of a new exile, Jews who fled former Communist countries and who, like earlier *Forward* readers, now find their lives divided between two worlds, one of them gone forever.

If our world were to suddenly vanish, would we be satisfied if the record of our civilization consisted only of its facts—of chronicles recounting who won what battle, or who won which election, or who said what about which scandal, or who was murdered and how? This is what news reporting consists of. Of course, reporting of this sort is essential to a functioning civil society. But as a record of human experience it is hollow, for it implies that the only thing worth remembering is who won and who lost. And this is what really made the *Forward* the newspaper of record for Ashkenazi Jews the world over: its record of private emotional experiences that would never make headlines. This record exists in the paper's published literary fiction. And now, for the first time, English-language readers are invited to enter that world.

Consider the very first story in this collection, "Golde's Lament" by Rokhl Brokhes. Anyone who has visited Ellis Island knows the basic facts of the mass migration of European Jewish immigrants to this country at the turn of the last century. But it is one thing to consider the statistics, read the documents, or visit the museums that have turned this migration into an official episode in American history. It is something else entirely to see this great departure through the eyes of Golde, whose chronically unemployed husband Leybe is leaving for America and saving desperately needed money by traveling with a female neighbor posing as his wife. Golde suffers silently until the night before Leybe leaves, when she bursts into uncontrollable wailing, her greatest pain a bottomless jealousy that she cannot admit to anyone. The story unpacks Golde's and Leybe's fears and regrets but also their generosities, the profound love revealed in their choices. In the subtle shades of their emotions, we twenty-first century readers recognize, with sudden humility, just how much our official records have infantilized these people, how much we have underestimated them, how little we know them. And this is only the beginning of this American Jewish story.

We know, or think we know, what it meant for these Jewish immigrants to turn themselves into Americans: to change languages, shed habits, and renegotiate religious, family, and work commitments. But we would never imagine it the way *Forward* editor Abraham Cahan presents it in the excerpt from his novella *The Additional Soul*. The story traces the paths of two Jewish immigrants: Shneur Zadobnik, a wealthy hedonist who rebuilds his wealth in America by operating a chain of bars and brothels, and Motke the Hatmaker, a poor fool whose failure to make it in New York drives him to small-town Pennsylvania. From that description you might think you already know this story, because the official record of American immigration is all about material triumph, success and failure announced at the bank. But that's not what interests Cahan. Instead he describes these men's "additional souls"—deeper spiritual dimensions of their characters that can expand or contract, and for which the radically different circumstances in America and Europe make all the difference.

In Europe, the pageantry of wealth included public charity as well as entertaining religious scholars and secular intellectuals. These rituals provided Zadobnik with spiritual enrichment: "The true humbleness, which would come upon him in a split second, the delicate feelings that fine company would inspire in him, the sweet elusive dreams of an honest, fine life—that was the sanctification of his good fortune." But in America, Zadobnik's wealth does not entitle him to spiritual perks, and his soul withers. Motke, meanwhile, had been a laughingstock in Russia, a pimp's lackey who playacted at madness as a way of coping with debasement. But in Pennsylvania, the narrator hardly recognizes him. Motke, though still poor, has remade himself in his new community as a respected man.

The story is a psychological dive into what it means to be a person when all of one's circumstances have been altered. If someone can change so much, is there such a thing as integrity of character or soul? In a story written in English, this might seem like a ponderous question. But Cahan's Yiddish makes this question much larger than merely a commentary on immigrants in America. It is the existential question about what makes us who we are—a question that Judaism has been asking for millennia. The novella's title, *The Additional Soul*, is an expression used to describe the spiritual amplification Jews are said to receive on the Sabbath. Cahan could have settled for social commentary. Instead he joins a three-thousand-year-old conversation about free will and destiny.

This depth of insight even appears in the *Forward*'s lighter fictional fare. Many Americans know the term "Yente" and think it is a Yiddish word meaning "busybody." But Yente is simply a woman's name—a name made famous by Yente Telebende, a fictional character in a hugely popular *Forward* humor series by the author B. Kovner that was later featured on the Yiddish stage and the *Forward*'s radio hour. Yente, her husband, and their children, are trying to survive in Brownsville, an immigrant neighborhood where many of the *Forward*'s readers lived. Making it in a new country was a challenge, but it also brought out people's true colors, including Yente's, whose philosophy of life seems to be an insistence on getting her way. Poverty and social mores never keep Yente from what she wants, whether she's faking an ethnic identity in order to confound a bigoted landlord, buying a new mattress she can't afford (and which her son soon burns for fun), or providing her own full-volume commentary on the Metropolitan Opera. Yente's children, too, have internalized her refusal to be refused by this new country. Her son Pinnie comes home with bags of coal the family desperately needs but can't afford. Convinced he's stealing, Yente forces her husband to follow the boy. He soon discovers his son's method: Pinnie taunts and provokes local merchants until they throw coal at him to make him go away. Pinnie thus heats the family's home all winter, as his mother praises him: "It's obvious: he's growing into a businessman." These stories are silly, slapstick, the opposite of profound. Yet reading them over a century later is an unexpectedly moving experience, because they feel so familiar. There is a seed within them of what has become an informal American Jewish identity: people uninterested in bowing to conventions, because conventions never served them well; people who see opportunities others overlook, because through inherited anxiety they are always looking; people who, after centuries of degradation, no longer take "no" for an answer. A paper of record might well provide the details of an immigrant group's political and economic challenges, as the *Forward* always did. But in the *Forward*'s fiction we find something greater and truer: a psychological record of the invention of American Jews.

That record took on greater meaning as the paper's readers became entrenched in America, and as they watched from a distance as their former world burned to the ground. The First World War and the Russian Civil War began the physical destruction of Eastern European Jewish life, complete with massacres on the Jewish home front and the mass conscription of teenagers into the jaws of violent death. One of the most wrenching stories here is "The Jewish Soldier" by the renowned writer Sholem Asch, about a company anticipating a battle. The company replicates the civilian Jewish world by including religious soldiers, secular soldiers, those in-between, and anti-Semites who harass them all. The battle itself is a horror, involving crushed bodies and severed limbs, the agony compounded as the amputees return home to find their parents murdered in pogroms. Like the facts of mass migration, we "knew" all this already. But we didn't know what it was like for Asnat, a young man whose assimilated Russian childhood leaves him desperately searching for honor, whose friendship with a religious Jewish soldier burdens him with regret, whose ultimate attempt at heroism vaults over tragedy into utter devastation. Stories here by the literary masters David Bergelson and Israel Joshua Singer achieve something similar with the Russian Civil War, a conflict whose numbing details come alive in stories that are not merely about trauma, but about what it means to live with humiliation; they serve as a guide to human dignity.

These and many other stories take us back to Europe, including gems like a never-before-translated tale by Nobel laureate Isaac Bashevis Singer, a beautiful fable by the eminent poet Kadya Molodowsky, and a standout by the literary giant Chaim Grade. Yet these fictional return trips to the old country, written by world-class talents traumatically severed from the world that formed them, are themselves American documents, reflecting the American Jewish community's absorption of refugees who could not entirely embrace the American credo of reinvention. These are not sentimental works based on nostalgia for a world destroyed. Instead these stories squarely face a reality that is far too dark for English-speaking American life.

There is a deep despair in Grade's "Grandfathers and Grandchildren," a story about a dying synagogue where elderly men resort to ruses to attract young students, or Sarah Hamer-Jacklyn's story "Compatriots," about two men who meet at the fiftieth reunion of their much-diminished *landsmanshaft*, a once-crucial organization supporting immigrants from a single European hometown. The *Forward* had been conceived as a newspaper for the future. But by dint of its language, the successful assimilation of its earliest readers, and the mass murder of the majority of the world's Yiddish speakers, within fifty years it had become a newspaper of the past. This is true even for the remarkable stories included here from the paper's recent years, like Blume Lempel's erotic "A Journey Back in Time" and Boris Sandler's unexpected "Studies in Solfège," both of which explore sexual affairs defined by their expiration dates. It may surprise Americans that there are no stories here that directly address the Holocaust, which for many *Forward* writers and readers was much too immediate for fiction. Instead, these post-Holocaust stories address something almost as wrenching and eternally relevant, a subject that American literature in English tends to avoid: mortality.

Ezra Glinter points out in these pages that "the American Jewish experience was largely a product of trauma." But this trauma goes much deeper than the cataclysms of the last century. It includes the fundamental tension between American and Jewish culture. America's founding legend insists that it doesn't matter who our parents or great-great-great-grandparents are, that what matters is what we do with the opportunities this country gives us, that we are meant to be self-made men or women without a past. This is what we call the American dream, and its promise is precisely what brought so many of our ancestors to this country. But Judaism has a very different founding legend. When God gave the Torah to the Israelites, it was received not only by that generation, but by all of their future descendants, who were also present at Sinai. This legend is exactly the opposite of the American dream. It insists that it indeed matters who one's great-great-great-grandparents were, and that one is entirely defined by the past. The central challenge of American Jewish life, one now shared by many other groups in this marvelously complicated country, is to thrive within this tension, to live one's life in a place where only the future matters in a community suffused by the shadow of eternity.

You may think you know the story of the American Jewish experience, its facts and timelines and famous figures and major events. But without this emotional record, the "living novel" of American Jewish life, you missed the part about what it means to be alive. So keep reading. We've got a story for you.

HAVE
I GOT A
STORY
FOR YOU

SECTION ONE

Immigration and Its Discontents

BETWEEN 1881, when the assassination of Czar Alexander II set off waves of pogroms across the Russian Empire, and 1924, when the Johnson-Reed Act shut down open immigration to the United States, nearly 3 million Jews made their way to America. These Yiddish-speaking immigrants came for many reasons. Some were fleeing pogroms; others, like *Forward* editor Abraham Cahan, came to avoid arrest for their political activities—or had already served time in jail. Many simply sought to escape poverty and to seek new opportunities in the "Golden Land."

Yet every immigrant experienced similar challenges. For each "greenhorn," the first order of business was to "ungreen" themselves—that is, to acculturate to American life. New arrivals had to learn a language, find a way to support themselves, and rebuild the communities they had left behind.

As a newspaper that catered to Yiddish-speaking immigrants, the *Forward* made it its business to smooth this transition. It advised its readers on American manners and fashions; it educated them in the country's history, geography, and political systems; it encouraged them to learn English as soon as they could. Perhaps most important, in its literary offerings the *Forward* gave them consolation; it assured them that others had gone through the same struggles and that the confusion and ambivalence they felt was entirely normal.

As a socialist newspaper, the *Forward* also sought to unify its readers politically and economically. For many of its readers immigration was not just an individual experience, but a collective opportunity. Whereas in the Russian Empire political activism was illegal, in America you could think, say, and vote for whomever you liked. Thus, the Yiddish intelligentsia turned itself into a generation of activists, lecturers, and labor organizers. Many of the stories published in the *Forward* reflected efforts at union organizing, labor conditions, and the economic ups and downs of American life.

Not all immigrants greeted their new experiences with enthusiasm, however. Although the United States was a haven from the violence and oppression of Europe, the perceived vulgarity and opportunism of America disappointed many new arrivals. And, as they discovered, immigration was not a one-time event, but a continuing experience. While parents aspired to their children's success, many of the stories that appeared in the *Forward* dealt with the frustration of older immigrants who become estranged from their Americanized children and grandchildren.

Viewed in hindsight, the Jewish immigration experience in America seems like a great success. But at the time, that success was hardly assured. Emotional trauma and material privation were not an exception, but a rule. For the immigrants struggling to find their footing in a new country, there was at least something to cling to when times got tough: a newspaper that told them they were not alone.

Rokhl Brokhes

1880–1945

Rokhl Brokhes was a short-story writer of depth and sophistication whose true contribution to Yiddish literature may never be known.

Born in Minsk to educated parents, Brokhes was taught to read Hebrew at a young age and immersed herself in works of Hebrew and world literature. When her father died when she was nine years old, Brokhes was forced to go to work as a seamstress, and she later taught needlework at the Minsk Jewish Vocational School for Girls.

Brokhes began writing fiction as a teenager and published her first story, "Yankele," in 1899. As a young woman, Brokhes married a dentist and moved with him to Saratov before returning to Minsk around 1920. After the Russian Revolution she continued to publish short stories in Soviet Yiddish periodicals, along with plays and children's stories.

Although two collections of Brokhes's work appeared in her lifetime, many of her stories remain uncollected. An eight-volume edition of her writing was being prepared by the state publishing house of the Byelorussian Soviet Socialist Republic in the early 1940s when the German invasion of the Soviet Union brought the project to a halt. Brokhes died in the Minsk Ghetto during the Holocaust.

In her fiction Brokhes often addresses the plight of women during times of political and social upheaval. "Golde's Lament," which appeared in the *Forward* on May 9, 1907, treats the subject of immigration from the perspective of a woman whose husband travels to America with another woman posing as his wife. The story was considered so important that the paper ran advertisements for two days announcing its publication and followed it with an essay by editor Abraham Cahan in which he declared it to be "the poetry of a suffering human heart."

Golde's Lament

(MAY 9, 1907)

Translated by Myra Mniewski

HE WAS SUPPOSED to leave this evening, but because of Peshke, their departure was put off until tomorrow's train.

The lamp burns brightly on the balcony. Everyone sits around the table talking.

Small talk. In the adjoining room Golde decides it's not worth paying attention, and stops listening.

She sits in her room. The beds are a tumble, disarranged. It's no small thing, this packing. The quilt and pillow have already been rolled up into a bundle. The children have passed out, asleep wherever—who has the wherewithal to keep an eye on them? The baby, with no one to comfort her, screamed her head off all evening. Golde's aged mother, also passed out on the hard bench behind the stove, is restlessly sighing and moaning.

Golde can't get comfortable either. She's already moved herself every which way on the bed, tossing and turning in all directions, unable to settle down.

A harrowing cry pushes to the surface. It recedes and pines. Her grief is huge and her pain immeasurable. He was supposed to leave today. But the delay is only until tomorrow.

How has it come to this, his going away? Does he really have to go? They'd been discussing it all winter, packing and repacking, trying to raise money for the trip—pleading and begging wherever possible, pawning or selling whatever was worth anything. He must go because all winter and all summer and all the previous winter and summer, and many summers and winters before that—entire years he'd searched for something of a concern, a position, some way to make a living, and couldn't find anything. He must go! The plans have already been made.

She feels herself aging—the emptiness of his absence, the fear of uncertainty, the distance their separation will bring. He is leaving tomorrow. Bundles are being carried out. The house is growing empty. Leybe is already gone. What is she worth without him? What does God have in store for her? She throws herself on the bed and bangs her head on the bedpost. She's finished—desperate, defeated. The bitter idea fills its measure, veils her eyes with a mournful gloom, pummels her mind as if with a cudgel—the unbearable thought of Peshke traveling along with him.

Golde knows this is an ugly thought. It's foolish; Leybe must not know of it. She must stop provoking herself. No one must suspect what lurks in her heart. She would herself like to deny it, not think about it, forget that Peshke is listed on his provincial visa as his wife.

Everything else recedes into the background. All the troubles she's been through—her worn-down sick children, the poverty that for the last few years has permeated every crevice—all of it is disappearing, withdrawing to a faraway place. The constant dread of not having bread for tomorrow is being displaced by the journey ahead. All she sees is a big ocean, heaving in its magnificence, stretching endlessly before her, with the blue firmament drawn out above it. And then the ship, with scores of portholes and numerous smokestacks. And who is sailing on that boat? Leybe and Peshke, totally different than they were at home, remade as new people. There they are, together, for everyone to see, the whole world thinking they are man and wife. And they're chatting and enjoying each other—having a good time. Peshke is laughing like a seduced woman, loud and boisterous, just like now, there, in the other room, where they all are.

The sounds from the balcony stimulate Golde's senses. The conversation, the singing, the laughter, sharpen the distressing images before her eyes. The horrific pain in her heart is growing unbearable. A murderous outrage is getting the better of her. If she could only find the strength, she would burst through the curtain and grab Peshke by the hair, hurl her to the ground, stomp on her. Leybe must not go with her! They can go without each other. How can you even compare them! Peshke is going to her husband, whom she has longed and pined for—a husband who's already sent her hundreds. And she's spent it. But he, Leybe, is going in search of bread, a piece of bread to nourish his poor, neglected health. He is leaving his wife and children aching and alone. Why is she laughing and afflicting his head with her yammering, garbling his feelings about his family?

Leybinke, she wants to say, you don't need her money. You don't need the twenty rubles she's lending you to make this journey possible. Is that why you've put her on your visa instead of your wife? Leybinke, in our poverty, money is certainly valued, and the twenty rubles will sustain you during the journey, but pay attention to my heart, what it's going through—how great my anguish is.

This is the chatter going on inside her—without words, soundless; just her choked sighs as she heaves and tosses in bed.

She is not going to share her lament with Leybe. He must not know of it. It's rash—crazy! She perceives the ugliness of her thoughts, their smallness, and wants to tear at her own flesh. Is this why her grief at Leybe's departure is so great? Who is this Peshke anyway? She's going to her husband. Did Leybe know her before? An unknown woman from another world? What a fine how-do-you-do! Had he ever mentioned her name before? Golde just talked about her in passing, counted her money and measured her fortune. She was jealous of her, begrudged her. When someone suggested Peshke sign on to Leybe's visa, they both, in their poverty, gleefully anticipated the twenty rubles. When everything had already been removed from their house, pawned and sold, when they had already exasperated and borrowed from everyone, Leybe was still discontent. He was despondent—a strange, unfamiliar person would get on his nerves on such a long journey. "When someone's heart aches he just wants to be alone, he doesn't want to have to talk to anyone," he said. And Golde tried to console him, saying, "Don't worry Leybinke, it will all work out."

But when Peshke came to bargain and negotiate a deal, when it was time to decide when and how they would go, on what day, through where and on what, that's when she suddenly felt all those other emotions. The conversations seemed to be only between the two of them—Leybe and Peshke. They were bound together, made sense only to each other. Her presence didn't matter one way or another. She was superfluous, unneeded. So she left the room, saying she had to check on the baby.

As she pressed up against the cradle, she felt her anguish for the first time, and since then it has not let up. Since then she's been continuously fighting back the tears that clutch at her throat. Whenever she gets a chance to get away from everyone, step away for just a little while, the tears pour out, pour out without letting up. Silken, bitter, hostile tears.

And when Leybe expounds on all the benefits of traveling with Peshke, a strange chill passes through her, taking over her whole being.

"You realize," he says, "how advantageous it is for me to travel with her. It even pays to wait for her until she has arranged everything. If it's to be her way, then so be it. My concerns are purely parsimonious, while she is a woman with money, with prospects. I cannot latch onto what she has, but when times are hard it will work in my favor to be connected to her. Her husband has already been there for a while. He is experienced and familiar with the conditions there. He will be able to advise me, point me in the right direction for work. And I'll have a hospitable place to come home to in a foreign land."

All that talk made good sense—she understands it, but searches for hidden meaning in his words nonetheless. She watches his facial expressions and listens to his cheerful banter, all the while not believing him, suspecting him.

She should have discussed everything with Peshke before their departure, but she didn't. While packing his things for the journey she was silent. Soaking some of his things in her tears, she hid them in his suitcase in her wild, insane fright. His departure hovered over her in a habitual nightmare and she became anxious and skittish—afflicted.

Leybe has also not been himself in recent days. He doesn't talk to her much either. He too is not all there, not conscious of what he's saying, forgetting what he was about to say. He just lies there lost in thought—awake the whole night. He's muddled, distressed, and angers easily.

And then there is Peshke, who never seems to leave their house. Either she's got something she wants to ask Leybe or she's got something to tell him. She hangs around all evening laughing and cackling. She's so loud the whole street can hear her. Tomorrow, tomorrow, they're going away. Tomorrow belongs to them.

"Dear mother!" she suddenly jumps up, "what am I going to do? I won't survive this! Leybe, Leybe, my Leybe, the father of my three babies. I will lie down in the doorway and tell them the truth. I will say, Leybe, kill me now, hack me to pieces, kill me, but not like this! I can't live without you! I can't! I won't even make it one day."

Golde grabs her head, tears pour from her eyes, the knot twists in her throat. Her heart is pounding. Her limbs turn limp and feeble.

"Golde, Golde, what's gotten into you!" her aged mother murmurs and creeps out from behind the stove. "You have little children, pull yourself together, why are you making yourself sick?"

Her mother is old and blind—she can't see what's happening to her daughter but she senses a weird tone in her voice. And the knot in Golde's throat unfurls in lament—a desolate wail.

And suddenly her room is filled. Someone has brought the lamp. They're all standing there: Uncle Berel; Fayvl, the neighbor; Mendel, Leybe's cousin; and the two of them too. There is Leybe, terrified. "What's wrong?" he asks. "Golde, what's wrong with you?" He tries to take her hand but she pulls away from him and buries her face in the pillow. She starts rocking ever more fiercely, totally lost in her torment—desperate, untethered.

"Golde, what's happening to you?" She hears Leybe's voice. "Why are you killing yourself like this? Why are you letting yourself go like this? Golde, Golde. Call the medic, the doctor. What's happening to her?"

His terrified voice calms her a bit, lessens her pain. But she won't open her eyes. She doesn't want to restrain the strange, wild sounds that are tearing out of her chest—let them scream, let them resound, let all the evil that has accumulated inside her pour out.

"*Feh*, disgusting," a voice responds. "I was also left all alone when my Zelig went away. I was also left alone. And I was certainly miserable and lonely without him. But look at me now—God has helped, I'm on my way to him now. Your Leybe is going away. He will reach his destination. He will make it and close the deal. And you too will be on your way to him before you know it."

"For sure, for sure! God will provide," the others chime in to comfort her.

But Leybe is silent. Who knows what he's thinking. And the icy void again pierces Golde's squirming flesh and she loses herself in a fresh lament—more forceful and wild and horrifying than before.

Golde went on like that for quite a while. No one was able to calm her for a long time. Some neighbors came in and rubbed her with vinegar, put cold compresses on her head, warmed her feet with a hot water bottle. The children woke up, were cradled and rocked, and went back to sleep. Everyone eventually dispersed.

Leybe sat with her for a long while, until dawn was already long on the horizon. He consoled her and begged her to be strong, to have faith, and to wait for a time when things would be better.

Abraham Cahan

1860–1951

ABRAHAM CAHAN, THE founding editor of the *Forward*, was the most influential Yiddish journalist in history, and an accomplished writer of fiction.

Born in the town of Podberezhi, in what is now Belarus, he moved with his parents at a young age to Vilna, where he received a traditional religious education. As a teenager, he developed an interest in secular literature and attended the city's Jewish teachers' seminary, where he became involved in radical politics.

Following the assassination of Czar Alexander II in 1881, Cahan's political affiliations brought him under the suspicion of government authorities. To avoid arrest he joined the thousands of Jewish refugees then fleeing the pogroms sweeping the Russian Empire, and immigrated to America.

In New York, Cahan quickly learned English and began a journalistic career writing for both the city's English-language newspapers and its nascent Yiddish press. When in 1897 a group of socialist editors and writers broke off from the existing socialist weekly to start their own Yiddish newspaper, the *Forward*, Cahan was appointed editor.

At the same time, Cahan was also writing and publishing fiction in English. In 1896 his first book, *Yekl: A Tail of the New York Ghetto*, appeared, and in 1917 he published his magnum opus, *The Rise of David Levinsky*. But although Cahan was the editor of the largest Yiddish newspaper in the world, his English-language fiction and his Yiddish journalism rarely overlapped.

One exception was *The Additional Soul*, a novella that Cahan serialized in the *Forward* between November 17, 1900, and January 19, 1901. The novella was comprised of fictionalized sketches of character types that he encountered in New York's Jewish ghetto on Manhattan's Lower East Side. In Jewish folk belief, a person receives an additional soul for the duration of the Sabbath. Cahan expands this concept to refer not only to an additional Sabbath soul, but also a more ethical and righteous soul that can exist at any time.

The following excerpt from *The Additional Soul* focuses on two such character types—Shneur Zadobnik, a rich immigrant who has lost the integrity he once had, and Motke the Hatter, a laughingstock who has been able to reinvent himself as a respectable figure. These two characters illustrate not only Cahan's distinction between those who have an "additional soul" and those who do not, but also the ways in which immigration allowed people to reinvent themselves—sometimes for the better, and sometimes for the worse.

Shneur Zadobnik
and Motke the Hatter

(DECEMBER 29, 1900–JANUARY 12, 1901)
AN EXCERPT FROM *The Additional Soul*
(NOVEMBER 17, 1900–JANUARY 19, 1901)

Translated by Jordan Kutzik

JEWS SAY THAT if you change where you live you'll change your luck, but is America really that different? What became of my fellow countryman Shneur Zadobnik here in America? I used to ask myself such questions when I was younger. Now I've stopped asking them altogether.

In the old country he belonged to the nouveau riche. He had already been rich for eleven or twelve years when the Russo-Turkish War[1] made him even richer. Money begets money, success begets success, as the Americans say. And luck? Well luck makes you lucky; it seems to reproduce just like cats do. Whatever Zadobnik touched was blessed. There's an old tale about a man who had the "golden touch"; whatever he put his finger on would turn into pure gold. Even when he caressed his daughter she became petrified—all that remained of her was a cold and silent golden golem, like Lot's wife, who became a pillar of salt.[2] In truth, that's how things go with millionaires. Whatever they touch is multiplied a thousandfold, and most of those things turn into petrified golems.

By nature Shneur was one of those folks who loved to have a good time. He wasn't a bad person. Complaining, sullying his reputation— that wasn't him. Stingy people have such joy from their treasure that for them it's like the manna the Jews ate in the dessert. The manna had all sorts of flavors: it was bread, meat, kugel—whatever you wished. For a true miser gold serves as his theater, his music, his honor and his love—every earthly joy wrapped into one. Shneur, however, was differ- ent. He sought delight in everything. He ate well, was used to having a nice glass of wine at his dinner table, was honored wherever he went, had the city's cantor perform in his home, loved his children and also the beggars, who loved him in turn. He found joy in everything. And this way of life was replicated in his business: if he gave away a thousand, he would get three thousand in return. He gave with an open hand and would donate hundreds to all sorts of charitable causes, but for every hundred he gave away, his heart would swell with a pride worth thousands of rubles.

The educated people in his city would say that he was an egoist. But he had a heart, and even his egoistic pleasures were intertwined with honest sentiment. He could be enraptured, Shneur; he had an additional soul. He would actually take pride in himself, take pride

---

1 1877–1878.
2 Genesis 19:26.

in his additional soul, just as his wife would take pride in the pearls around her neck. Just so long as he had one! It wasn't that big or healthy; it fact it was rather puny, but it was an additional soul, and a puny one is better than none at all.

The greatest Jewish scholars in the city used to gather at his house, and the proponents of *Haskalah*[3] would come together to see him. His children went to modern Russian high schools and he would feel right at home when educated young men visited to tutor them.

He had a good head on his shoulders. He was no scholar, not a true *Maskil*,[4] and certainly not an educated man. But he wasn't a delinquent, either. He listened a great deal and was interested in everything—partly because it suited his role, but mostly because he genuinely enjoyed learning things, and his mind took to it well. In short, he was like a relative to the scholars and a big shot among the proponents of the *Haskalah*. He was a patron, a supporter of education among the learned. He gave money to help poor boys go to modern Russian high schools and universities. He would pay a pretty penny for every book an author would bring him; he supported the yeshiva. Such a mixture of things is a true rarity. But Shneur Zadobnik was Shneur Zadobnik, and his house was among the finest. People therefore were jealous of him. They would hide their jealousy behind their eyes while gazing upon him with flattery.

He had moments when he would become truly enraptured. The very best of society would gather at his house, and at those times he would feel a certain genteel, refined spirit floating through his home. That would make him feel good inside. And since he felt goodness in his heart, he also became a better person as well.

Shneur Zadobnik often committed the ugly and wanton deeds common to the business world, but sometimes that refined spirit of his home stopped him. For instance, he was once squeezing the soul out of a poor, small-time businessman who was quivering in his arms when that same spirit touched him.

---

3 Jewish Enlightenment.
4 Proponent of the Jewish Enlightenment.

"*Feh*, it's not right," the spirit said, and Shneur released his victim and even helped him out. And in helping him, Shneur's heart went from loving and respecting himself to seeing goodness and gentleness in everything. At that point, he would flatter himself the same way the poor used to flatter him. But, as we've said before, he did have an additional soul, and when he would do something good, his limbs would feel warmer and his thoughts would drift somewhere far off, to more civilized places. He would imagine different things and lose himself in daydreams.

When learned men would come to his house and interpret biblical passages, Shneur would listen with a peculiar smile. The smile said two things at once. It said: "Speak words of Torah, speak! I'm a rich man and you are all paupers, so therefore I understand the meaning concealed in the small letters of your holy texts." At the same time the smile also said: "You all are bums and I'm Shneur Zadobnik, but my house is open to everyone." But little by little he would become truly interested in their discussion and forget about his wealth. He would ask about a point he didn't understand and listen with his full attention, with a shimmer in his eyes and color in his cheeks and with the dream of a better sort of life in his heart.

During those times he would, for a brief moment, become truly pious and make a blessing or say his Grace after meals with real devotion.

The same was true, however, when educated heretics would gather at his home. He would start off with that same smile of his but soon became genuinely enthused. And for the first minutes after they would leave, he would think over what they had discussed and believe with all his heart that he should no longer allow the religious men to come to his home—that religiosity, the Talmud, and all the other trappings of faith were nothing more than madness and darkness and that the only way to counter them was by spreading education and light. His enemies said that he was a hypocrite: a religious man among the pious, an enlightened man among the proponents of the *Haskalah*, and a godless man among the heretics. They didn't understand him.

The real story was this: Whoever visited his home infused him with a refined spirit. And this spirit would in turn refine his luck. The good fortune in his business dealings was like the body of his enjoyment, and this refined spirit was its soul. In his heart he divided his pleasures into two parts: one holy and one profane, one for the hallowed day and one for the other days of the week. The joys stemming from his wealth and the honor that it provided him, his revenge over enemies, the flavor of roast duck and wine, the pleasure he derived from everyone bowing and spinning before him—all of that fell into the section of his heart reserved for the profane. The true humbleness, which would come upon him in a split second, the delicate feelings that fine company would inspire in him, the sweet elusive dreams of an honest, fine life—that was the sanctification of his good fortune. We have six weekdays and the Sabbath, which comes but once a week. That's probably how it was with Shneur's happiness: it was six parts (or perhaps six hundred parts) egotistical joy with one part holy joy. But a tiny piece of an additional soul is better than nothing.

This all seems like typical bourgeois happiness. True, but bourgeois life is not the same everywhere. Look at what happened to Shneur's good fortune in America! He is also rich here and everything he touches does well here too. His star shines brightly, perhaps even more so than in Russia. But look a little closer: your heart will weep when you consider what has become of Shneur Zadobnik.

Shneur's wife died. He took a pretty young girl and became young again himself. Right afterwards, however, the wheel of fortune began to turn backward.

A large number of new merchants settled in Shneur's city after the Jews were driven out of Moscow and Saint Petersburg.[5] They were people who had been born in Shneur's hometown, but who had lived for many years in Saint Petersburg or Moscow and who therefore had money and skill in business. The competition was stark, and economic troubles grew so large that business collapsed altogether in the Jewish towns.

---

5 A reference to the anti-Semitic May Laws of 1882, and the subsequent expulsion of Jews from Moscow in 1891.

Many of Shneur's debtors went bankrupt. He lost nearly half his wealth and the other half began to melt away. Confusion broke out in many Jewish towns. The recently arrived merchants from Moscow and Saint Petersburg not only muddled up the business world, but also changed its style. The new businessmen were used to Moscow's customs, to wide-reaching management; they summoned a coachman in a totally different manner and cursed a tailor differently for not fitting a coat properly. In short: the wings of the old aristocracy had been clipped.

Because of his pretty young wife, Shneur wanted, as always, to live. But the wheel had already turned back.

His beautiful young wife had a peculiar sadness in her eyes, as if she had been fooled. This sadness cut Shneur's heart as if with knives. It spoke to him like a constant criticism, and the criticism dogged him as a constant thought: that he was no longer Shneur, that he had fallen out of the game entirely. It was terrifying. His mind clawed at itself.

A new idea began to take root: to immigrate to America. He would gather up his rubles as soon as possible, before they vanished entirely, and go with his wife and children to New York.

A certain class of Jew travels from Russia to America the same way that Americans settle in Europe. When an American earns "only" twenty-five thousand dollars a year and belongs to the upper class, he finds himself a home in Dresden or Munich, in Rome or Florence. Nobody knows him there and he can allow himself to live a bit more simply. Everything there is cheaper as well. There are entire colonies of this type of wealthy American in Dresden, Munich and several Italian cities.

It's the same story with fallen wealthy Russian Jews: at home they can't just do whatever comes along. But America is far from home and there's no shame in it. There may be many fellow countrymen here, but everything is permissible in America; nothing is shameful here. People know this in Russia, and embarrassed businessmen travel to America seeking refuge from their shame because everything can be done here and nothing is inappropriate, so long as you make a living.

The fallen Russian merchant therefore hopes to do big business with his few remaining rubles. If Chaim'ke the tailor could become a wealthy businessman there, if Borekh'ke the coachman's son-in-law could grow rich enough to own a factory, then certainly Shneur Zadobnik would be able to shake up the world.

At first his young wife did not want to hear about America. America was where tailors, coachman and all sorts of other poor people went. Why should she have married Shneur Zadobnik? She could have taken a young pauper and traveled far away with him. She never said any of this aloud, but the sadness in her eyes stabbed Shneur's heart like a sword. Her silence told him much more than if she had spoken.

He thought that he would lose his mind.

He didn't understand her well, however. She didn't understand herself, either. She had a womanly mistake in her heart. She wanted to travel away from home even more than he did. The eyes of the women in town, both those she knew and those of strangers, sucked the blood right out of her, just as her own eyes did to Shneur. It seemed that the women were teasing her, that they were making fun of her and the wealth that supposedly came along with her engagement.

Previously all of the women had been jealous of her, and now they were all taking joy in the fact that her husband's bread was landing butter side down. She was bothered more than anything by the words of pity she heard from her sister. She merely sighed at Zadobnik's state.

"Such a treasure!" she'd say. "Such a treasure! May God take pity upon him!" That's what her sister would say while sighing, and the young Mrs. Zadobnik knew in her heart of hearts that her sister loved every minute of it. Previously her sister had begrudged her for his wealth—she had made nice and flattered her, but it was just for show; now she was in seventh heaven because her sister had lost her status.

She would have flown to the other side of the world. Her shame was even greater than her husband's. She felt like someone who is tricked by a peddler who sells her a golden ring that is really made of brass.

Her anger at her husband was just as great as her disappointment over the brass ring, perhaps even greater.

Shneur wasn't lacking in character, and she felt joy in her heart when he started getting ready to leave. They came to America. As is usually the case, Zadobnik spent his first couple of years in America losing the few thousand dollars he had brought with him from the old country. Russian money is unlucky here. It has an odor of shame—not too much, but enough for the American business world to be unable to stand even the slightest whiff of it.

When Shneur lost his final rubles in America, along with the very last remnant of his dignity, he suffered for a year. The audacity of having tried to turn himself into someone! He stole; he borrowed from fellow countrymen and tore himself apart until he managed to open up a small store. What kind of store it was is difficult to say. He had some dry goods, some stationery, and even some Yiddish books. But Shneur used all of his abilities and all of his acumen to turn himself into a success. He was no longer a greenhorn. "Oh, if I only had the sense back then that I have now," he would say, shaking his head when he thought about the first few years he spent in America.

So what did he learn in those first three years? Why did he have to first pay several thousand dollars in "tuition"?

At first Shneur found himself constantly wondering. For instance, in the old country if he saw a well-dressed man who often went to the theater, lived in a nice apartment, had servants and could appreciate a good glass of wine, that was usually a sign that he was a gentleman, an educated person, or at the very least someone who aspired to refinement. Here though, he encountered men everywhere who were dressed and lived like Russian aristocrats, but who spoke with the most obscene language imaginable and acted like horse thieves. Their friends were pimps and many of them ran brothels themselves. When elections were held in the old country and people selected an alderman, you can be sure that he was among the finest citizens in the city. Here the aldermen, the legislators, were the lowest saloonkeepers; drunks and thugs wearing nice caps.

Shneur Zadobnik looked, shrugged his shoulders and felt his heart yearn for home.

In Russia a doctor is an educated, refined man. Here in the Jewish neighborhood most doctors were wild ignoramuses with the practices of a barber and the brazenness of the kidnappers who used to steal Jewish children to fill czarist army quotas.

In Russia a licensed attorney is a man who has graduated from a university and is well read. Here Zadobnik saw a whole gang of men with diamond rings on their fingers and chewing tobacco in their mouths. This gang of lawyers loitered in various criminal courts and in the neighborhood's two civil courts. They were old friends of the judges, and whenever a refined Russian lawyer worked in these courts, he found himself in a wretched situation and was rendered utterly useless.

Zadobnik looked around and wondered what kind of backward world he found himself in, and his heart was seized by longing.

He saw that people who owned houses of ill repute and saloons were the neighborhood elite, and the Jewish neighborhood was for Shneur all of America. (It is, in any case, the largest Jewish city in the world.) He saw that pimps were actually politicians and that these politicians were the closest friends of other politicians who were the best friends of more powerful politicians who were even more powerful than the mayor.

Shneur was bewildered. "Where the hell have I ended up?" he said to himself, heartbroken. A feeling of loneliness descended upon him.

He went to the synagogue seeking comfort in piety. But even that made him cry out in woe, for even the synagogue he found was part of a backward world and even there he was completely out of his element. He saw thugs and escaped thieves standing beside the Torah scroll holding pointers. In some synagogues pimps received the finest *aliyahs*[6] thanks to their work prostituting girls. Landlords of tenements packed full with whorehouses shared verses of scripture about divine revelation while true religious scholars suffered from want. Gangsters and parasites became well-fed reverends in fancy caps. Shneur saw with his own eyes how a storekeeper gave money to a band of tramps so that they would cheer for him as he left the synagogue, and when someone asked him how he wasn't ashamed of him-

---

6 A formal invitation to read from the Torah during a prayer service.

self, he answered, "Why does it bother you? It's an advertisement. This isn't Russia."

Shneur looked around and wondered. His heart was bitter and his ears rang with those words: "Why does it bother you? This isn't Russia." And his soul yearned and yearned.

He saw what kind of creatures Americans are. Before someone in Russia could turn around, here in America a huge business with a forty-story building and thousands of miles of train track would have been built. Which, ultimately, is a sign that Russia itself is a greenhorn.

He would stop and watch how five boys would carry more goods in five minutes than ten big men in the old country could have carried in an hour. The logic of it was simple: the box would be slid over a board that was angled downwards, dragged forward with a hook and placed into a wheelbarrow. The load would practically carry itself. If you needed to empty a wagon full of coal, you could just turn the wagon on its wheels, bend it over, and the coals pour right out into the basement all by themselves. It seemed so simple and yet no common sense was applied to such tasks in the old country. He wondered at it, and in his ears roared a voice louder and louder: "This is not Russia. One must be practical." In the old country the refined spirit would have told him, "It's not appropriate." Here there was no one to tell him such a thing; here everything and everyone murmured like a choir: "Nothing at all is shameful. You mustn't be a greenhorn."

Another acquaintance of his lived next door to a couple of prostitutes. When Shneur asked why he didn't move out, he answered: "I too once thought like you. But how do I know that it will be any better in another house? And why should what's going on next door bother me? In America there is a rule, 'Mind your own business.'"

When Shneur had a good look at what was going on around him, he would think to himself: "How did I end up here? May America with her masochistic ways and her pimps be cursed! What do I have to do with this?" In his loneliness the city with its forty-story buildings and its trains and its tricks, with its hustle and bustle and fashions, looked like some kind of fake flowers, like something counterfeit. A three-story house back in the old country had more good taste and substance to it than all of these towers that were constructed overnight. With houses in the old country people had time to get used to them and to learn to love and trust them. Here everything coalesced like drying spit: by the time you got used to something it had already been torn down and something new had taken its place. In the old country everyone loved the place where he was raised, but here nothing stays the same: if you don't see a street for several months you won't recognize it. They just tear everything apart and hammer it back together. Nothing is holy. Children have nothing to become attached to, nothing for their heart to yearn for.

Shneur's heart yearned for its former home. Tears would well up in his eyes.

Need breaks steel, as they say. Zadobnik learned to be practical. He studied the philosophy of "mind your own business." He saw that Russia is a greenhorn; he stopped yearning and assimilated. And just as a stone spins faster the further it rolls down a hill, so too did Shneur Zadobnik fall faster and faster into the morass.

A fellow countryman, for instance, asked him to repay a debt. He laughed at him and denied owing anything. The former refined spirit tried to speak to him with its weakened voice, saying, "That's not right, Shneur." But Shneur rejected the spirit, saying, "This isn't Russia."

And so it went, further and further downhill. The dry-goods store became a wholesale grocery; the wholesale grocery became a saloon. Shneur became famous and befriended Jewish bums. To have a saloon you must be "all right" with politicians and so he became close with the politicians.

As you already know, his second wife was a pretty woman. Well, he began to sense that the politicians and bums were going to his bar to see her. The weak, half-dead spirit used its last bit of strength to whisper, "Is this right, Shneur?"

Shneur answered: "Are they doing anything to her? This isn't Russia. In America you must not be proud. There is no Shneur Zadobnik here. In America everyone is equal."

He became a powerful figure in fraternal lodges, campaigned in elections for Tammany Hall, and did favors at the Essex Street Courthouse. The guests at his home were politicians and doctors who worked in brothels. His saloon was always full. He soon bought a property that was full of hookers. He sold a brothel and bought two more until he became one of the famous bail bondsmen for prostitutes and their johns.

By this time he had grown fatter and his character declined along with his obese body.

Before leaving the old country he had worked hard to make himself look young, and had groomed himself like a young man on account of his young wife. Now he wore diamond rings, bright-red neckties and shaved off nearly his entire beard. His face was adorned with remnants of beer and worthless company. It had become a rougher sort of face: meaty, red and somewhat sandy. In the old country he had also worn a tall hat, but his American stovepipe leaned to one side. His hands were usually in his pockets and he had even learned to spit like a true Tammany man. "What the hell!" he would often thunder, exactly like the alderman from his district.

If it ever occurred to him to consider his company, his feelings would answer for him: "Well, what's wrong? They're all doctors, lawyers and important people, the cream of the crop, not just random folks."

Morality is proportional. Even upstanding people have different morals in different generations, and morality also varies among different classes in the same generation. Rich men and prostitutes have their own moral codes. The number of hookers and johns in the Jewish quarter is so high that it is a world unto itself. The creatures who live in this world are surrounded by so many of their own class that they are simply estranged from the opinions and feelings of upstanding citizens. They have their own sense of morality, and they think about our sense of morality as something foreign. They have their own life; their own shame, and their own honor. And it is within this sort of life that some Americanized people like Zadobnik live.

Everything he touches turns to gold, and he is blessed in all of his endeavors. But what a difference there is between his American luck and his luck in the old country!

I once encountered him at the funeral of a fellow countryman. There were others from the old country there too. The sad moment had awoken Shneur from the hoo-ha of his American joys. The faces of the people who were abashed before him in the old country; the ringing music of the charity box; the cries of the orphans along with the noise of the funeral—it all reminded him of years gone by. He thought about the former Shneur Zadobnik without looking at his present with rose-tinted glasses. Walking with me behind the casket and speaking quietly it became clear that he saw things differently.

"You think that I don't understand," he said with a crestfallen tone. "I know perfectly well what kind of opinion you have of me, and you're right too! It would be a good thing of course if I could return home and become the old Shneur Zadobnik. But it's too late. God probably knows what he's doing."

A heavy sigh interrupted his words. In that moment a pure fire glowed in his heart. He yearned for his past. His ugly present disgusted him.

It truly touched me and I pitied him. I found myself feeling affection for him.

Several hours later he was back to being a Tammany man. The pure fire had been extinguished. The ringing of the charity box had been forgotten. And not a trace remained of the old Shneur Zadobnik.

IF SHNEUR HAD become boorish in America, there are others who have become more refined. It depends what circumstances a man finds himself in. Motke the Hatmaker was just the opposite of Shneur. In the old country he was on the lowest level. Motke the Hatmaker was his name for special occasions. Usually he was simply known as "Motke the Madman." He wasn't really a madman, however. He simply loved fooling people with all sorts of crazy acts that would drive everyone nuts. There are people who enjoy being spat upon so long as they get someone's attention. Motke was one of those people. Not long before his departure for America he worked in a hotel, bringing girls for the guests. It seemed that he had been born for such a trade: he was a natural broker, a lackey, a parasite from head to toe! Kissing the heel of the man who walked all over him was his tastiest delicacy. Making himself into a mountain of ash was the greatest sport.

I remember an incident I once saw. He had sold a peasant a hat and ripped him off when giving him change. Fifteen minutes later the peasant returned enraged. Motke pretended to be mute and gestured wildly, cursing with his hands and pretending to be afraid. The other hatmakers smiled as the peasant stood there confused, wondering if this was really the same man. Perhaps he had made a mistake. He continued trying to get through to him, but Motke bent down as though he wanted to tear a stone out of the pavement and knock the peasant over the head with it. One of the other hatters advised the peasant not to mess with Motke because mutes are dangerous people. The poor peasant became afraid and went home empty-handed.

Motke would often entertain the other hatmakers with his impressions of the various madmen who lived in our city's insane asylum, or other mute lunatics he encountered wandering around. He felt good when people laughed at his impersonations. Every day he would come up with a strange new routine: barking like a dog, oinking like a pig, knocking over various things that had not been tied down. People looked at him as if he were a hideous creature and he loved it. People considered him to be the lowest of the low and that was his pride and joy. I once witnessed another hatmaker eat half an apple and throw the rest into a disgusting puddle of sewage to see if Motke would retrieve it.

"He's not going to pick that up," the other hatmakers yelled so as to encourage him.

Motke smiled his vague smile.

"He's a coward, he doesn't have the courage to eat that apple," they yelled, driving him on.

In the end, Motke picked up the apple from the puddle of sewage and gulped it down. The hatmakers laughed uproariously and he felt like the hero of the day.

Once, when I had already been in America for quite a few years, I spent some time in a social organization in a small city in Pennsylvania. Among those I met there was Motke. I immediately noticed, however, that this was absolutely not the same Motke. He had a completely different manner of carrying himself, a totally different way of being. He greeted me very warmly and with a self-worth that did not match my previous conception of him. Wearing a strange smile he told me, without words, to forget about the old "Motke the Madman" and not to tell anyone about his old ways.

He had a sister and she was married to a very nice man. Truly good people went to her house and their little world was full of a beautiful spirit.

A greenhorn doesn't have his own sense of self in the beginning. He is downtrodden, shocked and coy. He isn't himself. During those first weeks when Motke didn't have the courage to get up to his old tricks, he had been treated not like a worm, but like a person, and that humane spirit set the tone for his American life. Being Motke the Madman didn't suit him here. I once thought that he had been born an ugly disgusting creature, but I was mistaken.

In the old country his fellow hatmakers had treated him like an annoying creature, and he got used to acting that way. Here he was treated from the first minute with respect, and he slowly began to respect himself.

He didn't become rich here; his brother-in-law and their friends are also poor workers, peddlers and agents. But they are among the richest in their souls and Motke was raised into that spirit.

At first I doubted whether the change would last. I thought that the old worm could still crawl out of him at any minute. But when I took a good look at Motke, I truly saw a new man. He conducted his life with true passion, as if he was trying to pay himself back for the years of self-debasement.

He was endlessly fascinating to me. I visited that city two more times, and each time I compared the two Motkes—the old-country Motke and the American Motke—with the two Shneur Zadobniks. Motke became dear to me. And Shneur? I used to think that I hated him here. No, I don't hate him, but my heart bleeds with pity.

Morris Rosenfeld

1862–1923

MORRIS ROSENFELD WAS beloved to generations of Yiddish readers as the preeminent "sweatshop poet," whose verses described the plight of working-class immigrants. As a prolific writer for the *Forward* in its early decades, he contributed not just poetry but also short stories, sketches, and belles-lettres.

Born Moyshe Yakov Alter in Stare Boksze, Poland (then part of the Russian Empire), Rosenfeld received a traditional religious education, which he continued in Warsaw, where he married and had three children. At age twenty he traveled to Amsterdam, where he worked as a diamond cutter, as well as to London and the United States, where he worked as a tailor.

In 1886, Rosenfeld settled permanently in New York, finding work in the city's garment industry. He also began writing poetry describing his own life and that of his fellow workers. His first poem was published in 1886, and his first collection appeared in 1888, followed by a second in 1890. In 1898, Harvard professor Leo Wiener translated and released a collection of Rosenfeld's work under the title *Songs from the Ghetto*, which made him briefly famous. Although Rosenfeld achieved renown during his lifetime as the "poet laureate of labor," he was rarely able to make a living from his writing and was forced to rely for much of his life on sweatshop work.

Starting in 1904, Rosenfeld became a regular contributor to the *Forward*, where he contributed numerous articles and short stories, in addition to poems. "Collecting Rent" appeared in the paper on March 2, 1911, and was republished the next year in a volume of Rosenfeld's collected writings. Although the subject of the piece is a landlord—a person Rosenfeld would normally consider a class enemy—the portrayal of Barnett Krepk is surprisingly sympathetic, even as it satirizes his capitalistic pretensions.

———

Collecting Rent

(MARCH 2, 1911)

Translated by Ross Perlin

HABIT, THEY SAY, is second nature—and the saying seems to be true as well. Thus was Barnett Krepk in the habit of collecting rent: he simply couldn't live without it.

For Krepk it was one of the two: either collect rent or die, God forbid. And indeed he would sooner die than miss a first of the month and not go out collecting rent.

"Collecting rent—you don't know what a delight it is," he often explained to the members of his family. "It's good for my health. May the hour never come, but if I ever have to stop being a landlord, I think I would do myself in!"

Krepk had once been one of the great up-and-coming real estate men—" quite the real estate man," as the ladies say; "a real estate man and a half," as the English say. At one point, he reckoned that if his tenants, their children and their children's children all belonged to him, he would have an army like the King of Romania's and wouldn't be afraid of going to war, even with Prussia itself.

Many times he fancied himself something of an emperor and his properties barracks, fortresses crammed with soldiers. He imagined that his tenants were his subjects, bound to pay tribute or soon settle accounts with their sovereign.

He could give an order, and they would be out on the street! And this little demonstration of power was nothing, just a trifle . . . An emperor, only an emperor could do such things . . .

"I'm off to review the troops," Krepk would say, chuckling, as soon as the morning of the first arrived. The little book with the rent receipts would be in his pocket, a stovepipe hat on his head, a gilded stick in his hand.

His face would light up with a smile, and he would set out for "the barracks" with a proud step, like a police lieutenant or a Cossack general.

But times change: kings are deposed from their thrones; nations come to nothing; colonels and even generals, heaven help us, fall off their horses and sprain their ankles, or get a bomb in the eye.

And Berl Krepk was sadly no longer "up on his horse." He now went about like someone defeated. He himself knew not from what— it was as if someone had given him the evil eye.

Yes, times change. At one time he was doing pretty well, he was an "allrightnik," though not much more than that. He had made it up one side of Mt. Allright, only for the ugly crash in the real estate business during the last financial crisis[7] to send him hurtling down the other side. He lost his shirt, lost face.

Those who had enough sense and courage to sell their buildings and lots before the panic broke out had gotten a good price and were now swimming in cash. But Krepk hadn't wanted to part with his houses. If he sold them, he would cease to be a landlord, would no longer be able to savor the collecting of rent. He would have money in the bank, but who doesn't have a bankbook in America? No! To become just a person like other people didn't suit him at all. There is something altogether different about property . . . A landlord is not a person; a landlord is . . . a landlord!

Alas, it had now been quite some time since Berl Krepk had gotten any joy from his properties. The ladder of success had suddenly

---

7 A reference to the Panic of 1907, also known as the Bankers' Panic or the Knickerbocker Crisis.

started shaking under him the way a fever patient shakes, and Krepk had fallen headlong from its rungs and tumbled down as it broke over his head. He was ruined. His earlier good fortune had collapsed like overcooked dumplings in a pan of hot water. He had almost nothing left, and as for what he still had—he had to do a song and a dance to keep it.

Even now he was still collecting rent, but oy, some collecting! What could he do? He had to do it, he was used to doing it, and habit is second nature, isn't that right, and so, in short, he collected.

From his whole earlier "kingdom" there remained just one single "palace" in one neighborhood of the city, which the real estate men called the "North Pole," since nobody lived there. You can't live there. The houses are ancient, decrepit, wheezing, without body or soul or the necessary conveniences, and on top of all that far from both trolley cars and subway stations. The population there was frozen through, as if they were up on the Arctic Ocean. The few characters who wandered around were the type who can get by without any apartment whatsoever, the sort who barely care where they sleep or which policeman's club they get decked by.

However many panes were in the windows of Krepk's building, the same number were all plastered with TO LET signs, but it helped like cupping helps a corpse. It was a rare event that anyone took an apartment there. As soon as anyone did walk in, you had to give him the first month free, and then he had nothing to pay with for the second, and the third he just didn't want to pay, and the fourth month he promised to pay by the fifth, and then the sixth month Krepk himself had to wait, because he needed a new mortgage. To get the mortgage, God help him, Krepk had to show that the building was not vacant and was in fact filled from top to bottom. By the seventh month the landlord himself had to pay for affronting the tenant's honor and moving him out. He would have to help the old tenant find rooms and give the new one a little cash, sparing no effort to hire a mover and pay the man's moving costs—all the while giving the old tenant loose change "for spending," or at least enough for the first few cases of beer. Nor could Krepk forget after all this to throw some coins in the charity box for ridding himself so easily of such a "bargain." It was only with God's help, for it might not be so easy to separate one-self from such a tenant, and first you might have to spit out your own lung before living to see two broken chairs and a tubercular mattress being carted off in a little wagon.

"For God's sake, Berl, get rid of this ruin, it's impoverishing us!" So Mrs. Krepk begged her husband, as you would beg a thief.

"Upon my life, brother-in-law!" said his wife's sister, a greenhorn. "Your fortune is worth nothing but trouble. You would have done better with such a building in Europe. To the devil with it! What do you need it for?"

"Papa, give it up!" the eldest daughter wept in English—and in Yiddish, "Daddy, let it go to hell!"

"Leave it, let it go, let it go to the devil," they all screamed at once.

"What do you want with me?" shouted the miserable Berl Krepk.

You can't blame Krepk too much. Habit is second nature. He was used to going around and collecting from his buildings, even when he was back in Europe. There he used to go into strangers' buildings. In America too, he would go around strange buildings for a long time, always collecting.

Later he collected in his own buildings, and yet still he went around collecting in foreign ones. And now that he had just the one building, he simply couldn't bring himself to abandon it. He couldn't sell it, and letting it to go to the devil would be a waste and a sin.

In truth, the Krepk family would have been a thousand times more fortunate without the property. The little Krepks would have been especially happy, and it's no wonder they were boiling with anger that their father took the whole dollop of *shmaltz*[8] that they earned and wasted it on the "North Pole."

The eldest daughter was an artist of the needle trades. She embroidered the tops of expensive women's blouses and earned thirty dollars a week. A second daughter worked for a fancy cap-maker and made twenty-five dollars a week. The youngest daughter was a ste-

---

8 Literally, "fat."

nographer and bookkeeper, making fifteen dollars a week. Two sons brought in thirty dollars a week, and on top of all this the Krepks had a cellar store, a basement full of woolen merchandise where the old Mrs. Krepk presided and earned. But whenever there was that rare extra penny, it went right into the empty property.

Interest on the mortgages, taxes to cover fire protection and water, repairs—the place was a sinkhole.

Here there was a ruptured ceiling and there, a chimney blowing up, refusing to let out smoke. By now it was just plain trouble and Krepk couldn't save himself. A drunken Irish tenant fell down the stairs and knocked out his own teeth—naturally the landlord was at fault for having such terrible stairs. Here an air vent was stopped up, there a water pipe burst. From sheer rage, an Italian had broken all of the doors along with their frames, using them to heat his oven; a Slovak, from some similar madness, had torn off the wallpaper and the plaster, along with everything else, and had blocked a critical vent. After that, the man informed the Board of Health that "there was something pungent" in the building. The man was afraid, horror of horrors, that he would get sick.

And so the city became involved, the police got mixed up in it, and Krepk received a warning that he had to overhaul the whole building, and if he did not, it would be condemned and no one would be able to live there anymore. He would simply have to go without tenants altogether and lose the little he still had.

The family rejoiced: perhaps now they would have an opportunity to abandon the wreck—but Krepk quickly convinced them that real estate would start booming again in no time, and they would be "all right" just like before. And in the meantime their father was still a landlord, and he would go on collecting rent.

B. Kovner

1874–1974

B. KOVNER WAS the pen name of Jacob—or Yankev—Adler, a humorist for the *Forward* for almost seven decades.

Born in Dynow, Poland, Adler received a traditional Jewish education until the age of sixteen, when he immigrated to the United States. In New York he found his first employment in a factory, before beginning a literary career in his early twenties. His first published pieces were two poems that were printed in the *Forward* shortly after its founding, which appeared under the pen name "Nesher," the Hebrew word for "eagle"—a play on the Yiddish meaning of his last name.

For the next seventy years Adler wrote poetry and short stories for some fifty-four different outlets, including the *Forward*. In 1911 he became a regular contributor to the newspaper, and was given the pseudonym B. Kovner by its editor, Abraham Cahan.

Under that name Adler became beloved to millions of readers as a writer whose sketches trained a loving yet satirical eye on life in immigrant neighborhoods such as the Lower East Side of Manhattan and the Brownsville section of Brooklyn. His recurring cast of characters included several who became veritable figures of Jewish folklore, including Peyshe the Farmer, Moyshe Kapoyer, and especially Yente Telebende, whose name became synonymous with the well-meaning, but annoying, female busybody.

In a series of sketches that spanned decades, Kovner portrayed Yente, her husband Mendel, and their son Pinnie, as they negotiated American rituals such as voting, going on strike, going to the opera, finding housing, and every other experience an immigrant family might undergo. While Kovner's portrayal of Yente may some-times seem misogynist by contemporary standards, it is a product of its time, and experienced immense popularity among both male and female readers of the *Forward*. The selection of pieces included here were all published in 1913 and 1914, and were collected in a book that year titled *Yente un andere shtiferayen* (Yente and Other Capers).

———

Brownsville Looks to the Heavens

(MAY 11, 1913)

Translated by Eitan Kensky

Brownsville, 7 a.m. People rush around half-asleep, some headed to the El station, some to the streetcars.

But over on Pitkin Avenue, men, women, policemen, and a couple of runny-nosed, filthy-cheeked small children idled in a circle, heads raised to the sky.

"What happened?" I asked a guy with a red beard.

"I don't know," he said to me and shrugged his left shoulder.

"Did something happen?" I grabbed a second man. This one had a black beard, but his ears were stuffed with cotton.

"Huh?" he replied. "Did you say something?"

"Did something happen?" I raised my tone.

"Don't ask me! I saw people staring up at the sky, so I looked too."

"What do you make of this crowd?" I turned and asked a young blond girl.

"Ask me something easier," she answered. "I was just passing by. I heard people talking, a commotion, a clamor, so I stopped here too."

Seeing as no one knew what was happening, I elbowed my way to a policeman. But the policeman also didn't know. "I saw a circle of people," he said. "I thought it was a fight, a fire, or some strikers who needed to get beat—turns out that nobody knew."

And with each moment the crowd grew and the racket boomed louder.

This was a regular picnic for the women: their mouths were busy, working overtime, asking God to keep the circle together forever. They were like fish in water.

Seeing that I was never going to make any sense of it, I spit and left for work.

On my way home for lunch, the circle was still standing, but the cops were gone. I found Yente among the women. Her face was unwashed, her housecoat was unpinned, and she carried an empty pitcher in her hand.

"Boy am I thunderstruck! Here he is back for lunch and I haven't even made breakfast," Yente spat out.

"Do you have any food for me?" I asked her.

"Fever!" Yente answered quickly, blood rushing to her cheeks. "I'm supposed to give him something to eat? And I suppose you won't accept pain and suffering? A real human being would see that I'm busy, that the house hasn't been cleaned, that I haven't sent the kids to school, that I had to pick up Pinnie at the station, because he disappeared from right under my hands. Just a kid being a kid, huh? He'll be a success just like his father—nothing but storm clouds ahead! Then he comes back, and asks me about food!"

"Who told you to spend half the day standing around with those women?" I grilled her.

"Just wait to see the 'kind' face I put on when I have to ask you questions! You'll think I'd never seen a person before, the way I'll deal with you. So you want to know how I got here? You really want to know? OK here, I'm saying! I was on my way out early in the morning with the pitcher to get milk, and I was about to go to the grocery when I saw it: the street black with people! I thought, Mrs. Kanarik had been caught with her boarder again, or Benny Zhuk slapped his wife again . . . I wouldn't wish it for the world, Mendel, but Benny is right. Day and night, she's out in the street gabbing with the women. Her house is littered in garbage and, not that I mean to gossip, but her greasy, filthy, empty-headed children swim around in the mud! And all she does is curse and slander and repeat every piece of gossip and upbraid her neighbors. And it's supposed to be a wonder that he slaps her?"

"Yente," I said. "You're going to make me faint!"

But Yente went on spreading rumors: "Yeh. I saw that the street was littered with people, I thought Mister Kanarik was fighting with the boarder, or Benny Zhuk was slapping his wife. So of course I wanted to know what was really happening, and I went, like this, with the pitcher in hand, and saw a bunch of Jews hanging around with their chins in the air looking at the sky, and I started to look too . . . And that's what I did: stand there, holding the pitcher in my hand and Pinnie by the ear. Suddenly, I feel someone tug at my housecoat. I turn around, and it's Fanny Keselpoyk and Sadie Bandura and blond Becky, and everyone has their kids with them. So they ask me: Yente, why is everyone just standing around? So I say, I don't know. People were standing, so I stood too . . ."

"Yente," I said again. "My heart is going to drop right out of me! Yente! It's one o'clock already. The whistle's blowing."

But Yente kept on talking: "So there, in the middle of all the commotion, I reach out and—can you believe how it hurt me as a mother?—Pinnie wasn't there! So I ran around and shouted, 'Has anyone seen my Pinnie?' Turns out that nobody's seen him. So I shout even louder, Pinnie, Pinela! Pinnie today, Pinnie tomorrow, Pinnie didn't answer! By then I knew: Pinnie was lost. And I ran over to a policeman and asked him: Have you seen Pinnie anywhere? The policeman asked me: Who is this Pinnie? So I said, My Pinnie, a little boy people call Pinnie!

"So he asked for a description. I said, 'He's a filthy kid, muddy, barefoot, disheveled hair.' He said, 'There's a kid just like that at the station house.' So without taking a breath I ran there and I looked— Pinnie! There he was sitting on a chair, washed, hair combed, with a lollipop in his hand, smacking his lips. A regular sport! I try to take him home, and he doesn't want to go . . ."

"Yente, the whistle! Without food, I'm growing weak! Yente!"

But Yente went on talking: "So I grabbed Pinnie by force and ran back to tell the woman that I got Pinnie, and in the meantime you came back. You know what, Mendel, I have some advice for you."

"What kind of advice?"

"Since it's already whistling and there isn't any time, wait a few hours and I'll make a regular supper for you."

Without taking a breath, I went back to the shop.

When I came back home for supper, I found Yente lying in bed with her head wrapped and a damp cloth on her throat. The kids were out in the street. The chairs were all knocked over, feet sticking out. The tablecloth was every which way. The sink was full of potato peels; the blanket was on the ground next to the bed and the broom and kashering board were on the blanket, and the picture of Baron Hirsch[9] was turned around with his face to the wall.

It was a regular museum!

"What's wrong with you?" I asked Yente, walking over to the bed.

"Too much running around today," she said. "Too much agitation. It gave me a headache . . . I didn't cook any supper. Mendel, can you get some powder for my head? There's a nickel on the bookshelf. Oy, my head!"

For dinner I ate Yente's delicacy: fever!

THE NEXT MORNING I found out that a Hebrew tutor had started the circle on Pitkin Avenue. He was on the way to synagogue for the early *minyan*[10] when he suddenly felt the need to scratch his beard . . . So he raised his beard to the sky. A bunch of Jews noticed a pious Jew

---

9 Baron Maurice de Hirsch (1831–1896), German-Jewish philanthropist and founder of the Jewish Colonization Association.
10 Prayer quorum.

staring at the heavens, and they started looking too. Little by little a circle of Jews and Jewesses formed—my Yente among them too!

———————

Yente Describes a Strike

(AUGUST 16, 1913)

Translated by Eitan Kensky

Dear Mendel,

We have a regular show here: All the male boarders departed and, in total, only one young man got off the train. Khone's his name. The world is his oyster! For a whole week, it was nothing but married women here. Khone is the only man on the whole farm.

He lacks for nothing.

All the women run after him like roosters chasing after a brood hen, or like you—may misfortune choke you—run after the *agune*[11] of Lewis Street.

All the women smile at him—at Khone, that is. They sit on his lap, go with him to pick blackberries, let him wrap his arms around them, let themselves be caressed, fondled . . .

In short, the whole week he, Khone, was the lone male among all the wives. Of course he went around with his head held high, putting on airs, proud as Count Pototsky.[12]

———————

11 A "chained woman" who cannot remarry because her husband has disappeared or refuses to grant her a religious divorce.
12 A mythical eighteenth-century Polish nobleman who converted to Judaism and was subsequently burned at the stake by the Roman Catholic Church.

But then Sunday came around: boy was he—Khone, that is—buried alive!

A real orphan.

Because, at that moment, each wifey, each Jewess, had *her* husband. They didn't speak a word to Khone; they didn't even look at him, like they didn't even know him.

He was lonely as a stone.

Poor Khone!

But, for that reason, last Monday, when all the men left again on the "husband train," and when the women came back from the station, and they started up flirting with Khone— again—Khone declared he was going on strike.

"I don't want to know you anymore!" He shouted severely. "I don't want to kiss you, caress you, wrap my arm around you, let you sit on my lap, go pick any blackberries with you or tell you any stories! If I'm good enough for you during the week, then I'm a man on Sunday too!"

In the end, the strike lasted from early Monday to dinner on Tuesday, and it was Khone who won.

The first one who gave in was a cute, black-eyed brunette, twenty-two or twenty-three.

She went up to Khone, took him by the chin and said, "Mister Khone, be a *mentsch*[13]. . . don't be angry . . ."

So Khone started to smile, caressed the girl's right cheek, and she saddled into his lap.

When the other women noticed the brunette sitting on Khone's lap—and that he was holding her, just like a "good brother"—they held a meeting near the stables, and it was decided to accede to all of Khone's demands.

And just like that, the strike came to an end.

---

13 Literally, "person."

Yente and Mendel Look for Rooms

(SEPTEMBER 20, 1913)

Translated by Eitan Kensky

So my landlord dropped in to visit my mother-in-law and said that me and Yente had to move out.

My Yente asked the landlord, "What, for example, do you mean by 'move out'?"

The landlord said, "By me, 'move out' means 'a change of climate.'"

My Yente asked, "And what, for example, do you mean by, 'a change of climate'?"

The landlord said, "What I mean by 'a change of climate' is very simple: you should search for another apartment, in a different house, on another street, and, if possible, in another city."

My Yente asked him. "What's the deal? Doesn't my mother pay you rent?"

The landlord said, "That's not what I mean. I mean, that—please, forgive me—you have too many children, wild children, who dance and jump and scream and fight and rip out the wallpaper and unscrew nails and remove faucets from the bathtub and handles from the door. Your Pinnie turns the house to rubble all by himself. I don't want to have it and *dat's all*."

Yente said, "Four children, you call that a lot? Look, my great-grandfather had sixteen, and my grandfather fourteen, and my father twelve."

"That may be the case," the landlord said. "But your grandfather and your father didn't live in my house."

"So what do you want?" Yente became incensed. "Am I, on account of your three rooms—with their cockroaches and bedbugs—to murder my children? You won't live to see it! My children are precious to me; I have no use for your three dark little holes!"

The landlord started to seethe, but Yente and my mother-in-law drowned him in curses.

The next morning, the landlord sent us an eviction notice.

From that we gathered that he was a beast who didn't understand jokes; that no upstanding person could do business with him. So I said to Yente, "Yente, let's go look for rooms."

Yente said, "awlright," and she called all the kids to come in from the street, wiped their noses, gave each of them a piece of bread with salt, and marched them back downstairs. "Go!" she said, and I died a little.

"Now that I've looked after the children," Yente said to me, "we can go."

First we marched to Osborn Street. We found a yellow notice on a door and we asked a guy who ran a coal cellar there, "How many rooms and how much money and are they in back or in front?"

The coal-Jew said, "No rooms. All the rooms are occupied."

So I said, "But there's a yellow notice on the door."

The coal-Jew said, "The notice was put there by the 'board of hel' because two kids on the stoop suffer from diphtheria."

I took Yente by the elbow and we kept moving.

On Belmont Avenue near Paul Street we found three rooms: only one window, no sink, and on the fourth floor. We inquired by the butcher.

The butcher said, "Twenty dollars with kids and eighteen dollars without kids."

Yente spat on the butcher and dragged me off.

On Sixth Street we found three rooms with two windows, on the fifth floor. The toilet was in the yard and the wash lines were on the roof. We inquired by the landlord in his rear dwelling.

The landlord asked what kind of *landsman*[14] I was.

---

14 That is, what part of Europe he originated from.

I said, "A Polish one."

He said, "It pains me greatly, but I do not accept any Poles because Poles are not fine people."

I said, "Much better people than you Litvaks!"[15]

He said, "There is no people finer than Litvaks."

I said, "I wouldn't do business with a Litvak even if you paid me a fortune!"

Words were exchanged and then he kicked us out.

We kept going. We found five rooms on Watkins Street.

"What country do you come from?" asked the next landlord, a Jew with a yarmulke.

Of course by then I was afraid to say that I was Polish. I said, "I am a Litvak."

"You're a Litvak?" he asked in a Polish Yiddish. "I don't accept you Litvaks because your heads are always looking to make sales!"

I said, "Litvaks are better than Poles!"

He said, "No people finer than Poles exists."

I said, "You! I wouldn't do business with a Pole if I was offered ten dollars for the trouble!"

He said, "You can leave."

Yente gave me a jab. "Come, Mendel. May he burn down with his house."

In short, we shlepped around all day. After a lot of sorrow, after a lot of angst, we found three rooms, a bath, and a letterbox, but small as a nest. There was barely room to put the kids down. There was no room for me and Yente. According to Yente's math, I am going to have to sleep with Pinnie in the bathtub.

---

15 Jews of Lithuanian origin.

How Pinnie Celebrated
Election Day

(NOVEMBER 8, 1913)

Translated by Eitan Kensky

VOTING DAY: the second I opened my eyes, crawled out of bed, grabbed a shave, showered, dressed in my Sabbath best and inhaled a cigarette, I ran out of the house to give my vote.

The second the drunk politicians saw me, they made eyes at me. They told me rumors. But I was steadfast and answered, "Mendel's vote is not for sale!"

On my way home, I met Yente on the street, wandering, moaning, holding her sides. I asked, "Yente, what's going on? Why are you moaning? Why are you holding your sides?"

She said, "That bed you gave me—I have just that kind of bed for you—like a grave! You call that a mattress—a sack with stones is what it is! Oy, my sides!"

"Is the mattress missing something?" I asked.

"What's it missing, you ask? Here's what you should miss: years of your life! It's missing being a little softer, a little newer, a little fuller."

"In this world," I said, "there are many bad mattresses. Look, Jonah the bookbinder has a mattress that's completely empty. All the straw fell out a long time ago and now he sleeps on the sack alone."

Yente said, "So, go and take up the cause with Jonah! I want you to buy a new mattress and *dat's all*."

"Yente, have patience. Wait until the kids grow, start working, bring home some paydays. When there's money, we'll go and buy a new bed and a new mattress. Pinnie will grow to be a real *mentsch*. He'll help us out, of course."

Yente said, "May you be punished, not Pinnie. Pinnie will be a musician," and her eyes lit up like lanterns.

I said, "Awlright, he'll give *lessons* and help us out."

Yente said, "Of course, in the meantime, we'll need to have a mattress."

I said, "And where, in the meantime, are we supposed to get money?"

Yente said, "I have a plan. Let's not pay the butcher and the milkman this week, or buy shoes for Fayvl—then we'll have money for a mattress."

I said, "Fine."

In short, Yente and I went off to the furniture store to pick out a fine mattress. Yente asked the price and the storekeeper said, nine dollars. Then Yente bid a dollar-and-a-quarter, then a dollar-and-a-half, and for three-and-a-half dollars she bought it. The storekeeper swore on his wife and his mother-in-law that he was losing money, a dollar out of pocket! But he had just that day settled his bills, and he could use the pretty penny.

I paid the storekeeper the money and told him to bring me the mattress around sunset: first we needed to steam-clean the beds with kerosene.

The storekeeper brought the mattress around five that night, put it down on the stairs, and left.

In the meantime, Pinnie, in honor of election day, decided to light a bonfire in the street and he needed something flammable. He saw a mattress lying in the stairwell—didn't ask anyone and didn't give it a second thought—grabbed the mattress, and immediately set it on fire.

In only a few minutes, our new mattress was engulfed by flames and Favyl, Isaac, Pinnie and their friends ran around it like poisoned mice and gathered up pieces of wood, papers, burlap, old chairs, baby carriages, and tossed them all onto our new, burning mattress, and the fire grew bigger and more festive, and Pinnie stood there and blew his big, tin trumpet and watched the crackling fire and burned up with pride.

And his cheeks were illuminated, as if by the Divine Presence, and his little heart was filled with inspiration, which he released through his tin trumpet; and the fire continued to rage, and his cheeks continued to gleam, and his inspiration trumpeted louder and louder!

———

Yente and Mendel and Mendel Beilis

(NOVEMBER 12, 1913)

Translated by Eitan Kensky

YENTE FLED FROM the street, flustered, seething, hooting and hollering.

"Mendel! Mendel! Take a listen to what's going on outside! Hear them shouting, 'Extra! Extra!' Every street, it's a commotion, 'Extra!' *I'llbetcha* a ship sunk again,[16] or a new Triangle Fire[17]—oh the horror! Mendel, why are you just standing there with one foot in the grave? Run outside and bring up a paper! You know how much I love to hear who's been murdered, burned alive, run over, or poisoned! Read something!"

I said, "Yente, I would read, but the kids aren't going to let me."

Yente said, "I'll drive the kids out into the street and then we're set."

---

16 A reference to the sinking of the RMS *Titanic* in April 1912.
17 The 1911 Triangle Shirtwaist Factory Fire caused the deaths of 146 garment workers, many of them Jewish women.

I said, "*Awlright*, kick them out!"

So Yente went and kicked out the kids and told them not to live long enough to come back upstairs.

Freed from the kids, I ran down and bought a paper and read:

"Kiev, Monday—Mendel Beilis[18] is free! The jury of twelve nobles reached the verdict that the martyr Mendel Beilis is not guilty."

Yente shook her head and said, "So what, you think that people will free you? You were a *shlimazel*[19] and you'll die a *shlimazel*. You'll see, when it comes time to free, they'll free that other Mendel, not you! No one will free you! Everything needs luck. If God ordains you to be a Mendel, then you better be a Kiev Mendel, not a Brownsville Mendel. May the Brownsville Mendels catch fire—they're good for nothing! Woe to the Yentes who fall into the arms of Brownsville Mendels!"

And she took a shot at my head with a couple of spicy curses.

I availed myself of the opportunity and continued reading.

"Local workers are opening a Mendel Beilis fund. It is thought that the fund will bring in a million dollars."

"What's that?" Yente said. "Will people collect millions on your behalf? Blows to the ribs—that's what people will collect for you, not millions! If you were a Mendel like that Mendel, things would be much better for me. My name wouldn't be so besmirched around the world."

I heard Yente like Haman hears noisemakers.[20] I kept reading.

"Kiev, Monday. As the jury rendered its verdict, Mendel Beilis 'not guilty,' the Jewish martyr turned pale and tears began to stream from his eyes."

Here Yente sighed and said in a sad voice. "Do you hear, Mendel. It's good that you weren't accused of anything . . . You have some luck, too, Mendel. Because according to what you tell me, not even

---

18 Menachem Mendel Beilis (1874–1934) was a Russian Jew from Kiev who was accused of ritually murdering a Christian child. He was acquitted at trial in 1913.

19 An inept or bungling person.

20 When the book of Esther is read on the holiday of Purim, it is traditional to try and drown out the name of the villain, Haman, with noisemakers.

the Russian 'sympathizers' are good people. Would they have made a fuss—over which Mendel? A Mendel is a Mendel! If a Berel fell into their hands, he would be in trouble! But tell me, Mendel, who is this Mendel Beilis who's got the whole world cooking? Wherever I go and wherever I'm standing, it's all Mendel Beilis. In the grocery—Mendel Beilis; at the butcher—Mendel Beilis; everywhere, Beilis."

I said, "Beilis is a simple Jew. A husband. A father of five children. A quiet man who was accused of slaughtering a *goyish*[21] child and using his blood for Passover."

Yente asked, "Who were the accusers?"

I said, "The Black Hundreds,[22] hooligans, anti-Semites."

Yente said, "May a single blow knock them all down!"

I said, "Amen."

Yente said, "Amen and Amen."

—

Pinnie Grows to Be a Businessman

(DECEMBER 13, 1913)

Translated by Eitan Kensky

PINNIE THAT LITTLE bastard!

Recently, Pinnie grabbed an old sack, slung it over his shoulder, and ran down into the street.

The frost was then raging, what terror!

---

21 Non-Jewish.
22 An anti-Semitic, ultranationalist movement in Russia in the early twentieth century.

A few hours later, he came back with a sack full of coal.

Yente asked him, "Where did you get that?"

Pinnie answered, "From the Italian."

"From which Italian?" Yente asked.

"The one with the coal cellar, on the second corner," answered Pinnie.

"Did you steal it?"

"No," answered Pinnie.

It was decided that I should watch him.

Meanwhile, Pinnie emptied the coals, flung the bag over his shoulder, grabbed a piece of bread and half an onion and ran down into the street.

Yente said to me, "Mendel, follow Pinnie and see where he goes. He should walk like you—on crutches! See where he comes into these coals. If he's stealing them, he'll ache for years. I'll shatter one of his ribs, chop off one of his sides, twist his arms off, make him into a cripple!"

I watched as he neared the coal cellar, took his position opposite the entrance, stuck his nose out at the Italian and shouted at him "Macaroni!" "Guinea!" "Monkey!" and ran off.

The Italian turned red and threw coals at him. Pinnie went and collected the coals, put them in his sack, and walked some more.

I followed him.

I saw him stop at a second coal cellar, where a Jew with a filthy face and a thin beard was sitting on the steps, eyeing a customer.

Pinnie started to taunt him. First he stuck out his tongue, then he took a stone and started to hack at the iron bars on the basement windows.

The man shouted, "Bastard, get out of here!"

Pinnie didn't hear him and kept banging.

The man shouted, raising his voice, "Bastard, get out of here or I'll rip your arms out!"

Pinnie pretended not to hear and banged louder.

Then the man became really angry and he snatched a big lump of coal and he threw it at Pinnie. Pinnie caught the coal and put it in his sack and then he started taunting the man again. The man threw coal after coal and Pinnie collected them all and put them in his sack.

And this is how he went, from one coal cellar to the next, until he gathered a sackful of coal. Then he came home and poured them out and went back to it.

It looked as if Pinnie would keep us in coal all winter. And not only coal; also in fruit and groceries.

See, he would go over to a fruit stand and start to needle the stand-keeper. The stand-keeper would start to get angry and throw at Pinnie whatever he had near him: a rotten apple, a pear, a banana, an orange. Pinnie collected them and brought them home and Yente cut them up and cooked them.

But Pinnie didn't rest and kept at it.

Here he took his position at a grocery.

And again, the same story: he sticks out his tongue, makes a "long nose," makes the fig sign . . . and the grocer rages, tosses a radish at Pinnie, an onion, a potato, a beet. Pinnie gathers them all up and brings them home.

In short, Pinnie made a big jump in our income: without him, it would have been very hard to come into our present luxuries!

And Yente was happy. She said, "The whole time Pinnie wasn't stealing, wasn't playing tricks; people were throwing it at him. *That* is proper and fine and we shouldn't get in his way.

As long as he gets it in an honorable way!

In conclusion, thanks to Pinnie our home is filled with the best of goods!

And more: how Yente swells with pride over him! "May his bones be filled with good health," she said. "It's obvious: he's growing into a businessman."

Rooms with Steam Heat

(DECEMBER 25, 1913)

Translated by Eitan Kensky

MY YENTE WENT nuts and said, "Mendel, let's move."
I asked, "Why?"

She said, "Because the rooms are cold. You can freeze to death in them. The wind blows in from all directions and the windows shake and you need three tons of coal to get through the winter. Remember, Mendel, how cold it was last year? Even the fire in the stove froze."

"Yes," I said, "I remember."

It was decided that we would go out and find rooms with steam heat.

We went together, me and my Yente.

We saw a "to let": rooms with steam heat. Inquire by the landlord, Mr. Fayfl.[23]

We went in and asked, "Are you Mr. Fayfl?"

"Yes," he said. "It is I who am Mr. Fayfl."

"How many rooms do you have?"

"Four."

"Perhaps five?"

"No, four."

"With steam?"

"With steam."

"With real steam?"

"With real steam."

"It can't be," my Yente said.

---

23 A play on the Yiddish name Fayvl and the word *fayfn*, to whistle.

The landlord grew angry. "Does that mean, you don't believe me? When I say steam, it's steam. With me there's no monkey business!"

"That's that," I said. "If you say it, then it's said. A landlord isn't going to go bluff."

"*I'llbetcha*," he said. "Landlords don't bluff."

I asked, "How much do the four rooms cost?"

He said, "It depends on how many kids you have. Without kids, I reckon, twenty-two dollars. With one kid, twenty-three; and with two, twenty-four. A dollar a kid."

I said, "And in case I have almost six kids?"

"What do you mean by 'almost?'"

"'Almost' means I already have five kids and the sixth is probably on the way."

"If so," he said, "the rooms will cost you twenty-eight dollars. I wanted to say thirty dollars, but I want this deal to be simple."

In short, my Yente offered him seventeen dollars and with the offer came two remarks: first, these aren't rooms, but holes; second, what, do you want us to work nonstop, you miser of a landlord?

The landlord started to make a show that he was losing money on the rooms, that this house was driving him into the poorhouse.

In short, we made a deal and a week later we moved in.

The rooms made my Yente swell with pride. "Now," she said, "we better keep our eyes open."

Her joy didn't last long. With the first frost, my Jewess ran to the heater and started to turn the knob. But no steam came out. The flat was as cold as the North Pole. Me and Yente and the kids trembled from the cold; our teeth chattered and chattered.

We went over to the landlord.

"Well, Mr. Fayfl, where's the steam? We're dying of cold!"

The landlord said to have patience. First, he hired a gentile, from Poland, to come and make the steam, but he didn't show; second, the engine is broken; third, coal's extremely expensive now—seven dollars a ton!

Meanwhile, we're sitting in "steam heat" rooms trembling from cold. One night we lay in bed with the comforter over our heads, blowing on our palms until morning. By the second night, my Yente and the kids went to sleep at her sister's and I was left all alone in the cold, "steam heat" rooms.

I would surely have frozen to death each night if I didn't go to sleep in my overcoat, with my fur hat on my head and with Yente's muff on my hands. In addition, I had to boil water, pour it into a rubber bag, and put it on my feet. When I got up in the morning, I shook pieces of ice from the rubber bag.

But of course the people from my hometown were jealous: such a pauper and he lives in rooms with steam heat!

Yente at the Metropolitan Opera

(MARCH 21, 1914)

Translated by Eitan Kensky

O N MY WAY back from the shop I told Yente that Benny the Operator sold me two tickets to the Metropolitan Opera House.

Yente asked me, "Mendel, what kind of house is that? A tenement house or a private house?"

I said, "Yente, it's a kind of theater, where the best singers in the world perform. That's where a man named Caruso[24] sings—and he gets two thousand dollars a night!"

"And so?" Yente said. "Are you going to give me two thousand dollars a night to sing? You should suffer two thousand blows!"

I said, "Yente, shut your little mouth and quit cursing."

Yente said, "I'll have you in the ground!"

---

24 Opera singer Enrico Caruso (1873–1921).

I said, "Yente, let's eat our supper and go. Time isn't standing still. You'll have time to curse me when we're on the streetcar or when we're sitting at the opera."

Yente said, "I'm afraid, Mendel, I might forget."

I said, "I'll remind you."

Yente said, "Get sick for a long time."

In short, we grabbed supper and Yente put on her stained skirt (she has a better one, but she didn't want to use it), and the small black cap with the broken feather, and, on top, a red wool cardigan sweater with torn pockets and without buttons, and on top of her sweater, her worn velvet coat, and we went to the streetcar.

Walking, I said, "Yente, now, if you want, you can curse me."

Yente said, "I'll have you in the ground!"

In the car, Yente tossed her head from side to side and seemed bored.

I said, "Yente, let's go outside, in the fresh air, you'll feel better."

She said, "May misfortune befall you!"

We made it to the opera full of such troubles.

Sitting up top in the last gallery, Yente started to get lightheaded, and she cried out, "Mendel, why did you move us up here? We can head downstairs; it's a lot better down there."

I said, "Yente, those seats are taken. Can't you see, the theater is full!"

Yente cast her gaze to and fro, considered the large crowd and said, "If God helped you have so many boarders, you'd make a nice living, huh?"

Meanwhile, they'd started to play.

At the beginning, Yente was impressed and kept her eyes on the stage. Then she asked me, "Mendel, why don't they sing Yiddish songs here?"

I shoved my elbow into Yente to get her to be quiet, hold her tongue.

But Yente didn't hear me and tossed a whole mountain of questions my way: "Mendel, why isn't there anyone here peddling soda water, peanuts, apples, oranges or bananas?"

"Yente," I said. "Don't twist my head with your stupid questions, let me listen!"

But Yente kept asking, "Mendel, would you like to have five rooms like those, with steam heat? Mendel, how much do you think it costs to carpet such a big floor? Mendel, why are the actors all singing at the same time? Are they trying to be done sooner?"

"Mendel, what are the women doing sitting over there with naked shoulders? It doesn't embarrass them at all? Mendel, why do they play so many violins, one is too few? Mendel, I feel a tug at my heart; can you get me a corned beef sandwich?"

"Mendel!"

The crowded started to laugh and shout and ordered her to shut her mouth, but Yente kept posing her questions.

"Mendel, what a pain you are! Why are you just letting me talk on and on without answering me? Mendel, what's this play called? Huh? Would it be too much of a bother for them to speak Yiddish? Mendel—"

By then my nerves had gotten to me and I shouted at her, "Yente, quit pestering me with your questions! Be quiet and pay attention!"

And Yente stayed still for a while and started to listen. When the first act ended, I noticed that Yente had fallen fast asleep. Her head was tilted back, her mouth was agape and she snored. People were staring at her and laughing. I enjoyed it and let her sleep. I decided not to wake her.

The second act ended and they were in the midst of the third. The crowd was astounded by the chanteuse—and Yente slept like after a bath!

During the last act, a tall, beautiful singer in a white satin dress bedecked with pearls performed. She sang like a bird in the forest at the break of day. And a kind of whistle sound trailed her.

At that moment, the theater was so quiet you could hear a pin drop. Everyone sat there enchanted, with bated breath, listening to her throat imitate the whistle, and the whistle imitate the singer . . .

And just at that moment, Yente began to dream a horrible nightmare. She shuddered and started to shout in her sleep, "Mendel, what a pain you are! Mendel, Pinnie is standing on the roof! He's going to fall and die, Mendel! Mendel!"

Then a terrifying uproar broke out! People shouted from every direction: "Throw her out! Throw her out!" And soon a special policeman came and ordered us to go. Or, to be precise, he kicked us out.

On the way home, Yente couldn't stop wondering why rich people were so smitten with the opera.

Roshelle Weprinsky
1895–1981

Roshelle Weprinsky was a novelist and poet associated with *Di yunge* (The Young Ones), a group of like-minded New York Yiddish poets and writers in the early twentieth century.

Born in the town of Ivankiv, in what is now Ukraine, Weprinsky attended a religious elementary school and later a Russian-Jewish high school in Kiev. In 1906 she immigrated to the United States, where she attended night school and began writing poetry. Her first pieces, influenced by "sweatshop poets" such as Morris Rosenfeld, were published in a variety of Yiddish periodicals, including the *Forward*. She published several volumes of poetry in her lifetime, starting in the 1920s and continuing until the 1970s.

For much of her life Weprinsky was the partner of poet Mani Leib, who was also a contributor to the *Forward* and a member of *Di yunge*. Weprinsky described the group in her 1971 novel *Ven di hent kraytsn zikh* (*With Arms Crossed*) and in a volume of correspondence with Mani Leib, which was published in 1980.

In the two stories included here, which appeared in the late 1930s and early 1940s, Weprinsky makes use of a lyrical prose style to evoke the difficulties of adjusting to an adopted homeland, even decades after arrival.

Annie

(AUGUST 6, 1939)

Translated by Myra Mniewski

I N THE SHOP where Annie worked, there were other middle-aged women just like her. Hardship had brought them back to their places at the machine. But Annie hadn't yet noticed them. She was confused and felt lost in this new place, not yet accustomed to the noise. She was like a worm exposed to the bright light of day after being flushed to the surface by a rainstorm, and she squirmed in the unfamiliar light of the shop. She felt the world's eye focused on her like a magnifying glass, examining her from all angles, exposing her fraudulent and worn-out self. So she bent closer to her machine, as if wanting to merge with it.

That's how it was at the beginning. And even later, when Annie had already grown accustomed to the peculiar din and noticed the other women around her, the sight of whom actually brought her a bit of comfort, she was still not able to form an intimacy with the shop. It remained strange and unfamiliar to her, as if she had never been there before. But her hands remembered the work. As if from a distant dream her fingers naturally curved towards the fabric. It was remarkable how things happened on their own, without her, as if she wasn't even there. The cogs clacked, the wheels roared, the foreman yelled over it all, but she heard nothing. It was as if she was in her own home tending to all her little interests, her husband and her children.

Yes, her husband—how pale he'd become lately. A strange pity overtook her. How ashamed he must feel about her going back to work and him staying home, doing nothing, unable to find something to do. His gaze was downcast whenever he talked to her. And the sound of his voice changed—it became thinner and milder. When he addresses her by her name, Annie, the tenderness in his voice practically chokes her. Her old feelings surge up for a second and her eyes twinkle for a bit. She forgets about her burden for a minute. And when they are alone, just the two of them, it's as if he wants to win her favor with caresses, in order to compensate for the other things he's not giving her. Annie feels shame for allowing those moments to subsume her. She doesn't want to think about it anymore, so instead she conjures up her children and occupies her mind with them.

"Come Reyzele, it's time to shampoo your hair! She's pretty good for a fifteen-year-old girl whose mother can't look after her so closely. I'm busy—you can see for yourself, you might try helping out in the house a little. Yes, like that."

And then immediately her thirteen-year-old, Ayzikl, appears before her. His hands and feet have grown large recently and his voice has become so deep that she hardly recognizes him. And as usual, whenever he comes to mind, she is overtaken with worry over the soles of his shoes. Every three weeks they need to be resoled because of all the ball playing he does! And his appetite—there should be no evil eye! "Here my son, have a piece of bread with butter." And *sha*. What is she going to make for supper today? She'll have to stop at the butcher's on her way home. And at the grocer's and the green market. How she would love to make something special for her little one today, her ten-year-old, Perele, may God bless her! What an angel she is! Oh how she would love to buy her a wool dress with her next pay, one with pleats like everyone is wearing now.

Annie's fingers are suddenly aware of the warmth of the material she is in the middle of sewing. Her fingers begin patting it, as if it actually was the dress her Perele was going to wear.

The shop around her is roaring, in tumult. But the hubbub she hears is not hers; it's a foreign sound. In the evening the elevator takes her and the other workers down and pours them out into the throng. The closer she gets to her house, the closer she is to reality.

And even though, in the mornings, when Annie gets up, and her bones hurt as if someone had banged on them, she is nevertheless eager to go to work. The small pay that she now receives has inspired many needs and desires. She has more contact with the rich city now. She passes display windows loaded with marvelous things. Her eyes see, and her womanly heart fills with desire.

"May the season stretch out a little bit more," Annie says to herself. "Then maybe, maybe, maybe . . ." and she pictures all the beautiful things she would buy for her children.

But the work was cut off abruptly, out of the blue. One morning when Annie arrived at work, the shop was strangely quiet. The workers who had arrived before her stood there with their hands hanging by their sides, like the wheels of a stopped mill. Not a thing was in motion. The silence in the shop hung like unwritten handwriting: SLACK.

The foreman, indifferent, addressed everyone as if individually: There's nothing to do. Whoever wants to, come back at noon. Something might come in for an hour or two.

The workers stirred themselves and quietly shuffled out.

Annie gazed at the older seamstresses intensely. Their faces looked half-softened from years of being housewives and half-hardened from the shop. But everyone's hands hung down dejected and heavy.

Annie remained standing downstairs in the street. She squinted against the brightness of the day. Her clothes looked worn-out. She thought about where to spend the few hours until noon, because after all, a couple hours of work might come in then; it was hard for her to go home. Her desires had been dealt a sharp blow.

Dejected, she proceeded with slow steps in her worn-out shoes until she wandered over to the corner of Fifth Avenue, where she found herself face-to-face with a richly decorated store window. Stopping in front of it, her eyes widened. And even though she wasn't in a position to buy anything, she nevertheless allowed herself to enter through the opulent glass doors that didn't stop revolving until she was inside.

The glitter and dazzle that greeted her eyes felt like a heavenly kingdom. Expensive articles and big bargains were on display. Her heart attached itself to what the wooden or waxen mannequins were wearing. Annie lingered at every table. Everything she saw she needed! This table had everything for her Perele: dresses and sweaters for school; gloves of pure wool; a woolen hat; a soft little scarf to wrap around her neck. She handled all these things with motherly kindness, stroking them and turning them inside out. Are these gloves really of pure wool? she marveled. Yes, they're made of pure wool! Annie's face brightened. In her mind she'd already tried all these items on her dear Perele. Might this sweater be a little too tight for her dear child? She was totally occupied in this way when a salesgirl's head appeared from behind the counter:

"Can I help you, Madam?"

"Huh? No, no thank you."

As if caught in a spell, Annie moved on. Presently, a half-dozen wax figures dressed in expensive coats took her breath away. Annie's bedazzled eyes took them in all at once but fixated on one in particular. This is it! This is exactly the coat for my Rosele! It was exactly the one she'd been dreaming of, with that little fur collar! What a beauty!

Annie's feet sank deeper into the soft gray carpet, as if they were planted there. She stared at the coat for so long, until she became terribly close to it, and she went to pat it. She spotted a loose gray thread on its left sleeve and carefully removed it, patting down the sleeve and feeling as though the coat was now all but hers.

There was nothing left to do but go look at that pink dress again; perfect for Rosele's graduation. And right next to it—a black taffeta dress fitted on a dummy with a middle-aged face, curly gray hair, and a motherly smile, saying to Annie, this dress is for you! At this, Annie's face lights up, her wrinkles smooth out and she feels good. She proceeds rhythmically on the soft gray carpet as if at a ball, not conscious of her direction. An escalator takes her up to the next floor.

She is now in another world. Menswear of all sorts; dark and earnest suits, not as approachable. Annie stands at a distance. Her Ayzikl, her husband—how beautiful he would look dressed in these things. She feels her heart beating lightly. A salesman is coming towards her.

She avoids him by moving aside and proceeds unnoticed into the furniture department.

A new spell totally enchants her. She hasn't bought a new piece of furniture since she got married. She hasn't even dreamed of it. Her husband's wages hardly covered the most essential pieces, and recently everything's been getting threadbare. Their beds look like they're on chicken legs. And right here are all the wonderful things she needs, right here before her eyes. Entire rooms furnished with deep soft chairs; low expensive beds made up and covered with pillows, drapes on the windows and pictures on the walls. And a deep calm and restfulness permeates everything.

Suddenly, Annie experiences an utter tiredness in her bones. Oh how she would love to rest and stretch her legs out. She bends down to pat the soft chair, as if she actually was about to buy it and, as if to try it out, she sinks right into it. A sweetness travels through her limbs, a feeling like she won't be getting up anytime soon. She looks around and sees that no one is in the department at the moment. She is there alone. She stretches her two tired legs and sinks deeper into the plush. She half-closes her eyes in the deep softness and silence, only to fall asleep. But no, she's not asleep. She's sure of it. Dreams start to jumble in her head—daydreams. She's at home on the plush gray carpet wearing the black taffeta and smiling affectionately. Guests come over and she invites them to sit in the comfy armchairs. Rosele appears in the pink dress; it's her graduation. Annie picks the gray thread off of Rosele's coat sleeve. And there is her husband, calling her, with such tenderness in his voice. But she pretends not to hear, not to understand, because guests are arriving and squeezing her delicate hands. Ayzikl and Perele stand in the distance, all dressed up and looking beautiful. Ach, how great it is to be a mother, to be a woman, oh how good . . .

Her head suddenly falls back—she feels as if she's falling! Where is she falling from—is she falling asleep? No! No! Wait! Something inside her screams. What time is it? Where's a clock?

With great effort, Annie forces her bloodshot eyes open. Her eyes are burning, irritated from fatigue, but she quickly scans the walls looking for a clock. Finally she sees one on a far-off wall. It's twelve o'clock.

Annie jumps up from the sunken armchair as if pricked by needles. Only one thought resounds in her head: Let her not be late! Two hours of work would also be good!

———

By a Far Shore

(MARCH 15, 1942)

Translated by Myra Mniewski

THE OCEAN HERE, where the palms are green, where the sun shines the whole year, where the air is as mild and gentle as the breath of a child—the ocean here is so soft and gentle; it doesn't storm, it doesn't fling its waves as if it were trying to shed parts of itself, it doesn't tumble with thick foamy lips, it doesn't bite into the shore as if releasing all of its suffering rage. The ocean here, under this endless blue sky, stretches out peacefully, reclining quietly, softly spreading out, whispering so softly and calmly—as quiet as the old folks who sit by these shores of Miami.

The old folks like to sit by the seashore and look out far across the sea, thinking muddled thoughts, remembering fragments of memories. Their former lives are like tales from *A Thousand and One Nights*. One moment you're born and growing up in a tiny village across a faraway sea with no inkling of the wider world. The village, fenced in by faraway skies, where women toil at their clay ovens, stoking embers with their pokers, rocking little ones in rigid cradles, nursing them until they're already walking, the little ones going over to their mothers' breasts and grabbing them to their mouths as if they were hunks of bread. And inside the women, in their bellies, yet another little soul rises like leavened dough, already pushing its way into the world, moving the women to yet again prepare a cradle.

The men have gone to the markets to do business, traveling over the countryside in sleet and snow, making their way to the nobleman, to bow to him, their eyes brimming, feeling no bigger than a worm, thinking this is how they will endure life forever. But then they are crossing wide oceans to arrive at a big, free country, their eyes wide and bright. Their hands get moving, they begin building—stores and houses, upright and square, in a frenzy, at the same feverish pace as baking matzo for Passover. Opulent houses sprout up and it is still not enough. Children are educated, molded into honorable people who then become estranged from their parents.

And suddenly, with the speed of a dream, everything changes. Everything disappears with the wind. And now they are old and as helpless as children. No place had been prepared for them. They remain wanderers, having transmigrated to yet another faraway shore, a shore where it is eternally summer, where a strange golden holiday shimmers before them. Every day, in their holiday finery, their tribe plods with canes in their hands, their businesses closed forever. And yet, a frail, muted longing pulls at their hearts, as if craving to retrieve something from their dreams, but they can't quite grasp what it was. How did this happen? Their bygone lives appear before them like rubbed-out handwriting. Their aged eyes flutter.

The old folks move closer together. They want to be with each other. That way they might hear something from someone. Some news. So they sit here in this little park by the faraway Florida shore. These former doers and builders who were once magnates sit in the sand or on benches, shaded by the palms that sway in the gentle breeze, their thin branches crackling like dry, old fingers.

Those sitting on the sand expose those parts of themselves that are in pain—the parts they have come here to heal. Each one of them exposes her old body to the sun as if it were God's eye, so that it should see them and work its miracle.

Also sitting there are old folks in their holiday best. These ones are sitting on benches. Nothing hurts them, only old age. They are probably aware that there is no cure for that, that old age cannot be healed. So they seem to be as lost as the others, as they whisper quietly among themselves, their lips like weak waves.

Two old women have shuffled up to each other on a bench. They've been watching each other for a while—have acknowledged each other. One of them is older than the other. The older one is close to seventy. The younger one—around sixty. The older one is not a greenhorn anymore. She's been coming here for years already and always loves to meet new people, especially since this year there are fewer of her old acquaintances and this one here looks familiar.

"Excuse me," the older one volleyed out the first question, "weren't you here last year?"

"No, this is my first time here," the younger one answered, a little lost.

"Is that so."

"And you? You were here last year?" The younger one was surprised at the older woman's temerity, to undertake such a journey a second time.

"Me? I've been here many times already," she replied, and it was impossible to tell from her tone if she was bragging or ashamed.

"When did you arrive?" the older one asked again.

"The day before yesterday. And you? You got here a while ago," the younger one guessed.

"Yes, quite a while ago," the older one replied. "Where are you living, seeing that you've only just arrived?"

"Over there," the younger one turned and pointed to a white, flat-roofed building, partitioned into small rooms and even smaller kitchens.

"You don't say!" the older one rejoiced to her new neighbor. "I live in the building right next door."

"Really."

The two women remained quiet for a while, looking down at their laps, since it was no longer necessary to scrutinize each other's faces. There was no need to further examine each other. They'd already gotten to know one another. Their congeniality made them feel familiar. After all, some time ago they had lived the same life, breathed the same air, cooked the same treats, thought the same thoughts, had the same worries. That way of life had by now practically vanished, but it was still present in their faces, and they recognized it.

"If you'll pardon my asking," the older one again took the lead, "are you, God forbid, suffering from some ailment, or have you come for no particular reason?"

"Do I know?" the younger one muttered. "The doctor said the heart maybe, a little bit."

"Really," the older one answered, grasping that this one here was not of her class.

"And you? What ails you, that you've been coming here for how many years now?"

"Me?" The old woman looked away absentmindedly, staring into the air. Then she added, "You understand of course that an old person is not a young person; when a pot is used for a long time it gets worn down and battered. It hurts and sometimes it coughs too, but by no means can I complain about my health, at my age—no."

"Then do you come here because you like it?"

"Do I like it? Yes and no. What's liking it got to do with anything? Wherever a person is used to living, that's where she likes it."

The younger one felt a heaviness in the older one's tone and her curiosity was piqued.

"Please, pardon me for what I'm about to ask you," the younger one said, taking on the older one's boldness. "But do you live with your children back home?"

"Children!" her elder blurted out. "I have only one child—a one and only daughter, may she be healthy and well! May no Jewish children be deprived of a life like hers. She lives like an aristocrat! If only I had more children! Not to wish it on anyone but they haven't stayed close to me."

"And you don't live with this daughter? You don't get along with your only daughter? Forgive me for putting such questions to you."

"Get along?" the old one repeated, as if to herself. And why not let the younger one ask her such inappropriate questions. Let her, on the contrary, it felt good to talk about it.

"Live in peace together?" she said again, as if to herself. "No it's not a question of getting along. Why shouldn't we get along? I lived with my daughter for years, even then when she lived in the Bronx. But then my son-in-law hadn't yet worked himself up, my grandchildren were still little then, and I was younger then too. My dear woman, you get it, don't you," she said, putting her hand on the younger one's knee. "Work, I had enough. And I was happy too. I was used to working and taking caring of a big house. And if I occasionally got lonely, because my daughter often entertained high-minded, clever folks, I would go out and meet up with my former girlfriends—my friends. I had people to talk to. Now, you understand, it's a whole different story."

"What goes on now?" the younger one asked with interest.

"Now," the older one resumed weaving her yarn, as if she needed to unburden herself completely—a person mustn't shut herself off, it's hard to exist with locked lips— "Now, since my son-in-law, there should be no evil eye, has achieved such success, my daughter lives on Central Park West. The grandchildren are grown, perfect Americans. They don't understand a word I say. A Negro in a white cap wanders about through the house, on the parquet floors; the furniture is constantly being changed—everything has to be the latest style! You get it, my dear woman, an old piece of furniture like me is out of place there. Sometimes I even let out a little cough too, like an old person. Could I possibly fit into such a scene? I ask you my dear woman! They haven't thrown me out, by no means. My daughter is kindhearted, my son-in-law too. It's not that—there is just no place for me there; not in the house and not outside, where the gentiles and their dogs roam about. And lately my daughter has been traveling a lot. She used to go to Europe all the time. That's where the party was—Europe! Then when that became unfashionable it's just trips; every so often a trip! So I get stuck with the Negro staring at me like a puppy at its father. I never see my grandkids. Do they need me or care about me? So then my daughter convinced me to come here; she said it would be good for my health. So I let myself be persuaded, even though I was scared. It seemed like the end of the world to me. But on the other hand, what did I have to lose? And so now I can't even remember how long I've been coming here. And believe me, it's not like you disappear here— we're among our own people here. In the summer my daughter rents me a room by the sea or in the country also among my people. So now I'm constantly traveling. You understand, I'm a traveler."

"No need to confess," the younger one cut her off. "Believe me, it could be worse."

"Of course—God forbid! I'm not complaining," the old one retorted. "I'm not the only one who travels around like this. Do you see the old folks sitting on those benches? They all gallivant around. They come here every year, not because they're sick, but because they're old. Their children didn't feel right about putting their aged mother or father in a home; respectable folk don't look kindly on that. And in their posh homes there's also no place for them. So they send them around—winter here and summer there. So the old folks travel around. I've given it a name: The Traveling Old Age Home . . . Ha, ha, ha! I should have it so good! I gave it that name myself! But listen to this, there's a very old one here, she got tired of roaming, so now she stays put right here. Winter and summer she sits here all alone like a stone. She cooks herself her bit of food and makes her bed up tidy. When Friday comes, she welcomes the Sabbath for herself with challah and fish, blesses the candles and comes here and sits on a bench all alone. I'll point her out to you tomorrow. She's as quiet as a dove—talks very little. *Nu*, what's this little bit of life that's left us worth? Ha! I'd better not go astray with such talk."

"Why talk that way? You shouldn't talk that way! Believe me, the world is good; and sweet even to the aged palate. And this here is a true paradise! The air is a joy here! May we only not need it," the younger one ended quietly to herself.

But the older one caught her last words and cracked up, laughing silently, the skin on her neck scrunching up like an old elephant's. "Ha-ha-ha, I scored a good one with you! That's well put: may we not need it. May I live not to!" and she again cracked up, furrowing her aged neck.

The younger one didn't understand what was so funny about it all.

The two of them again fell silent, looking around at those who slowly, one by one, were getting up from their benches to go home. They looked like shadows gradually descending into town. The sun was about to set and an early evening breeze floated in; the sea rippled gently and all the colors of the rainbow played off it. The lights further uptown were already flickering on; the entertainment spots, winking electricity from afar, enticed everyone to the nightlife that was about to get going. Young people and middle-aged folks began moving uptown. Women in flannel pants and colorful jackets; men, their collars open, their heads bare and tussled, proceeded in the soft evening air, as if on wings, or more like moths to the evening flame.

"We should go already," the older woman said, spent and in need of nourishment. "We have to go prepare our bit of food. Come, are you going? Let me at least find out what your name is!"

"Mine is Mrs. Bloom," the younger one replied.

"And mine is Mrs. Diamond. Let's go, Mrs. Bloom!" And they both got up from their bench and went on their way, like two old friends.

Sarah Hamer-Jacklyn

1905–1975

SARAH HAMER-JACKLYN, one of the *Forward*'s most popular writers, was born in Radomsko, Poland, to a Hasidic family. In 1914 she immigrated to Canada and settled in Toronto, where she attended public school and received private tutoring in Jewish subjects.

At age sixteen Hamer-Jacklyn began a career as an actress and singer in Toronto's Yiddish theater. Her acting career took her to New York, where she married, had a son and eventually divorced. Her literary career began at age thirty-four with the publication of a story titled "A Shop Girl" in the newspaper *Der tog* (*The Day*). She continued to write for many Yiddish periodicals, including the *Forward*, and published several collections of stories.

"Compatriots" appeared in the *Forward* on August 3, 1952, and was included two years later in her collection *Shtamn un tsvaygn* (*Roots and Branches*). It tells the story of two older men, both of whom were once involved in their *landsmanshaft*—a social and mutual-aid society based on common geographical origin—but whose lives have since diverged, and who now find themselves longing for their younger years.

Appropriately enough, the story appeared on the same page of the newspaper as a column titled "Question and Answers About Social Security."

Compatriots

(AUGUST 3, 1952)

Translated by Rose Waldman

ARON KAUFMAN PACED tensely around his house. He absolutely could not decide what to do. Should he go to tonight's fiftieth-anniversary banquet for the Zlotkover Society or not? Well, could he just not go? He'd built this society, after all! Hadn't he given fifty of his eighty-six years to his Zlotkover compatriots? And he'd even been president for a quarter century. It was true, he'd derived a lot of satisfaction from his compatriots, but he'd also suffered plenty of anguish. The last few years were becoming even worse. The language less Jewish, his compatriots ever more like gentiles. They hadn't even come by to give his deceased wife her final honor. Only a handful had come.

So many times he'd made the decision not to attend the gatherings. He'd resolve that when the usual postcard arrived, inviting "Dear Sisters and Brothers" to the meetings, he'd throw the postcard out and turn his back on their English-language invitations—he wouldn't go! But later—he could never quite account for how it happened, couldn't remember at all—he would somehow find himself at the society's gathering. Sitting there in a corner as if at a stranger's wedding, he would feel agitated and nostalgic for his past leadership, for when he was young, active, and standing at the helm. He'd been the president, and only Yiddish was spoken.

He glanced at a Yiddish newspaper and tried to read the editorial, but his brain couldn't handle it. He began reading a lighter article, but then realized that once again his mind had wandered to thoughts of his compatriots, today's fiftieth anniversary, and the wonderful past . . . The newspaper slipped out of his fingers. His eyes gazed into the distance, and a curtain suddenly seemed to open on a time fifty years ago. He saw himself as a naïve eighteen-year-old in New York. He'd fled his small Polish town right after a pogrom, then underwent all the difficulties of a greenhorn immigrant. Yet difficult as it was, how could it compare with the hellish terror of pogroms and the constant struggle for a piece of bread? Still, he couldn't help but feel nostalgia for his hometown, wistful for the dear memories of his childhood years.

In New York he'd learned a skill: he became a "cloak operator."[25] He became friendly with a "finisher" in the shop, the beautiful black-eyed Clara, and they soon fell in love. Together they fought for the union and helped organize the shop. Later they went on strike and marched on the picket line together, went to lectures, listened to enlightening words from Morris Hillquit,[26] Joseph Barondess,[27] and Ab. Cahan.[28] A year later he married his Clara and together they had a happy life. Soon after their wedding, he began organizing the society. His humble home on Broome Street became home to every greenhorn compatriot. The newcomer would stay there until Aaron found him a job and a home, until he ungreened himself and become a bit of a *mentsch*.[29] It was at Aaron's home on Broome Street that the first gathering for the founding of the Zlotkover Society was held. Two years later, Aaron's old friend from home, Chaim Brikman, arrived. Chaim became Aaron's right-hand man. They both worked hard to advance the society, to make it stronger and better. When Aaron Kaufman

---

25 A sewing-machine operator who worked on ladies' cloaks.
26 Morris Hillquit (1869–1933), born Moishe Hillkowitz, was a socialist politician and labor lawyer.
27 Joseph Barondess (1867–1928) was a labor leader known as the "King of the Cloakmakers."
28 Abraham Cahan (1860–1951) was a socialist journalist and the longtime editor of the *Forward*.
29 Literally, "person."

became president, Chaim became the secretary, and both invested a great deal. They visited the homes of their compatriots, called and demanded dues, organized picnics and "package parties," collected money, sent matzos for Passover back to Zlotkov, sent money for the ill and for orphans. And if it happened that one of the compatriots had begun to "forget" his wife and children from back home, Aaron and Chaim reminded him. Often they'd send boat fare to those wives and children and apologized and made peace within the broken family.

Aaron had four children, but who had the time to devote to them? His wife Clara raised them and performed all the household duties while he led the society. With his own eyes, Aaron lived to see a tiny handful of compatriots grow into a large organization that numbered more than four hundred individuals.

Later his dear friend Chaim Brikman married an American girl, and they rode off to the far West. He bought a piece of land and so transformed a long-held dream into reality—he became a farmer. In the beginning, Aaron would receive letters often, and so he knew that things were all right. A child was born, and then another. But gradually the correspondence dwindled down to nothing. Only to the big Society celebrations did Chaim send a check, and so they all knew that Chaim had lucked out and had become a wealthy farmer.

Aaron didn't begrudge his friend's riches; he was happy for him with all his heart. The only thing that bothered him was that he'd lost such a dear brother and dedicated activist.

With the passing years, many of the compatriots worked their way up. From lowly workers they became shop owners. From peddlers, businessmen making their own deals. Aaron Kaufman, too, had the opportunity to become partners with a fellow countryman in a tailor shop. But he turned down the chance because he felt he'd be betraying his other compatriots. Who would lead the society if he were to abandon it to manage a shop, with all of its business deals and headaches? And when his wife argued that other compatriots were doing exactly that, he explained to her that they weren't presidents, merely soldiers, and often not even that. Someone had to be on the alert and protect the society.

Indeed, Aaron protected it staunchly. He guarded even the Yiddish language with watchful eyes, refusing to allow any speeches in English. And if a fellow asked a question in English, Aaron quickly cried out, "I don't understand what you're saying. Here we understand only Yiddish!"

If the fellow insisted, Aaron explained to him: Why speak a poor English if he could speak a rich Yiddish? True, one was supposed to learn English, but that was for the outside world. Here, it was their hometown. In Zlotkov people speak Yiddish, *mameloshn*.[30] And here it was Zlotkov . . .

Later the changing of names began. Spitalnik became Mr. Spit; Edelman turned into Adel. And when Aaron Kaufman's presidency was through, there suddenly arose a jumble of half Yiddish, half English. He protested, shouted, banged on the table. His compatriots reminded him that his own two sons—one a doctor, the other an engineer—had also shortened their names from Kaufman to Kay. And so, he was forced to bite his lip and remain silent.

Years flew by. Through watery eyes and with a heart heavy, Aaron Kaufman watched his society become some sort of "lodge." The older compatriots dispersed, un-greened, and set out on other paths. Many died, and the young ones seemed foreign, distant, impossible to reach. A new world, a new flavor. The old ones kept slipping away somehow, moving ever farther and becoming ever stranger.

So he'd come to the gatherings sometimes, mingle, gaze at the president's chair where he once sat and ruled with a firm hand. And near him had been seated, like ministers, the society officials: the secretary, the "hospitality" chair, the recording secretary. Today, though, they were strange chairs, strange people. The old ones had died, and even those who were still alive were dead to the former Zlotkov Society.

---

30 Mother tongue.

Thoughts of nothingness crawled through his mind. Oy, he thought, sighing, if only his wife were still alive, he'd have someone to talk to. But no, he was alone. The house was dark. Night had fallen a long time ago, but he had not yet put on a light.

Aaron got up from his chair and flicked the switch. The room flooded with light. He squinted against the brightness, walked past a mirror and remained standing there. Gray hair. Not too long ago, it seemed to him, he had a head full of black curly hair, a tall svelte figure, sparkling brown eyes. He was still tall, only a bit skinnier now. The eyes, he thought, were the same, but covered with glasses that concealed deep wrinkles. He carelessly slipped on his coat. Perhaps he'd step into the theater, or visit the children. No, he would not go to his children. They always went away on Saturday and were never home.

And Aaron Kaufman decided he'd take a stroll.

The air was pleasant, refreshing. He walked and he walked and suddenly found himself near the entrance of the large hall where the banquet was taking place. Perhaps he should go in? He'd certainly find many familiar faces . . . surely. No small thing, a society's fifty-year existence!

He went in. A large, brightly lit hall. The music played. Such a festive crowd. It looked cheerful. Young couples were dancing odd, offbeat dances. What a strange crowd this was. No one familiar. Such youth! Perhaps he'd stepped into the wrong place? Rumba music. Beating on castanets. Young people twirling wantonly. No! This could not be the Zlotkov Society. He'd stumbled into a dance hall among young couples.

"Hey. Look out, mister."

Aaron apologized.

Excuse me. Was this his society? Sure, sure, certainly; right there in the corner he recognized his compatriots. Just a few. What a foreign, motley crowd . . .

"Today we'll be awarding a prize for the best rumba dance!" a blond young man announced.

He looked like a complete *sheygets*,[31] Aaron thought. Who was he? An English "entertainer," most likely.

All at once Aaron felt someone's hands covering his eyes. "Guess who?" the man said.

"I don't know."

"Guess."

"Well, really, how should I know?"

The voice sounded familiar, but Aaron couldn't remember where he'd heard it before.

"You give up? Huh?"

"I don't know," Aaron said.

"All right. Look."

Aaron turned and saw a tall elderly man with a wide hat, like a cowboy's. A wrinkled face, browned by the sun. Trembling, Aaron cried out, "Chaim Brikman!"

They hugged each other, fell upon each other's shoulders, and kissed like two long lost brothers.

"Heavens, Brikman, what brings you here? You look like a baron!"

"So if I'm a baron, you shouldn't be calling me Brikman, but Mr. Brick."

"Oh, you too?" Aaron asked, astonishment fixing him to the spot.

"No, not me too. Only my children."

"Mine too," Aaron reassured him. "Somehow, it was as if my heart was telling me to come here today," he marveled. "Tell me, good brother, what brought you here to the Zlotkover compatriots after so many years?"

"I missed it. All those old memories . . . I saved up a lot of money, my friend, but I lost my wife. The children scattered, got married to *shiksas*.[32] Didn't want to live on the farm. And when they come to visit, they're alien to me. I'm an old Jew, deserted on a rich estate.

---

31 A derogatory term for a non-Jewish male.
32 A derogatory term for non-Jewish women.

I gnaw away at the large fields and drink from the oil spring. It all became too boring, so I sold it all. What else should I have done? Find an old gentile woman? I want to be back among Jews. Among our own. Perhaps I'll get to know a younger woman here . . ."

"I lost my wife too," Aaron said sadly. "I have four married children, may they be healthy, grandchildren, I'm proud of them, but I'm lonely, I'm alone."

"You aren't alone. You're with your compatriots and with memories of Zlotkov. You meet, spend time together, reminisce about how it was back home. This is New York, a melting pot, there are places to go. I was alone, with the empty field and a big empty house. But you, you have all of Zlotkov here. I envy you."

"Nah, this isn't the same society you remember. Forty years have passed since you left, Chaim. Go ahead, look around and tell me if you recognize anyone."

Chaim craned his neck, carefully scrutinizing the faces of the people around him, and paused at a pretty middle-aged woman. "There's Chanaleh, Moshe Gittel's," he said, "the shoemaker's daughter."

"No. That's not her. That's Moshe Gittel the shoemaker's *grand-daughter*!"

"I could have sworn it was Chanaleh."

"No. It's Chanaleh's daughter."

He looked around again, then paused for a longer time when he spotted an elderly man. Confidently, he said, "That's Shmuel Berel the water carrier's son, Moshe!"

"Wrong! It's Shmuel Berel the water carrier's grandchild. Asher is his name."

Chaim Brikman remained standing dumbfounded. After a minute he said, pleased, "Well, we haven't aged as much, especially me."

"Yes, my friend, we've changed too. Become gray. A bit wrinkled. A bit stooped . . . Well, you definitely look more vigorous than me."

"I still feel young. Strong and healthy. You have to understand, I lived out on the field, in the free air . . . But I'm not going back again. I already sold everything and came here to New York to set-tle down. To be with old friends and compatriots. And you, espe-cially. I've missed you. And I want to live among Jews." He suddenly became quiet, lost in thought. Then he asked, "How long since your wife died?"

"Two years now."

"You're alone?"

"Yes. Alone."

The commotion and din grew. It was difficult to hear each other's words.

"Why shouldn't a young man like you look for a decent woman to marry?"

"A young man? Me?" Aaron Kaufman gaped at him, astonished.

"Well, if you count all the years, it won't work. You've taken an early old age upon yourself," Brikman shouted into his friend's ear.

All at once, it turned quiet. The blowing of the saxophones and beating of the drums stopped.

Chaim Brikman stood up and put on his cowboy hat, drawing everyone's attention. They stared at him with curiosity. Some of the older compatriots recognized him, and soon a circle had formed around the cowboy. They barraged him with questions, and Brikman gladly regaled them with descriptions of the far West, of a farmer's life, and how you discover a *gusher*. He defined the word: it meant an "oil well."

Suddenly, there was a bang on the drum. The blond young man announced through the microphone that they'd now be playing the new Spanish rumba and prizes would be awarded to those who danced the prettiest. The orchestra burst into song, the castanets thrummed, trumpets blared, trays clattered, and soon the entire crowd in the hall was rocking and swaying. Waves of people danced past Aaron and Chaim. In the crush, amidst all the jostling, they got pulled into the dance circle. Brikman grabbed onto a flustered woman and kicked it up with her, skipped about and with great enjoyment tapped his feet to the beat of the castanets.

With tremendous difficulty, Aaron Kaufman stumbled out of the human wave, sidled off to a corner and waited patiently for his friend.

After the dance, Brikman—sweaty, happy—ran to find Aaron. He spotted him from a distance and cried out: "Why are you hiding? Let's dance!"

"Dance, of all things? I want to go home."

"Already?" Chaim pleaded. "You know what? Let's go for a stroll. I want to look again at the city where I spent my first years as a greenhorn."

"Fine," Aaron agreed, and they both set out upon the New York streets.

The night was mild. A clear, starry sky and a full moon floated over the tall buildings. Chaim Brikman stopped, inhaled the fresh air, and gazed about him. "How delightful," he said, "to be alive in this world! Only the skyscrapers are blocking my view of the sky. Take me away from this gentile neighborhood. Let's go back to my good old streets, Forsyth Street, Allen and Delancey Street." His tone was wistful.

They walked slowly towards the Jewish neighborhood, while Chaim Brikman told Aaron all about his children and how they'd married Christian girls. His grandchildren knew nothing of Jewishness and one of his daughters-in-law, a religious Catholic, actually took the children to church. He himself also frequently forgot when it was a Jewish holiday. "But here it'll be different. Now I'm back home. Back among Jews."

Aaron abruptly stopped walking and said, "Here you have it—Forsyth Street."

Chaim looked around, stunned. He saw an unfamiliar wide street, a garden with benches and a children's playground on one side; on the other side, there were new buildings, modern stores.

"You're making fun of me or what? You're fooling me, brother. Off with you! I want to see Forsyth Street. I want to see the dear old crooked tenements with the fire escapes, with the laundry hanging on clotheslines in the street."

"You won't see those anymore," his friend interrupted him. "They're gone, along with our greenhorn years and our youth."

"Well then, take me to Delancey Street." He refused to give up.

"It's not far. We're almost there."

They walked silently, each lost in his own thoughts.

"Right here's Delancey Street," Aaron Kaufman announced.

Chaim looked around, shrugged his shoulders. Strange. All strange. Tall brick walls. New buildings. New shops. "Oy, unrecognizable," he cried. "Let's go to East Broadway. That's the place I always think of as the Land of Israel."

"There, my friend, it is dark and silent now. Come to Allen Street. It isn't far. After all, that's where we once lived."

They arrived at Allen Street. This street, too, Chaim didn't recognize. "It somehow became wider. And it looks so clean. With benches and strange shops," he lamented.

"The world moves forward," Aaron said, "becomes modernized, with atom bombs . . . What did you expect? To still find the tramway maybe, pulled by a horse? Yes, the world moves ahead; only we go backwards. We're already riding away from this fair."

"I hate hearing such silly talk," Chaim protested.

From Allen Street they went to Eldridge Street. Brikman became happy. Here and there he recognized little houses, old, twisted, with fire escapes, laundry hanging. And there! Right there was the house where he once lived! And the same store on the ground floor. He was as happy to find it as if it were a good old friend. Suddenly they heard a song wafting from the old tenement. They drew closer. The song was coming from a wine cellar. They stood listening silently. Aaron wanted to continue on their way, but Chaim didn't let him. "Shh, shh, let's listen," he said.

A melancholy, tearful voice floated over the quiet night street:

The wordless Yiddish tune will live forever
As long as the world will stand
Our grandfathers gave us our Yiddish song
And so it will go on, from land to land.

"Are you hearing these words?" Chaim Brikman cried, awed. "This is the old, good wine cellar that I remember from my greenhorn years! Dear song! Golden lyrics!"

He tugged at his friend's sleeve. "Come," he said. "Come downstairs and let's drink to a new life. To our old friendship. And to all our compatriots."

With firm, steady steps they both walked down the stairs to the wine cellar.

SECTION TWO

Modern Times

M ODERNITY CAN BE seen as the subject of nearly all of modern Yiddish literature. Ever since Sholem Aleichem's Tevye the
Dairyman anguished over his daughters' life decisions, Yiddish writers have been depicting the clash between Jewish and non-Jewish cul-
tures, between traditional lifestyles and contemporary ones, between
the values of older generations and those that succeeded them.

No one felt these struggles more acutely than the readers and writers of the *Forward*. Just as the first wave of immigrants "ungreened"
themselves and became alienated from the families and communities
they had left in Europe, so too their children, born and raised in
America, found themselves estranged from their parents' religious,
cultural, and linguistic backgrounds.

These issues weren't confined to the United States. In the years
before and after the First World War, both American and European
Jewry confronted the rise of Jewish socialism and the labor movement; the entry of Jews into higher education and the professions; a
swiftly changing relationship to traditional Judaism; the challenge of
Zionism; and new and different forms of both emancipation and anti-
Semitism. That nearly every writer in this collection had a religious
education as a child but turned towards secular culture as an adult
illustrates the spirit of the times.

All of these issues came to the fore in the journalism of the Yiddish press. In literature, however, one theme predominated: the ever-shifting terrain of romantic and sexual mores. While the days of arranged marriage were mostly past, and the effects of radical politics and first-wave feminism were in the air, traditional values were still strongly present. For the cosmopolitan young men and women writing and reading these stories, sex and romance presented a constant negotiation between propriety and desire, social expectations and personal fulfillment.

Here the women who wrote for the *Forward* occupied the most important role. While many male authors also addressed these themes—canonical writers like Hersh Dovid Nomberg and Avrom Reyzen are representative here—they were often taken up by women, who expressed their own fraught situations. Female authors were so prized that the *Forward* took pains to highlight the gender of its contributors. And while their work exhibited a wide range of attitudes, we find in these stories skepticism of the new order and a subtle but harsh critique of male behavior.

Here art reflected the conditions of writers' lives. But life, no doubt, also took its cues from art. As readers struggled to make sense of the rules by which romance was conducted in twentieth-century America, they looked to the *Forward* to point out the possibilities and pitfalls of their unprecedented freedom.

Hersh Dovid Nomberg
1876–1927

FEW YIDDISH WRITERS played as many different roles, both literary and political, as Hersh Dovid Nomberg. He was a writer of fiction and poetry; a journalist, essayist and literary critic; an architect of political Yiddishism (a term he coined), and, for a time, a politician and representative in the Polish parliament.

Nomberg was born in the Polish town of Mszczonow, known in Yiddish as Amshinov and home to a prominent Hasidic movement of the same name. As a young adult, Nomberg experienced a crisis of faith and, at age twenty-one, left his wife and son and moved to Warsaw. There he pursued a secular education, taught himself Russian, Polish, and German, and began writing Hebrew literature.

With the encouragement of I. L. Peretz, Warsaw's preeminent Jewish literary figure, Nomberg switched to Yiddish and became acquainted with other young Yiddish writers, such as Avrom Reyzen and Sholem Asch, with whom he shared a Warsaw apartment. His early works were often published in both Hebrew and Yiddish, and included poetry, short fiction, novellas, and literary criticism.

Setting a pattern of lifelong travel, the first decade of the twentieth century saw Nomberg move between Germany, France, Switzerland, and Lithuania, before relocating once again to Warsaw. In 1908 he attended the Czernowitz Conference in support of the Yiddish language, where he proposed a compromise resolution between Hebraists and Yiddishists that proclaimed Yiddish "a" national language of the Jewish people rather than "the" national language.

During the First World War, Nomberg became active in the Yiddish secular school movement, and helped found the Association of Jewish Writers and Journalists, of which he became president in 1925. Shortly after the war he helped found the Folkspartey (People's Party), which advocated for Jewish cultural autonomy in Eastern Europe, and for which he served as a delegate in the Sejm, or Polish parliament, between 1919 and 1920.

In the early 1920s, Nomberg traveled widely in North America, South America, and Palestine, although he never settled permanently outside of Poland. Having suffered from a chronic lung ailment for much of his adult life, Nomberg died in Warsaw at the age of fifty-one.

Although he published widely, Nomberg's main journalistic outlets were European Yiddish newspapers and few of his pieces appeared in the *Forward*. "Friends," which appeared from February 24 to 26, 1912, is one of Nomberg's few contributions to the paper, and features the moody, intellectual character types commonly found in his work. Known as a "fligelman," or "winged man," after a character in his 1903 story of the same name, such figures are typically estranged from their surroundings and rendered impotent by circumstances beyond their control.

Friends

(FEBRUARY 24–26, 1912)

Translated by Seymour Levitan

I

YES, IT WAS jealousy, nothing else. He caught himself feeling it, and it was no secret to him.

He'd begun to hate his friend, his best, possibly his only friend, who had shared his loneliness for years. He couldn't look him straight in the eyes, couldn't speak two words to him without faltering, couldn't bear to see his face. Every look, every grimace, irritated and provoked. The mild smile on his friend's lips, the smile he used to love so, now struck him as false, hypocritical, unbearable; the clever, thoughtful remarks, flat and parroted.

It wasn't yet a full year after his marriage, and every day he was more in love with his wife. He, the lonely man already past thirty, could hardly believe that the love of a one-and-only woman could offer him such profound happiness, could turn gray days into bright, intoxicating holidays, make him drunk with delight and with new, untried, unimagined blessings.

It was a lucky choice, and it showed that he had good taste. Etta wasn't a glowing or flashy or flamboyant beauty. She dressed and carried herself so modestly, was so withheld, that at first glance she hardly made an impression. Now he knew that she had hidden her beauty just for the man she had chosen. The graceful lines of her body, the delicate neck, the round, beautifully shaped arms that seemed made to embrace—all of it was a secret revealed to him little by little, a bookful of poetry and brilliance that he leafed through page by page, drawing new enchantment from it.

He was happy. The business that he'd managed alone for the last three years was going not badly, his clouded eyes cleared, he was more cheerful and fresher, he'd been given a second youth.

Happy people have a natural desire to see their friends happy. People who have married happily want their friends to be engaged. It was this feeling that prompted him to look up his old friend, a Yiddish poet, and bring him home. He didn't do it, for God's sake, to be boastful, to show off his happiness. He wanted with all his heart for his friend to drop his dreams, be practical, marry and be happy just like himself. And he would see.

There was a time when he was himself involved with literature, was hungry, always alone, bitter, and philosophized very much about life, while life tossed him aside into a narrow corner. Finally he'd caught himself, and now he was so happy.

In the quiet at home after supper, when he and Etta were still at the table, when the lamp was bright and the street noise that reached them was like a rhythmic pulse of life, when he loved to stroke Etta's bright hair, search out her small ear and kiss it slowly, peacefully—he would tell her about his former life and about his friend. He described him as very deep and clever, told about his wandering life, and to his great joy noted that Etta understood the kind of person he was and was interested.

Along with the beauty of her body, he discovered every day in this woman he loved more fineness of soul, more intelligence and appealing good sense. This girl he had taken out of a dress shop was quite perceptive, understood people, and with womanly instinct judged them remarkably clearly. She was not at all a stranger to the workings of the psyche.

Once when he read his friend's poems to her just before bedtime, there were tears in her eyes at some of them. And he was thankful that without knowing it, his friend had helped him uncover so much sensitivity in his Etta.

"Why doesn't he come up to us?" she asked. She'd only seen him once. Soon after their wedding he paid his respects, sat altogether a half-hour and never showed up again.

"He's a wild person. He doesn't like the calm and quiet of home, he either wants the street noise, the crush of people, or to be entirely alone. You know, Etta," he added smiling, "we're after all petty bourgeois, everything about us is petty, homey and sweet."

And he kissed her, and she put her delicate, bare arms on his shoulders. "You're good . . ." And while she sat on his lap, she went on talking about his friend. "Poets live a completely different life. They fly—fly far off, and they think another way entirely. I'd be afraid to live with a poet. He has such a strange look . . ."

"You mean he has a look that frightens you! Go on! He's good-hearted."

"No, I know. The goodness shows in his eyes. But when he looked at me, there was something so strange about it, the way a chicken or a dog looks at you."

"A chicken or a dog? Is that the way you think of him? You're *bad!*"
And he kissed her again on her lips. "Go on, go on, you don't understand." And she slapped him on the arm.

"I mean his look is so strange, so far off—totally different."

He looked at her amazed, enchanted. She had expressed it so well, caught his old friend's look exactly!

When he ran into his friend some time later, he brought him home, and from then on he was a steady visitor. And that's when it began.

Jealousy entered quietly, unnoticed, stole into his heart, and like a sickness that you have without knowing it, grew until it was ripe.

II

ETTA WAS IN her bed, asleep. The apartment was dark; it was long past midnight. He tossed from side to side and couldn't sleep. It was his first sleepless night, the end of his happy days.

What had he actually noticed? Nothing. It amounted to nothing. His friend drops in often. Well, yes, but he had invited him so often, and after all, he's a solitary person, and Etta is interesting and beautiful. Somehow his friend's eyes, his chickeny or doggy eyes, had acquired a strange glow. But wasn't it foolish, petty, to be obsessing about it and poisoning one's own life? Absolutely foolish and petty.

What else? When his friend hovers around Etta, there's a smile on her lips that he doesn't understand. Again pettiness—she's become a woman, the girlish reticence has melted like mist. This is how a mature woman smiles, like mother Eve, who gratified her curiosity with the forbidden apple. Just two hours ago, as she grew tired and sleepy, he was overtaken by such strong love for her that he held and kissed her passionately, to the point of forgetting. And in the midst of it he saw the smile on her lips, the new smile, and he sobered.

Now he knows the true meaning of her laughing eyes. There's a new beauty in his Etta. He knew her so little before this, and every day he discovers something new. Right! What a petty fool he is! To harbor suspicion of her and insult her this way in his thoughts—his one and only Etta.

And so what if Etta's fingers brushed his friend's hand. It was accidental. She was handing him tea and wanted to pass the sugar to him. It was an accident! And he's just nervous, nothing more. The check that bounced today . . . Somehow he hears the train whistle, he even thinks he hears the noise of the wheels . . . he had no idea the train was so close. Etta is sleeping, but not restfully, it seems. He can hear her breath, broken at times.

He calls quietly, barely whispering, "Etta . . ." And she answers immediately:

"You aren't asleep? What's wrong, Chaim?"

"Nothing. I've been sleeping. I was dreaming. What time is it?"

"It just struck two."

"Two? You know? I don't remember whether the gas is turned off tight." He came up with this story about the gas intentionally. He wanted to see Etta's face, to read it. He turned up the gas and went over to her bed.

She was lying curled up in the blanket and the pillow. And when he came over, she turned to him, her head completely curtained by her bright hair. He brushed the hair from her face and felt he was doing it not with a lover's hand, but with the cold hand of an investigator and judge. He wanted to see her. But her face, a bit tired and beautiful—beautiful! beautiful!—told him nothing about what he wanted to know.

"Do you love me, Etta?" She opened her eyes and looked at him. God! Wasn't this the chickeny, doggy, distant look that she described when she spoke about his friend? And what did the cold smile mean? With tragedy and shakiness in his voice that even he could hear, he asked again, "Do you love me, Etta?"

"You have to ask that at two in the morning? Go to sleep, love." She stroked his head, and he obeyed like a child, turned off the gas and lay down. "Love," that's what she said. He repeated it to himself a hundred times. "Love," but how was it said? What lay in it? Was this just a way of soothing, the way one soothes a foolish child? "Love" and not "dearest." Why not "dearest"? Foolishness! But why wasn't she sleeping? What unsettled her?

At the very worst it would only be that she was in love with this friend, yet nothing had happened. But if not, her sleep wouldn't be restless. That was clear! Tomorrow he had so much work to do, and, as if in spite, he couldn't sleep. It struck three and then four and his nervousness increased. He was bathed in sweat, his head was pounding.

"Etta . . ." he called out quietly, but with pleading and despair in his voice. But there was no answer from the other bed. Etta's breathing was even, regular. She was sleeping.

And he was attacked by oppressive anxiety and dread. How would this end? What would come now? This was it, jealousy, and it was just beginning. More and more would follow . . . clouded days, sleepless nights. It would be hard to pay the price for his few months of happiness. Yes, nothing on earth is free of charge. Why should he have deserved a second youth? This was how he had to pay for it!

It would be best if he met with his friend tomorrow and told him plainly: "Look, we're old friends, we can talk openly. You've destroyed my happiness. I was the happiest man on earth just a while ago, and now I'm the unhappiest. Now I toss and turn in bed, covered in sweat and trembling all over. This can't go on, do you understand? It has to stop. Sorry." And would his friend smile quietly and take his measure with his distant chickeny or doggy look? Let him! The point is that he wouldn't come up anymore.

At about six he dressed and made himself tea. His head was horribly heavy. He had a slight fever. Like a trained dog, he kneeled beside his wife's bed and laid his tired head on her. He wanted her to wake but didn't want to wake her. Quietly, calmly, he lay that way. The tea on the table grew cold, the sun shone in at the sides of the window shades, a strand of light stole over Etta's face, and she woke, startled. "What's wrong, Chaim?" There was fear in her voice. "Nothing, Etta. I couldn't sleep, so I made tea." "But you're trembling." She sat up in bed. Her half-uncovered young body overwhelmed his senses. He fell to her and kissed her hotly and forgot himself in her arms.

And at night the three of them sat together, he, she and his friend, and played cards. He was sleepy and wanted to break off and say goodnight, but his friend's eyes had a strange, lively glow, and Etta smiled. Yes, this was the new beauty that he'd discovered in her—a cold, clever smile.

III

HE WAS TORMENTED by jealousy but even more by uncertainty. He didn't dare speak a word about it and had nothing at all to hold on to.

It seemed to him that if he were only sure it had happened, that his Etta belonged to someone else, his situation would be much more bearable than it was now, when he was flung from one extreme to the other, from love and trust in his wife, to jealousy and distrust. It would be a misfortune, a terrible misfortune, a black abyss would open for him, as if there were nothing left but to throw himself in. But he wouldn't be feverish and choking on his pain like this.

"What's wrong with you, Chaim? Go see a doctor," Etta would say.

"It's nothing. It comes from loving you so much." And he would try to smile as he said this. It was meant to be a kind of apology for being cooler to her now.

And his friend's eyes kept on glowing, his distant look came near when he spoke with Etta. To him, to her husband, Etta smiled, but she laughed out loud when his friend was there. She wouldn't have laughed like that before, he thought. I don't like it. It's too bold, too unrestrained for her, it's out of harmony with who she is.

Once after his friend left, he let himself remark, "I never heard you laugh the way you laughed today." Something like an angry fire lit up in her eyes and was extinguished at once. She said nothing, as if she hadn't heard what he said. And only after a while she sat down next to him, stroked his hair and smiled, and once more soothed him the way one soothes an angry child.

"You don't like the way I laugh, Chaim? Your nerves are bad. You should see a doctor." With that, the encounter ended, and once again, a tormented, sleepless night. And in the morning he asked himself again, what reason do I have to be suspicious? And once again he beat his breast within himself for thinking this way about his wife.

Two months passed like this. If the first months after his wedding were the happiest in his life, these last two were the most upsetting. He felt that he lacked the endurance and strength to suffer any-more, that it would all suddenly blow up like a compressed explosive. A catastrophe was coming, surely. He would go crazy, he would kill himself, or there would be a terrible scene. Something had to happen.

And in fact something did happen. He can't recall exactly how it came about. She came home, complained about a headache, lay down in bed, was sick, and died. The day after taking ill she wasn't clear in her head, and she died that way, in uncertain circumstances. It happened so simply and so much beyond comprehension. After that came old women who sewed shrouds, candles were lit, and afterwards they took her out and buried her. He followed after her funeral and said nothing and didn't even weep. Somehow his friend came over to him with his eyes full of tears. Why is he crying? He couldn't under-stand. Everything else was totally simple, each thing following the last the way it goes—she was sick and died and was buried, and when he returned home, Etta wasn't there any longer.

Her bed was empty.

He fell into a hard, heavy sleep, but suddenly woke, as if from something awful, and suddenly he seized his head and began howl-ing between the four walls and the empty bed that heard him. How did this happen? When did it happen? How? He couldn't even say exactly how many days she'd been sick. It flew by so quickly, came out of nowhere.

This is death, death, he said to himself, as if he just now properly comprehended the import of the short word. That's what it is—death.

His friend came in, pale, depressed, his eyes red. "Chaim! This is such a tragedy! No one had any idea . . . Such a young life, such a blossoming life . . . and suddenly! Who could have thought it?" And with frightened, uncomprehending eyes Chaim looked at him and answered, "Yes, that's what it is—death."

They spent the night together. His friend sat down next to him on the bed and slipped off into sleep leaning against his shoulder. Chaim leaned back on the bed to let his friend's head slowly sink into the pillow. The physical closeness of his friend eased things for him. And in that way they both slipped into sleep late at night.

IV

HE HAD TO get his brother to run his business while he left the city for a summer cottage. Not alone, but with his doctor, who feared for his mental state.

Nothing distracted or interested him. He couldn't speak more than brief, abrupt words to anyone but his friend. His friend did in fact visit often and spent time with him. They spoke mainly about Etta. He was sure that her like never was in this world. Such harmony within and without, such capacity to love, such a hidden, delicate, interior life. When he said these things, it seemed to him that his friend responded and understood, and that eased his pain.

"Aah, what do you know, what do you know about her beauty! The most beautiful image in marble hasn't got it. The world lost a work of art when she died!" And his friend heard him out, nodded and said, "She was the most beautiful woman I've ever met in my life." But with these words something broke apart in Chaim's heart. A shudder ran through his body. The old jealousy was ignited. He'd held Etta in his arms—he!

Shattered by the old doubt that suddenly awoke, he left his friend with the excuse that he wanted to rest.

And new nights of torment began for him, and like a worm, doubt gnawed at his heart. Old scenes awakened in his memory. With precision he recalled his friend's and Etta's every hand movement, every expression of their eyes, their looks, their smiles, and weighed and measured it all and again tried to get to the truth, and as before, he was hurled from belief to despair, and as before, after the most bitter despair came self-reproach—that he was petty and foolish, that he had no grounds to be suspicious.

And uncertainty, the most frightening of all the torments, plagued him again. It was as if the longing for his lost happiness stepped aside. And as if to confirm his suspicion and increase his uneasiness, his friend stayed away for a few days. And when his friend finally came, he couldn't control himself any longer, and with despair and pleading he pounced. "You have to tell me the truth. It's all the same now, she's no longer alive. Tell me, was she yours? Tell the truth . . ."

But his friend looked at him with his distant look and answered, agitated, as if trying to escape from a trap, "What are you thinking? What are you thinking? It never happened. It's a fantasy, your sick fantasy," and Chaim nearly started to cry.

"I'm such a low-down person! I suspected her, I suspected her!"

"Calm yourself, Chaim!"

Chaim really did want to calm himself, but a short time later he began to feel that the recurring doubt wouldn't go away, and he asked again, "But tell me, what makes you talk about the beauty of her body?" His friend responded as if surprised.

"What?"

"Nothing, sorry."

And so he was left with his uncertainty again. Just to calm himself a little and not plague himself with the same thought day and night, he felt instinctively that it was better not to see his friend. Let it stay like this, in the dark, let it be a secret, let the dead be forgotten together with their secrets. Anyway, he thought, I'm not looking for any more happiness, all I need is to forget, just to forget!

Returning to the city, he avoided his friend. Now the real grief began for him, the long, choking longing for Etta. Her figure pursued him. He felt depressed and alone in the world, alone forever. This loneliness and longing would never leave him. A third youth wouldn't happen.

On mild evenings when the grief wouldn't stop and he felt a sleepless night coming on, he would go out to the cemetery and walk around near the grave of his dead wife, with his eyes on the star-filled sky. Thoughts about the past of everything, of the earth on which he walked, of the millions of stars that sparkle up there—that everything passes, fades and dies, young or old, ripe and weary or fresh and eager for life—comforted and quieted him.

And on one such evening at the start of November, he encountered his friend, whom he hadn't seen for some time, at his wife's grave. On her grave lay fresh flowers that his friend had brought.

In a split second it was clear to him that his friend had hidden something from him, both during Etta's life and now after her death. Yes, it had happened.

He was confused, jealousy flared up again in his heart, he looked on in a threatening silence. But his friend got control of himself and said, "It's now exactly six months since she died. I brought her flowers."

"Flowers? Did you love her that much?"

"Don't be angry, Chaim. Let's not be angry here by her grave. It's not the place for it. Let's have respect for her and for what's sacred in our own lives."

"So is that it? Did you love her?"

"Don't talk in that tone! Yes, it's true, I loved her, and the most splendid part of my life is gone with her. And nothing is left."

"And did she love you too?"

His friend was silent for a while, but afterwards went over to Chaim, took him by the arm, and quietly, with a tone that came from deep inside him, said: "Don't be angry with me, my good friend. It's love. It's a power beyond our understanding and our best intentions. I loved her like no other woman in the world."

"Oh there isn't another such woman in the world!" Chaim blurted out, and as he spoke, the burning hate towards his friend vanished.

It was autumn. There was a chill breeze. At the edge of the horizon the moon floated up as if bathed in blood. The trees creaked, and the last leaves were torn off by the wind.

"I haven't forgotten her. She's right here in front of me as if she were alive, with her graceful body and her blond hair and the wonderful expression in her eyes." But Chaim couldn't bear to hear his friend speak about Etta. He pulled his arm away and left without saying good night.

But a few months later they met again, as luck would have it, and even now—years have passed and both are growing old—they sit together and remember Etta. And with time they have grown so accustomed to this that they speak about the open and hidden beauties of the deceased and are unembarrassed, like two brothers talking about a sister dear to them both.

Avrom Reyzen
1876–1953

ONE OF THE most influential figures among the second generation of modern Yiddish writers, Avrom Reyzen was a prolific
contributor to many Yiddish publications, including the *Forward*.

Born in Koidanov, Belorussia, Reyzen belonged to a prominent
Yiddish literary family that included his father, Kalmen, his brother,
Zalmen, and his sister, Soreh.

Reyzen received a traditional religious education, as well as tutoring in Russian, German, and other secular subjects. He began writing
in his early adolescence and corresponded with the leading writers of
the preceding generation, including Yankev Dinezon and I. L. Peretz. His early work appeared in pioneering Yiddish periodicals such
as *Dos Yudishes folks-blat* (*The Jewish People's Paper*) of Saint Petersburg
and Peretz's *Yudishe bibliotek* (*The Jewish Library*). In 1895 he was con-
scripted into the Russian army, where he served in a military band
before being released four years later. He then moved to Warsaw,
where he became one of the most active Yiddish literary figures in
Europe, publishing copious amounts of fiction and poetry and serving as the editor or publisher of numerous journals and publishing
enterprises.

In 1911, Reyzen moved to New York, where he began contributing
regularly to the city's Yiddish press, including both the *Forward* and
the Communist *Frayhayt* (*Freedom*). In 1929, Reyzen, together with
many other writers, broke with *Frayhayt* over its coverage of Arab
attacks against Jews in Hebron, and he subsequently wrote primarily
for the *Forward*, where he contributed a new short story each week.

Although much of Reyzen's writing was included in two sets of collected works that appeared in 1916–1917 and 1928, much more remained uncollected, including "Who Will Prevail?" The story appeared in the *Forward* in daily installments between July 26 and 30, 1913, and was republished later that year in the Warsaw newspaper *Der moment* (*The Moment*), between September 12 and 24.

Although the story takes place in Warsaw, and features a young Reyzenesque protagonist, its themes are not much different from the fiction that Reyzen and other writers wrote in an American context, particularly when it came to the subject of sexual and romantic relationships in a postreligious environment.

Who Will Prevail?

(JULY 20–30, 1913)

Translated by Ezra Glinter

I

WHILE LOOKING FOR a room, Meir Hecht, a brown-haired young man around twenty years old, of taller than average height with an intelligent, sympathetic face, stopped by the entrance to a quiet Jewish street and read: "A room for a bachelor in the courtyard, third floor, number nineteen." He entered the courtyard and, after looking for the number on all of the doors, found it at last. He went up the stairs.

The corridor was narrow and the stairs had become crooked with age; Meir Hecht considered it a defect, but he didn't turn back. "Let me see the room," he thought, "maybe it will be better inside." He stood outside the door with a half-covered number 19 and searched for a knocker, but there was no sign of one. He knocked with his fist instead.

The door opened from the inside and a middle-aged woman appeared in the doorway, holding an unpeeled potato and a knife in her hand. Seeing the woman, Meir Hecht wanted to retreat without a word, but she stood solidly in the doorway and demanded:

"What do you want, young man?"

"A room . . ." Hecht stammered.

"You're in luck! There is in fact a room to rent," she said. "Did a friend tell you about it, or did you see it on the gate?"

"On the gate," Hecht answered briefly.

"You see, Goldele was right. She said we should hang a sign."

Hearing the name Goldele, Hecht imagined the kind of pretty Warsaw brunette he often saw on the Jewish streets. His face took on a friendly expression and he said:

"Could you be so kind as to show me the room?"

"I can certainly show it," the woman answered. "When you have merchandise you need to put it on display. Come, forgive me."

She stepped over the threshold into a large room, which must have been the parlor. There was a wide table and in the corners of the room were two made beds and a sofa, which was covered with a dark quilt. At the end of the room by the wall stood a few old chairs.

"This is the dining room," the matron said with satisfied look, "but we sleep here also. We are, thank God, not a large household— just three children."

"And the room is where?" Hecht asked, already a little uneasy.

"There's a little room here also," the woman answered good-naturedly. "Why shouldn't there be a room? True, it's not a big one, but that just makes it warm, like an oven. Come, forgive me."

She made a turn to the right and stood by a curtain. As if with witchcraft, she parted it in two, and revealed a tiny room.

"Ach, it's too small," Hecht said with surprise, looking at a bed and table that took up the entire space.

"What do you need a bigger one for?" the woman asked. "This seems right to me for one person."

"But there's not even enough room to put in a chair," Hecht scowled.

"You could put three chairs in here," the matron said defensively. "You just need to push the bed a little bit into the corner. And anyway, what do you need all those chairs for? You can sit on the bed."

"Sometimes I need to read, to write," Hecht muttered.

"Be reasonable," the woman persisted. "Couldn't you read and write just as well in the dining room? There's nobody here all day. He works, Goldele my daughter works, and the two boys go to school . . ."

Hecht looked again at the little room—it seemed more like a stall. But then he thought about this Goldele, and about whether something might happen with her . . . How old would she be, exactly? How could he go about asking?

"So you have three children, they should be healthy," Hecht said. "Two boys and a girl. How old are the boys?"

"The boys . . ." the matron screwed up her face, "how old are they? One, Leybele is seven years old, and Gershonke, nine years . . ."

"And the girl, I assume, is a year or two older?"

"Oh, what did you say? The girl is already almost nineteen years old."

"I might, it seems, take the room," Hecht decided. And he asked coldly, "What will this little room cost?"

"What can we arrange for you?" the woman bargained. "I'll tell you the truth. Until now two workers lived here, they slept in one bed, and I charged them five rubles. You will presumably live here alone, without a roommate."

"God help me!" Hecht exclaimed. "It's too small for myself. Taking more roommates—nothing could be worse!"

"*Nu*, so what should I do with you?" the woman smiled goodnaturedly. "For you, I'll take four rubles. That's not too expensive," she added, afraid that she might have undermined herself with too high a price.

"Good." Hecht was agreeable. "I'll move in today."

"You could move in already," the woman agreed.

Hecht took his money from a purse. He had a five-ruble note, which he gave to the woman and asked for a receipt. She gave him a ruble back and, looking at him, inquired:

"I forgot to ask. Are you a worker, or something else?"

"Something else," Hecht said with a laugh.

"Can we know what, for example?"

"A teacher."

"A teacher?" she said, and seemed to swell up with pride at the fine profession practiced by her new lodger. "You are busy the whole day, I imagine."

"Yes, I am a little busy, a little free, however I make it," Hecht answered.

She gave him a friendly look and said: "Do you know German?"

"What do you need my German for?" Hecht asked with a smile.

"Did I say I need it? What do I need German for? I only mean for my Goldele. Polish she knows not too badly, but she wants to learn a little German. She goes through different streets after work and it's good to know German also. Do you think she could learn?"

"Oh, with great pleasure," Hecht agreed. Living in the same house, he wouldn't even ask for money.

He left to get his things.

II

FEELING HAPPY AND full of high hopes, Hecht went back to his old dwelling to get his small suitcase. It was a winter afternoon; in spite of the frosty weather, the sun, which stood very high in the sky, shone on the snow, which lay in heaps by the sides of the street. Under the sun's rays the snow glistened with a mild submissiveness, and the streets smelled like the onset of spring.

Hecht went through the noisy Jewish thoroughfare, whose clamor made him even happier. With sure steps he walked farther and farther, looking at the face of each girl he passed. Some glanced back at him, some acted as though they didn't notice him, and a few looked at him with a friendly expression. One even smiled at him, and his heart melted. He felt the need to touch a girlish hand. As soon as he met the right girl, he would, with heated sincerity, declare his pure, everlasting love.

In front of his eyes appeared the image of that unknown girl named Golde, with whom he would live in the same house. In his old apartment he had felt so out of place. The mistress was always angry and her husband was a fanatic. He always lectured Hecht for not being religious. He had lived there for two months and it felt like he was in prison. On top of that, the man snored loudly at night.

Now he was going to live with simple, everyday folk. Their house was not especially well decorated, but for that reason it was much more comfortable. And the little room was so pleasant . . . a person could really feel good in that room. Sunk in these thoughts, he came at last to his old lodging.

He entered the house, went up the stairs, and picked up the suitcase he had already packed the day before, and which was standing in the kitchen. "Be well!" he shouted through the house. The mistress came out. An old woman in a thick wig, she cast a suspicious glance at him and answered coldly: "Go in good health . . ." and waited until he was gone.

Hecht wasn't bothered by the coldness of his former landlady. She was already so far off and so foreign to him—as though she was dead! Going down the stairs, he looked in the direction of his former spot and murmured to himself: "Two months of life gone." He looked back as if he wanted to bid farewell to those two months, and then left the courtyard, forgetting about them forever.

Turning into the crowded street, he ran into a porter standing at the intersection, wearing a thick rope belt. "Young man!" the porter called out. "Perhaps I can carry that heavy suitcase for you?"

"No thank you, it's not heavy," Hecht answered pleasantly.

"You, young man, don't thank me," the porter said, insulted. "It would be better if you gave a Jew some way to earn a pound of bread."

Hearing the porter's brazen but justified words, Hecht looked at him and, noticing his wrinkled, worn-out face, said guiltily, "Actually, take it."

The porter's face cleared up like a cloudy sky and he smiled broadly. "For a young man like you it's not appropriate to carry a suitcase by yourself."

"What do you want for it, my friend?" Hecht asked warily, fearing a high price.

"We won't have to go to court over it," the porter joked. "How far is it?" Hecht told him the name of the house. "I won't fleece you," the porter assured him.

Hecht already regretted what he had done. Who knows how much the porter would ask for? In total he possessed exactly one ruble. And the first day in a new house without any money would be terrible. But the thing was already done, and he couldn't take it back. He reassured himself that the man seemed to be honest and that he wouldn't cheat him. The porter could see that Hecht was no wealthy young man. At last they arrived in the courtyard.

"Here it is," Hecht said, and tried to take back his bundle, so that the porter couldn't hold it hostage. The porter was no fool, however. He became stubborn and insisted on taking it all the way to the door.

"It's not right for you to carry it yourself," he said.

Hecht decided to give him a twenty-five kopek piece. "If only he'll take it!" he worried. But he remembered that when he took a droshky[33] it cost him a forty-groschen coin, and this couldn't possibly be more than a droshky. A fifteen-kopek coin would be enough, he decided, and rejoiced over the ten kopeks he would save.

When they entered the house it was already dark, and the mistress had lit the lamp. "Where should I leave it?" the porter asked, holding onto Hecht's bag the entire time.

"Leave it where it is," Hecht answered, and started digging around in his pocket. "What do I owe you, my friend?"

---

33 A type of Russian carriage.

"Do I know?" the porter scratched his temple. "I'll say, for you, ten kopeks."

"Five would be enough," the landlady butted in.

But Hecht, happy at the low price, took the porter up on the offer. "I'll give him the ten kopecks. Here you are—go in good health."

The porter took the coin and looked at it from all sides. "Thank you, good sir," he said, and left.

"You gave him too much," the landlady muttered in a motherly way. "It was only worth five kopecks."

Hecht was moved by her friendly tone, which he had not heard in a long time. "Oh, so what?" he said. "What is five kopecks worth to me?"

"Don't say that," the landlady said, sticking to her position. "Money is money. My Golde is also like that, she always wants to give more. She never bargains, never. I always fight with her about it." With those words the woman looked at the clock. "It's already five o'clock, she should be home from work soon."

Hecht perked up with interest. He stood in front of the small mirror and straightened his whiskers, and then his tie. He noticed that his collar was not especially white, and excused himself.

"Might I go clean up a little?"

"Yes, why not. You can do it here in the house, or in your room . . ."

Hecht took his suitcase with him to the room, opened it up, and from a small paper package took out a clean white collar. Before the trip he had already combed his youthful black hair. He went back into the big room and looked at himself in the mirror. His ears glowed from excitement. He noticed this and was pleased.

Going back into his little room, Hecht lit a candle that he took from his suitcase and went through some of his books. He laid them out by the room's only window, which, as luck would have it, had a wide sill. A few of the books he put on the little table. He also set up an inkwell with a pen, and put out a few long, blank pieces of paper. That was how he decorated his room.

III

FIFTEEN MINUTES PASSED. Hecht sat in his room and looked out through the window onto the small, square courtyard. A single gas lantern was already lit and it shone on him weakly. He looked at everyone who entered, and if it was a young girl his heart beat fiercely—until she turned towards another house and Hecht realized that he had been mistaken.

At last he noticed a young woman, wearing a small hat with a feather on its side, enter the courtyard. She was smartly dressed but with modest taste. She looked in the window and saw the strange young man and, as it seemed to Hecht, took note and walked faster. A few seconds later he heard from his bedroom the sound of a fresh, ringing young voice, though he couldn't make out the words. "She has arrived!" he said happily to himself, getting up off the spot.

Entering the rest of the house seemed unfitting, however. After all, he didn't know yet who she was. Chasing after her before the time was right wouldn't be helpful. Instead, he would do the opposite— play the role of an indifferent, cold-blooded man, and if it turned out to be worth it, he wouldn't run away.

While considering how to best conduct himself at the first encounter, he heard soft footsteps near his room. Hecht cautiously pulled aside the curtain and saw her. He looked at her in fright. She looked at him pleasantly and curiously. Then she smiled and her big, black and somehow dreamy eyes twinkled good-naturedly.

"You are our new lodger?" she asked, taking hold of the conversation with a smile and not finding anything else to say.

"Yes," Hecht answered curtly and, heartened by her friendly glances, asked back: "And you are the daughter of the house?"

"Yes, I am the daughter," she presented herself, giving him her hand in sister-like fashion.

He grabbed it thirstily, pressed it, and exclaimed, "It cheers me know such a fine girl as yourself!"

She took a step forward and laughed.

"I already please you?"

The question made Hecht feel lost, but he quickly recovered himself and answered with a smile, "I didn't say that you please me, only that you cheer me."

"What's the difference?" she laughed.

"There's a big difference."

Golde wanted to say something in response, but her mother called her suddenly from the kitchen.

"Golde! Come here, daughter!"

Golde, smiling sweetly, excused herself, saying that she would come right back.

Hecht remained in the little room, feeling very happy. A smile stretched across his face, and his ears glowed and stuck out from happiness. He wanted to go into the house and continue the conversation but was held back by the thought that it had been enough for a first meeting. Golde, he thought, wasn't going anywhere.

But Hecht couldn't sit still for long. He decided to go down to the street, and to the restaurant where he could get something to eat and could share his new experiences with his friends. He put on his old, but not overly tattered, coat and went out. No one was in the main room anymore; it was half-dark, and Hecht heard the ringing of spoon on a plate coming from the kitchen. He guessed that Golde was eating now.

He went into the kitchen. Golde seemed embarrassed to see him. She put down the spoon and said with a smile, "You're going already?"

"Yes . . . I still have a lecture to give . . ."

"The gentleman gives lectures," Golde's mother said, butting in from her seat on a kitchen stool.

"A teeeecher," Golde said, stretching out the word with a mixture of respect and impudence, looking at Hecht and smiling the whole time.

"You don't like teachers?" Hecht said, smiling back.

"Oh, just the opposite," Golde said. "A teacher is a very fine profession. A teacher is also an intelligent person," she laughed.

Hecht felt like he should be insulted, but the mother interrupted.

"She's starting up already with her little bits of wisdom. She's already that sort of person—for her there's no difference between an elder and a youth, no simple person and no scholar." Becoming more vociferous, the mother went on, "You don't know so well the gentleman who allows you to speak this way. This is no Chaim!"

"And who is this Chaim?" Hecht asked with feigned indifference.

"Also a lodger of ours. We set up a little bed for him here at night. He comes in at nine o'clock."

"Chaim is an ordinary tailor," Golde declared with finality. "You surely don't like tailors?" she asked, lifting her gaze searchingly to Hecht.

Instead of answering, Hecht asked back: "And you?"

"Me? I am a tailor myself."

"A fine comparison," the mother chimed in. "A woman tailor could be the mistress of a household also. But the young man is a tailor the son of a tailor."

"And you have a greater pedigree?" Golde said with a chuckle, needling her mother.

The mother smiled back, looked over at Hecht and asked earnestly, "Were your parents workers or householders?"

Hecht swelled up at the thought of his lineage, and answered proudly, "My parents were fine householders, and my grandfather was a rabbi."

"Te-te-te," the mother twittered and picked herself up from the stool. "Indeed, an impressive pedigree."

Golde also looked at him earnestly and opened her big eyes wide and child-like.

"You must know Hebrew, too?"

Hecht smiled. "Yes, but so what? I know Gemara[34] also, and could have been a rabbi, if I had wanted."

"But you are a nonbeliever," Golde said thoughtfully.

"Ah, that's another question. Now I must go."

"And when are you coming back?" Golde asked earnestly, giving him a friendly look.

Her questions and her glances made Hecht bold. "In a few hours

---

34 A component of the Talmud, redacted circa 500 C.E.

from now," he said. And, almost involuntarily, asked, "Will you still be here?"

"Yes, certainly!" she assured him.

"In the meantime, Adieu!"

"Adieu! Adieu!" She repeated the word, which she didn't often have an opportunity to use. But she also shook her head from side to side, as if she was joking.

Hecht went to the door and left. On the other side he heard Golde say to her mother, "An intelligent one."

He smiled happily and went down the stairs.

IV

IN THE LITTLE café where Meir Hecht was a regular, he met a few of his friends sitting at a small table. He sat down, ordered something to eat and with a gleam in his eye announced: "I moved into a new place today."

"Mazel tov!" roared his friend Bloch, a mystically disposed little man with a small freckled face.

"Indeed, mazel tov!" Hecht sang out.

"And what's the big deal?" asked a second friend, Shapiro.

"No big deal," Hecht answered. "A small room, poor people . . . but there's a girl there who is a complete wonder. A simple child, but very interesting."

"So, a girl," Bloch murmured. "No wonder you're so pleased . . . you don't want to have a minute's peace!"

"There's no harm done," Hecht answered. "It's just more pleasant to live in the company of the fairer sex. A house without a beautiful woman is like a ruin."

"So put up a *mezuza*[35] then," Bloch joked ill temperedly.

"A pretty girl is better than a *mezuza*!" Shapiro laughed.

---

35 A piece of parchment inscribed with biblical passages that is affixed in the doorways of Jewish homes.

Hearing the comparison made Hecht lively. "I wouldn't want to kiss a *mezuza* these days, but this girl in my place, I want to do more than kiss . . ."

"A great find!" Bloch joked. "But she would be beneath my station."

"Yes, perhaps!" Hecht said, and his eyes sparkled. "But I'm of a different opinion. Ach, if only there was money. Money! Money! Money!" he shouted.

One of the customers at the café turned towards the little table in shock. Bloch got angry and mumbled, "Don't scream like that. People are staring."

Hecht was embarrassed and excused himself. He called to the waitress, paid for his meal, put the leftovers securely in his pocket, and went to the door. Bloch called out after him, "Give us your address, so we can come by sometime." Hecht turned around, wrote his new address on a scrap of paper and left.

When he got back to his new home, it was already ten o'clock at night. At the table he found a few new people, along with Golde and her mother. There was her father, the two boys, and the other tenant. Hecht wished them a good evening, not knowing exactly how to behave.

"Daddy! This is our tenant!" Golde said cheerfully, presenting Hecht to her father.

"So it is," said the father, a forty-year-old Jew with a worn-out but ruddy, healthy-looking face. He held out a broad, strong hand. "How do you do?"

Hecht stuck out his small white hand, which seemed to be swallowed up by the father's. At the same time, he noticed how the first tenant stared at him unceasingly, and he felt uneasy.

"And I'd like to introduce myself!" the other tenant finally exclaimed, with simple modesty. "My name is Chaim Kulka." A little man with a wild name like "Kulka" made an unpleasant impression on Hecht. With a feeling of revulsion he held out his hand, before turning back to the father.

"You've just come back from work?"

"Oh, I've been here for an hour already," the father answered happily. "I always come home at nine o'clock. *Nu* . . . you little rascals!" he said, turning towards the two boys, who were sitting at the table with their eyes fixed on the new tenant. "Time for bed!"

"Bedtime! Bedtime!" Golde urged them.

The boys complained, and eventually one of them, getting angry with Golde, threatened her:

"I'll tell on you!"

Golde went red. "What will you tell?" she demanded.

"I'll tell that on Saturday Chaim kissed you!" her brother chattered innocently.

Golde went red as fire. Hecht looked at Chaim with anger, then at Golde with reproach, and finally said to the boys with a smile, "Now, one mustn't tell tales . . ."

"Whatever he's babbling about, let's hear it!" the mother chimed in.

"And if yes, so what?" the father said, taking up the issue. "Chaim is no stranger . . ."

"But it's a lie!" Golde defended herself, and turned redder.

Chaim looked at her with scorn.

Hecht stayed seated for a few minutes and finally, saying good night, went to his little room. He sat down on the bed, moved the table closer, lit the lamp and began leafing through a book.

But he could not read. The letters jumped here and there, up and down, and trailed behind them the image of the pretty, fresh young Golde . . .

V

TWO HOURS LATER, everyone in the house was asleep. But Hecht was still sitting by his table, reading, writing, and rubbing his brow. At last he heard a quiet whisper. His blood flamed up. He could hardly control himself and strained to catch a word.

"Leave, Chaim, leave . . . I don't want to," Hecht heard Golde whisper.

"Why not tonight?" Chaim whispered back.

"Just because . . . I don't want to. Take your hand away. Don't touch me."

Hecht's face glowed. He strained his ears again, but once again the house was silent. He stuck his head out between the curtains of his room, looked furtively around the house, and saw Chaim standing by the table like someone who had been struck. Golde was sitting, holding in her hand a little book. Hecht stayed still and waited. Eventually, Chaim went off in the direction of the kitchen, where he had his bed. Golde was alone.

Hecht coughed heavily and sat down on his bed. Golde coughed back—as if she wanted him to know that she was waiting, and that she wanted him to come sit and spend some time with her, once Chaim was asleep. A few minutes went by. Hecht peered through the curtain with excitement. He saw Golde sitting by the table leaning her lovely head on her elbows. As if a mysterious power was urging him on, he picked himself up and entered the room.

Golde looked at him with a loving smile. Hecht wanted to say something, but Golde gestured at him to be quiet. Her gesture was the greatest assurance. Hecht felt like he had been waiting for this moment. He hadn't known what it would be like, but now he felt like it was the eve of some great, beautiful holiday.

He remained quiet for a few moments. Then Golde stood up and whispered, "Have you read this book?"

Hecht took the book in hand. It was a sensational Yiddish novel. He smiled and said, "I will give you better books than this."

"I know you have good books," Golde said softly, and looked into his eyes.

Hecht looked back at her lovingly, and asked gravely, "Who is this Chaim?"

She turned red and answered: "He's lived with us for two years already—a worker, a tailor. We are friends."

"And not more?"

"Oh no, absolutely not!" Golde said emphatically.

Hecht was quiet for a moment and then whispered to her quietly, almost in her ear, "You are really better than him."

Golde turned red and lowered her eyes in embarrassment. Hecht took her by the hand, and she didn't take it away. Quite the opposite— to his great amazement she gave his hand a strong squeeze. But the next moment she seemed to remember something and quickly tore her hand away.

"A good night! I'm going to sleep."

"A good night!" Hecht answered, and went off like a victor to his room.

The next evening, when Hecht returned to the house, he didn't see any sign of Chaim. This made him happy, and he laughed to himself. True, the young tailor couldn't stand in his way, could never be any real competition. But it was better that he wasn't here.

Hecht went to his room and picked up a German book, which he carried out to show to Golde. She took it with delight and said earnestly, "This is in German!"

"Yes, German!" Hecht replied.

The father, who was already home, put out his hand and said, "Show me, show me, let me see what it looks like."

With great deference he took the little book in his hand, turned a few pages and said sagely, "It must be an important book!"

"Yes, very important," Hecht affirmed.

"Jacobi[36] says that German is the greatest language in the world."

Golde moved closer to hear what the scholarly Hecht would say. He smiled and exclaimed, "German is a very beautiful language, but there are even more beautiful ones. French, for example, is even more beautiful."

The father furrowed his brow and solemnly asked, "If that's so, could you tell me what kind of language French is? German I've

---

36 Carl Gustav Jacob Jacobi (1804–1851), the first Jewish mathematician to be appointed a professor at a German university.

sometimes heard spoken, but French—never. *Nu*, so say a few words, let's hear how it sounds."

Hecht was in a tight spot. He didn't know any French. But if he didn't say something for these simple people he would ruin their esteem for him, and who knew if Goldele, who looked at him now with such affection, wouldn't suddenly cool towards him. He stammered the few words he had picked up.

"*Bonjour. Monsieur. Pardon. Merci. Mon ami. Au revoir, mon ami!*"

"*Oy vey!*" Goldele's father enthused. "Such a beautiful language!"

Golde looked at Hecht with amazement and veneration. Hecht took note and, beaming, turned to her.

"You like French?"

"Oh, it's so pretty, so pretty . . . please teach it to me."

"Very good, I will teach it to you," Hecht assured her good-naturedly.

"What do you need French for?" the mother said, butting in. "It would be better for the gentleman to teach you German."

"Certainly," the father said, agreeing with his wife. "What do you need French for? German will be useful to you." Then, rethinking the matter, he added, "Everything a person knows can be useful." He believed strongly in education. "If only I knew at least a bit of Polish. Now that would come in handy!"

"Now in your old age you figure it out," the mother joked. "Chaim also doesn't know any languages, and so what? There's no shame in that."

Golde blushed and said, "He really is a vulgar youth."

"*Nu, nu,*" the father winked at her meaningfully. "Don't speak foolishness. Chaim is a fortunate bachelor—he works and he earns."

"Where is he, so late?" the mother asked.

"You miss him?" Golde said ironically, turning to her mother.

"I should miss him?" the mother replied. "He's not here, is all I'm saying."

As she spoke, Chaim walked in. He said good evening quietly, wiped his face with a white cloth and boomed out: "Working late!"

"Why's that?" Golde's father asked.

"Just . . . because . . . one has to make money . . ." And he was silent.

VI

A FEW WEEKS passed. Hecht and Golde grew closer from day to day. When everyone else was asleep, she would go to his room and spend time sitting with him on the bed.

The first kiss didn't go well. Immediately after Hecht had given her a weak peck, she jumped up and ran out. Hecht had to plead and promise her that he wouldn't do it anymore. But eventually she let him try again, and on recent evenings she would go into his room when he was already lying in bed, covered up with the blanket, and he would pull her to him and kiss her. She only whispered softly, "Don't kiss so hard . . . they'll catch us."

And Chaim kept coming back late in the evening, greeting everyone and then going immediately to sleep. To Hecht he said nothing. He would only sometimes cast a sidelong glance at him and smile.

"Why does he smile like that?" Hecht often asked himself, and couldn't find an answer. But he felt that the smile implied something sinister.

One time, when Hecht came home in the evening after he had been at the café, telling his friends that Golde was practically his, he found everyone sitting at the table in high spirits. He wondered what the reason was for the exceptional good mood but couldn't figure it out. He looked at Golde, seeking an explanation, but she smiled and kept her eyes down, saying nothing. At last Chaim stood up and said, "We should also show it to Mr. Hecht—he would appreciate such a thing."

"Indeed, we must show him," the father agreed, "but what then? He's no expert in that."

Golde smiled and went to the cupboard, from which she removed a small box and brought it with a little laugh over to Hecht. He opened it with trembling hands and saw something sparkle.

"Take it out! Look at it! Look at it!" Chaim demanded with irritation. Seeing how Hecht didn't move a finger, he took it out himself, held it up and turned it around. "Do you see?"

"He bought it as a present for Golde—a hundred rubles he paid!" The mother pushed her way forward and her eyes glowed from happiness.

"Try it on!" Chaim told Golde. She rolled up her sleeve and put it on her wrist. Her beautiful arm sparkled and looked even richer and more beautiful.

"Beautiful, truly!" Golde said, turning to Hecht.

"A very . . . very . . ." Hecht mumbled and didn't know what to do. Should he stay here among these people, who suddenly seemed so distant and strange, or run back to his café and be among his friends—Shapiro, Bloch and the others.

"Tell me, what do you call a jewel in French?" Chaim asked suddenly, turning to Hecht.

Hecht knew that Chaim was making fun of him. Blood flowed to his face as he turned and said, "How does a person like you come to be interested in French?"

"Au revoir, ton, bonjour." Golde sang out the few words she remembered. Hecht didn't know if she was mocking him too or was simply expressing her happiness. He smiled absently and stammered, "Not like that . . . you don't say *'ton bonjour.'*"

"Such a business over how one speaks," Chaim defended her. "She may not know grammar, but the bracelet suits her, don't you think?"

Hecht finally came to himself. His pride reared up and he exclaimed: "I don't care about such foolishness!"

Golde, drunk from happiness, looked at Hecht and said warningly: "For you it's foolishness, because you didn't give it to your girl."

"Oh, they don't believe in it," the father said in defense of Hecht. "Educated people have other things to give."

"Yes, yes, educated people have other gifts," Chaim said sarcastically and stuck his hands in his pockets.

Hecht turned around, went by himself into his room, and threw himself fully clothed on the bed. His face burned. He could have hit someone on the head with a hammer. He felt beaten down and badly fallen. A tailor, just a youth, had bested him. Like an evil bird, the thought pecked at his brain.

The image of Golde swam before his eyes. He tried to drive it away, but a longing for her filled his entire being. She would no longer come to his room. She would not come!

He cast a glance at the table. There lay several books in no particular order. They looked pathetic and ridiculous.

Hecht buried his face in the pillow as though he wanted to hide from the world and from himself. But the talk and laughter from the house still reached him. Even deep in the pillow, he saw Golde clearly, with the bracelet on her arm, and Chaim by her side.

Yente Serdatsky
1877–1962

Y ENTE SERDATSKY, ONE of the most important literary contributors to the *Forward* in its early decades, chronicled the lives of Jewish immigrant women in numerous stories published in the 1910s and 1920s.

Born Yente Raybman in the town of Aleksat, near Kovne, or Kaunas, Lithuania, Serdatsky was educated in a religious elementary school for girls, as well as by private tutors. Her father was an educated furniture dealer, and the family's home was a gathering place for Yiddish writers.

At age thirteen Serdatsky was apprenticed to a seamstress and later ran a grocery store while she continued to read literature in German, Hebrew, and Russian. Following the Revolution of 1905, Serdatsky moved to Warsaw, leaving behind a husband and three children. Her first published story, "Mirl," appeared that year in the Warsaw newspaper *Der veg* (*The Way*), and attracted the attention of writers such as I. L. Peretz.

Serdatsky immigrated to the United States in 1907, settling first in Chicago and later in New York, where she ran a soup kitchen. She also began publishing short stories and sketches in a variety of Yiddish periodicals and came out with a collection of selected works in 1913.

Serdatsky was a regular contributor to the *Forward* until 1922, when she got in a financial dispute with editor Abraham Cahan and stopped writing for the paper. Only in 1949 did she begin publishing again, this time in the *Nyu Yorker vokhnblat* (*New York Weekly*).

The three stories included here all appeared in the early 1920s and portray women at various stages of life: two unmarried young women who worry about the intentions of the men who have become their self-appointed guardians; a widow who decides not to pursue further romantic entanglements; and an older woman struggling with the psychological effects of isolation and old age.

———

The Devoted Cousin

(JUNE 6, 1920)

Translated by Jessica Kirzane

THEY WERE SISTERS. One was now twenty-five, and the other was about a year younger. A few years ago, when they arrived here from a small town in Poland, they were very beautiful, young and fresh with color in their cheeks, sparkling black eyes and thick dark hair. They are still beautiful now, although they work all the time and their lives are not easy.

Like all poor young people, they came here for a reason. Their parents were poor. They were the eldest of the children; they had four younger siblings and more were on the way. They did not have many friends. The aunt with whom they came to stay was religious, and they couldn't stand to stay with her for more than the first few weeks. They had another uncle and aunt whom they also didn't like, and as soon as they found work they rented a room from strangers. Just as it began to seem as though the girls were going to end up living entirely alone and friendless, a cousin appeared who had been living here in America for many years. He had never written to them when they were living in the old country with their family. They had assumed they were entirely estranged from him. He was nice to the girls.

The cousin was close to forty years old, and he acted almost like a father to them. They behaved casually towards him, and he thought of them as younger sisters. He was a kind bachelor, a short, thin man with a dark face and eyes as black as theirs. He wore glasses because his eyes had grown weak from too much work. He was learned. For many years he had worked in a shop and in the evenings had studied to become a doctor. That was his greatest desire. Later he changed his passion and instead became a manager at the shop. It was a position that paid well and commanded a lot of respect, much more respect than a doctor's diploma. But he had not foresworn books—reading was not only his habit; it was his need. He had simply exchanged his difficult textbooks for easy, pleasant literature. This was more comfortable—he was able to imagine himself in the company of all types of interesting people.

Aside from books, the cousin held one desire sacred, and that was to be free. He was always aware, always careful, to be sure that no one had control over him. He did not drink or play cards, did not smoke, and above all he kept away from women. Oh, what temptations lie in a glance from a pair of brown or black eyes! If you return it even a little you become an eternal slave to a woman, a child, a boss in your workplace, even a boss in your home. No, he would not do this! It was for this reason he was careful not to live in the homes of any young landladies, where other older bachelors looked for love without attachment, and he made no acquaintances among families because there are young women in every family who might make eyes at him. His landlady was almost always a graying Irish woman, and when he needed some amusement, he went to a play or a concert. There he met other unattached people like himself. Sometimes they bored him to tears. He didn't think love for sale was good or right, but sometimes it helps a man remain free.

When his cousins came over to America, he stayed away from them for several weeks and considered the situation with caution. Then he decided that they were no danger to him. He had never had a sister, but he was sure that his feelings towards them were warm and calm, like one might feel towards a smaller, younger sister. By nature he was a good man, and he saw no reason why he should keep his distance. They were his relatives after all, and there are dangers threatening young, morally upright women from all sides. It was only right that he should quickly come to their aid.

Having decided this, he carried out his decision. The first thing he did was find them a "clean" place to work, in a shop run by Mrs. Weisman. Few men worked there so the girls would be spared their hungry, lustful stares, and wouldn't have to listen to their off-color jokes and dirty speech.

After taking care of their workplace, he turned his attention to the home where they had a room. Everything there was just as he would have wished it. It was a large, nice, airy room in the home of a childless couple who were busy all day at work. They still live there today.

With both of these things taken care of, he enrolled them in night school and several months later, when they could already understand some English, he began to bring them easy books to read. It didn't bother him when they read in Yiddish, but things would be easier for them if they could get used to the English language.

In this way he was good to them, and time went by.

EVERYTHING WOULD HAVE been fine, except that he was greatly worried about their leisure activities. He was particularly worried about the younger sister. The older sister had a more serious nature and was content with her work, her books, and on Sundays going to the theater not far from their home. But it was not so with the younger sister. She was lighthearted, with sparkling eyes and joyful laughter. Her figure was light and breezy, her legs moved as though they were propelled by the wind. She liked to get out of the house, to laugh, to dance.

Before he even had time to think, the younger sister had gathered a bunch of young men around her. God knows where she found them. They buzzed around her like bees. If only they had been well-mannered young people, but they all looked suspicious, fresh . . . One evening she didn't follow her sister home but instead went off with one of the men to a dance.

The cousin, being a good and reliable man, saw no other way. He took it upon himself to instruct the young woman and show her the world. When she was with him, the young men scattered like flies fleeing smoke. This didn't bother her because her cousin was very good to her and took her out to different places several times a week. He was also happy and smiled and enjoyed himself. When she was by his side, he was sure that nothing bad could happen to her.

Because he was a good and honorable friend, he also wanted to take the older sister out, but she refused. When did she have time for such things? She needed to clean her room and take care of her laundry. She could not allow herself to buy ready-made clothing, since sewing herself cost a third as much and she could send the few dollars left over to the poor and sick instead of buying such extravagances. So she bought all kinds of fabrics and made beautiful clothes for herself and her sister. When she had a little free time, she paged through a book. If her younger sister did not have such a lighthearted nature, she might have made more demands on her, but her sister needed to be out and about.

The older sister was not home alone for long, since her cousin introduced her to one of his friends. The friend was a kind, gentle bachelor, and the woman would have fallen in love with him if her cousin had not already warned her against it. "Doraleh," he said to her after the man's first visit, "you must know that you should not fall for him, he can only be a teacher and a dear friend to you, and nothing more."

The older sister smiled a lonely smile. She already knew this, because she and the friend had discussed it a while ago. It had taken him a long time until he was willing to come into her home. He was an exceptional man, with wealthy parents. Yet he hated wealthy and idle society, and the tumult of married life. He bought and read many books. Among many other things, he believed that a man and a woman should only be dear friends and that they should not arouse in one another any other feelings. "Maybe he is right," the girl thought. She was quiet and serious and became withdrawn with her dear friend, the bachelor. He began to come to her several evenings a week. In this way she was saved from her loneliness.

The bachelor was very interesting. His father was a rich businessman. He had two brothers and two sisters, all older than him. They were all married, bourgeois, rich people. He did not like them and did not see them often. He was the youngest son and his father loved him very much, but he felt more affection for his mother. She was an old, gray, simple woman. She had a lonely smile and her voice was weak and filled with motherly gentleness.

His father was entirely different. At one time he had been a Russian student and had dreamed of high ideals. But his success made him just like all other businessmen. He played cards, drank wine, and the rest of it. But he did not like these rich, morally loose people. He probably still had a desire for higher living. You could tell because of his deep love and devotion to his youngest son. He loved and doted on him because he buried himself in books and engaged with another world.

The bachelor himself dabbled with books. He wanted to be a poet. If he had been a painter, he would have known the meaning of his existence. He thought about this often, and worried that he was living without purpose. There was no subject that he needed to study. He hated business, and he could not become a teacher or a leader because he was afraid of being in front of a large crowd of people. He often walked around with his head bowed, thinking. His greatest pleasure was to buy a new book, and he hoped it would explain to him the hidden secret of his being.

His few friends had until now been intellectual men like himself. Now he also began to count the gentle, lonely young woman among his friends. He was happy that she aroused in him no other feelings. He spoke with her like he would speak to a good friend. She listened to his every word and this made him even more pleased. He was simply happy. The only pity was that she knew so little. Every now and again he brought her another book, but she didn't read very much. She did not have much free time.

THE COUSIN AND his friend never considered getting married, and this was no secret to the women. The women did expect to get married, and this was no secret to the men. When the men were alone together, they would speak about the women's futures. One would worry out loud: "They should get married! How long can a woman remain single? No more than thirty years. After that she has to have children. It would be a sin if all women decided to do what we have done and let the world collapse without a future." He thought to himself and then added, "It is also better for an elderly lady to be the wife of an honorable older gentleman, the mother of married children and a grandmother to beautiful grandchildren, ha-ha! How would my mother look if she were still unmarried? An old maid!"

The cousin agreed that his friend was right, the sisters needed to get married, it was already time. But until someone proposed, the two men would stay by their sides. The older sister would be lonely without his friend and the younger sister might stray from the right path if he left her alone even for a minute.

The cousin thought for some time. After that he began to worry: he had a difficult mission, but he felt called upon to make it work. The way he behaved with the younger sister, he felt that she forgot sometimes that he was her cousin and almost old enough to be her father. She flirted with him, kissed him, threw her arms around his neck. How could he let her go on in this way?

His friend understood his difficulties. His face burned with embarrassment, his eyes glimmered and grew damp with sympathy, he warmly pressed the cousin's hands and, moved, said quietly, "my pure, idealistic friend!"

THE WOMEN ALWAYS went to bed late and got up early in the morning, so they had to cut their conversations short in order to get to sleep. This time, though, the younger sister had more to say. As usual, she began her conversation like this:

"Doraleh, are you sleeping?" she asked in a gentle, singsong voice. Her voice was a gentle, soft, sunny monotone, and her older sister awoke.

"Don't say anything, Lucy, we have to sleep. It's late!"

"So what if it's late? We can sleep in, we can get up when half the day is already gone, your boyfriend will take care of the damage!"

"Leave me alone!" the older sister said angrily. "He has never offered me money and I would never take any from him!"

"Then why do you accept books from him?"

"It's permissible to take books. They are for the human spirit."

"Leave me alone with your human spirit!" the younger sister responded petulantly. Both were silent, but this didn't last long. She asked again, worriedly, "Doraleh, what will come of this? When will we get married? We already have gray hairs."

"Who knows when? It will happen."

"When will it happen? Year after year goes by just the same."

The older sister stifled her own worry and anxiety. It seemed to her that her sister was just a little child and that she must come to her aid, calm her, and drive away her fear and worry. She began to tell her that they had plenty of time, that even women less attractive than they would not be concerned that a good, attractive, respectable man would come along.

They were quiet for a while longer and it seemed as though the younger sister might have fallen asleep, but all of a sudden she blurted out: "Doraleh, why should they not marry us?"

"You know, Lucy, that they do not ever want to get married, so why would you bring up such a useless idea?"

"Why would some other man want to marry us if they don't?" The girl was getting riled up.

"It is a matter of taste. Some men prefer to remain free and others don't mind chaining themselves up."

"Tastes can change," said the younger sister, almost to herself.

They were quiet again for a while, each thinking to herself of all the possibilities. The older sister imagined herself in a wealthy home. A servant did all the hard work, and her husband, a beloved man, a fine and honorable man, was always by her side. They read books together, they had a beautiful, rich life, and eventually there would be children—a little boy . . . a little girl . . . and more and more.

The younger sister saw herself in almost the same picture. He, the cousin, became a wealthy businessman: there was a wealthy home, silk clothes, jewelry, dances, and after a time a child, a little boy with blue eyes and curly hair . . .

The younger sister's mind worked quickly, and she came quickly to the realization that all of these good things did not depend on her, but on him. It made her angry and uncomfortable, and it made her think of all kinds of plans as to how she could make him bend to her desires.

A while later she turned suddenly to her sister and said, "Doraleh, don't be mad at me, tomorrow I am going to look for a new room to stay in. I don't want to live in the same room as you anymore!"

She waited to hear her sister's surprised outcry, her angry words, her curses, but to her surprise the older sister put her hands over her head and smoothed her hair. In the quiet of the night they had both arrived at the same thought.

They did not go through with it because the cousin saw the danger in their plan to have separate rooms and did not allow it. "Such a young, lighthearted girl should not live alone!" he said to the other bachelor. The man agreed with him and shook hands with him heartily.

The Young Widow

(AUGUST 1, 1921)

Translated by Jessica Kirzane

S HE WAS THE wife of an enlightened worker. They lived modestly and peacefully. They loved one another and they loved their only child fiercely. They never dreamed of other loves, other joys, as dissatisfied enlightened people from the Jewish quarter often do. He had eyes for no woman aside from his wife, and she never so much as looked at another man. But the devil lurked behind this peaceful life and waited for his chance to steal it all away. He did not have to wait long. A trifling incident occurred: the husband caught a chill and was laid up in bed. A week later he was carried away from his house for his eternal rest.

The young wife was saddened but did not become distraught. After all, was she alone in the world? She must live and hold herself together for the sake of their son. In a few months she had already arranged everything: she sold her home and sent her son to boarding school. She found a room to rent for herself and went to work in the same position she had held before she was married. She worked in a small shop where they made women's clothing to order. The proprietress of the shop was a middle-aged woman. She had a troubled past that had caused her hair to go prematurely gray and her brow to wrinkle. Now she was rich, but she did not want to give up her work. In the noise of the machines she could more easily forget the difficult experiences of years gone by.

When the young woman returned, the proprietress took her in with a spark in her eye and quickly gave her a position. It seemed as though she had been waiting for her, and maybe she had been. Many women who left the shop in order to marry later returned when bitter fates forced them to share in the woman's solitude—and there they remained for many, many years.

The young woman was happy to be offered work in her former position, but she was sure that she wouldn't stay too long: she was young, pretty, genteel, and frugal. A real treasure for a man who wanted to marry and have a quiet and comfortable life. She could not be expected to mourn her husband forever, and if the right man should come along, she would go with him.

When several months had passed and the "right man" had not speedily appeared, she did not despair. She never spoke of it and it seemed as though she wasn't thinking about it, either. With a clear head and with a clear, calm mind, she conducted her life with the mechanical regularity of clockwork: she spent her days at work and spent the few free hours after work in her room sewing clothes for herself and for her child. She went to bed early so that she would rise refreshed, with a spring in her step, a healthy body and a clear head. Even on Sundays she had a regular way she spent her time: this was a path that led to a small town outside of New York. There, among the trees and flowers, was a bright white house. Attached to the house was a large veranda decorated with colorful flowers and before it was a large front lawn strewn with toys and cradles for children's exercise and play. Blond women in white dresses with quiet movements and motherly smiles on their faces watched over a few dozen children. The children were clean, well behaved, and attractive, and their happy voices filled the blue, quiet air with joy.

One of the children waited for her every Sunday. He ran to her with arms stretched wide: "Mama dear! Mama darling!" She kissed him quietly. His cries upon seeing her died down and he played with his toys. She looked around and saw how quickly the day was passing. On the way home she thought that her child seemed even more beautiful than before, and that he was living a better life than children who are raised by their parents in a poverty-stricken home. The peace she felt about her child dissipated as she sorrowed over her hus-

band's passing. But her mind told her that she must be content to
work to support herself and her child. She followed this logic, went
to bed early and awoke the next day ready to work. Her hands flew,
and the needle glimmered in the sun like a thin shimmer of light
refracted through a diamond.

IN THE HEAT of summer the proprietress would close her shop for
several weeks to go away somewhere. This way the workers had a bit
of rest, although they weren't paid for it. The first summer the young
woman waited impatiently for this break because she had decided to
go to the mountains. As a girl, she used to travel almost every summer and would have a happy time, but after her wedding she stopped
going because there was no money to spare. Now she had sewn beautiful summer clothes and bought colorful accessories with great care.
She often found herself blushing: she hoped that something would
come of her efforts . . .

Instead of the four weeks she had anticipated, she spent only
one week away. She returned because she was sure that she could
not relax away as well as she could at home. She had a huge room
and a comfortable bed all to herself. In the morning there was no
need to hurry to get up: it seemed an insult to obey the alarm clock
that summoned her to eat. All she wanted to do was lie in bed
and look out the window at the blue sky and the green mountains
and listen to the birdsongs; to doze off and to weave a sun-soaked
dream.

From her room at home she could also see the blue sky because she
lived on the highest floor in the back. The sun streamed in through
the windows, and she had to let down the green curtains in order to
shield herself from a flood of golden sunlight. Golden flecks of light
pierced the curtains and covered the furniture and the walls. The
fine linens seemed bleached in the sun-flecks and looked as though
they were woven with gold. The idea that she did not need to get up
to work caused a sweet sleepiness to pour over her body. She lay with

half-open eyes and in her half-sleep her dreams were sweet, peaceful and filled with a rosy glow.

She hardly noticed at all how the weeks passed. Afterwards she returned to work, and her life proceeded like clockwork, day after day, week after week. At the beginning of the next summer, a little tired out from her year of constant labor, she often thought about the few weeks of rest that were approaching. This time she didn't even consider going to the mountains. She only dreamed about the early mornings during which she wouldn't have to get up early to work and could sleep and dream to her heart's content.

That time did come, but this summer she was not fated to enjoy peaceful sleep and carefree mornings. She had begun to suffer, because on her lonely, difficult, but peaceful life's path she encountered not a wolf, not a bear, not any other kind of animal, but a man.

THE PROPRIETRESS DID not treat her workers well. She paid them low wages for long hours of work. And she was also very strict. There was no one who would rebel because the married women whose misfortunes had brought them back to work were content to have a stable position where they felt at home, and the young female workers hoped to leave the shop soon. They expected no help from anyone. Then the eyes of justice looked down on the exhausted workers and the union sent one of their clerks to organize the shop.

The young man considered the workers as he spoke to the proprietress. His experienced eye landed on the young woman. He decided that he would speak to her and she would help him with his work, which did not promise to be easy.

He had not made a mistake. He didn't have to speak with her long. She understood everything related to work and capital, but she advised him to wait before acting, because in a few weeks the shop would be closed and it would be easier to organize the workers when they were back in full force. They had to meet several times in order to talk it all through. By then they were already drawn to one another: she as a person who suffered and he as a person who had become used to caring for the oppressed and the suffering. They had plenty to talk about aside from the shop. It is easier to conduct difficult, complicated conversations in quiet surroundings, and since it was spring, they began taking walks together in the park.

The rest happened by itself. The two young people fell in love. But she, despite the strong temptation, had not allowed him to come to her room. She always parted ways with him before it was too late at night. Her mind told her that she must do this, and she always obeyed this thought.

The young man had a wife and children, but this did not prevent him from frequently falling in love with other women. He did not hide it from the young widow. According to his reasoning, he had done nothing wrong, and the more he spoke with her about it, the more justified he felt: he must have a home where he could rest, a wife to care for who would love him unconditionally, and children who would love him all his life and keep his strivings and ideals alive after he was gone. His love for other women was the holiday of his life, the inspiration behind his daring work for the sake of the masses. The perfume of other women drove away the pessimistic thoughts that buried themselves under his contentment and dwelt there.

And what about her? Would the romance also bring inspiration and joy to her life? He was sure of this: she was exactly the type who must live the life of a free and independent woman. Not all women have to be housewives, just like not all hens and birds should sit day after day in their nests watching over their eggs. She had already had a husband, a house, a child. Now she should lead the life of a free songbird, bringing joy to herself and others.

He described for her the life of free, independent, intelligent women: they think a lot about their work, become artists of their craft, earn a lot of money, go to the opera, to concerts, and spend time in cafés having intellectual conversations with knowledgeable men who relate to them as they would to close friends; they enjoy all of the luxuries they could possibly have, and even those who are not as beautiful as she is wield power in affairs of love.

The woman's heart pounded in her chest, but she did not agree to it, although if it hadn't been for her child she might have given it a try. But for the sake of her child, who must be raised with a strict sense of order, she must remain a respectable widow or legally marry a husband who could be a father to the child.

The first few days after she made this decision she suffered greatly. Then the pain of it started to ease. A few weeks later she was entirely at peace with her choice and her haggard face wore a smile, as do the faces of all idealists who go through a trial and come out triumphant. The heat exhausted her and she impatiently awaited her few weeks of rest. She needed them now for her body and for her spirit.

ON THE FIRST night of her vacation she slept soundly and easily. When she awoke, the sun did not smile down on her because it was a rainy day. The gray air, filled with moisture and heat, brought with it discomfort and unrest. She remained in bed. Against her will her eyes wandered over the furniture and walls. The wallpaper was dusty and cracked, the dresser and its chair had long lost their color, and the mirror was full of specks that had accumulated after years of hanging on the wall. She felt she should put up new wallpaper and install new furniture. She had been thinking about it for several weeks already but there was nothing to be done about it, as it wasn't really her house.

Her house? Did she need to have her own house? She began to go over in her mind the words of her former lover, and before she was able to recall her own responses to that conversation, she had fallen asleep. She did not have good dreams. Real-life events spun around her in a gray whirlwind: her husband, his sickness, his death . . . Something scared her and she started to run. Her legs did not follow her commands, but she still felt she had to run because something dangerous was behind her. Suddenly she saw herself at the top of a tall mountain. She looked into a valley and her heart clenched in fear . . . What was this? In the valley she saw piles of eggs and on them sat hens. No, they weren't hens! It was her sister birds, Aunt Deborah, the proprietress for whom she worked, the woman from whom she rented her room . . . Why were they looking at her so sorrowfully? With so much longing? With tear-streaked faces? . . . They called out to her . . . but how could she go to them, when the mountain's side was so smooth and so tall? She bent down to tell them something and lost her balance, and her limbs froze in fear. Her heart skipped a beat. She fell down like a stone and woke up.

She was afraid to go back to sleep. She got dressed. It was quiet in the house. The landlady had traveled to the mountains and the landlady's husband was at work at the shop. She gathered together a bundle of work, but the warm gray air made her hands moist and her arms heavy and her sad thoughts grew like mushrooms in damp air.

She left the house and went into the street. She decided to go to the department store to buy some things for her child. She had left it all for her free time. But she was unable to go. She walked around the house and into a nearby park. She went to a picture house, but they were showing a long film and she didn't have enough pennies to watch it. There was nothing interesting showing in the second picture house, but at least it was cool, so she stayed and nodded off.

When she left her seat, she found that it was a bright day outside. The sky was clear; the sun quickly dried the rain-soaked streets. People flooded into the streets like a mighty stream that had been dammed up and was now released. It was evening, the sun was setting, and the bright light together with the masses of people made her tired. Her vision blurred, and she remembered that she had not eaten all day. She had no desire to go into a restaurant. Nearby there was a delicatessen. She went inside and bought a salty, peppery bite to eat. When she got home, it was already almost dark outside. The smell of the flavorful food whetted her appetite, and she began to eat. Her thoughts wandered far away, and she forgot herself and lost track of time. Later she awoke from her reverie when her arms and legs grew heavy and her head began to hurt and she felt a burning, tingling sensation in her mouth and neck. She drank a lot of water and only felt worse. It grew later and later. She lay down but could not sleep. The more sleep grew unattainable, the more tightly she felt bound by the desperation of her family life. It had been torn apart, and she could not see how it could ever be made whole again.

———

She Waits

(JANUARY 9, 1922)

Translated by Jessica Kirzane

S HE WAITS FOR him. Night after night she looks outside, teary-eyed, lying in wait in the darkness, following every shadow. At the slightest noise her heart pounds: he is here! But he is not here. He does not hurry, and she waits. All day she looks out the window and thinks only of him. She has a lot of time. There is a rocking chair by the window in her bedroom. She sits and looks out the window. She sees many other windows of tenement houses with fire escapes that connect one apartment to the other with narrow iron stairs. The window looks out onto an empty gray lot where they plan to build an open-air summer theater, though in the meantime it has stood empty for several years.

All of the neighbors look at the empty lot with pleasure, because it allows them to freely see the blue sky flecked with sunny gold. She looks at it more than anyone else because she has a lot of time and thinks only of him.

When will he come? What roof will he climb down from? What courtyard will he crawl out from? Surely he will come from the house across the way, because it is on a quiet street. He will come on a dark night. His tall figure will be hidden by shadows, his eyes will flash like phosphorous, he will move quietly in the darkness like a gentle wind blew him in. She will hear his breath from the other side of the building. He is inside! He will come into the room like a plume of smoke, his eyes like two spears piercing the bed where she lies, and he will go straight to her, straight to her . . .

She is not waiting for a lover. Certainly not now. At one time she had waited; she had not believed that she would waste her whole life waiting for a man. He would come, he would be gentle and honorable. He would speak words of love to her and warm and gladden her sad and longing heart.

But he never came. Now she is a woman over fifty with gray hair. She has an air of hard work, of a sorrowful life without a shadow of love or joy.

Without a shadow of joy? No, she cannot say this. At first she was happy with the child she bore. Later, though, she understood more about the child: he grew up to be exactly like his father, with his attitudes, his nature. His father loved him. He took him to the theater, on walks, and later took him to work in the shop where he was a foreman. They both seem foreign to her, and she to them. Her son was married long ago. His wife is healthy, coarse and unrefined like he is. His wife's mother, a widow, is just like her daughter. They are all the same. He—her husband—whiles away his free time. She is not friendly to her son and his wife and they never come to her home.

Her husband is a stranger to her. She hated him from the first moment she saw him. In those days, in the village they called home, a girl had no say. Her parents told her to get married, and so she got married. Her parents rushed her into it. They saw the way she looked at the neighbor's son, a tall, blond non-Jew, and it made them look as though they'd seen a ghost. She still smiles when she thinks about it: she even kissed him a few times and once he snuck into her room through the balcony. It was a dark night. He wanted to steal her away to a church but she didn't go with him. No one knew about these things. How did her parents come to suspect something? How?

She was married. It happened. Silently she braided her hair. In the early years in New York she worked very hard and she never complained. Now she has nothing to do. For years her husband has not even allowed her to do laundry. He carries it up to the Chinese laundryman and brings it back himself. She is also not permitted to cook. There are many restaurants, so why should he burden a weak woman, especially if he would also get no pleasure from the food? She won't go to a restaurant? Then she should eat at home. It is easier to prepare food for one person than for two or three . . .

When her son was married, her husband freed her from another task: he made his bed in the front room on a leather sofa that served as a bed during the night. He felt comfortable and she was freed from the work. She had waited for this kind of freedom for many years. It came a little too late, but she felt relieved, as though someone had removed a clump of gluey tar from her body.

FROM THEN ON she has had a lot of free time and has stopped sleeping at night. She isn't upset about it; she sleeps many hours during the day. Around lunchtime tiredness steals around her like a thief. It wraps around her weak body and carries her soul away to that faraway world from which she came. She lingers for hours in that other world, and then she awakens, walks with quiet steps across the kitchen, washes her face, her hands, has a quick bite to eat, puts the few dishes back in their places, and goes back to her bedroom. She sits in the rocking chair and looks out the window.

From there she sees many things. The neighbors in the tenement houses do not know her although she has been living in the apartment for years. But from the laundry pegged to the lines, she knows almost everything that goes on in each house: above her they are bleaching new swaddling clothes; they must have a new child. To the right, a story above, new silk dresses with blue and green stripes wave in the bright sun. There, an Irish woman moved into the house. By looking at the laundry she can tell who is coming and who is going from the homes. She also sees, hanging from the line, a housedress made of dark cloth, so she knows that the lady of the house has grown old and tired and that the happiness in her heart has faded away.

In the evenings the laundry is taken into the homes, and the courtyard once again appears large, the sky blue, the windows aflame in the glare from the setting sun. The naked walls are covered with golden rays. Many windows are open. Mothers and children stick their heads out of the windows to enjoy God's world.

It is then that she leaves the window. She goes down into the street to buy something. It is already dark by the time she returns. She has something to eat again and then returns to her seat by the window. But she doesn't stay there for long. The neighbors' windows, lit up from within, display sorrowful portraits: a man with a gloomy face sits over his bowl of food while his wife runs from the table to the oven, from the oven to the table. A woman in glasses sits in the lamplight and darns a pair of dark-colored socks. Children pore over schoolbooks. A grown girl knits a sweater and her face is pale, sad, worried.

She leaves the window and lies down in bed. She extinguishes the flame, tucks herself under a blanket and waits for sleep. Sleep does not arrive in a hurry. It has more deserving people to comfort. Sleep visits her during the day. She lies still and waits. Later she hears her husband unlocking the door. The floor shakes with his heavy steps. He turns on the light in his room, rustles the pages of his newspaper for a while. Later she hears the bed creak under his heavy body. In the dark he falls asleep.

She smiles sadly. He thinks she is asleep when he does not see a light in her room. It is easier this way. What does it matter to her if she sees his red face with its huge nose? Once, when motherly love warmed her heart, she would leave the fire burning. Then his footsteps would approach her door and his gravelly voice would grind out, "Malke, are you asleep?"

"Not yet," she would answer weakly. He would open the door and stand in the doorway with downcast eyes and she would ask, "How is Mendel?"

He wouldn't tell her much about Mendel. She gathered, though, that he was all right. Her husband would go back to his room. His wife would put out the fire. Sleep would not hurry towards her. Her warm motherly heart would stir her thoughts so that they swam in her brain like little grains in a pot cooking over a low fire. Then they would congeal into a gluey paste, and she would fall asleep.

THIS WAS HOW her quiet, sad life passed by until a short while ago. There was a crisis in the country.[37] People went hungry, without clothes, without a roof over their heads. And they started to hear about murders, robberies, thefts. Stories like these also reached her ears: in one house a thief snuck in through the dumbwaiter. It was still light outside. The lady of the house looked out the window and saw him with a knife in his hand. She fainted with fear and he escaped.

In another house the doorbell rang in the middle of the day.

"Who is it?"

"A peddler selling old wares."

The good-hearted lady of the house opened the door and he grabbed her around the neck. In a certain house a robber snuck in through the window by the fire escape, went right to the bed where an old lady lay, and started to search under the pillows. The lady woke up. She had a weak heart and died from fear.

She had heard these and similar stories at the grocery store and the butcher shop, and she'd smiled peacefully. She has no reason to fear thieves. She has no jewelry, and if her husband earns money, he keeps it in the bank. Nevertheless, when she got home, she tested the door to make sure it was locked well, turned the key on the dumbwaiter, and sat as always by the window. As she sat rocking there, she suddenly stood up and closed the window, locked it, and then tried with all her strength to pull it open. It did not give. She let go and sat back down. It was the first time in many years that a happy smile played on her aging face. She was happy because she was safe, secure, like someone sitting in a warm house when it is frosty outside, who

---

37 A reference to the Depression of 1920–1921.

doesn't have to go out to buy food because she has everything she needs right at home.

Before she fell asleep she tested the locks again. Then she lay down in bed and let the fire burn. Later she heard him come in as usual. She heard him close the door. The key made the right noise in the lock. When she sensed that he was standing by her door, she forgot to ask about Mendel and said right away, "Please, Berchik, before you go to sleep, check to make sure you have closed the door properly."

"Why now, all of a sudden?" he barked in his gravelly voice.

"I've been hearing about thefts, robberies . . ." she explained with a quavering, almost young-sounding voice.

"I know what you are worried about! Your jewelry, your clothes, your expensive butter . . ." he barked with displeasure, as he stormed away with heavy steps.

She listened once more. He hadn't double-checked the door. It grew dark and she heard his bed creak. "What a brutish man," she thought. "Everything is a joke to him." She decided to get up and try the door herself if he would not. In the meantime she began to feel tired and drifted off to sleep. Suddenly she awoke with a start. She thought she heard the rope of the dumb waiter being lowered. She listened closely. It wasn't the rope, it was her husband turning over in his bed. How her heart was pounding! She stayed awake until her heart quieted. It took a while, and a little light had already started to shine through her windows when she finally fell asleep.

She slept late and the day went by for her like a wooden fruit bowl emptied of its contents. She had no desire to sit by the window and she was unable to fall asleep for her midday nap. In the evening she went shopping. She again heard the horrible stories of murder and robbery.

How would a thief know if she was rich or poor? This thought occurred to her and she started to check all of the locks. She calmed down, but soon she had second thoughts—what is a lock to a thief? One tap with a chisel and it would open. She grew cold and did not want to sit by the window, so she lay in bed long before it was night. Under the blankets she grew warmer. She could see the neighbors' windows from her bed. The reddish rays of the sun lit up the door-ways and the shadows of the night grew long. They looked like burn-ing black tar, and she was suddenly seized by fear. Dark pieces of laundry hung from the line. Men's trousers tangled in the wind, one trouser leg here and one trouser leg there, like witches. She wasn't happy about this. She stopped looking and fell asleep. Later she shook herself awake when her husband came in. Her heart pounded. When his bed creaked, her heart pounded again and it took a long time for her to calm down.

The fires went out in her neighbors' windows. It grew late. She jumped out of bed like a young girl and ran barefoot to the door, to the dumbwaiter, to the window, to be sure that everything was locked tight. She tucked herself back in bed, lay with open eyes, torn entirely from her sleep, and her eyes followed another shadow danc-ing on the wall. Suddenly she stirred. In the house across the way, on the fire escape, she saw him. Him, the thief! He snuck in through the window. She heard a scream. He was probably already clutching his victim's neck and choking her . . .

As she caught her breath, she saw that it was only another man's suit hanging out to dry, and the cry had come from a homeless cat. But a few nights later when she was half-asleep, she thought she saw him, the thief, at her own window. It was him, him! He leapt like a young deer over the ladder of the iron fire escape. He was tall, thin, with fiery eyes. His strong arms pressed against the lock, but it would not budge. Then he came in through the window like a curl of smoke and went straight to her, straight to her!

And this is how she sees him, night after night. Him, the tall, thin, terrible, wonderful thief . . . It seems as though she is waiting for him, but he never comes because a thief is not a young lover who clambers through the windows in the dark night because of love. He goes where he can be sure that his gallantry will be rewarded with jewelry and gold.

Lyala Kaufman

1887–1964

THE LITERARY CAREER of Lyala Kaufman is often overshadowed by that of her father, famed Yiddish writer Sholem Aleichem, and that of her daughter, novelist Bel Kaufman. But Lyala Kaufman was an accomplished and prolific author in her own right, publishing thousands of short stories in the *Forward* over a period of more than thirty years.

Born Sarah Rabinowitz in the town of Belaya Tserkov, in present-day Ukraine, Kaufman attended high school in Kiev and university in Geneva. In 1909 she married Yiddish writer Michael J. Kaufman and moved with him to Berlin, where he studied medicine. Their daughter Bella, later known as Bel, was born in Berlin in 1911.

Around 1912 the family moved to Odessa, where there was a burgeoning Hebrew and Yiddish literary community. Ten years later, following the Russian Revolution, Kaufman and her family escaped from the USSR and immigrated to America, where they settled first in the Bronx and then in Newark, New Jersey.

Kaufman's first published writing was a remembrance of her father in the *Forward*, but she soon began contributing short stories as well. Over the next three decades she published approximately two thousand such pieces, mostly dealing with twentieth-century Jewish American life. Although these stories made her a well-known figure to the readers of the *Forward*, none of her writing was ever translated or collected into books.

The selection of pieces included here, mostly dating from the 1960s, deal with the lives and problems of a wide cross-section of first- and second-generation immigrants, including women, children, and the elderly. In such pieces Kaufman demonstrated her ability to capture the concerns of the full spectrum of *Forward* readers, from teenagers going on first dates to grandmothers delighting in their newborn grandchildren.

At Prayer

(APRIL 30, 1929)

Translated by Ri J. Turner

SOREH-FEYGE, AS SHE was called in the old country—here in America they call her Mrs. Merliss—woke up this morning in a particularly bad mood. For days now, she has gotten out of bed grumpy, bitter and gloomy. In fact, why deny it—almost the whole time she's been in America (nearly a year now) she has felt down-hearted: practically since the very first day. She doesn't like it here. How can that be? She herself doesn't know. She is supposedly surrounded by kin, by her very own flesh and blood, and yet . . .

Her daughter-in-law Lizzie is, apparently, the same old stocky, goodhearted, foolish Leah'ke—yet she is also somehow not the same. She's gotten a little too smart here, and it irritates her mother-in-law. Back in the old country, she used to look up to Soreh-Feyge. "Mother-in-Law, what's your opinion? Mother-in-Law, how do you feel about it?" But here, a different kind of "Mother-in-Law" comes out of her mouth. "Mother-in-Law, you don't know a thing about it, everything is different here. Mother-in-Law, that's not the way they do it in America." And Soreh-Feyge hears the derision in her voice.

Yes, that's how it is—Soreh-Feyge, who was always the clever one, seems to have turned into a fool here. No matter what she says, the grandchildren burst out laughing. The older one looks down and makes a strangled face, and the younger one snorts openly into his fist, choking on his laughter—despite the fact that their father Benny fixes them with a warning glare. In those moments, it seems to Soreh-Feyge that even Benny's eyes flicker with glints of mockery. Yes, she's become a fool in her old age, the clever Soreh-Feyge! They started laughing at her the moment she stepped off the ship—"that old grandma with a kerchief on her head."

Anyway, why the Devil did she come to live with them? Who needs her here? She should have lived out her years in her old familiar *shtetl*.[38] All right, so her husband died and left her alone—so what? She really wasn't lonely there. The whole town knew her and respected her.

And here? Her son and daughter-in-law invite guests—in English they call it a "party"—and every person who walks through the door is some kind of . . . well, they're not Jews and they're not gentiles. Only the Devil knows what they are. You think there's any logic to it? Some of them don't even understand Yiddish! But none of them drives her crazier than that old harridan, the *shiksa*[39] with the shorn head—only the Devil remembers her Jewish name—who makes herself out to be some kind of aristocrat, and calls Soreh-Feyge nothing but Mrs. Merliss. For her part, Soreh-Feyge is willing to swear that back in the old country the old biddy used to wear a wig.

Her son, Benny, likes to explain that every country and every land has its own customs, and that the *treyfniatshke*[40] still keeps a perfectly kosher kitchen . . . a likely story! Soreh-Feyge wouldn't accept even a glass of tea in that house! Even at her own daughter-in-law's she keeps a separate kitchen—east, west, and never the twain shall meet. She has her suspicions about all those glasses and jars stamped like medicine bottles from a pharmacy: "Kosher." No, she puts no stock in that . . .

---

38 Small town.
39 A derogatory term for a non-Jewish woman.
40 Meaning, a non-kosher woman, or a woman who doesn't keep kosher.

Every morning when she prays the morning service with her good old *Korbn-minkhe* prayer book[41] in hand, Soreh-Feyge pleads with God to forgive her if something in the house is less than kosher—after all, no matter how hard she tries, she's no match for America!

But it's strange. Even the prayer service isn't what it was at home—the prayers themselves are somehow foreign. Maybe it's because she's perpetually irate—or because the room in which she prays now is so different from the room in the old country where she prayed for so many years. She tries to focus on her prayers, but she cannot. Against her will, her eyes flit critically from one object to another. Why did the children feel the need to squander so much money? Her heart sinks when she looks at the mirror on her dresser. What use is a mirror to an old bag like herself? They probably bought it in order to have a laugh at her expense.

She looks out the window with eyes full of accusation. Boys are running around in the street, making a racket—sheer chaos! Such slovenliness! A memory flashes before her eyes: the dear old alleyway at home, paved with dust, with an eternal mud puddle in its midst. Her heart clenches as if seized by an icy fist. Hot tears drip onto the old prayer book, and all the letters run together until Soreh-Feyge can't make out a single word. How strange that even the prayer book itself, her old *Korbn-minkhe* which she has used for so many years—even the prayer book is no longer what it once was. It looks somehow out of place in its new environment. Such an old prayer book! Back at home it hadn't looked quite so old.

"Mother-in-Law! You really should get a new prayer book one of these days," her daughter-in-law said at one point. But Soreh-Feyge shot her a contemptuous look and called after her, "Once a fool, always a fool . . ."

The more she prays, the more her heart fills with a dried-out acrimony. Towards whom? Towards all of them . . . her silly daughter-in-law, her son Benny, the mirror on the dresser, the old *treyfniatshke* harridan (God only knows what her name used to be), and maybe

---

41 A prayer book with Yiddish translation, commonly used by women.

even towards the Master of the Universe Himself, who seems to have abandoned her in her old age.

Nevertheless, she *will* pray! To spite them all, she will pray! Let them laugh at her—but this is the one thing that not one of them dares take away. *This is hers!*

"No, I *won't* let you have this!" she barks, stabbing the tabletop with her finger. "I'm not giving this up! It's mine!"

And quick-quick, her bloodless lips whisper the dried-out words of the prayers, which fail to refresh her soul—instead, they only exasperate her more.

But then, abruptly, as if remembering the necessary words at long last, Soreh-Feyge raises her turbid eyes to the ceiling, and with her whole heart speaks passionately to God Himself.

"Master of the Universe! Master of the Universe! May they all die a horrible death!"

And she feels immediately that a stone has lifted from her heart, and everything is already much more bearable.

A Country Girl

(JULY 1, 1952)

Translated by Ri J. Turner

IT WAS RIVELEH's idea to spend the summer on a farm. She herself had grown up on a farm, surrounded by forests and fields.

Three years had passed since she had come to New York. She, Riva (or Riveleh, as they called her), had been married for two years—very unhappily married. For her, a country girl, marriage to a city boy was no trifle. It was just as her aunt had predicted, the New York aunt who had taken Riveleh in.

Something had happened to Riveleh at home: a simple farm boy had courted her, but her parents weren't willing. Riveleh had argued and wept, but they had beguiled her with the grandeur of the city, the promise of a new life . . .

So she, the poor relation, had come here to live with her rich aunt. She had understood on the very first day that it was a trap—a despicable trap.

Her aunt was pleasant, hospitable. But a chill radiated from her hospitality—the chill of pity. And Riveleh could not tolerate anyone's pity.

The aunt tried to impress her bumpkin niece with the wonders of urban life. "You see," she boasted, "we don't have to milk cows here—instead, a bottle of milk pops up every morning behind the door. And do you see this pot? It cooks without water. And this one . . ."

Riveleh looked on and thought of her home in her village: in the background the forest, in the foreground the wide meadow and the river where she used to rendezvous with her sweetheart.

When she first arrived in the city, Riveleh was a curvaceous girl with ruddy cheeks. Her aunt took on the task of "turning her into a person."

"Don't eat that, Riveleh, you're already too fat. Here in the city, people prefer the slender look . . . Don't sulk like that, Riveleh! Here in the city, people prefer girls who are cheerful . . ."

In short order, Riveleh saw that her beloved auntie would just as soon be rid of her. Perhaps for that reason, she let Irving, her English teacher, give her a kiss.

Her aunt looked thoughtful when Riveleh told her about it. Then she said, "I don't get the impression that you two are serious."

But when Irving began coming over every evening, Riveleh's aunt called her into her room "to have a chat." She said: "You are the daughter of my only sister, and I am responsible for you. I don't think that a match with Irving is going to bring you happiness. You are not his equal!"

Riveleh wept. She thought to herself, "I don't think this is an auspicious match either. But after all, I can't say 'Dearest Auntie, it's you yourself who are pushing me out the door into the arms of the first man who will have me . . . '"

Not knowing that her words were tearing open an old wound, her aunt continued her speech. "It would have been best if you had married someone from your village!"

That evening, Riveleh lay in her city bedroom, "equipped with all the latest conveniences," and wept bitterly, remembering her friends from home—and one of them in particular.

She decided to marry Irving. "He's a good man!" she reassured herself. "I just don't understand him that well yet. After all, he's a city boy . . ."

Riveleh strove with all her might to become a city girl—to lose weight, to smile constantly like her new friends, and to bake delicious pies for her husband.

By the end of the first year, she could chatter along with the best of them, and her husband was satisfied with her. But she continued to cower before her aunt's pitying gaze. Apparently, Riveleh's aunt didn't find her slenderness convincing—nor her laughter.

In the winter months Riveleh was preoccupied with housekeeping, and her husband spent his time at work. But summers were more difficult. Irving had his summer vacation, and she, Riveleh, could think of nothing to say to him.

"He's a good person!" Riveleh tried to convince herself.

She got thinner and scrawnier—not on purpose this time. It just happened.

When the second summer came along, she was afraid it would be just as bad as the first. She longed for familiar landscapes—she remembered the sound of birdsong in the early summer mornings, and the way the fragrance of the forest permeated everything, and the cascade of pinecones falling from the trees . . .

She cried silently, out of earshot of her city husband. He would call her a "country girl," the way he did anytime he was dissatisfied with something about her.

And Riveleh reflected upon how fortune had deceived her. Lady Luck had offered her a fine, noble person in the form of the peasant boy who had stirred her first womanly feelings. But in the end, the fickle Lady had swapped him for another. (Oh, how thrilled her country parents were by her "good fortune"!) This second man played a skillful game of tennis and baseball, but—Riveleh admitted it to herself for the first time—he was an utter bore.

"What shall I do? What shall I do?" Riveleh wrung her hands. Just then, an idea flashed into her mind. Why not travel with him to a farm? On a farm they would understand each other better, they would get closer to each other, deep in the woods, next to a murmuring brook . . .

So they went. They went to a farm that he knew of, not far from New York City.

How Riveleh's heart pounded when they arrived at the farm! How many sweet memories rushed through her mind! There were the cows! Dear, sweet cows! She, Riveleh, had gone three years without seeing a cow. What a darling cow! And so similar to her old cows at home, my God! A rooster was crowing somewhere . . .

"And here we are!" said Irving, leading her to a house. A group of people were sitting on the porch. The men were in short trousers and the women sported knickers—and the whole group was playing cards.

Everyone greeted Irving as one of the gang, and the hosts were overjoyed to see him—not least the farmer's daughter, a tall girl with brightly painted lips.

Riveleh looked around: "So . . . where is the brook?" she asked Irving.

"The brook? Right! . . . But you can only get there in a car!"

"And the forest? Where is it?"

"The forest? The forest is back in your old village!" he laughed. "Go on, put on an outfit like the ones they're wearing. This crowd doesn't like country styles."

A few days passed. Tennis! Ball! Cards! Irving found it all terribly exciting, and steered the farmer's daughter around the place right under Riveleh's nose. Riveleh escaped to the barnyard every chance

she got, to visit the cows and the chickens. There she wept silently—
she mourned the past and she mourned her present loneliness. She
was a stranger, even more so here than in the city.

As she reminisced, the desire to flee overtook her—to flee back as
soon as possible, to flee home.

Riveleh decided to write to her aunt. She wrote a long letter,
acknowledging that her aunt had been right, she should not have
married Irving. She was unhappy, and would her aunt please take
pity on her and explain how to recover her freedom—how to separate
from her husband?

Her aunt answered with a long letter of her own. She wrote quite
affectionately that she, Riveleh, was the daughter of her only sister,
and therefore the responsibility for Riveleh's good fortune lay upon
her shoulders. To recover her freedom was impossible: it would be too
expensive. Thus wrote her aunt. She, Riveleh, must accustom herself
to her new life and forget all this foolishness. And if Riveleh didn't
like it there on the farm, she, the aunt, could recommend another
place with more conveniences. There they had a special porch for
sunbathing, and every room was equipped with hot and cold running
water. It would be just like being in the city . . .

———

To Go, or Not to Go?

(OCTOBER 12, 1960)

Translated by Ri J. Turner

L IBBY WAS IN a fix.

It was the first time in her eighteen years of life that she had
been asked on a date. The date was supposed to be in a bachelor pad

down a back alley. No one could be allowed to find out about it—not Papa, not Mama, not her older sister. Especially not her older sister!

The day drew nearer, and Libby had not yet decided: should she go or not go?

She wanted to go so badly! For the first time in her life, she wanted to be alone with a boy—with Billy, as she liked to call her twenty-two-year-old beau.

She felt she would die from the anguish of thinking about it. What should she do? If she went, they'd certainly kiss and neck in a secret corner, hidden from the rest of the world. But she was afraid. She was afraid of all of it: What if she met an acquaintance on the stairs? What if her parents were to find out? What if her older sister were to guess?

Her older sister! On the morning of that fateful day, she looked at Libby with suspicion in her eyes.

"How come you're so dressed up?"

"I'm not dressed up!" Libby's skin mottled white and red. "Quite the opposite! I'm . . ."

"Indeed, the opposite?" Her sister's eyes pierced her like cold daggers. After all, the two of them shared a room, and she, Libby, had nowhere to escape from her sister's severe gaze.

"Why aren't you eating? Are you ill?" Her mother felt her forehead at dinnertime. And her father muttered into his plate, "What do you expect? She runs around for days on end, scarcely showing her face at home."

Libby's heart sank. She had been on the verge of asking permission to "see a movie with her girlfriends" that evening . . .

What should she do? Her throat filled with suppressed tears. How unlucky she was!

The minutes ticked away, faster and faster. Soon it would be evening . . . But suddenly a strange calm descended upon her. Well, it wasn't meant to be, apparently. Maybe it was better this way? She had heard so much from her mother—and in a different vein, from her older sister—about the kinds of misfortunes that can happen to girls when they aren't cautious and visit fellows in their apartments. She got chills thinking about it—all those ruined young women!

Not meant to be! Oh well . . . so she would stay at home, lie down on the sofa to read a book. The appointed moment would pass, and that would be the end of it. It wasn't meant to be!

Libby lay down on the sofa, picked up a book, and began to read. But Billy's face swam up between the lines. The letters looked like his eyes, and the lines of text—his whiskers. Her heart pined for the lost kisses.

She peeked over at her sister, who was lying on her bed, also reading. Phooey, if not for her sister!

But then she had an idea. What if, for example, her sister were to fall asleep? Just a little longer staring at her book, and she surely would! "Sleep! Sleep!" Libby sent the thought at her sister.

She went pale with nerves. Maybe it was meant to be after all!

She stole glance after glance at her older sister, lying in bed, mercilessly awake.

"God in Heaven! Put her to sleep!"

And just then, the miracle happened! Her sister's eyes fluttered closed. Another minute, and she had fallen into a deep sleep. The book made a quiet rustle as it fell from her hand.

Libby slid off the sofa.

"It's meant to be! It's undeniable—God Himself arranged it!"

And without making a sound, as quiet as a mouse, she slipped out of the room.

———

The Grandmother

(NOVEMBER 14, 1960)

Translated by Ri J. Turner

S HE STILL MANAGES to drag herself around, but barely. She can barely see and barely hear, but nevertheless, she offers a daily commentary about every member of the household.

"You came home late again yesterday! Where were you?" she asks her twenty-year-old grandson.

Her victim laughs. "Grandmother, when do you sleep? Never?"

She doesn't grumble, never complains about the changing times, doesn't wax poetic about the olden days. On the contrary. She admires the new world and she has no nostalgia for the way things were in her day.

"Grandma! You're a card!" That grandson of hers kisses her wrinkled cheek. "Grandmother, tell the story about how you fell in love . . ."

And for the hundredth time the grandmother tells about how she was sent to a matchmaker at age thirteen, was engaged to Grandfather (who is already long, long gone to his just reward), how she had feared that she wouldn't recognize him, considering that she had met him once and only once, and that a veil blocked her view at the wedding canopy. It was not until afterwards that she really saw him face-to-face.

"I wept with fear, but he said to me, 'Don't be afraid, why are you crying?' So I said, 'I want to go home . . . ' And he replied, 'You musn't. You're married now. I didn't want to get married either, but everyone has to—I'm already fifteen years old, after all . . . I'm afraid too.'"

Her grandson giggles. "All right, but when did you fall in love?"

"Just then, at that moment . . . that's when I fell in love."

The boy howls with laughter. How hilarious their grandmother is. She mixes up past and present. Sometimes she turns to her older son, Michael, saying, "Take your warm scarf, my child, and wind it snugly so that you don't catch cold again, God forbid."

"When have I caught cold, Mama?" asks Michael, a vigorous sixty-five-year-old man with broad shoulders and wide, powerful hands. He could probably pick Grandmother up with one hand and wave her in the air like a *Kiddush* cup.[42]

"What do you mean when? You mean to tell me you've forgotten your lung infection?"

Michael guffaws in his timbrous bass. "But Mama dearest . . . that was a good fifty years ago. I was still a child then—ha ha!"

"Humph! You think you're not still a child?" she scoffs, tipping her little gray head back to look up at him. "You'd do better to obey me and wrap up your neck."

Michael is now married to his second wife. The household's primary misunderstandings break out between the grandmother and the second wife, Ethel.

"Sarah honey," the grandmother says to her affectionately, "don't you think it's a little chilly in the house?"

"Oy, Mother, I've already told you a hundred times that I'm not Sarah. My name is Ethel! Ethel! Ethel!" she yells.

"Oy, oy, oy!" The old lady catches herself, and remembers suddenly that Sarah, Michael's first wife, has been dead a long time already. Yes, it's true. This woman standing before her isn't Sarah. And she goes on to remember how she led her Michael to the wedding canopy with the sixteen-year-old Sarah, only yesterday, it seems. A beautiful bride, that Sarah—a diamond. But Sarah is no more; someone else has taken her place, someone called Ethel—yes. Yes, how could she have forgotten?

---

42 The cup used for sanctified wine on the Sabbath and holidays.

"Please forgive me, Sarah honey," she says. "I forgot."

She forgets sometimes. Yes, her memory has gotten a bit weaker. On the holidays, when all her children and grandchildren come to visit, and the little ones run boisterously through the rooms—sometimes then, the grandmother seizes one of them, a nice little plump child, and clasps him to her breast, caressing his little head for a long moment. Then she asks, "And whose is this one?"

Her question is answered only with thunderous laughter. Apparently, she said the wrong thing . . . she smiles disconcertedly and fixes her blondish white hair, which has crept out from under her white kerchief. "They're laughing again . . . every little thing makes them laugh."

Yes, she has begun to forget. She lifts a spoon to bring it to her mouth, and suddenly forgets what to do with it. And the soup spatters the tablecloth in the meantime. Ethel is displeased. "She's too old," she complains to her husband.

Also, they don't believe her, the grandmother, even when she does remember something correctly.

Once, when the children and grandchildren all came over to visit, the grandmother picked up a little tot, an infant (whose could this one be?), looked him over with a broad smile and assured everyone:

"He's the spitting image of Michael! Michael was just the same . . . The same little nose, the same little mouth . . ."

"Stop it, Mother!" Ethel cut her off angrily. "You're being ridiculous!" But the grandmother was beside herself. Why did no one believe her? She dug in her heels and swore up and down: "I'm telling you, he's the spitting image of Michael!"

It was the truth. A mother can forget a lot of things, but she will never forget how her first child looked on the first day of his life.

Poor Sammy!

(MARCH 12, 1962)

Translated by Ri J. Turner

SAMMY SITS WITH Helen the entire evening and suffers, poor thing. He suffers for a lot of reasons: because he is only sixteen and Helen thinks he's a baby (she's fifteen); because he has a name that's as common and boring as "Sammy"; and, more than anything, he suffers because he's in love with Helen and he wants to kiss her more than anything . . . but she can't seem to take the hint!

"Our English teacher," she says, swinging her oxford-clad foot, "is a real dumbbell. We pay no attention to her and do whatever we please."

"And our math teacher," answers Sammy in his deep bass (his voice changed just last year), "is so strict that anyone who says a word gets a zero on the spot."

He looks deep into Helen's teasing gray eyes and thinks, "How do I make her understand? This is the real thing—I'll love her for the rest of my life. When we grow up, we'll get married."

"You're a funny boy," says Helen, swinging her foot. "When I grow up, I'll be a teacher." And as if answering his unspoken thoughts, she adds, "I'm never going to get married!"

Sam's heart gives a throb. "Why?" he asks, shocked. "Everyone gets married."

"What's the point? Really, answer me that."

Sam doesn't know how to respond. He just knows one thing: he wants to kiss her at least once. Some of his friends brag about such things, but he doesn't believe them anyway. How in the blazes does one do it? In the movies, on the screen, it looks so easy. But in the movies they're usually standing, and in this case Helen is sitting. It's impossible to do it like this!

He stands up and goes over to the window. Maybe she'll figure it out and come over too.

"It looks like it's going to snow again," he says. "Just take a look at those clouds."

But she doesn't get it. She doesn't budge an inch.

"I haven't practiced yet, for my piano lesson I mean. My piano teacher is a dumbbell too."

Sammy understands that this is a hint that it's time for him to leave. And still he hasn't kissed her—just like yesterday and the day before yesterday.

He makes up his mind and sits down opposite her. It seems to him that she's radiating a kind of warmth.

"Helen," he says, leaning towards her, "Helen!"

Helen's swinging foot connects with his side. Sammy gets the message. He has failed.

"Dumbbell!" Her voice echoes in his ears as if it had come from far, far away.

THAT NIGHT, SAMMY lies down but can't fall asleep. Some kind of weight, like a heavy stone, lies over his heart. He has wept already, embarrassed by his own tears. It would be good to become a famous doctor, or a professor or pilot, and win Helen over that way. Then she would understand what a mistake she had made. Or on the other hand he could die, so that she would know that it was because of her, it was her fault—and then she'd poison herself. "Oh, women!" he mutters contemptuously to himself, but the sense of heaviness does not dissipate. How miserable he is, how forlorn!

His mother enters and sits down on the side of his bed.

"What's going on, darling? You seemed so downhearted all evening. A bad grade, huh?"

She bends over him and feels his forehead, caresses his cheeks, gives him a kiss.

"You're my whole life, you know that, right? You're my diamond . . ."

Sammy is suddenly flooded with warmth, the same warmth that radiated from Helen. His mother clasps his head to her breast. He grabs on to her neck and kisses her, kisses and kisses . . .

"Mama, my mama . . ."

The more he kisses her, the lighter his heart feels.

"I CAN'T FIGURE out what's happening with Sam," his mother says to his father while she undresses for bed. "He's gotten so strange, poor thing."

"What's the matter?" his father asked with his eyelids half-closed.

"I don't know," she says, sitting thoughtfully on the bed.

"Eh, I'm sure it's nothing!" says her husband, and shuts his eyes the rest of the way.

Soon he can be heard snoring. But Sammy's mother is still sitting on the bed, deep in thought. Her son's eager kisses had called forth a murky unease. She thinks and thinks.

"Oh! I'll start giving him cod liver oil," she decides, relieved. She hurriedly puts on her nightgown, and soon she too is fast asleep.

Her Dowry

(MARCH 26, 1962)

Translated by Ri J. Turner

FROM EARLIEST CHILDHOOD, ever since Paula could remember, she had known that her mother was amassing a dowry for her. "Dowry" was an oft-repeated word in the quarrels between her mother and her father, who could not seem to agree about Paula's future.

Her father, a handsome jolly man and a spendthrift, always used to joke about money with her frugal mother.

"What does a beautiful girl need with a dowry? After all, I took you without a dowry!" he used to tease her.

"No, it's better for Paula to choose a man with a dowry in hand, so that he'll respect her! It's easier to save a little money for the child now, rather than spending it later on you know what . . ."

Her mother always stopped at that point, without clarifying her meaning.

Paula loved her cheerful father more than her stingy, pragmatic mother, even though he was rarely home and almost never brought her treats—whereas her mother was always with her and provided for her every need.

Paula was drawn to her stylish, perpetually festive father like a fly to honey.

"Your father is an actor, he performs on the stage!" her friend once told her, and Paula was quite insulted.

"Mama, tell me, is it true that Papa is an actor?"

"And how!" her mother answered, with her typical opacity. "Especially offstage . . ."

She had a tendency to speak in half-sentences when talking about Paula's father. Cryptic, unclear.

"If you have money, you'll be able to choose a man who loves and respects you," her mother told Paula often, while combing her curly hair. She had a tendency to speak querulously to Paula, as if complaining to herself.

"Will I be beautiful?"

"That's not so important, as it turns out. I was beautiful once, and what did it get me? A girl has to have a dowry. That's the main thing!"

And she gave Paula a strange, probing look, as if attempting to foretell her future.

Paula grew accustomed to the idea that a girl must have a dowry—that her dowry, or lack of one, would determine her fate.

At school she constantly boasted to the other children that she had a dowry. Most of them did not understand the word, but Harold, who was quite a handsome boy, walked right up to her once and said, "How much?"

"What?"

"How much is your dowry?"

Paula did not know.

She came running to her mother. "Mama, how much is my dowry?"

"Don't worry your little head about it! It's enough!" Her mother stroked her curly hair and smiled with satisfaction. "When you grow up . . ." She lapsed into her usual half-sentences. "I'm looking out for your interests . . . And it would be more, if not for those scheming flibbertigibbets . . ."

"My mother says I have a lot and I'll get even more," Paula told Harold, and she could see from his face that he was impressed.

But she soon began to have doubts. As it turned out, her first adolescent love affair fell apart on account of her dowry.

Leon with the freckles and the strong teeth vacillated between Paula and her friend Clara. He wrote love letters to both of them on the new typewriter that someone had given him for his bar mitzvah.

Paula was put out. This wasn't how it was supposed to work. She alone should be his sweetheart—she, and no other! She stamped her foot and scolded Leon with abandon. At the end of her speech, she played her trump card: "I have a dowry and she does not!"

But Leon showed his strong teeth in a display of contempt: "I'm never gonna marry a woman for her dowry!" And from then on, he sent his typed love letters to Clara only.

Paula wept bitterly about that—but then she wiped her eyes and thought with a sigh: "Anyway, I'll still come out on top, because I have a dowry . . ."

AS PAULA GREW up, she became a beautiful girl—everyone said so. When she went out arm in arm with her father, to the theater or to a restaurant, everyone surrounded them, paying compliments.

"With a face like that, and with your figure . . . you're just destined for the stage!"

Paula nestled closer to her father, pleased. Everyone was always boasting about her future career. But on the way home, her euphoria would dwindle.

"See here, don't tell your mother!" her father always warned.

But her mother interrogated her at length, refusing to let her sleep until she told the whole story: Where had they been? Who else was there?

"And the one with the long earrings—was she there too?"

And even though the one with the long earrings had sat with them throughout the entire evening, Paula answered bravely, "With long earrings? I don't remember anyone like that . . ."

"Sort of pale, thin . . ."

"I don't remember . . ."

"That's the one all the money goes to, instead of . . ."

Her mother was against it, but after Paula finished school, she moved to New York to attend theater classes.

TRUE LOVE SMACKED Paula in the face much sooner than expected. It hit her like a whirlwind—a wild storm that tore through her, stirred her up, and left her in ruins. When all was said and done, she washed ashore like a piece of rotting driftwood.

Paula wandered home, dejected, miserable and disappointed—in her talent, in the stage, and in love. By then her father was no longer living with her mother. They had separated. Her mother, who had become even more pragmatic in her old age, took one look at Paula and knew exactly what had happened. Wringing her hands, she lamented, "My little girl! What did they do to you down there? Woe is me! It's all your father's fault! The sin is upon his head! The blood is on his hands!"

Paula was scrawny and her eyes were dull. Biting her lip, she managed to force out a few words:

"But Mama . . . he . . . he promised me . . . I believed him . . ."

And no one could get another word out of her. Who was the "he"? That question she would not answer.

Paula wandered around the house like a shadow, frozen with indifference. Every now and then she heard her mother whisper to someone, saying that she should be married off as soon as possible. Thank God, at least she was no pauper. She had a dowry . . .

Miriam Raskin
1889–1973

ALTHOUGH MIRIAM RASKIN'S stories often focus on the inner lives of everyday women, her own life was anything but ordinary.

Born in Slonim, in what is now Belarus, Raskin became politically active as a teenager, joined the socialist General Jewish Labor Bund, participated in the Revolution of 1905, and was imprisoned for a year for her political activities.

In 1920 she immigrated to the United States, where she published her first short stories in the literary and political journal *Tsukunft* (*Future*). Her first novel, *Tsen yor lebn* (*Ten Years of Life*) was published in 1927.

In the 1920s Raskin began publishing serialized novels and short stories in the *Forward*. A collection of those pieces, published in 1941 as *Shtile lebns* (*Quiet Lives*), earned widespread praise from Yiddish literary critics, including *Forward* editor Abraham Cahan, who wrote a laudatory review of the book. The same year, Raskin published another novel, *Zlatke*, which told the story of a female revolutionary much like her younger self.

In contrast with her own early life experience, Raskin's stories for the *Forward* focused on the lives of ordinary Jewish women in America and were written in a relatively unadorned American Yiddish idiom. In both "She Wants to Be Different," which appeared on October 27, 1943, and "In the Automat," which was published on February 7, 1966, Raskin focuses on the hidden desires of two single women, both of whom are content with their lives but still yearn for something more.

She Wants to Be Different

(OCTOBER 27, 1943)

Translated by Laura Yaros

EVERY EVENING, AT exactly seven-thirty, Novick would arrive at Eva's house. He called on her to go out with him, to the theater or to a concert. Eva would put on her coat and hat.

"Where are we going today, Novick?"

"Wherever you like, Eva," he answered. His voice and whole demeanor conveyed the impression that he was prepared to give her everything in the world.

Novick was a good-natured, quiet man who worked as a book-keeper in an office. His wife was dead and he now lived alone.

Eva was a tall, good-looking woman, with black, shiny hair. Her whole bearing conveyed the image of an independent, strong-willed person. Eva had been married at one point, but was long separated from her husband. She ran her own business, a beauty salon, and was reputed to be a capable and clever woman.

Novick was in love with Eva. Once, at an opportune moment, he blurted out something about getting married. He spoke in his quiet, dull voice: "This is no way to live. A man alone, and we're also getting older . . ."

He showed her calculations indicating that his salary was enough for two people to live on comfortably, and if she wanted to continue with her business—the beauty salon—he would not stop her.

Eva then looked at Novick, at how his chubby, expanding figure sat in a low chair, at his thinning hair glossy and slicked back, at his expressionless, lackluster eyes. She thought: no, this was not the man she could love. She quickly brushed him off, saying, "Novick, you know that I don't want to be tied down to a house, or to the duties of a housewife. I prefer to live my life as it is now."

Eva loved her free and independent life, to be able to do things the way she wanted, with no one having any authority over her. She wanted things to be different for her than for all the other women she knew, and deep inside her lived a vague hope that something unusual would still happen to her.

Even in childhood, Eva had been headstrong and obstinate. She did not like how her parents lived in constant poverty and worry. Eva herself began working from the age of fifteen and earned good money; her bearing was proud and conveyed a sense of self-worth. She got married before the age of twenty. Her husband had his own ambitions. He believed in working at his business and wanted his wife to keep house, cook tasty meals and be prepared to raise his children.

Eva did not wish to give up her job and become a housewife. She felt it was too soon to settle down to a staid existence. "Is this all there is?" she fearfully thought. She was not the type to bend to someone else's will, and thus felt obliged to separate from her husband.

Eva did not like to remember those years of her married life, and thinking about them for long was a waste of time. Her days were now filled with hard work and all kinds of new interests. She lived on one of the busy streets in the big city and her name was printed on a finely crafted sign placed in the window of her apartment: Eva Rosen, Beauty Salon.

Eva's days began very early. Her time was budgeted and scheduled. So much must be devoted to personal grooming, and so much to eating meals. When the women customers began to arrive, Eva was already prepared for them, neatly and impeccably dressed, energetic and cheerful. On the little table by the mirror her accoutrements were already laid out in various bottles and jars, like in a pharmacy. The regular customers wondered about Eva, "How can she do this? Where does she find all that time?"

"Oh, it's easy," Eva replied, with a clever smile, "You just need to have a system."

Her skillful fingers worked quickly. This woman needed a manicure; that one wanted a wave; and yet another, a massage. The women left her salon beautified and rejuvenated. They trusted Eva's excellent abilities and good taste, and willingly put themselves in her hands. The women who were more intimately acquainted with Eva would ask her for advice about their personal lives; they looked up to her, imitated her way of dressing and of carrying herself.

"It's up to each woman to keep herself youthful and pretty," Eva liked to say, accompanying her words with a clever, aloof smile, and it seemed as if she knew more than she could say.

When her workday came to an end, she quickly put her equipment in order and tidied up the room. Now it was time to rest. She lay down on the divan and closed her eyes. By her side lay her small wristwatch. She would rest like that for fifteen minutes, and take five minutes to rub her face with a salve to wash away the signs of fatigue from her face. Then she would make supper, throwing something together from the bits of leftovers she found in her icebox. At exactly half past seven, the doorbell would ring, Novick would appear and they would go out somewhere.

Once, it seemed to Novick that Eva looked tired, and he suggested, "Maybe we won't go anywhere tonight, Eva?" He looked her in the eyes.

Being alone with Novick for the entire evening was no great pleasure for Eva, and she spoke up: "Let's go to a restaurant somewhere on Broadway."

Novick gave in immediately. He was goodness itself. He found nothing too difficult to do for her and hoped to win her heart with his devotion and perseverance. Eva often found his excessive devotion repugnant. Her harsh and uncompassionate nature clashed with his submissiveness and melancholic manner, which she disliked. She fretted as to why she did not put an end to their relationship, except, somehow, she instinctively knew that without him things would be worse, and that it was easier to socialize with people when she was not alone but had someone by her side.

Eva enjoyed sitting in a restaurant on the fanciest, busiest street, where the pulse of the big city felt very strong. The fast-paced life was in tune with her nature and resonated with her, along with the teeming crowds circulating back and forth before her eyes. She especially liked to be there late in the evening, after the various entertainments and theaters let out, when young and old were drawn there, lively and festive.

Eva and Novick greeted many friends and acquaintances. They took a few tables and everyone acted like one friendly family. Eva's friends were all married people, staid and well-established. The women always admired her—a woman such as Eva, who showed no signs of aging. One woman, already a little shabby and older-looking, stared at her penetratingly, as if to discover the secret to her youthful appearance. "Who looks as good as you, Eva?" she remarked.

Eva knew that this woman was thinking about her unfettered, unmarried life. Did she envy Eva, or was she being catty in some way? However, Eva answered this woman with a restrained smile, "Well, I can't complain. I'm doing pretty well."

New acquaintances came over to their tables and their circle widened. Eva obtained new clients. She recorded addresses in her little book and made appointments. She did this with much tact and dignity, speaking fluent English. Her own makeup was not overly garish and she was dressed elegantly and very tastefully. She was a real personality.

Eva never failed to attract male gazes. Young and old sought out conversation with her, and complimented her. Eva was then at her best. She could be witty and knew just what to say to everyone. With a smile from her dark, shining eyes, she unwillingly becoming the center of attention.

Novick behaved like a perfect gentleman. He was the first to offer a cigarette or fetch a chair. Novick also liked telling stories, but his recounting always lasted too long to hold his listeners' attention. Eva often had to interrupt him in the middle with an impatient gesture. "Oh, Novick!" she would exclaim.

She'd heard the story so many times already. Novick would cut off his remarks mid-sentence and stay silent for a long time.

As the evening grew late, Novick took his watch out of his vest pocket and brought it over for Eva to see.

"Don't you think it's time to go home, Eva?"

"Yes, you're right, Novick," she laughed.

They said goodbye to their friends. Novick helped Eva with her coat and accompanied her home. Later, when Eva was alone in her room, her heart stirred with all kinds of emotions. She believed she could appeal to people, that her personality could stimulate and provoke restlessness in men's hearts, and envy and jealousy in women. She felt superior to all the other women, and their envy did not bother her. There was something else: it seemed to Eva that her current feelings were only temporary, that something wondrous and unusual was in store for her—a vague hope, a fantasy instilled in her since childhood.

In the Automat

(FEBRUARY 7, 1966)

Translated by Laura Yaros

O N A SUMMER's evening, Miss Posner sat down at a small table in a restaurant to eat her supper after a turbulent day at work. She enjoyed spending an hour or two in the automat.[43] She was a saleslady

---

43 A fast-food restaurant where food is served from vending machines.

in a women's clothing store, and all day she had to stay on her feet and deal with the women customers. Here she could relax.

Miss Posner was not in a hurry to go home. She knew that her clean, neat, comfortable room would be waiting for her. She reserved moviegoing for Saturday nights, when she didn't have to hurry to get up early the next morning and when the whole next day would be a relaxed, leisurely Sunday.

Miss Posner enjoyed eating her supper alone upstairs, on the balcony of the automat. It seemed to her that a better class of people sat there. She often felt as though she was sitting in a theater and from there she could look down below, as if from a gallery, and observe the stream of people coming and going. Today it looked like more people than usual were stirring down there, but on the balcony it was quieter, with fewer people.

To one side, an elderly couple was sitting at a table. Both were gray-haired, but the woman was more vivacious. Miss Posner saw her bringing up her tray of food. She positioned the silverware and placemat as if she were at home. The husband scowled at the food, but his wife appeared to know better what was good for him, and making faces would be of no help. It amused Miss Posner to observe them. She always enjoyed seeing how other people lived and what they did, rather than thinking about herself.

A little further away, three young women sat down at a table, eating their supper, happy and laughing, and they looked joyful simply because they were young and had much to talk about.

A woman in a red hat sat down by the balcony railing, keeping a sharp and persistent eye on the restaurant entrance below. She was definitely waiting for her friend, who would be arriving at any minute.

There was a lot for Miss Posner to see. Two young couples came upstairs and sat down to supper at a table, but something strange occurred. Of the two young women, one was prettier, cheerful, and was behaving provocatively, in a bold yet poised manner. The two young men gravitated and spoke only to her. The other young woman, quiet and withdrawn, remained sitting as if in shadow.

The prettier young woman wore a small watch on her wrist. One of the young men took her hand, wanting to know what time it was. Miss Posner knew very well that it was not the watch that interested him, but the fact that he could take her by the hand and gaze into her eyes. The other young man did not want to give up, and told her something amusing, at which she laughed heartily.

Miss Posner felt very sorry for the other young woman, who remained sitting quietly, left out. Where could such a game lead? One of the young men was her boyfriend, so why should he flirt with the prettier woman, the one who behaved so provocatively? The two couples ate their supper and left, and Miss Posner remained seated with her thoroughly cleaned plate, quite disturbed by how life could be so hard. She thought regretfully about every young woman who had been wronged.

Meanwhile, even more people entered the restaurant. Three of them, two women and a man, approached her table, as if they wished to wait for her to finish her food and leave the place free for them. She saw this from the way they looked at her, staring vacantly as they waited for her to leave already.

Her glance told them, "No, I'm not done."

She put down her hat and newspaper on the chair and went to get another coffee. Passing a mirror, she looked at herself for a while— what would make these particular people insult the way she was dressed? She was pretty enough and stylish and looked no worse than a thousand other young women.

When Miss Posner came back up with her coffee, the three dis-respectful people had already gotten a place at another table. The woman in the red hat who sat by the railing continued to look down at the entrance door. She was stubbornly waiting for someone who apparently had promised to be there.

An elegant and very beautiful young woman now sat in the old couple's place. Her dark, gray eyes spoke volumes. A man swiftly approached her, although empty tables were now available. He sat near her and spoke to her briefly. He probably asked if he was disturb-ing her, and she, with a smile, allowed him to sit near her. He rested his elbow on the table and they looked at each other for a while—a "he" and a "she," both young, slim and good-looking. They would fall in love, that was as clear as day. Miss Posner was captivated by the scene; it could be said that she was witnessing the beginning of an event.

It did not last long before another man approached their table. The woman took him by the hand familiarly and looked guiltily at him. Could he be the real boyfriend? Miss Posner covered her face with both hands; she did not want to see the jealous scene that the real boyfriend would make, seeing his woman with another man.

Something entirely different occurred. The men were good friends. They both went downstairs into the restaurant and returned with trays of food, and then all three sat down at the table. The woman and the two men ate their supper together peacefully.

It was already late, and in the restaurant below it grew quieter and the people fewer. Everyone had somewhere to hurry off to. The woman in the red hat by the railing, who waited the whole time and looked below at the door so tenaciously, had also already stood up. The person she had waited for would not be coming today. Miss Posner also intended to go home, but she lingered a while longer.

A young woman arrived carrying a book under her arm, and an older man followed behind her with a tray of food. Miss Posner could see them close up. The young woman appeared to be about nineteen or twenty. She had a delicate profile and lovely long, blond, shiny hair. The man was older, with a shabby appearance and thin gray hair over a high forehead. He maintained a very benevolent demeanor in front of the young woman and seemed to want to please her. Miss Posner looked at him resentfully. She had always disapproved of an older man and a young woman developing a close relationship.

The man appeared to be a music teacher, and the young woman his student. As they ate their supper, he picked up the book that the woman had held earlier. He turned a page and began to explain something to her, leaning towards her. The young woman appeared interested and she nodded her head attentively, but soon she caught herself, realizing that it was already late.

"Oh, dear!" she exclaimed, looking at the clock on the wall.

She stood up. She needed to go home. He still tried to delay her, taking her by the hand, but she quickly put on her coat, said goodbye and departed, leaving him alone.

Miss Posner was happy with this outcome; there was no need for him to harbor any fantasy that he could become close friends with the young woman.

Later, when Miss Posner traveled home on the subway, she was already tired out, but she was satisfied. It had been an enjoyable evening.

SECTION THREE

World on Fire

THE AMERICAN JEWISH experience was largely a product of trauma. When the first waves of Eastern European Jews began immigrating to the United States in the early 1880s, they were often fleeing pogroms; subsequent disasters over the next several decades set off further waves of immigration. Starting with the outbreak of the First World War, European Jewry found itself in a near-constant state of crisis, with the Russian Revolution and Civil War, Stalinist persecution, the rise of Nazism, and ultimately the Holocaust.

All of these tragedies were covered in detail by the *Forward*. Although it was an American newspaper, its writers and audience were still closely tied to Europe. The *Forward* employed many writers—among them celebrated literary figures like Sholem Asch and Israel Joshua Singer—who sent dispatches from Jewish centers like Warsaw and Vilna. It would have been a rare *Forward* reader who didn't have family in the old country and who didn't worry about their welfare.

It didn't take long for the news on the front page to make its way into fiction. Sholem Asch's "The Jewish Soldier," a novella about Jewish members of the Imperial Russian Army, appeared in the newspaper in November and December of 1914, just months after the outbreak of the First World War. Shortly after the end of the Ukrainian War of Independence (1917–1921), modernist writer

David Bergelson turned the multiparty conflict into a series of stories that he wrote from his new home in Berlin. Years later, when Singer addressed the same period, his prose read as though it too had been written in the midst of the event itself.

This did not hold true for the Holocaust, however. Even as the full extent of the tragedy became known, it did not become a major subject of fiction. This was not because the *Forward* was indifferent or oblivious to the catastrophe—far from it. Throughout the war the paper carried reports of destruction coming out of Europe, and it was among the first news organizations to report on the full extent of the genocide. After the war the *Forward* had many Holocaust survivors as contributors, including Elie Wiesel, who wrote news articles, political commentary, and literary criticism. But in the decades following the war there was little in the way of Holocaust fiction.

Perhaps this made sense—the trauma was too great and too recent to fictionalize at that moment. The full horrors of the ghettos and concentration camps were still fresh; making up stories about them may have seemed superfluous, even taboo. But in time some writers did address the subject, at least around the margins. Even here, although these pieces are often structured and presented as fiction, it is apparent that they represent the authors' own experiences. In some cases, there was nothing to tell but the truth.

Sholem Asch
1880–1957

Sholem Asch was one of the most influential Yiddish novelists of the twentieth-century, as well as one of Yiddish literature's most popular writers in translation.

Born the youngest of ten children in Kutno, Poland, Asch received a traditional religious education until he left school at age sixteen. With the help of Moses Mendelssohn's translation of the Bible, he taught himself German and, after moving to the town of Wloclawek, began writing in Hebrew. In Wloclawek, Asch supported himself as a letter-writer for the town's illiterate residents, an experienced he later described as his "advanced schooling" and an opportunity "to peer into the hidden corners of life."

In 1899, Asch moved to Warsaw, where he met I. L. Peretz, who encouraged him to write in Yiddish. Through Peretz he also became acquainted with other young Yiddish writers, including Hersh Dovid Nomberg and Avrom Reyzen, with whom he shared a Warsaw apartment.

In the early years of the twentieth century Asch continued to write in both Hebrew and Yiddish, publishing his first collection of Hebrew stories in 1902 and his first in Yiddish in 1903. The next year he published his novel *A Shtetl* (*A Small Town*) in the newspaper *Der Fraynd* (*The Friend*), and also began writing for the Yiddish stage. In 1903, Asch married Mathilda Shapiro, the daughter of the Hebrew writer Menachem Mendel Shapiro. The couple had two children: Moses, who went on to found Folkways Records, and Nathan, who also became a writer.

In 1908 Asch visited Palestine, and in 1909 he traveled to America, where he began writing occasional pieces for the *Forward*. Upon the outbreak of World War I, Asch immigrated to the United States, and became a regular contributor to the newspaper.

"The Jewish Soldier" appeared from November 21 to December 4, 1914, just months after the outbreak of the war. It showed not only Asch's considerable talent for writing historical fiction as that history was unfolding, but also to capture the cultural, social, and religious divisions among European Jews, and their corresponding attitudes towards the conflict then sweeping through the Jewish towns and cities of Central and Eastern Europe.

Over the following decades Asch continued to serialize his major novels in the *Forward*, including *Motke the Thief*, *Uncle Moses*, and his *Three Cities* trilogy. His writing usually appeared once a week, on Saturdays. After the war Asch returned to Europe, living in Poland, France, and Weimar Germany, although the *Forward* continued to be his main journalistic outlet.

Asch also had a significant career as a dramatist, and his work frequently invited controversy. His most famous play, *God of Vengeance*, portrayed a homosexual love affair between a prostitute and the brothel owner's daughter and was produced in Berlin by Max Reinhardt in 1907. When the play was produced on Broadway in 1923, the producer and lead actor were arrested and prosecuted on obscenity charges.

With the rise of Nazism in the 1930s, Asch returned to the United States, where he came into conflict with *Forward* editor Abraham Cahan over his novel *The Nazarene*, which portrayed Jesus as a religious Jew, and which Cahan interpreted as promoting Jewish conversion to Christianity. When the book appeared in English translation in 1939, the split between the *Forward* and Asch became irreparable.

Asch published the next two works in his Christological trilogy—*The Apostle* and *Mary*—in the Communist newspaper *Morgn-frayhayt* (*Morning-Freedom*), although he later resigned from that publication to protest the persecution of Yiddish writers in the Soviet Union. For the last years of his life Asch lived in Bat Yam, Israel, and died in London at age seventy-seven, one of the most popular and controversial Yiddish writers in modern history.

———

The Jewish Soldier

(NOVEMBER 21–DECEMBER 4, 1914)

Translated by Saul Noam Zaritt

IT WAS THE most bountiful year in memory. And the year was at its most glorious—the height of summer. Everything in the fields and meadows and gardens and orchards was ripe and plump, waiting to be harvested and stored in the granary, though the granaries and yards were themselves already overflowing with the produce that had been harvested. The apples weighed branches to the ground. The big-bellied watermelons shimmered in the warm sand and appeared golden orange in the sun; the vine leaves, already overripe, had turned yellow. The grains of the field had already long been gathered and stored in piles in the granaries, waiting for the threshing machine. The plump sheep wandered about the harvested fields and munched on the forgotten and leftover stalks. But the grains would wait in vain for the thresher. The ripe blue and moist plums woke early each morning with wonder to find their fallen friends lazing about on the ground, not understanding why the gardener hadn't yet gathered them in barrels. The heavy vines bent their thin yellow-singed branches towards the earth, waiting impatiently for someone to pick their fruits. Even the sheep, which the young shepherd had guided to the river every night, sat down now in the water, picking at their curly wool in the water and sand, not knowing why no one came to shear them and free them from the great burden that had grown upon their backs.

But the grains in the yards and the fruit on the trees would wait in vain for their masters.

One pleasant afternoon, the county clerk came to the center of the village's main street and called the peasants from the fields with a trumpet so that he could read aloud for them a proclamation sent from the city. Twenty-four hours later, the farmers from the fields and the gardeners from the orchards had changed into their military uniforms. Everyone now looked the same. There was no more peasant, no more fisherman, no more blacksmith, no more carpenter—all had become soldiers, covered from head to toe with armaments. All of the roads and all of the rivers led them from the villages and cities to kill or be killed.

For decades the factories had been manufacturing weapons. Tens of thousands of men had made a living from this enterprise; with their wisdom and diligence they had forged large cannons out of metal and bronze and equipped them with enormous grenades filled with dynamite and other destructive materials. Great wise men sat sequestered away in rooms where they deliberated day and night on how to make bigger weapons and bigger bombs, which would be filled with even more terrible things that could bring about more annihilation.

And now strong horses, four harnessed to each armed vehicle, trotted across the moist, black fields of the Polish province of Kuyavia. The previous day, cavalrymen had set off in advance of these troops. The riders had been brought from the distant sun-flecked land that lies in the valley of the Terek River, below the Caucasus Mountains. The brave hunters had left behind the light-filled and joyous meadows along the Don and Terek rivers, where they would ride with ease on their horses in the surrounding steppes. They had been led here and then sent ahead to search out the enemy. Scores of men followed them, all of different nationalities and lands—Russians, Ruthenians, Lithuanians, Poles, Jews. All looked the same now, in the same gray, earthen uniforms and each with a rifle in his hand and a knapsack on his back. After them came the heavy cannons trudging through the dark moist earth. The great, strong horses groaned in their harnesses as they dragged the carts upon which the metal bombs and bullets were loaded. And after these streamed countless field-kitchen wagons, polluting the air with their smoke. The herd of beasts that accompanied them kicked up clouds of dust. There were also wagons of the Red Cross that carried the sick, a few more horses and automobiles, and wagons that stored bread, cabbage or hay, and so on and so on, endlessly . . .

General L.'s army, which had chased the enemy into the Polish Kuyavia province, had stopped to rest in a large field under a small mountain range. The army was now in reserve and waited its turn to go to the front. In the meantime, the soldiers had grown restless on account of the constant movement, having had to run from one field to another, without shooting a single bullet and without looking the enemy in the eye. Until now the army had been continuously rushing from place to place; there had not been enough time to spend a full night in a single encampment or even to have a warm meal. A few times, when the command had come to get moving, they had even been forced to throw out the food that had been prepared in the kitchens. The explanation in the order they received was that the enemy moved quickly when there was no fighting and that the enemy could not be allowed to settle in and fortify itself. But all of this hurrying, the endless waiting for battle and searching after the enemy, caused the soldiers to be more exhausted and irritated than if they had been under fire by cannons. But just now an order was given to set up the tents for some rest. Scouts had discovered that the enemy had taken up a strong position under the mountains and it would be difficult to drive them out. The army was also too tired to attack, so the order was given to rest here, in the position that had been taken, in order to prepare for an offensive that would take place in a few days.

SOON THE FIELD of cabbage, where the army was stationed, became a fully established encampment, as if the soldiers had permanently installed themselves there. The air carried the smoke of the field kitchens, which were positioned in the middle of the camp. The pungent smell of meat and melting fat wafted from the kitchens and teased the soldiers' appetites. Scattered about, the soldiers scrubbed their tin bowls, pans and utensils with dirt, idling around the boiling pots. Soldiers tossed their clothes off near the tents, took off their boots and stockings, and the smell of the food mixed with the stench of sweat and grease. These aromas gave the camp a homey atmosphere and there was a feeling that they were going to stay here a while. Looking around, one saw soldiers everywhere, some busy setting up tents, others taking off their boots—and each one ready to eat.

Among those idling around the pot of the fourth company of the forty-eighth infantry regiment was the Jew Asnat, who had been a soldier for over a year. He checked on the overflowing pot and then turned to go to his little corner, where he had settled with his fellow soldiers. But he was interrupted by the following scene:

Two short Russian soldiers, Asmin and Kozlov, had pinned down the arms of the Jewish soldier Levin, and the Cossack Arbuz was shoving a piece of pork into his mouth. The Jew clenched his teeth, his eyes bulged and he kicked at the soldiers. The smell of the unkosher pork had nearly caused him to vomit, and he was afraid he might relax his clamped jaw. The warm saliva that had gathered in his mouth was making him gag so the Jew started spitting everywhere, and the soldiers started laughing and shouting:

"Eat! You need to eat! You put God's food to shame—it was prepared for men to eat, not animals."

"Don't let him loose—he has to eat—he must, he must . . ."

Asnat stood watching for a moment. The image of the poor little Jew, flailing about pathetically in the hands of the soldiers, had moved him in a strange way. Without thinking, he seized the Jewish soldier and wordlessly pulled him from their clutches. The other ones looked at him with wonder: they saw that he was a more experienced soldier than they were, so they deferred to him; they let go of the Jewish soldier. Asnat took Levin with him and sat down in a corner. Asnat calmly ate his food. The Jewish soldier rested for a bit, lying on the ground and catching his breath after having wrestled with the other soldiers. Then he got up and started reciting the afternoon prayer. Asnat looked on, observing how the Jewish soldier swayed devoutly without fear or shame, and how it didn't bother him that the other soldiers were looking at him in bewilderment, laughing and showering him with insults. Asnat had now become uninterested in his meal. He poured his food out, smoked a cigarette, and lay back on the ground.

When the Jew finished praying, he sat down at a distance from the others and took out a flask of water. He washed his hands and then started eating a piece of stale bread with cheese that he had kept in his coat.

Asnat marveled at the Jewish soldier's devotion to his religiosity in the middle of war. He came up to Levin and asked him:

"Say, Levin, are you a rabbi? Is that why you're so religious?"

"A rabbi?" Levin laughed. "You have to be a rabbi in order to be a Jew?"

"But how can you manage when a war is going on?"

"What is there to manage? The Lord of the universe helps those who want to serve Him. Whenever we run into a Jewish supplier, he usually gets me some Jewish food. I get by."

"And what do you do when we're on the road?"

"I pray on the road, whenever I can."

Asnat was silent for a minute.

Levin interjected earnestly:

"If not now, when you're constantly in danger, then when else would you maintain your Jewishness? In the blink of an eye you can be called to the heavens, God forbid . . ."

Asnat saw that the Jew firmly believed in the World to Come. When it came to pass, he would be ready, and Asnat was envious of him.

"Do you have a wife?"

"A wife and two children," the Jew sighed.

"So?" Asnat asked.

"So, are we not in God's hands? If you're destined to live, the bullets will miss you; they will pass you by and have no power over you.

And if not, will it help if you hide? They will find you in your hole when your time comes," the Jew answered, confidently and calmly.

Asnat marveled at him with envy—this Jew maintains his faith even under enemy fire, among non-Jews, believing that a different power guides him on his way and determines his fate.

"Does this mean that you have no fear of death?"

"No fear?" Levin replied. "Of course I am afraid of the day of judgment. But what can you do? I do what I can. When we set out in the morning, I recite the confessional prayer. I ask the Lord of the Universe that if it is to be today, that at least I should merit a proper Jewish burial; and if I am not fated to have a proper burial, then at least I hope I have the mind to say 'Hear, O Israel!'[44] because they say that the enemy's bullets leave you mindless and soldiers die without sensing it. Is this true?"

"I haven't heard about it," Asnat answered.

They were both quiet for a moment and looked at the setting sun. Here and there you could see the smoke of the campfires in front of the tents with the soldiers circled around them. From some of the campfires you could hear a somber song of longing that reminded you of your homeland. From other campfires one could hear healthy laughter and the joy of youth. The whole camp was sunk in a cloud of smoke and dust that rose up from the campfires, and the clouds stood out against the red setting sun.

Asnat spoke up:

"And do you wear *tzitzis*,[45] the four-cornered garment?"

Levin was embarrassed.

"What kind of question is that? Of course I do."

"I've heard it said that when a Jew dies he is buried in a *tallis*.[46] Even the worst Jew is buried in a *tallis*. It's a kind of Jewish flag. Is this true?"

---

44 Deuteronomy 6:4, "Hear O Israel the Lord our God the Lord is One," is traditionally said by religious Jews as their last words.
45 Ritual fringes worn on the corners of a four-cornered garment.
46 Prayer shawl.

"Of course it is. And if it is His will, God forbid, and it comes to pass, I will cover my eyes with my *tzitzis* so that they'll be able to tell that I am a Jew." Levin pointed to his *tzitzis*, which he had taken out from under his uniform.

"Meaning, under the Jewish flag?" Asnat said with a solemn smile and then became pensive.

The evening was cold, and some of the campfires had gone out. It became quiet and night swept over the camp.

They remained together a little while longer in silence. It became dark. Then the trumpet sounded and the soldiers, one by one, retired to their tents to sleep, as they too were tired and sleepy.

AFTER THE SOLDIERS had all gone, Asnat remained sitting alone at the entrance to his tent. Night had already settled upon the camp. It was a bright and cold night. The two leafless poplars on the top of the hill looked like fearsome demons in the moonlight, and the tents, spread out across the field, scattered their shadows. A few fires still smoldered, and a few soldiers wrapped themselves in their coats and wandered between the tents, looking like shadows themselves. A few voices could still be heard calling out to one another. Asnat was tired and sleepy, but the soldiers' voices unnerved him and left him uneasy. He went into his tent. His comrades, one-year veterans like he was, had already fallen asleep wrapped in their coats, and the tent had become warm from the steam that rose from their young and healthy bodies.

Asnat tumbled into his little corner, put something down underneath his body, encased himself in his coat, and burrowed his face into the ground, not feeling the moisture of the dew, which, regardless of the tents, had still settled on the trembling cabbage leaves. He quickly fell asleep.

He remained sleeping for a couple of hours. But the dew had formed on the ground, making the turf dense and moist, as if the earth had been softened like lime. Asnat immediately began to feel the moisture as it seeped into his coat and into his clothes and then reached his body. At first the moisture was pleasant, soft. But soon his body became cold and his feet began to tremble. Yet his thirst for sleep was so strong that he went to war against the moisture and was able to defeat it. Asnat turned over, looking for a corner of the blanket that was still dry, slipped it underneath his body and fell asleep again. But quickly that corner too became wet and Asnat felt as if some worm was underneath him, biting him. He got up, took hold of the lantern hanging in the tent, and shined the light where he had been sleeping. He saw that he had been slogging his feet in mud—a mixture of black earth, trampled grass, and water. This disgusted him and he didn't want to lie back down. But he longed for sleep, so he gathered together some straw from where the guns were stored. But the spot he had now chosen was so narrow that he had to hold his feet with his hands and lay his head on the guns. He fell asleep like this for ten or fifteen minutes, which felt to him like a long, long time. But he suddenly felt so cold that he tore open his eyes. His sleep vanished entirely, and he opened the slit in the tent to look out and see if it was dawn yet.

The night was black, the moon had disappeared somewhere, and blackness was all around. The tents looked like demons, and the few soldiers who wandered among them looked like the amputated limbs of ghosts. On the distant horizon shined the light of a beacon, and he didn't know if it came from the Russian or the enemy camp. The light gave him a pang in his heart, reminding him of the danger he was in. The fear of death, which he did not notice during the day in the camp or on the road, when among his fellow living soldiers, now fell upon him suddenly in the silence of the night with sleep all around him. He became terrified of this light that shone from the beacon. He closed the tent flap, fell back on the straw and tried to go back to sleep. But now he could not fall back asleep. Sleep was gone and he began to think. Random thoughts and recollections flew through his mind. He recalled the soldiers' conversations, remembered scenes from his childhood, and his entire life went before his eyes in the dark of the night.

He thought of his childhood, which had passed unhappily. He had loved no one because he had no one to love. His mother was busy bearing children her entire life. She birthed twelve children and had no time for any of them: she was taken up with her sickness, which the doctors were never able to properly diagnose, sending her from one expert to another. His father was an egoist, caring only for himself and his affairs.

The children were left to take care of themselves. The parents' duty of education and upbringing consisted of doing all they could to ensure their children were accepted into the gymnasium. But as soon as they happily saw their children dressed in school uniforms, they figured they had fulfilled their obligations. From time to time they would take interest in the marks he received in school, though not because they wanted to learn more about his abilities or his progress. No, they wanted to find out if he was going to receive a gold medal, which would then lead him through the gates of the university.

And he remembered the unhappy day when he brought home from school a "2" in Russian grammar. His parents then used all their resources to procure a tutor for him in Russian language, even going so far as to hire his teacher from school.

He had nothing in his childhood to love. Not his studies, which had quickly turned into a way to boost his career; not faith, since his father, the "liberal," had kept his children far from religion, except on certain formal occasions when he brought them to the Reformed synagogue on Rosh Hashanah and Yom Kippur and they became bored by the Jews in prayer shawls making supplications in an incomprehensible language.

He remembered that as a child he was fascinated by the heroes of Russian history. He devoured children's books about the great deeds of Peter the Great, Mikhail Kutuzov,[47] the Cossacks. In his childish naïveté he was proud of them and often thought that when he grew up he would also become a hero.

---

47 Mikhail Kutuzov (1745–1813) was a field marshal who defeated Napoleon during the French invasion of Russia.

But then his father dashed this dream. He recalled the moment as if it happened yesterday.

He was reading a book about Napoleon in Russia and how Kutuzov had defeated him. Asnat burst into his father's office and exclaimed:

"Papa, do you know who defeated Napoleon? Kutuzov, Papa . . ."

His father looked at him, puzzled.

"And why are you so pleased that Kutuzov defeated Napoleon?"

"What do you mean, Papa? He saved Russia!"

"Such good news. Did you hear, Chana," he said, turning to his wife, "Kutuzov defeated Napoleon. Rejoice, Chana, rejoice."

Asnat remained standing in the middle of the room and felt strange . . . he would remember this moment for the rest of his life.

Only when he was a little older did he begin to understand that there was little to celebrate about Kutuzov and the other Russian heroes who had beaten down the Poles, the Caucasians, and the Siberians. And it wasn't his parents who told him any of this. He learned from his own experience that as a Jew he had nothing to celebrate in his life, nothing to make him proud. He had no history of his own, and foreign history remained distant from him. And even learning— the process of coming to know the world around him—became only a tool through which he could get a coveted mark of 5 in order to reach a higher class and from there go on to the golden medal.

And so his youth passed without joy, without light, and without love. He recalled that he often had the feeling, especially in front of his classmates, that he had been born with a handicap, though he could not figure out what exactly his defect was. He was as young, healthy, and happy as the rest of his friends, and he lacked for nothing—and yet he felt ashamed in some way in front of them. He had no claim against anyone, apparently no one had been the cause of the defect. He was born this way, but he felt to this very day that he couldn't forgive his father for it. He didn't love his father as other children did, or as he would have wanted to. And then, he recalled, something in him changed. He became older. The teachers despised him and his fellow Jewish students and made things difficult for them. This bound him to his Jewish friends. And not just the students. He remembered that he began to take an interest in the old Jewish woman who delivered butter and eggs to their house, and with the Jews who came to his father's office, though he could never understand them or love them.

Then the tragic times came.

He was just a small boy, but he felt it so deeply . . . the Jews were beaten . . . He heard wild and terrible things. The times left a deep impression on his whole life. From then on, life was more somber, though somehow more interesting. He began to love the oppressed and the downtrodden, seeing himself among them. His life and his learning took on a new meaning. One needed to live and learn for those who were beaten down. He became determined, no longer ashamed in front of his friends, no longer a cripple. The opposite— he had more than they did, he was stronger than they were. He was the oppressed one. From then on, his life had a purpose, he felt he had something to search for. He began to study in earnest—not for his father, not for the golden medal, but for himself. He read serious books and soon felt as if he had grown up. Though it remained unclear to him, he felt a responsibility, not for the golden medal, but for something deeper, something inside himself.

He studied with the knowledge that he would not continue on to university. He cared little for the teachers and the other students and the entire school. When he finished the gymnasium without the golden medal, his parents now thinking that he was a failure, he went abroad. There he met others like himself, others who thought as he did, though he did not speak much with them. He went through everything for himself alone, living only with himself.

He attended an Austrian university with many other Russian and German Jews. He had few friends and he did not join a party. He couldn't find a place for himself among them. His experience of the world became incomprehensible to him.

When in Russia he despised all things Russian. He could smell the dried Jewish blood wherever he went, and he waited impatiently for the day of revenge for all of the insults and misfortunes perpetrated against the Jews. But when hearing the speeches of the Austrian and Galician Jewish students, he would repeatedly feel hurt. An inexplicable stubbornness took hold of him to oppose their diatribes and instead praise Russia and present himself as a warmhearted patriot.

To this day he doesn't understand this stubbornness. In his heart he wished the worst for Russia, but as soon as he heard the foreign students' pronouncements, he would feel sick and try to prove that Jews in Russia had it better than Jews in Austria. In the heat of debate he would start to praise the breadth of the Russian soul.

This stance made him many enemies, separating him from everyone. He did not want to go back to Russia—he had nothing to return to. He wouldn't have been able to attend university there and he would have had nothing to do. So he had to remain in Austria. His friends were aware of this weakness and took advantage of it.

In time political friction developed between Russia and Austria. Often he heard the Austrian Jewish students express their yearning for a war with Russia. They saw in Russia not only their country's enemy, but also the enemy of the Jewish nation. But to Asnat, it all mattered very little. In those days he rarely showed his face, not knowing what to do. He also couldn't just stay in his room. He was jealous of the Austrian Jewish students who could give speeches, who had someone to fight against. He felt as one who stands alone in the street. He had no one with him. Asnat was a nation unto himself, a nation of one.

What happened next is what brought him to his current situation.

It was in the halls of the university. Relations between Russia and Austria had become tense. There were rumors that war could break out at any moment. He saw how agitated and excited the students had become: everyone was singing patriotic songs and signing up to be drafted into the army, Jews included. He was jealous of them because they had a homeland, a land worth fighting for. He would have been so happy to be like them, and here he was, standing alone, while the world swirled around him. Everything was in motion and he felt unmoved.

Didn't he live on this Earth? Why did he feel so lost, so alone? He had no one by his side. And as he stood like this, a friend approached him, a Jewish student from Galicia—a good friend, a good Jew, and a

Jewish nationalist like himself. He patted Asnat on the shoulder and said:

"Asnat, we're going to make them pay for everything: for the pogroms, for the shame of our daughters, for all of the bloody injustices, for the long war that they have waged against us, for everything. We'll make them pay for everything. Asnat, the day of judgment has come."

His eyes gleamed with the joy of vengeance, and Asnat saw how his Jewish heart flamed within him.

And Asnat shot back:

"You will take your vengeance without me. You will find me on the other side."

"Asnat, what is wrong with you? Stay with us, we're taking revenge as Jews."

"I also want to have a homeland. I also want to belong somewhere, I'm also made of something."

He got on the first train back to Russia. There he willingly gave in to everything. But that was all so long ago.

THE DAWN EMERGED through the wet dew. The sun had begun to dry out the dampness of the night, and it had now become cold and brisk. Asnat came out of his tent, looked at the red morning sky and was happy that it was day. The camp had already begun to stir. Soldiers were spreading out their blankets in the sun to dry. Others were washing themselves and scrubbing their tin bowls. Their appetites had also awakened with the morning, but having nothing to eat yet, the soldiers had meanwhile turned their attention to their bowls.

Since daybreak one could hear from afar the constant firing of cannons, whose echoes sounded dully in the brisk morning. For the first time, the shooting, now so near, made an impression on the soldiers. All were alert, and small circles of whispering soldiers had formed across the camp.

The morning was so beautiful though, the sun warming the

green countryside. The nearby shooting, combined with the calm and pleasant landscape, made a strange impression on Asnat. He had not gotten enough sleep and was now frozen from the cold, so he looked for a patch of sunlight and stood there to be warmed by the sun's rays.

Soon Levin came by with two soldiers from the same company in tow, Levinson and Kahanovski, wrapped in their still soaked and wrinkled coats. They also had not slept much, but they seemed worked up and agitated by the shooting. Levinson's Jewish eyes showed fear, running like water into the caverns underneath them; his nose was pale and he pulled pensively at his short beard. Levin looked about dumbly and contemplatively, and one could almost discern a Hasidic smile on his thin, pale lips. The third one, Kahanovski, looked altogether different from the rest of them. The cannon fire had caused an excited curiosity to show on his healthy, dark face. His black eyes glowed, and his facial expressions and lively gestures betrayed a certain restlessness, like the impatience of a hunting dog who watches as his master reaches for his gun.

"Do you hear it, Asnat, do you hear it?" Levinson asked, referring to the cannon fire.

Asnat was silent.

"Of course he hears it. Is he not a soldier?" Kahanovksi said with joy.

"And why are you so happy?" Levinson asked Kahanovksi nervously.

"You can hear the explosions," Kahankovski curtly answered with a wink.

Levinson was the company's intellectual. He wrote all of the letters the soldiers sent home and read to them the letters they received. He kept them informed about politics and knew much about Judaism. Kahanovski was the opposite; he was known to be young and stupid and from an uneducated family. And Levinson had grown accustomed to Kahanovski obeying him and showing him respect. Now, with the cannon fire, which had scared Levinson, Kahanovski's boldness unnerved him.

"Why are you so happy? You're going to your certain death. Look at how joyful he is when he hears the explosions. Be happy, be happy."

"I have no fear," Kahanovski shouted. "I am a soldier and all of my brothers were soldiers. As soon as you become a soldier, you have to imagine yourself earning a ribbon or two, not like Aranovich, who knocked out his teeth because he didn't want to serve, or like the little Jews of our town who stayed up nights before the draft saying Psalms and harming themselves so they wouldn't be taken as soldiers. My father served Czar Nicholas as a soldier and so did all five of his sons. When I was drafted, my father bought me a sack, stuffed a pair of new boots in it, a few shirts, a needle and thread, added a few rubles for the road and told me: 'Go serve the czar with honor and listen to your superiors. Be a good soldier and all will be well and everyone will love you. And when you come to a city, find yourself a poor young woman from a proper home, get engaged, and you'll find what to eat. The girl will do your washing. But make sure not to make the girl unhappy, she's a Jewish maiden after all.' I'm doing what my father told me: I'm a good soldier, I've received a ribbon, and my superiors love me. That's how it is, brothers! Once you've become a soldier, be faithful to the czar!"

"But for what?" Levinson raged. "For the rights they're supposed to give us? For the pogroms they wage against us? Because they drive us out of the villages and expel us from the cities like wild dogs? The gentiles make war, they fight for a reason—they have a fatherland, an emperor. What are we serving for? Why should we give up our lives? If we are victorious, will we get anything out of it? On the contrary, they won't even let us live in the conquered territory."

Everyone was silent.

"I don't know anything about rights. I only know that I am a Jewish soldier and I need to obey my superiors. And when my superiors say go to war for the czar and for the fatherland, I go. I'll fight as long as I have strength. If they give us rights afterwards or if they don't—the responsibility is theirs. I do what I can—I fight for the fatherland."

"For the fatherland," Levinson said with a smirk and turned to

Levin. Levin had meanwhile washed his hands, taken out his *tefillin*,[48] which he had brought with him, and moved to a corner to pray.

"Levin, do you want to fight for the fatherland?"

Levin continued to pray and did not answer.

Asnat looked at Levin with envy, saying quietly:

"His life is better than all of ours. He has more than all of us."

"What do you mean?" Levinson asked.

"He has a god. His god is his master, his god is his homeland! Levin," he called to Levin, who was in the middle of the Eighteen Benedictions,[49] "what would you say, Levin, if they let you go home right now so you could sit and pray, day and night, in the study house? Hey, what would you rather do—look into some difficult passages in Maimonides or sacrifice yourself for the fatherland?"

"So you see now who a Jew's boss is, where his homeland is," Asnat continued, turning to Kahanovski. "A Jew has no homeland—his homeland is the Jewish God, right, Levin?" Asnat then turned to Levinson, who seemed to suddenly have a religious look about him.

"Of course," Levin agreed. "All other peoples have kings of flesh and blood and our king is God."

Kahanovski was silent a moment, not knowing how to respond. The youth's whole body seemed to tremble with excitement. He then remembered something and called out:

"But Levinson, how is it that you've suddenly become religious? You've always laughed about God."

"That's not true," Levinson replied. "I never laughed about the Jewish God."

Asnat mused for a moment: "But is it really true that a Jew has no homeland, only a spiritual and divine one? Is a Jew truly without a homeland? And what should a Jew who no longer believes in God do?" Asnat said all this as if to himself.

Aranovich then arrived, pale and frightened. Aranovich was a tall and strong young man, but toothless, which made his healthy face

---

48 Phylacteries.

49 The essential part of the Jewish prayer service, said three times daily.

look like a broken window. He approached the group quietly and spoke with the tone of one speaking of the dead.

"Do you know they're burying the dead from the battlefield just below our camp?"

"Where did you hear this, Aranovich?"

"The soldiers are all going to look now, but they won't let them. Look, from that hill you can see everything."

They looked over and saw tens of soldiers standing on a hill and looking down into the valley.

"It looks like we've come close to the front, and today or tomorrow our turn will come to fight. I didn't think it would happen so quickly," Levin said. "I thought there would be peace first."

"Brother, you're going to go to the front to shoot Austrians!" Kahanovski answered, smacking him on the shoulder.

"And why are you so happy?" Aranovich asked him.

"Why shouldn't I be happy? Our commander said that it's a great honor for a soldier to go to the front. The emperor himself depends on the soldier that goes to the front and the emperor gives him his due. Why shouldn't I be happy?"

"Look how happy he is to get killed or to kill another Jew," Levinson motioned to the others.

"I don't understand. You didn't know why you were sent here?" Asnat exclaimed. He had been quite stirred by Levinson's answer. "We are soldiers and we've gone to war. We don't know who lies in wait on the other side, whether it's a Jew or a Christian. We only know that the enemy is over there, the enemy of our country. And the soldier who doesn't shoot at them is a traitor and deserves to be hanged. Kahanovski, you're right. Give me your hand and we'll go together to shoot the Austrians and we'll earn a Cross of St. George. You're right, once you're a soldier you have to be a good soldier. If not, you bring shame not only on yourself, but also on the entire nation to which you belong."

"You see, you're right," Aranovich responded. "We, Jewish soldiers, need to fight hard so they won't be able to say that Jews are cowards. We need to fight and give our all to show the anti-Semites."

"No, not for the anti-Semites," Asnat called out. "We need to fight for ourselves. Because we are men and we want to be thought of as men."

"Of course, of course we need to faithfully serve the emperor," Levin enjoined. "The rabbi told me when I last saw him that I should serve the czar faithfully, that it was a *mitzvah*[50] and an obligation."

Everyone was silent for a moment.

But Aranovich still trembled from fear and said with his hands more than he said with his mouth:

"Go over there and see how they're being buried. Like dogs. Look, look!" the young man called out with a shudder, and covered his eyes.

"OK, OK, let's go," Kahanovski replied. "Come on, Asnat, aren't you going to see how they bury the Austrians?"

"Of course I'm coming," Asnat said, standing up.

"Wait, I'm coming too," Levinson smiled. "Let's see what my burial will look like." He also stood up to go.

"It's forbidden to talk like that," Levin said quietly.

"And you, Aranovich, aren't you coming?" Kahanovski said cheerfully to the pale young man.

They climbed the hill where many other soldiers were already standing and looked down on the wide field. From a distance they saw fresh earth dug in very long rows. Jews in black overcoats with small Jewish hats stood with shovels in their hands and covered the graves with dirt. Next to them stood guards with guns in their hands, prodding the Jews at their work. Soldiers' clothes, guns, and other possessions lay around the piles of dirt, and military carts were brought to gather everything up. The whole field was trampled. Next to the trees lay broken branches and bullet-ridden tree trunks. The wounded trees told the story of the great massacre that had taken place here better than the things strewn about the ground. The trees, destroyed at the very height of their blooming, seemed almost like children who had known nothing of what was going on or its purpose, but had been forced to remain where they stood without any chance of escape.

---

50 Religious commandment.

The soldiers were not allowed to look on for very long. They were driven away from the hill: command was afraid that death would frighten the young soldiers.

When Asnat and his friends returned to their previous spot, they found Aranovich sitting with Levin. Levin held a prayer book in his hand and recited Psalms while Aranovich lowered his head to also look into the book and repeat each word after Levin, like a student with his rabbi.

The scene left a wild impression on the other soldiers. They knew Aranovich as someone who had always laughed at Levin's piety and often bothered him while he prayed. Aranovich was suddenly reciting Psalms! They all sensed the earnestness in his reciting of the Psalms, and so they dispersed wordlessly, not wanting to disturb them.

ASNAT WAS RESTLESS the whole day. He wandered about dejectedly, unable to find a place for himself. It wasn't the field of death that had gotten to him, but that he had somehow lost track of the reason he had decided to become a soldier. When he had first made the decision, he hadn't exactly understood it either, but he had felt that he had done the right thing. Now he had lost that feeling, and it seemed to him that it was all nonsense. The conversation with Levinson had reminded him of the many episodes he had witnessed of Jews being persecuted, and in particular of how they had driven his father out of the forest he himself had purchased. His father, the great timber merchant, had registered as a citizen through a poor, drunken non-Jew, a privilege for which he paid weekly. There were so many incidents, not of outright rage, but of small acts of vengeance and everyday abuse. And maybe they were right, that a Jew has no homeland and will never have one. So let the nations of the world devour one another—what does it matter to the Jews? They should hide themselves in a cellar and observe with indifferent expressions on their faces as they're passed like slaves from one master to another. What difference does it make whom they serve?

And he was ashamed, not for his young life that he had put in danger for nothing, but of his feelings. It seemed to him that the commanders were laughing at him, that the Jew Asnat had thought himself privileged enough to become a soldier and wage war for his "fatherland."

ASNAT LAY ON the ground and watched as Aranovich, Kahanovski and many other Jewish soldiers, whom he knew had never prayed a day in their lives, all gathered around Levin. Their praying gradually became warmer and more devout. Levinson, the intellectual, who had always laughed at God, also joined in, taking a prayer book in his hand; he had also become devout all of a sudden. Aranovich was crying—the tears poured from his eyes and his face twisted in sorrow, as if he was taking great pity on himself.

The group of soldiers became quiet. Levin recited out loud the confessional prayer, and all the soldiers repeated after him, pounding their chests. Some cried, some became pensive, and others were silent—but everyone was serious. After the confessional prayer, the soldiers kissed and shook hands, as if it were Yom Kippur at the *Kol Nidre*[51] service.

Levinson approached Asnat.

"So, Asnat, give me your hand and forgive me, even if you don't believe in it."

Asnat silently shook hands with him.

After the Russian Orthodox prayer service also concluded, the feeling in the camp became a bit lighter. The soldiers became livelier and more cheerful, and they sat down with each other as brothers. Lunch was eaten in groups, and Jewish and Russian soldiers continually kissed one another, sang songs and wished one another good luck. The camp was filled with a feeling of brotherhood. The officers

---

51 The first prayer service on Yom Kippur, the Day of Atonement, and one of the most solemn occasions of the Jewish year.

and lieutenants mingled with the soldiers, exchanging salutations and joining the fraternal atmosphere. Arbuzov, a bit drunk from the excitement, went up to Levin, kissed him and other Jewish soldiers and repeated again and again:

"Pray to your God, pray, you Jewish soldiers! He is our God too, pray that he help us, pray that he save us."

And to his comrades, the Russian soldiers that had come with him, he explained:

"Each person has his God and his way of praying to Him."

"There is only one God in the world for all of us," a Jewish soldier exclaimed.

"There is only one God," the Russian soldiers answered.

"Come let's embrace, brothers."

"We're all brothers."

And the Jewish soldiers kissed the Russian soldiers, the medics, and the orderlies.

"Yesterday you humiliated him," Arbuzov said, while crying on Levin's shoulder, to the soldier who had stuffed a piece of meat in Levin's mouth. "Go, Ivanov, go and make up with him."

"Make up with him, Ivanov," the other soldiers called out in response.

Ivanov, the huge, strong gentile, approached, full of shame, and offered Levin his hand.

"Kiss him," Arbuzov shrieked, "kiss one another!"

Ivanov and Levin kissed.

"That is how it should be," the other soldiers said in agreement.

ASNAT LAY DOWN on the field alone. He had seen the brotherhood and the true humanity with which death had bound one man to another, but he could not take any part in it. He was frustrated with himself that he couldn't disregard all of his thoughts and, like Levinson, throw himself into the brotherhood and forget about everything in an instant. He also wanted to kiss the other soldiers, but he just wasn't able to. It seemed to him that if he were to do such a thing the feeling of it wouldn't be true, as if he was doing it to ingratiate himself to the other soldiers. He felt that his heart was racing; he wanted, in that moment, before they departed maybe never to see one another again, to shake someone's hand. But he didn't have anyone. He hated Levinson the intellectual, and Levin was too religious for him. But he couldn't stay alone in the field any longer. The soldiers had already taken note of him, and he was afraid that they would consider him too proud. He stood up and left the Jewish soldiers. He remembered Kahanovski and said to himself: yes, with him I have to say my goodbyes. Asnat went looking for him. He found Kahanovski sitting in a corner talking with Aranovich. Aranovich had finished crying and now was trying to comfort himself. His eyes showed a hopeless despondency and he kept shaking his head back and forth. Kahanovksi sat next to him, offering comforting words.

"Look, Asnat is here too," Kahanovski said to Aranovich. "He's more educated and wealthier than us, and yet see how he goes into battle without fear. None of the soldiers are afraid; see how courageous they are. We're all going into battle. You must hope that you'll live, that you'll shoot them, and that no bullet will catch you. You have to be brave. You're no child."

"But I have a little girl back home and I want to see how she grows up, what she'll look like when she's older. I so much want to see all of this, but I know I'll never see her again," the young man answered in unending despair.

"But Aranovich, we all have fathers and mothers! We're not dead yet! What's gotten into you? Look at me, look at Asnat, look at all the other Jewish soldiers."

When Kahanovski took his leave from Aranovich, Asnat went up to Kahanovski and said with an awkward smile:

"So, Kahanovski, give me your hand. Maybe we won't see each other again. You're in the seventh company, right?"

"Yes," Kahanovski answered. He then became pale and offered his hand to Asnat.

"Do you have anyone?" Asnat asked.

"I have a fiancé that I love."

"You're happier than me. I've got no one."

"No one?"

"Well, yes, I do have a little sister that I love."

"Give her this chain when you come home," Kahanovski said, taking the chain off his watch.

Asnat looked for something in his pockets to give Kahanovski. He couldn't find anything except for a small ribbon that his sister had given him to remember her by. But he didn't want to give it away. He remembered the golden watch, a present from his father for finishing school. He took it out of his satchel and gave it to Kahanovski.

They kissed one another and went their separate ways.

Asnat went into his tent and took out from among his things the handkerchief that he had brought with him from home so he could have it near him when he needed it. He didn't want to die with strange clothes on his body, or to simply bleed out on the sand. He placed the handkerchief near his heart and prepared himself for the road.

In a half-hour the company left the cabbage field behind and went into the line of fire.

THEY WALKED ACROSS the field they had looked down upon just the day before from atop the hill. It was clear that a devastating slaughter had taken place there over the previous two days. The field was all trampled and long rows of freshly dug earth stretched across it. The half-broken trees stood with their bullet-ridden, still-smoldering branches hanging like corpses swimming in their own blood. The field was a beet field and the beets had not yet been harvested. The red and white beets had been kicked around and trampled, their green leaves like dirty rags. Among the beets you could find soldiers' uniforms, hats, satchels, rifles, swords, and every once in a while a dead body or a part of a dead body. Old peasant farmers and their wives and daughters gathered up the beets from among the scattered objects and put them in piles while Jews in black cloaks and small hats gathered up the corpses and carried them to freshly dug graves. The beets that were still whole were gathered for later use while the trampled ones were left on the ground to rot with the corpses.

The soldiers walked silently, though they had been commanded to sing. Here and there you could hear a lone voice, but no one else joined in song, and soon the lone voice went silent as well. Then they came to the mass graves where the Jewish men stood with shovels. They had paused for a moment from their labor and stood to the side with their shovels in one hand while saluting the regiment with the other. The soldiers began jumping over the ditches, and as they leaped, they looked down at the dead soldiers piled one on top of the other, some naked and some in their uniforms. Dead faces stared at them with small and innocent open eyes. The earnest dead faces seemed to tear themselves from the dirty uniforms. A few soldiers stopped to look into the ditches, but those who wanted to jump after them pushed them forward. This is how the regiment proceeded past the mass graves.

They also came across huge black holes in the ground that from a distance looked like great puddles of mud. But when they passed near these holes and examined them more closely, they pulled back startled: inside they saw a cauldron of human and horse intestines. From within the seething black mess, which the soldiers could hardly comprehend, human faces and limbs protruded, emerging from underneath a horse that had been torn apart with its guts oozing over everything.

At first they came upon a single black ditch and then moved past; but soon they started appearing with greater frequency. The landscape was covered with these muddy ditches, and the soldiers had to navigate their way between them. They knew that the ditches had been made by the enemy's bombs, but each soldier comforted himself by saying that he would be spared from such an end. How they could convince themselves of this no one knows. But the young, healthy life force within them protested and refused to fall into such a filthy cauldron, where death was so foul; in their fantasies they imagined a freer and better death.

The sun began to set on the horizon. The landscape became flatter and wider, and the sky curved over the earth, the glowing red of the horizon reflecting everywhere.

At a corner of the sky there appeared a pale patch that hung above the landscape. Something had appeared, and it was difficult to tell from a distance whether it was houses, mountains or more forest. The closer they came to the patch of white, the more it became clear that it was a cloud of smoke which rose from the ground and into the heavens. The soldiers understood what it was. Some of their hearts began to beat harder, others were already indifferent. The road had become easier to walk on, and the graves and long ditches were fewer. But from time to time one had to jump over a dead soldier who had been left in the field. The dead soldier, with his rifle in hand, and the fact that they would come upon him so suddenly, so unexpectedly— this terrified the soldiers more than the black graves. Each soldier's imagination had become overactive: I could be just like him . . .

The road became more treacherous, the ground trampled and worn. The soldiers' legs sank deeper into the sandy earth, which was covered in patches of clover that stuck to their boots. It had become dark, but the atmosphere was homey, even joyful. They passed by several wagons, horses and automobiles. High-ranking officers stood on top of a hill deep in discussion. One could see suddenly that there were many of them, that regiments were coming from all directions, and that there were all different kinds of soldiers—infantry, cavalry, artillery. They didn't know exactly where all of these soldiers had come from, but it seemed to them that the entire world was full of them. As far as the eye could see, the landscape was packed with soldiers. Torches and flares had been lit in various places, and each one illuminated the soldiers' faces. One could hear in the distance the constant sound of shooting. Boom! Boom! Boom! But one hardly noticed the sound anymore; it had been drowned out by the noise of the soldiers, the wagons and horses, the cars racing past like devils. It was all so exciting, you forgot that you were ever afraid. There were so many of them!

But they didn't remain there for more than a moment. They passed over the noise and rush of the other soldiers and proceeded to a village whose houses were boarded up. Not a soul could be seen. The church steeple was burning and no one thought to put it out.

They came to a spot just below the village and suddenly saw before them a black field overgrown with something, though it was too dark to tell whether it was trees or human beings.

Suddenly a flare streaked over their heads and lit up a green forest, the brightness revealing trembling leaves and soldiers overlooking a meadow. In a moment it was dark again and they felt something pass over their heads with a gust of wind.

The air was torn asunder by a great noise. The projectile could be heard again as it fell with a dull thud into the earth, taking a few trees down with it.

The soldiers continued on and another car raced past as if possessed. The trotting of horses could be heard nearby, though who or what was riding them remained unknown in the dark. Their boots came down on something—maybe a stone? But no, it was something softer, something unknowable . . .

They went further into the darkness. Then suddenly another flash of light appeared over their heads. You could see your comrades like it was day—Aranovich's pale face—and then your eyes were blinded and another gust of wind passed overhead.

The noise this time was lesser. Some soldiers fell into a ditch, others collapsed by your side, their feet giving way. But they continued onward. Another flash of light, another gust of wind. Your head wanted to tear itself from your body, but some thought fell into your mind, the recognition of your friends' voices—"God, help me . . ."—but still you went onward, ever onward, until you came to a ditch. There you found the others. Orders were given to lie down in the ditches or to dig new ones, and all the soldiers threw themselves into the earth.

All around it was quiet. In the black night you could hear the piercing sounds of shooting, and again and again there were flashes of light and gusts of wind followed by a screeching noise, as if the bombs wanted to awaken the air.

The soldiers lay in their trenches for a long time, protecting their heads with sand. In the distance you could see small fires where the enemy was stationed. But the command was given not to shoot until ordered to do so—this had something to do with tricking the enemy into abandoning its fortified position. They wanted the enemy to think that we had retreated after their heavy bombardment of our position the previous day. Meanwhile, overnight, we had quietly added reinforcements so that if the enemy should even think about moving out of its position to encroach on our territory, we would take them in close combat with our bayonets—since we felt much stronger in such a fight. But the soldiers couldn't hold back, and they exchanged some fire with the enemy, their shots echoing in the darkness of the night.

When Asnat found his way into the trenches, he felt something soft underneath him. At first he drew back in fear, and then he heard a voice: "Have mercy, brother." He turned and noticed a soldier.

"Give me something to drink, brother," the soldier moaned. "I'm dying of thirst."

Asnat gave him his flask and the soldier took a drink.

"What's wrong, are you wounded?" Asnat asked him. "Why haven't you been evacuated from here?"

"There's no time, no one came to ask. Everyone here in this trench is either dead or wounded. Bombs fell the entire day, like thunder. God's curse, brother, God's curse has been set upon the world."

"How did they let us trample on people, on living people?" Asnat asked.

"We too trampled on dead bodies. Look, there is someone else under me. He was warm for most of the day, he drank all my water, and I used my shirt to dress his wound. Now he is cold. He's bled out. He's been cold since dusk, God have mercy on him. He was a Catholic, Valentine Stekhovitsh was his name, from the eighty-seventh rifle regiment. I remember all of this very well. He asked me before he died to remember his name and to notify his regiment so they can write to his mother. Now I pass on his name to you. Remember it, I repeated it a whole day. Remember my name too: Ivan Maladets, from the fourteenth rifle regiment, the sixth company. Remember it well, remember . . ."

"You'll yet live, brother! We've arrived, so many of us have come—we'll take revenge for you!"

"No, dear brother, no. I won't live to see it," the wounded soldier coughed. "You might, but I won't! I have no blood left. It's coming hand over foot, like a warm river. And there's no water left. I've drunk all of it and I'm thirsty for more."

"Wait, I'll move him from underneath you, so you'll be more comfortable," Asnat said.

"No brother, don't do it. He's safer here. Out there the grenades will blow him to bits and even God won't recognize him. The face of God will be destroyed. He won't be accepted in heaven. Let him be. Have mercy."

"Where is your wound? Show me and I'll dress it for you," Asnat said.

"There's nothing left to dress it with. I've used everything I have. My blood is running out. Everything is wet."

"I have a handkerchief here," Asnat answered him, taking out the handkerchief he had attached to his chest. "Take it."

But the handkerchief didn't help. Blood from the wound was everywhere, and his clothes and the mud had become one mass that bound his body to the ground. After a short while, the handkerchief had disappeared among the rest of it.

Asnat felt connected to the soldier after he gave him the handkerchief. And the feeling did him good. He had never imagined that war could be so cruel and terrible, but for a moment it did not bother him that he had come to know the terrors of war.

He became happier and prouder of himself, and not a trace was left of that ugly feeling or those superstitions that had exhausted him during the day. Now he no longer hesitated or overanalyzed; he just sat in the dark and felt the ground underneath him, the black, cold earth, and he had the feeling that he wasn't going to war for anyone—only for the land. For the land upon which he was born, and upon which his father's father was born, and upon which they had always lived. For her and only for her did he now sit in the trenches, not letting anyone take her away. This is what connected him to the wounded soldier whom he did not know, and who might very well be his enemy or someone that he may have offended; or maybe he had taken part in pogroms against Jews. But the land brought them together. The two of them—no, all three of them, since Asnat now remembered Valentine Stekhovitsh—were defending the strip of land upon which they were born.

He looked into the dark night that stretched over the land, and it seemed to him that he had set out to free this strip of land from the black and terrifying night. In the distance the enemy's fires still shined, flickering like the eyes of a poisonous snake that had taken hold of his mother's neck. Asnat had come to free his mother from the snake. He had the feeling that the earth was sick and that was why she had been so cruel to him—it was only because she had that snake around her neck. She needed to be freed from the poisonous flames that appeared in the distance. He now felt inside himself the strength and the courage to go over there and stamp out their fires with his feet. He felt that he was young and strong and that he could free his sick mother from the poisonous snake.

And so he lay for half the night in his trench, passing the time in thought and looking into the black night and into the fires across the field. The wounded soldier did not stop groaning and asking for water. Asnat had already asked for his neighbors' flasks of water though they too had wounded comrades who were dying of thirst. For a while the wounded soldier was quiet. It appeared he had fallen asleep. Asnat was about to wake him when all of a sudden he called out:

"Brother, I feel I've made a turn for the worse. Make the sign of the cross over me, before I die."

Asnat thought for a moment, and then made the sign of the cross over the wounded soldier while explaining: "I'm no Christian, but even so . . ."

The soldier was silent for a minute.

"What, you're a Muslim?" he asked suddenly.

"No, a Jew," Asnat answered back.

"Oh, a Jew," the wounded soldier responded, as if to himself. "Well, it's all the same to me. There is one God in this world. Kiss me, it's so painful to die alone."

Asnat and the soldier kissed.

"And don't forget Valentine Stekhovitsh, a Catholic, and Ivan Maladets, an Eastern Orthodox. Repeat the names, or you'll forget."

"And Asnat Meir, a Jew," Asnat said to himself.

And then the soldier was silent.

After a half-hour Asnat started to feel cold. He turned and nudged the wounded soldier, but the soldier did not respond. Asnat prodded him with his hand and asked, "What's with you? Can you hear me?" but he did not answer. Asnat was seized by fear. Instinctively he moved away from the dead body, but he could not remain calm. He very much wanted to see the soldier's face. The whole time they had spoken, his face had been hidden in the ground. But Asnat was afraid of turning him over, despite his curiosity. Lighting a match was forbidden, so the enemy would not know their position. Finally, he lifted the dead man's head and looked deeply into his face by the faint light of the stars. In the dim light he looked just like Arbuzov from his company, and it seemed to Asnat that Arbuzov was in fact lying there.

The rest of the night Asnat remained cold and felt like he had been abandoned.

THE LANDSCAPE BRIGHTENED with the first rays of morning light. At first Asnat felt a dampness all around him, and he didn't know whether it was dew or the blood of the dead soldier. Then the horizon reddened and everything was covered in fog. And soon from among the clouds the field and a few trees appeared, and then a tall rampart made out of dug-up earth topped with white structures. Immediately an order was given to shoot. The whole front exploded with fire. The blasts deafened the ear and all senses were deadened. No one knew or had any sense of what was going on; all they could see was a white line where everyone aimed their weapons. Something flew over their heads and to their right and left, but no one paid it any mind. As in a dream, they were vaguely conscious of something flying by them while their thoughts were focused on the white streak across the hills.

After a short while the command was given to advance a few meters forward into the next trenches. Asnat saw other soldiers running, so he ran after them into the trenches and then into the next ones that they had abandoned. Like the other soldiers, Asnat dug deeper into the ground to pile the dirt above his head to protect himself and then continued shooting.

Asnat looked at his people's flag, which was carried with them to each position. Wherever the flag went, he knew he had to follow. He was conscious of his actions and did as was expected of him. But he felt nothing: all of his senses were focused on one goal. Every once in a while the flag would rise up over their heads and run forward and Asnat would follow. But each time there were fewer soldiers with the flag. They sank into the ditches that opened under their feet. He then saw how the flag tottered and fell to the earth. A thought flew through his mind:

Levin with his *tzitzis*, the Jewish flag—every Jew is buried wrapped in this flag . . . Asnat sprang from his trench and ran towards the flag. Something flew past him and stung him along the way, as if he had been burned, but he continued running. He felt as if he was running to save something essential, not a man but something more than a man, and if he were to save it he would save the land under his feet. He ran forward, another stinger, another burn, and a searing sensation around his head. But he felt nothing; it seemed as if he had lifted up the whole earth with all the fallen soldiers. He waved the flag over his head and ran forward.

Again something whizzed by him and he felt another burn. Now it felt as if his head was burning, his hair too and his face. But he continued to run. He looked around to see if anyone was running with him. He saw no one behind him, it was as if everyone had sunk into the earth. Suddenly he came upon the white strip. He saw some movement, figures starting to run at him. He stood standing for a moment in the field with the flag in his hand. There was no one around him, everything had faded away. And his head was burning—soon the flag would begin to burn as well.

From a distance something sparkled and trumpets sounded. He came to himself and charged the enemy. He could see how the small people from the other side started running at him. They were coming quite close. He turned around and started running in the other direction with the flag.

Over his head little flames flew by. The earth was full of holes, full of ditches. In one ditch there lay spread out a pair of *tzitzis*. He wanted to cry out: Levin! But he just jumped over the ditches with the flag in his hand. He tripped but continued running.

Gradually everything became lighter. He felt as if he had wings. And he flew off with the flag and the soldiers were flying with him on flaming horses. He too had a flaming horse. He jumped with his horse over the dead in the black ditches.

Suddenly he fell off his horse. He wanted to get up and continue running . . . on the ground . . . but the fire was already extinguished. Two soldiers took him under his arms and dragged him, with flag in hand and covered from head to foot in blood, to the general.

The general tried to speak with Asnat, but he could not understand him. He thought only of having seen the *tzitzis* as he jumped over the trenches, and how the *tzitzis* looked among all of the faces . . .

When he opened his eyes, he found himself in what seemed to be a huge field crowded with beds. Soldiers dressed in white looked at him. There was a great noise: the sound of groans came from every direction. In one corner a soldier cried out in a loud voice. It seemed to Asnat that he was on the battlefield and that the soldiers in white had been placed in beds in the trenches. He looked up to the ceiling, expecting that something would fall from the sky, and by instinct he felt the compulsion to grab for his rifle. He made a quick movement and immediately felt a searing pang in his head, in his sides, in his feet, as if he were being stabbed with spears. He then remained still, indifferent, and his head and heart became empty.

Someone spoke to him from the bed next to him.

"Soldier, what regiment are you from? What battlefield?"

He understood the question, and he thought that he had given some sort of answer, but the solider asked again:

"Soldier, what regiment are you from? What battlefield? Can you hear me?"

"A Catholic, a Russian, and a Jew," Asnat mumbled to himself, so that the one talking to him couldn't understand.

Soon a young woman approached him, dressed in white (everyone looked like soldiers to him), and spoke to him in plain Yiddish:

"You're going to live, Asnat, you're going to live. The head doctor himself is taking care of you. The operation was successful. The doctors are doing all they can."

Asnat didn't understand what she was talking about.

He drank some kind of liquid that she gave him and his sight became clearer. He realized that he was not in a field but in a very large room filled with beds.

"Where am I?" he asked quietly.

"You're in the Warsaw Jewish hospital. Everyone here knows about you, the newspapers are all writing about you. You're a hero Asnat, a hero. We're all proud of you."

Asnat didn't quite understand what she was saying, but just hearing her voice made him feel better.

"And the governor came by asking about you, the general and the high-ranking officers too. Everyone is talking about you. And they've hung a Cross of St. George over your bed. The general himself came and hung it here. We're all proud of you, Asnat, that you're a Jew. All the Jews are overjoyed."

Asnat now began to understand, but he had a strange feeling. It seemed to him that something was missing. Some part of his body was missing—but this wasn't what bothered him. He felt as if the missing body part was trembling, moving somehow, looking for its former place. And that trembling came from where his legs used to be . . .

Slowly and quietly he felt around with his hand under his blanket and he noticed something strange: he couldn't find his legs . . . they seemed to be there, he could feel them, they were trembling . . . but he had no idea where they were. They were hiding somewhere. He had a funny thought: *he* was sitting in one bed and *his legs* were in a second bed . . . Can one's legs be taken away from one's body? But, still, he could feel them, he felt the nerves . . . something was tickling the pinky toe of his left foot, he had an itch there. He searched with his hand, slowly, for his legs . . .

Suddenly, it all became clear to him. He trembled and asked the young woman uneasily:

"What, did they cut off my legs?"

The young woman became pale. Two enormous tears formed in her eyes. She bent her head over his and kissed his forehead. Her tears dampened his face and she said quietly:

"You're a hero, Asnat. You're a hero."

A moment later the doctor appeared, having observed the scene from afar. He took the Cross of St. George down from the wall and gave it to Asnat, declaiming with a cheerful tone:

"The general entrusted me with the task of presenting this to you, in the emperor's name, upon your waking."

Asnat held the steel cross in his hand for a minute: under the blanket he could still feel the nerves of his amputated legs . . . He thought to himself: would he really never walk again? He had the sense that in a minute he would jump out of bed—that is how strongly he felt his legs.

A FEW WEEKS later Asnat was released from the hospital. During his time there he had become a real celebrity. But other heroes like him soon came through the hospital and attention shifted away from him. With time he became somewhat used to his wooden legs and his two crutches, which he had already begun using in the hospital. The longing for his own legs faded and he slowly got used to walking on his prosthetic legs. He began to grow fond of his new legs. Often he had the strange feeling that the nerves of his natural legs were now trembling within the cold wood, and so he even began to love his new wooden legs.

He couldn't stay long in the hospital. Thousands of others now needed his bed. He was sent to a small town, far away in Russia. There he was still an attraction. He waited in the town for his father to come and take him home. He had sent his father several telegrams, but he had yet to receive an answer. He had heard already in the hospital that his town, Yanov, which was not very far from the border, had been overrun a couple of times by the Russians and then by the Germans and that the town had been destroyed. But where was his father? Where was his mother? Where was his little sister?

Jews from the town he was stationed in cobbled together a few rubles, enough to send him home. He traveled for two weeks in freight cars until he finally reached Yanov. He didn't recognize the town. The trees in the surrounding orchards had all been cut down; the fields and the roads had been destroyed; the market was burned down; the chimneys looked like black demons between sunken white walls. Here and there a few houses still stood with knocked-out windows and torn open walls. There was no one on the streets, save for a few soldiers, who had built a fire in the middle of the market square and sat around it, warming their hands. He searched for the ruins of his father's house and saw from a distance the walls of his mother's bedroom; he recognized them from the white wallpaper. The frame of a photograph still hung on the wall. The courtyard was strewn with beams and pieces of the building. Stones and straw were scattered everywhere and among them he found his mother's silk dresses, a wig, a holy book, and a broken table.

He left the ruins and wandered the streets, searching for someone, anyone. But he found no one. Just a few hungry dogs roamed around the market looking at him with crazed eyes, not understanding why everything was like this. At the end of one street he noticed the old study house. It was still standing, as it had before, and a light was shining in its windows. He went inside. A single candle was burning and a few old Jews, in thin, torn coats, were shaking—from the cold, from fear, from hunger—while sitting around the enormous cold oven.

His entrance awakened the old Jews. They gathered around him, at first fearfully, warily, and then they began to recognize him, and he them: two of them were Reb[52] Yosef Rozenkrants, the wealthiest member of the town, and Reb Chaim Sokhatshever, his in-law. He barely recognized them—they had been proud homeowners, the finest Jews of the town. Now they looked like beggars or vagabonds.

Everyone was quiet for a moment. Reb Yosef wiped the tears from his eyes with his sleeve and said:

"So, Asnat, this is what we've come to!"

"And where is my father?" Asnat asked.

The Jews were silent and looked at one another. Suddenly, Leyb the synagogue caretaker called out:

"Why should we hide this from him? He should know. He has to say the mourner's prayer. Asnat, your father is no longer among the living."

"Why?" Asnat protested.

"They let him have it. He was barely able to crawl his way to a Jewish grave."

"Who did this to him?"

"The Cossacks."

"Did they shoot him?"

"No, worse."

"What happened? Tell me!" Asnat ordered.

"They whipped him to death!"

Asnat bit his lip and was silent. They were all silent for a while.

"And where is my mother?"

"Your mother is upstairs in the women's section with the other women. They're cooking something warm for us."

In a few minutes there was a scream, like the howl of a wild animal when it is wounded. This was Asnat's mother, who burst into the study house with a wild and weary look on her face. She had just

---

52 Yiddish for "Mr."

heard that her son had returned and now filled the study house with a mother's cry.

"My child, my child has come back!"

She fell upon him from one side and his sister fell upon him from the other, and for a while she wasn't able to get a single comprehensible word to come out of her mouth.

All of a sudden she noticed his wooden legs and in a frenzy she fell to the ground and grabbed his legs and screamed out with an almost inhuman voice:

"Look, look what they've done to my child! My legs, my golden legs!" And she kissed his wooden legs. She embraced them, pressed them to her face, and covered them with motherly tears.

Asnat stood as if struck by lightning. He tore the steel cross from his uniform and held it out in his hand. He exclaimed, as if to himself:

"Is this worth a father or a mother? Is this worth my two legs, my two legs of flesh and blood?"

And he held the cross as far away from his body as he could.

Asnat had wanted to throw the cross away, but he remembered that he had done all of this—had gone to battle—not for them but for himself, for Ansat. He put the cross back on his chest and showed it to his mother.

"I lost my legs, Mama, but I got a medal."

His mother tore the cross off his uniform and howled like a wounded, wild animal:

"Look everyone. My legs, my two legs of flesh and blood—for a cross . . ."

David Bergelson
1884–1952

D AVID BERGELSON WAS one of the great Yiddish modernists of
the twentieth century and, for a few years in the 1920s, a high-
profile contributor to the *Forward*.

Born to a wealthy family in Okhrimovo, in what is now Ukraine,
Bergelson lost both of his parents as a teenager and was subsequently
raised by his older brothers. At the age of nineteen he moved to Kiev,
where he helped the city become a center for modern Yiddish culture.

Like many Yiddish writers, Bergelson began by writing in Hebrew
but switched early on to Yiddish and never published his Hebrew
works. His first published book was *At the Depot*, a novella that
appeared in 1909 and received plaudits from literary critics. Four
years later his novel *The End of Everything* (also translated as *When All
Is Said and Done*), a masterpiece of Yiddish modernism, established
him as one of the most important Yiddish writers of the period.

In 1921, following the Russian Revolution and the Ukrainian War
of Independence, Bergelson immigrated to Berlin, where he joined a
large expatriate community of Yiddish-speaking writers, artists, and
intellectuals. It was there that he met Abraham Cahan, who invited
him to write for the *Forward*. For the next five years Bergelson became
a regular contributor of short stories and novellas, although he often
argued with Cahan over the frequency of his publication, which he
depended on for his livelihood.

"On the Eve of Battle" appeared in the *Forward* in 1923 and
extended a narrative about the insurgent leader Botshko and his rag-
tag band of Red Army fighters, whom Bergelson had introduced in

the *Forward* in 1922. Set in rural Ukraine in the late fall of 1918, when the forces of the Ukrainian nationalist leader Symon Petliura were perpetrating vicious pogroms against Jews, the story focuses on Aba, a young Jewish wagon driver, who joins Botshko's regiment for protection, only to have his courage and sense of loyalty put to the test in the midst of a murderous rampage.

In 1926, Bergelson's differences with Cahan reached a breaking point, and he quit the *Forward* to write for its Communist competitor, *Frayhayt* (*Freedom*). Bergelson stayed in Berlin until 1934, when the rise of Nazism convinced him to move first to Denmark and then to return to the Soviet Union. During the Second World War he was active in the Jewish Anti-Fascist Committee and helped edit its publication, *Eynikayt* (*Unity*).

Although Bergelson initially benefited from Soviet state support for Yiddish culture, like other Yiddish writers and intellectuals, he soon became the target of Stalinist persecution. At the beginning of 1949 he was arrested, and was subsequently imprisoned and tortured for more than two years. On August 12, 1952, Bergelson was executed along with twelve other Yiddish writers and cultural figures, a date that became known as the "Night of the Murdered Poets."

On the Eve of Battle

(JANUARY 29–FEBRUARY 6, 1923)

Translated by Ellen Kellman

I

ANDRIUK WAS SHOT by blond Fritz with the Cossack sidelock; he shot him with a strange, sudden swiftness, as though he was compelled to hurry, or else the whole affair might come to naught. And the forty-year-old Andriuk, with his wrinkled, deceitful face, had just developed a cataract in his left eye. He got it from a stab wound during their hasty retreat from Aleksandrovke to Kislok at dusk on Saturday. Now it remained in everyone's memory how, before death, this very cataract had gazed on them entreatingly, as if it were both beseeching and reprimanding them: "Didn't I serve loyally, ah, Comrades? And why shoot me now? For a trifle—for a little theft from a peasant in the village."

And along with the cataract, Leyzerke—Lazar Popov, the military commissar—a strict and upright officer—remained in everyone's memory. Even though no one had heard him order Fritz to shoot Andriuk, it was obvious . . .

With his hands in his pockets, Leyzerke went out all alone to talk to the many peasants who were creating an uproar around headquarters, and promised to pay for all the damage that his retreating "great ones"[53] had caused in the village, and even for Andriuk's theft, and everyone saw how the peasants obeyed him and dispersed.

From that moment on, Leyzerke's reputation began to rise like yeast.

In the squadron they discussed everything:

"We will stay longer in Kislok."

"More men will be coming."

"The military commissar has ordered it."

And Botshko asked him:

"So, does this mean that Comrade Popov is waiting for a communiqué and money?"

Leyzer responded in brief:

"We wait."

He no longer acquiesced to anyone—he had always been an upright fellow.

From then on no other thefts were heard of in the village. Suddenly the members of the squadron became much older and quieter.

---

53 A reference to the Bolshevik forces.

And when Botshko went over to the barracks, they listened to what he had to say and looked at him with newly virtuous eyes; they had coalesced because of Andriuk's misfortune. Immersed in the muted grayness of the village, a few short winter days passed. The memory of the small town of Aleksandrovke, from which they had pulled back, was still fresh, as was Andriuk's cataract, which had grimaced drily and begged for compassion before death. And it seemed that compassion would come later, compassion would still come.

Just as before, the nights reek of sweaty barracks, of bodies that never get undressed, that lie around on the floor and fill the primitively heated building with the sound of snoring. Late at night, when they stretch out fully, they give off a choking stench, a mixture of an unclean animal cage and a smoldering charcoal lamp. And at that moment, Elik the slaughterer's son wakes up. He retreated here from Aleksandrovke with Leyzerke because his party ordered him to, and also because it's all the same to him where he gets killed—at home or somewhere else. Just before he wakes up he senses that he is choking—that there is no air to breathe. In total darkness he lights a match and kindles a little green flame, briefly making the barracks visible, as if through smoke. In this pitch-black game of blind man's bluff, the door creaks and Elik finds a seat outdoors on the earthen bench, wraps himself in his shabby short coat and stoops, stoops down like a Jew. Above his head an unfamiliar night sky, quiet and rustic, alternately starry and cloudy. As though under no one's jurisdiction, blind sleeping houses are silhouetted, but from far beyond them, a long, drawn-out, vigilant, nocturnal whistle is intermittently heard. From the granaries and fences opposite, Leyzerke approaches in his gray military greatcoat with its slit down to the soles of his feet. And as always, when he goes out late at night to check the positions, he is not alone. Two non-Jewish lads from Kislok—heavily armed, blank-faced youths—follow him like loyal Hasidim.[54] A few

---

54 The term "Hasid" (plural, Hasidim) refers to a follower of a charismatic ultra-Orthodox leader, or *rebbe,* but any loyal follower of a charismatic leader can be called a Hasid in Yiddish.

days earlier he and Elik had a short conversation about Andriuk's violent death.

Leyzerke: "You'll see, Elik: what a regime! . . . What a regime!"

Elik smiled through the hole that was left when his front tooth was knocked out: "Yes, indeed, it's already spattered with blood."

Since then Leyzerke has been avoiding Elik. From the distant darkness his voice is heard.

"Who's smoking there, out of doors?"

"It's me, Elik."

"Why are you sitting out here?"

"It's stifling in the barrack."

A pause.

It seems that Leyzerke is reluctant to leave, but hesitates to go over to Elik.

"You have to get used to it."

And he disappears into the village to check the sentries' positions. One might think that Leyzerke came over to the barrack for no particular reason. But a while later, a member of his heavily armed escort came running, and asked about Aba, a robust fellow from the local area—a strapping, ruddy-faced guy.

"Isn't there someone by that name among you?"

"There is, there is."

ABA, YEKHIEL-MOYSHE THE coachman's boy, the second Jew to join the squadron, was a lethargic fellow, like an unemployed worker. He had been among those who personally witnessed how Fritz raised his rifle to shoot Andriuk. But when he was asked if Leyzerke had given the order, the coachman shrugged his shoulders dully and lazily turned away.

"What does it matter to me?"

And at that time, it appeared that Aba would not want to pledge his loyalty without a good reason—that he actually joined the "great ones" only because he was promised that they would soon go to the big town in the valley, where his fiancée lived. And as soon as he got there, that would be the end of the whole business. So Aba slept soundly during the long nights, like a superfluous sleepyhead—a silent sign that he had come along partly for a purpose and partly out of idleness. He mooched around lazily the whole time, noticing that from the nearby plundered town of Granov young escapees kept on arriving, and were given guns, and that large, powerful gentile youths from Kislok were joining the squadron. The others told him:

"Around thirty of them, aren't there? And everyone with his own horse."

So he answered coldly:

"Who cares?"

It was as if a more enthusiastic answer would be enough to strengthen his bond with the "great ones." He felt like an outsider among them, but it seemed to him that the group was peculiarly warm and welcoming. Aba thought: "They give out bread, they do." And also meat, and when they cook, they offer him a portion, and actually, he's a stranger here—the fifth wheel on the wagon.

But on that predawn morning, Aba's lethargic body felt how it was roused too vigorously from sleep, and whoever was doing the rousing was too enthusiastic, and was an expert rouser.

They ordered him to get dressed, shouting:

"Faster! They are waiting for you outside."

Aba thought he was dreaming in the gray outdoor dawn. All night, frozen white pellets had been falling quietly, like light snow, and Leyzerke was standing there waiting, in his gray military greatcoat with the slit down to the soles of his feet, as the pellets fell, and asked Aba whom he knew in the surrounding villages. And he dispatched Aba to Zekharye the wheelwright's place in the large village of Lisht-shinovke and ordered him to scout out what Petliura's[55] retreating

---

55 Symon Vasylyovych Petliura (1879–1926) was a leader in Ukraine's fight for independence following the 1917 Russian Revolution. During the late autumn of 1918 and the winter of 1919, when the story takes place, Petliura's forces perpetrated murderous pogroms on Jewish inhabitants in many rural areas in Ukraine. Bolshevik fighters engaged them in combat and were thus viewed as protectors by many local Jews.

units were doing there. Officer Klimenko, who was Leyzerke's close friend, and Botshko himself were standing there with him. Both looked very sleepy, but it appeared as if they had decided on the whole thing yesterday, and they had only come out to have a look at Aba in his worn-out gray greatcoat. They told him to pull his peasant's cap down lower. They asked him:

"Ready?"

And while Aba pulled his red coachman's belt over his hips, Botshko gave an authoritative whistle, stepped forward, looked intently at Aba, straightened up, and gave an apparently fervent order:

"Right shoulder forward, march!"

Aba obeyed in silence; he was still a soldier under gentile command. He started walking, but still felt very sleepy. He didn't understand clearly why they were sending him to Zekharye the wheelwright in Lishtshinovke, and what he was supposed to do there. He strode through the fields, and the deeper the damp gray fog became, the more his mission faded from memory. He only knew that he must avoid all the villages—it was dangerous—and even if he took detours everywhere, it would still only be a mile or a mile-and-a-half to get to Lishtshinovke. And from there, it was only about four miles to the large town in the valley, where his fiancée was a servant in an inn. She was a bad-tempered person and he, Aba, would wager: "Just let anybody else try to make a pass at her." Now, as always, Aba made no decision about it. He just sensed that he had no desire to go back, and that, even now, in the midst of this deadly situation, it was wonderful to stride towards his bride as he was doing at that moment. He once came to her on just such an early gray morning and found her all alone behind the inn, bending over a basin that she had just emptied out. A pair of crows had settled down near her, and a pair of pigs came running, attracted by the smell of the upturned basin.

"Scram! she yelled at them angrily. Scram!"

She herself was barefoot, with an ample bosom. Her sleeves were rolled up, her legs bare, her sleepy face with its narrow eyes dull and dark, and smelling unwashed. Always quick to anger, she spoke very little but rapidly, so rapidly that an outsider could hardly understand her at all, and as she spoke, she blinked her eyes.

"Well, well, Abke!" she remarked abruptly. "What brings you here, ha? Abke?"

II

ABA STEPPED QUICKLY through unfamiliar fields. All around him uninhabited tracts of land seemed to flow together in a cascade, and there was no one, no one who might notice the red of his coachman's belt from a distance. The day—cloudy and dark, shrunken, was very much like a short Friday—a day that waits for a snowfall, and no snow falls. The tracts also seemed shrunken. As Aba approached the large village through the fields, something wintry and deathly glanced at him. A strange silence had descended upon the houses, gardens and lanes, as though someone had just died in the middle of the day, and the whole village was waiting and listening for church bells to begin tolling. They glanced at Aba even more silently in the wheelwright's half-gentile, half-Jewish little dwelling.

The wheelwright and his wife were both seated on a small sofa near the tepid stove, the soles of their shoes outspread, and it seemed as though it was a fast day in the house. No one was cooking breakfast. The window shades were lowered, although it was daytime. The children played off to one side, dejected and speaking in whispers, as though they had been admonished by parents who were observing the seven days of mourning after a death.

"Quiet! Quieter . . . Look how cheerful this one is."

And when they finally said something to him, Aba, it sounded indifferent and aggrieved.

"So where are you headed, ha? Aba . . . The devil is driving you to your bride in the middle of such a calamity?"

"Stay here, you ass! You'll leave your head on the road. They are murdering people everywhere around Yanovke and Granov." And their sad eyes looked not at Aba, but at the lowered window shades across from them.

"Listen to what happened to the molasses maker, will you?"

And his stubbornness made Aba unyielding.

"I'm going on. I don't give a damn about it!"

But it seemed that he knew the molasses maker. He lived in a house with a tin roof, a mile or so from the village. The day before, the molasses maker and his son-in-law had been found murdered behind the house, and Molly, his mute daughter, had suddenly begun to speak. She had run barefoot into the nearby woods with her infant in her arms. At night she rapped on the priest's door and said: "I want to convert to Christianity." But when he opened the door for her, she was no longer there. Peasants are saying that she knocks on their doors at night and says: "Open up, I am barefoot with my child in my arms." And when they open the door for her, she is no longer there. She disappears. She has lost her mind . . .

"And the murderers are free as birds. They are right here in the village."

From time to time someone in the wheelwright's house raised a window shade a tiny bit to watch the *petlurovtses*,[56] who were gathering on the square across the way.

"The scoundrels—they keep coming."

"Just look at how many there are!"

So Aba also looked in that direction, but all he saw was caps, long mittens and broadly cut pantaloons of red and green silk that might be used for theater costumes.

"Damn them!" he cursed, "what a calamity!"

In the middle of the village, next to the school, a hungry white goat, an elderly one, was tethered. Petliura's retreating divisions had brought her there from the decimated town of Granov. She blinked

---

56 Forces loyal to Symon Petliura.

her sad, stranger's eyes at the unfamiliar village. Inside the building, in the classrooms, a headquarters had been established during the night, and the "general staff" was getting drunk. Every little while, bits of shattered windowpanes were thrown outdoors by members of the elite, private party, a party which lasted a day and a night, as if there were girls and dancing. And all around it was unnaturally dark; indifferent houses, covered with light frost; innumerable roofs, like mute blemishes in the stillness; and a pensive cross in a far corner of the village waited for a snowfall, and still no snow fell. Outdoors it got darker and darker—night came on.

At the wheelwright's house, an oily nightlight flickered. In the darkened room faces became pallid, as if during a fast, and they were still discussing the molasses maker's daughter Molly, who lingered by a little fire in the woods, barefoot, with her child in her arms, and if anyone came near her she would run away.

"She's lost her mind, ha? Lost her mind . . ."

"And apparently she took bread along with her . . . she did, she did."

Aba sat across from them with an open, salivating mouth, and his eyes narrowed. He looked and looked at them, and finally dozed off, apparently from listening for such a long time, and from muted melancholy. And the moment he dozed off, unfamiliar footsteps were heard approaching the house—hard footfalls in sturdy masculine boots. Several voices started talking at the same time; a sturdy shoulder tried to push in the door, and suddenly someone started banging hard, first on one window, then on the other. Aba trembled, opened his eyes, and was unable to recognize any of the people around him. In the little house a pair of hands were being wrung—the wife's hands. The hands spoke in a human voice:

"Oy, it's terrible, it's terrible! . . ."

Someone's eyes rolled upwards with great bewilderment, as though below them someone was slitting his throat with a knife. And in the same instant, Aba's whole body sensed that it could no longer remain in the house. It was too confining for him, as if he were in a cage that was about to be closed forever. If there were only one or two of them outside, he would attack them with his bare hands, but he heard the voices of seven or eight men out there.

"Damn them!"

III

MOVING NIMBLY AND silently to one side, Aba entered the dark back room of the house. He felt around for the ladder, located it in a dark corner and climbed up into the attic. There he stood stooped over for a while and listened: the intruders were already in the house; they spoke loudly, very loudly; their voices exploded in anger. His body stubbornly moved further away. Through the sizable opening in the chimney, he scrutinized the roof of the adjacent stable and moved over to it. There, in the soft hay that filled the ventilated hayloft, it was much warmer, darker and quieter. The only sound from below him came from the wheelwright's two horses. They stopped chewing for a while, as though what was happening in the attic reminded them of the retreating Germans, from whom the wheelwright had bought them for a pittance. And in the stable not even the tiniest rustle was heard. Aba craned his neck and listened for sounds from the stable's exit for a long time, until it began to feel strained. Weary and drowsy, he rested his head in his hands, and just as he dropped off to sleep, many tiny bits of fear began to approach him. His body lay among them as if it were naked. He awakened late at night. Around him there was a dreamlike murmur, as if enclosed in barbed wire; a rifle suddenly fired off a round, paused and fired again, but when he listened, it was entirely quiet around the stable. To the left of the stable, where the wheelwright's house was, someone banged the door hard, and a female voice suddenly burst out in wild hysterics, as though the woman was unwillingly following someone who was violently dragging her outside. For a while the voice seemed to hold itself in check, to immerse itself in acute terror in the deadly night air, but it soon broke off, suddenly ending with a strangely quiet, womanly sigh.

"Oy, woe is me, woe!"

And once again there was silent, deathly numbness in the infinite void of the surrounding night.

Again, Aba woke up in great terror, this time in gray daylight. It seemed to him that Zekharye the wheelwright was groaning and begging for a drink of water. But when he looked around, he found no one, and he, Aba, was himself very thirsty. He climbed quietly down and went outside. Now, in the gray, drowsy dawn, with the first crowing of the cocks, was the best time to make his escape. He walked quickly downhill to the misty, waterlogged pathway at the end of the wheelwright's long garden, but he suddenly noticed several of Petliura's cavalrymen trotting their horses across from the little bridge. They were riding in a bunch, like a group of spies returning to the village after a night of reconnaissance. Aba suddenly bent over double and moved to one side. Still stooped over, he vaulted a fence into a non-Jew's garden. He didn't know whether the cavalrymen had seen him or not. He lay there a while listening. They were still talking loudly at the beginning of the low-lying path next to the little bridge. Curses resounded there, like dull metal, and it was too late to escape: they were starting to cause a stir around the houses. A wagon was moving loudly somewhere, as though over paving stones, and far away, at the far end of the village, church bells starting tolling as if it were Sunday. It was already full daylight. The rising sun barely gave off warmth and was hurrying to the brightness of midday. And the outdoors was letting go of its frost.

ABA LAY IN a non-Jew's garden in a pit that had once been a cellar; disoriented, he sat on a pile of last year's garbage and listened; in the village, he heard the clip-clopping sound of more and more horses' hooves—Petliura's cavalrymen were arriving.

One side of the pit was covered with crooked branches, with thin twigs, and through them the sky was visible, as if through *skhakh*.[57] It was a clear, early winter sky, turned newly blue and transparent, which draws one to the fresh outdoors, but the day itself was a reminder of everything that had happened the night before, and was sick, strangely sick, like him, Aba, sitting there in the pit without a cap on. He didn't know where he had lost it: by the fence, or in the wheelwright's hayloft. And he thought ceaselessly about the wheelwright's two horses, who stood abandoned in the stable. At night, when darkness fell, he could catch one of these horses and quietly ride back to Kislok, to the "great ones." But only if the dog that was chained up in the peasant's yard stopped barking, and if no one caught him in the pit where he would be hiding all day.

IV

DURING THE DAY two of the marauders walked drunkenly by, very close to the fence, not far from the pit where he lay. Coughing victoriously, they greeted a village girl in a courtyard, stopped to welcome a new arrival to their band, cursed each other to the heavens and disappeared. By then it was getting close to sundown. Church bells started tolling in the village and then went silent. Just then some Christian girls, apparently playing, trudged among the frozen grasses near the pit; they tramped all around, but didn't approach it. They chattered to each other so peacefully and childishly, and it still seemed to Aba that they were distant, distant—they, the playing girls and he, Aba, lying in the pit—they, the playing girls, and the wheelwright's abandoned house, which stood nearby, off to one side. At dusk a moth-

---

57 The term *skhakh* refers to the branches used to cover a *suke*, or booth, in which Jews dwell during the weeklong holiday of Sukes, the Feast of Tabernacles. A *suke* is intended to offer only temporary shelter. Bergelson's reference to *skhakh* underlines Aba's precarious situation, even as he benefits from the protection of the branches covering the pit.

er's voice was heard shouting to them from a distance, from the house at the top of the garden on the hillock. The voice called them now, as always, calmly, to a home-cooked meal of potatoes. The children walked calmly towards the house. But suddenly a noisy commotion was heard in the middle of the village. The commotion got louder and louder; it flooded the streets and then concentrated itself again in one distant spot. Hundreds of voices strengthened it there. They were quarreling over something, rasping like dogs. Somebody was getting beaten there, somebody was screaming. Aba felt as if barbed wire was receding from around his naked body and dispersing. The danger that had lain in wait for him here for an entire day was now transferred to someone else, a stranger, there in the very center of the great commotion. He stared into the dark emptiness around him, and slowly began to climb out of the pit.

IN THE LIGHT frost, there was the smell of cold apple peelings and a new sheepskin. In the middle of the village, steam from fatty marrow bones and tallow rose from the two iron stoves at the headquarters of the "general staff." And there were many, many marauders in the village.

Masses of them were standing in the square, choking on their own odor—an odor of stale iodine and sweat. They were jostling one another to get close to the music coming from a large harmonica, around which couples were dancing. At dusk, somewhere horses were kicking in resistance to being hurried towards a low corner of the sky, which was burning like the fires of hell. Somewhere the land was being trashed with the shells of sunflower seeds and the cores of cabbages. And loud, rude laughter arose whenever a peasant girl tried to leave the entryway of her father's house. And suddenly shouting voices were heard:

"Chase him, chase him!"

"Don't let him through!"

In a scattered tangle, the first pairs of feet hurried towards a stranger's wagon, which had appeared in the middle of the road in the far corner of the village.

"Halt, halt!"

And everyone else followed them. They poured out of the houses and yards. Booted knees vaulted deftly over fences and made their way over to the stranger's detained wagon.

"Don't let him through!"

"Unharness his horses!"

"He wanted to escape!"

The crowd around the wagon grew larger, as if swollen with rainwater, encircling and constricting it; they cursed the occupants furiously, pushing with their fists and struggling to get to the two men deep inside the crowd. They were already quite hoarse and exhausted from defending themselves in half-choked, grating voices, with arguments and more arguments. Someone kept on demanding and demanding, talking them blue in the face in an unending stream of words.

It got late: the moon rose. Then, from the center of the crowd, someone led out a pair of tired, unharnessed horses. They were taken to the village, as if after a peaceful court verdict, and the tightly packed rows of men dispersed and scattered. Rather than walking away, they moved furtively, vanishing in a blur, like a subsided swelling. Everyone in the village was already asleep, but Aba stood hatless, all by himself, in his tattered gray greatcoat. He stood stiffly, leaning into the pensive cross at the entrance to the village, watching with nocturnal eyes.

Across from him, on the spot where the fight took place, only a sizable empty wagon remained, wretched, unharnessed, with its shafts sticking out and its reins spread over the ground. And two battered creatures were tinkering with it: one of these characters was tall and wore a short jacket and boots. He was lively, like a young, well-trained soldier who obeys orders and says little. He kept cupping his palm over his nose and looking up to the moon to see if it was still bleeding. The other was of medium build and wore a black greatcoat. He kept on fiddling shortsightedly with the straw in the wagon and tapping its boards as one taps a container with a false bottom:

"It's here!" he said, "it's all here!"

The visor of his student's cap was pushed to one side. His distracted, half-Tatar face looked as if he had not had time to shave in weeks, and there was little room for his shining black pupils in his small, narrow eyes. They seemed to say:

"There isn't time . . . there isn't time . . ."

"How are you?" he kept asking the tall one. "Does it hurt? Ha? Does it hurt?"

Aba stole slowly closer and closer to them, but completely without fear. Both of them had been chased and beaten, just like himself, Aba. His body gravitated towards them, perceiving no danger. He stood close to them, his arms folded, watching with nocturnal eyes. And suddenly his glance met that of the tall one in the short coat and boots who was facing the wagon; his eyes met the other's dully, fearlessly. Aba moved quietly back to the cross, but the other guy kept slowly coming nearer, with his forehead down, as if to butt him, and with his very large, strangely unfamiliar eyes, stared a while at Aba's face. A pause. A voice put a question to Aba very quietly, as if entreating him to disclose his secret:

"You seem to be a Jew. Ha? . . ."

Quiet.

"You seem to be a Jew. Ha? . . ."

V

FEELING NO FEAR, Aba swallowed. It seemed to him that he was imitating the tall man's quiet voice precisely. He spoke with a twang:

"Well, yes."

He waited a moment, and added:

"What's the story, then, ah?"

The very large eyes noticed that he was hatless.

"How did you happen to get here?"

Aba said this. But now both strangers were standing next to him.

They murmured to each other, glanced at Aba and murmured some more:

"And is it far to get to the 'great ones'?"

"What's the story, then? . . ."

"We need to get there."

"I'd say it's about fifteen versts."[58]

"No further?"

"Listen, man, I've come from them."

Once again they made a silent inspection of Aba, followed by quiet murmuring and further inspection.

"Can we get a pair of horses?"

"It's better to go on foot."

"No, we must have them."

"What for?" Aba moved sideways towards the wagon, appraising it with a coachman's knowing eye. "Are you transporting cargo?"

"We are."

"So here's the thing." Aba started scratching himself. He looked around.

"There is a pair of horses in the wheelwright's stable . . . They murdered the wheelwright here just last night . . ."

Aba continued: "So what's the plan? Before we get the horses, we have to drag the wagon around the whole village to the little bridge near the low-lying path, and I am afraid . . . and I'm hungry . . . isn't there anything to chew on?"

They gave Aba bread and took a look at the bridge. The young man in the short jacket and boots started off, and then together they pulled the wagon towards it, the young man and the chewing Aba in the harness, while the distracted one in the student's cap pushed from behind. In the moonlight, Aba led the horses out of the stable and harnessed them, and the man in the student's cap kept urging him to go faster.

"So maybe they're expecting you?" Aba asked.

"And if so?"

---

58 A verst is slightly more than a kilometer.

"I heard it said that we are waiting in Kislok for a communiqué and for money."

And the strangers exchanged glances.

"Is there someone called Popov with you?"

"There is: he's a military commissar—a Jew, they say."

"And is Botshko there?"

"That's it then, ah?"

"Move it, it's right, it's right."

All three of them threw themselves into the wagon and they left the village by a sandy road that led up a high hill. Now the two strangers called each other by name: the one in the black greatcoat was called Petruk. The other one was called Zalkind. After climbing the hill, they avoided the main highway and traveled by a narrow side road, which petered out in the wide tracts of land, as if on a steppe. There the horses started to stumble, and both strangers hunched over and became silent. Aba sat hatless in the wagon, his feet tucked under him, like the driver he was, and drove ahead lazily. He kept thinking of the village receding behind him, and Zekharye the wheelwright's little half-gentile, half-Jewish house, which stood there facing the school:

"I should have at least gone over to Zekharye the wheelwright's, at least to have a look . . ."

He regretted what had happened to Zekharye the wheelwright, the way you regret the fate of a tight-lipped Jew, an old guy like that, who never said a soft word, but you knew, of course, that he was loyal, and you could count on him. And he also felt a quiet, nocturnal sorrow about the molasses maker in the tin-roofed house outside the village. He kept glancing over at the small forest as they approached it. High above, the moon was shining more brightly than before. Below, among the trees, it seemed to him that there was something very red and lively over there, like a tremulous little fire, but a cold one, like frost that became invigorated late at night; like the cold light that poured down from above, from the moon. The closer one came to it, the further away the little fire moved. It shifted away and fled into the forest. Aba gazed at it for such a long time that he nearly fell asleep. They were already very close to the forest. And suddenly, Aba swayed in his seat, and with an anxious shudder, dully opened his eyes wide. His other senses were still deeply asleep, but his eyes remained open and what they saw was like in a dream. At the entrance to the woods, in an empty area where the trees had been chopped down, among stumps that were withering beneath the moon, a shadow moved from one spot to the next, and a figure in a skirt, strangely light and float-ing, ran off barefoot with a child in its arms, floated out from among the trees on one side, and immediately disappeared among the trees on the opposite side.

"Whoa!" Aba suddenly stopped the wagon and jumped down.

"What?" Came the frightened question from the startled strang-ers. "What happened?"

But it was strangely quiet all around. Moonlight poured down from above onto the wood, and in its gray depths there was not a rustle, no fire, and no movement. Just then Aba looked around, as if waking up:

"No, nothing . . ." he replied.

And walking back from the front end of the wagon, Aba pretended that part of the harness had torn, and he was repairing it with great effort, tying many knots so that it would not tear again.

THE NEXT MORNING:

A piece of red material flies high above the little headquarters of the "general staff" in the middle of the village of Kislok. It has been fluttering since very early in the morning, like a freshly made *kimpet-fon*,[59] floating very charmingly on the crackling little waves of air. It is creased in many places, and in every crease there is joy:

"An end to staying in one place."

A breeze blows from the river, and the mouth of the breeze, full

---

59 The curtain or tapestry that traditionally surrounds the bed of a lying-in mother and her newborn infant. Amulets are hung from the curtain to protect the baby from evil spirits.

of humidity, smells of a putrefying Christian cemetery. Again it's dark outside; the weather is very dirty and damp. Boots are slogging through the village, and in addition to that, in a low-lying side lane, shoulders are bent to the ground and an experienced hand, smeared with fat, scours and scrubs. Troops are readying the cannons for battle once again. And across the way, in a large, muddy yard, near little houses that serve as barracks, they are currying "government" horses with new enthusiasm. And new arrivals (from Kislok and nearby villages) are listening: the troops are joking about the "general staff" as one would about a boss who has suddenly become rich and can pay their wages.

"Today the communiqué arrived, and cash, cash."

"Two of them came."

And Aba, the guy with the red belt, brought them.

Aba wandered sleepily around the muddy yard, still caught up in a short dream from earlier. He stood there like a stranger, like a bystander, facing the street with a very sleepy face, spitting sourly and angrily, as after a binge of drunkenness. In a far corner, there is a herd of "government" horses. They stand there with narrowed, dozing eyes and yawn in the rain. And Aba has a close connection with three of them. One—the Jewish smith's—is small and dirty. And two are the wheelwright's: large, with very short, disheveled, painful tails, shorn necks rubbed raw by the harness, and lean, pleasant-smelling hindquarters. Aba looked at them with sadness, as if they were orphans, remembering the calamity of the past couple of days.

"Stand still, you!"

Speaking gruffly, with a nasal twang, he bent down to examine one of the horses. He freed the horse's foot, which was tangled in a rope, and it didn't kick him in the abdomen, as a horse should deserve in such a case.

"Aba!" someone called from behind him. "Go!"

"You're being called to 'headquarters.'"

Aba set out lazily, like a coachman who brought off a rescue from a disaster the previous night and was now about to hear what his bosses had to say about it. But at "headquarters," everyone had been together since dawn, gathered around Petruk and the second guy, who wore an unusually gray expression, and who, when he looked at someone, seemed to confront his eyes the way one would confront an animal with horns. Klimenko, the officer who wore a greatcoat over his undershirt, stretched himself out with a smile on his lips, as if he had just heard the end of a long story, and Leyzerke and Botshko also took their ease:

"The first pay packet," they said, "goes to Aba."

"Aba deserves it."

"Well done, Aba!" And they praised him, praised him robustly.

Aba still felt like a stranger, an outsider. He stood among them, vague and awkward, as he had at his *ufruf*,[60] when wagon drivers had raised a toast to him. They gave him money and apples. He looked at the money in one hand and the apples in the other, and remembered his bride, who worked at the inn in the big town in the valley:

"Well, and what's taking so long about getting to town?" he suddenly asked gruffly. "When will we ever get to town?"

---

60 An *ufruf* is the call to a bridegroom to read from the Torah in the synagogue on the Sabbath preceding his wedding. The ceremony is followed by a celebration.

Israel Joshua Singer
1893–1944

ALTHOUGH ISRAEL JOSHUA Singer died at the young age of fifty-one, he retains his place as one of the major Yiddish novelists of the twentieth century and, along with his younger brother Isaac Bashevis Singer, one of the most important literary contributors to the *Forward*.

Born in the Polish town of Bilgoraj, near Lublin, Singer grew up in Leoncin, where he received a traditional religious education. When he was fourteen years old, the family moved to Warsaw, where Singer attended the yeshiva of the Ger Hasidic sect and worked as an unskilled laborer. At yeshiva Singer took an interest in Hebrew and Yiddish literature, and in 1918 he moved to Kiev, where he began publishing his first stories and novellas.

In 1921, Singer returned to Warsaw and published "Pearls," a story that attracted the attention of *Forward* editor Abraham Cahan, who reprinted the piece in the newspaper and invited Singer to become a regular contributor. Years later Singer wrote of Cahan that he was "the first person who gave me any recognition or reward."

Singer continued to write for the *Forward*, although his early articles were mostly journalistic reports written under the pseudonym G. Kuper. In 1924 he wrote a series of articles about Jewish life in Galicia, followed in 1926 with a series about the Soviet Union. Singer was also active in Warsaw's Yiddish literary community and helped found the city's main literary organ, *Literarishe bleter* (*Literary Pages*).

Singer began writing fiction again in 1931, after meeting with

Cahan in Berlin, and that year he began serializing his novel *Yoshe Kalb*. In 1933, Singer immigrated to the United States, where he continued to write novels in serialization for the *Forward*, along with stories, novellas, and journalistic pieces.

"Bakhmatsh Station," which appeared in the newspaper from October 14 to 20, 1943, is among the last things Singer wrote for the *Forward* before his death in February 1944. The story takes place in the middle of the Ukrainian War of Independence, which pitted a range of forces against one another, primary among them Bolsheviks, Ukrainian nationalists, White Russians, Germany, Austria-Hungary, and Poland. The period was also marked by infamous pogroms against Jews.

In his depiction of the war Singer conveys not only the chaos of the period, but also the promise the new Soviet state held out to its Jewish citizens. Although that promise was ultimately betrayed, "Bakhmatsh Station" illustrates why the Soviet experiment offered such hope in the first place.

Bakhmatsch Station

(OCTOBER 14–20, 1943)

Translated by Anita Norich

THE FORMER BANK, built to resemble a temple, was full of men, women, children, boxes, bags, papers strewn about and typewriters. In front, near the one remaining picture of the bank's founder— a magnate with sideburns and medals—hung badly printed pictures of bushy-haired Karl Marx, bald Lenin and pointy-bearded Trotsky. Over them hung a red flag with white letters declaring that the Soviets were in charge of everything.

The carved marble walls and columns were covered with a seemingly endless number of announcements and decrees, printed or written on poor-quality paper. Among the official decrees there were many private requests from people who had lost their loved ones and were asking for news of them or of their lost possessions or even for a place to sleep.

At the barred cashiers' windows, where people used to withdraw money, sat badly dressed clerks and unshaven, unkempt young men or short-haired young women. The rows of people in front of the windows were long, weaving, full of men and women evacuated from Kiev, the city by the Dnieper that had been occupied by the Polish military. They were abandoned, sleep-deprived, weary, broken, lost people in a strange place, and they besieged the officials' windows, asking for bread, clothing, a corner in which to lay their heads. Others were searching for their things, which they had lost while fleeing, or their relatives, from whom they had been separated in the chaos of leaving their homes. Men were looking for their wives, women for husbands, parents for children. The clerks, unsure of what to do with these people, sent them from one department to another, demanding documents or asking them to come later, tomorrow, next week. Any time except now. There was one woman, small and thin as a child but with a grown-up, pale face that seemed to consist only of eyes—unbelievably large, sad, half-crazed eyes—who would not stop going from window to window, from one person to another asking everyone about her husband. She had met him just one day before the enemy's assault and, the next day, lost him while fleeing the city.

"What's his last name?" people asked her. "Where is he from? What does he do?"

"I didn't ask him, dear people," she answered. "I only know that his name is Seryozshe, that he's a dear man, and that he has blond hair and blue eyes."

Despite how overwhelmed they were, the people in the bank couldn't stop laughing over these identifiers in that land full of blond, blue-eyed people.

"How is it possible not to know the last name of your own husband?" women asked her mockingly.

"His name is Seryozshe, and he's a dear man, my angel," the madwoman kept answering. She continued to go from person to person, even though everyone laughed at her. She wouldn't let go of a dirty dog, a sickly thing that she held in her arms and petted, murmuring soothing words, like a mother comforting her firstborn. "Don't worry, my darling. We'll find our beloved Seryozshe," she said to the dog who lay there, a dumb, sad animal. It seemed as though the dog knew that it wouldn't last long in the world.

I was one of those who sought their lost families. The attack on the Ukrainian main city, where I had been living, came as suddenly as a thunderbolt. Just a few days earlier, the commander of the city garrison had assured us that, just as a pig can't see its own tail, so the enemy would be unable to see the main revolutionary Ukrainian Red city. Workers even covered the streets and buildings with red in honor of the approaching May 1 celebrations. Suddenly, just a day or two before May 1, the Red Army retreated and the city was quickly evacuated.

I was sick of pogroms and insults from the soldiers in Petliura's[61] and Denikin's[62] armies and all the other warring factions that robbed and murdered the Children of Israel whenever they entered or left that "Holy City." I didn't want to suffer through the arrival of yet another army, so I took my family and fled wherever my legs might carry me.

At the train stations, men fought with fists for a place in a freight car. Women tore out each other's hair or fainted. Children whined. People flung themselves onto the trains through doors and windows. I don't even know how it happened, but my family was packed into one of the cars. When I wanted to follow them,

---

61 Symon Vasylyovych Petliura (1879–1926) was a leader in Ukraine's fight for independence following the 1917 Russian Revolution.
62 Anton Ivanovich Denikin (1872–1947) was a general in the White Army during the Russian Civil War (1917–1922), fighting against the Communist Reds.

a soldier stopped me with the shiny tip of his bayonet, which he pointed at my emaciated chest.

"Not another step. I'll stab you!" he said.

Looking at his hardened face and expressionless eyes, I could see that he meant it. The train left. In all the tumult I didn't even catch a glimpse of my disappearing family. All that remained for me and the thousands of others left behind was the sound of the clanging wheels and the sight of steam.

It was as chaotic near the boats at the shore of the Dnieper as it had been at the train station. On one white boat, the captain had planted himself at the helm and, using a megaphone, begged everyone to have mercy and stop trying to board.

"Comrades, the boat can't hold anyone else," he warned. "It will sink."

No one listened to him and, like great waves, they pushed themselves onto the boat.

I went along with the wave and boarded. The sailors were running around like madmen, using their fists to force the crowd away from the sides of the boat and into the middle. "Get away, you devils. You'll weigh down one side and capsize the boat!" they yelled.

The steamboat moved slowly, panting and whistling continuously. On the green shore of the *shtetl*[63] Kanev, from which a white memorial in honor of the Ukrainian poet Shevchenko peered at us from the hill on which it stood, bullets rained down, shot by soldiers hidden among the cliffs.

"Sailors, full steam ahead!" the captain yelled.

We left the lovely but dangerous banks of the Dnieper, passing by Cherkasy, Kremenchuk, and all sorts of other cities and towns. After a trip full of stops and starts, we came to Ekaterinoslav, the town that Prince Potemkin had built for his queen and lover, Catherine the Great.

I wandered around like a lost soul in that pretty southern town on the Dnieper, spending the nights in Potemkin's Park and the

---

63 Small town.

days in all sorts of offices with really wild names. I stood in long lines and tried to find out where the train with my family had gone. No one knew. There was not a single thing in the country that a civilized human being could use: no telegraph, no mail, no telephone, no train. The military had taken over everything. The entire town was overrun by hordes of Budyonny's Cossacks,[64] who were trying to rid the Ukrainian capital city of the enemy. Riding on small Siberian horses, they were traveling in endless rows, sunburned, dusty, curious and wild, unshaven, with forelocks and one sidelock. Even though the sun was blazing, they wore fur hats and coats. They carried rifles and spears, daggers, and silver swords and knives. Accompanying the men were their equally sunburned, dusty, curious and combative wives. Loudly, they all sang their long, savage songs about the Ural River, about fighting and carousing.

> Past the Urals, past the river
> Cossacks marched.
> Hey, hey, fight on.
> Cossacks marched.

The new, inexperienced city officials, overwhelmed by the chaos caused by new laws and orders that changed daily, didn't know what to do with the flood of people and baggage streaming from the neighboring evacuated towns.

"We don't know. Come later. Leave us alone." Those were the answers they gave from behind their barred windows.

I spent days running from office to office and finally found my way to a senior official. After the first few words of my request, he cut me off with just one Russian word: *zamkompoevakyug*. I wanted to ask him what that incomprehensible word meant, but a Red Army guard told me to leave because others were waiting.

---

64 Semyon Budyonny (1883–1973) was a Soviet military leader. Isaac Babel's *Red Cavalry* stories are loosely based on his experiences with Budyonny's troops.

With great difficulty, I finally learned that the word was the abbreviated title of the commission's delegate charged with overseeing the evacuation from the southern battlefront. I needed to direct my request to him.

After days of waiting, I finally got to him, that "*zamkompoevakyug.*" He was just a young man with girlish red cheeks lightly covered with light, downy hair. He sat with his hat on his head, surrounded by clouds of tobacco smoke.

"What was the number of the train your family was traveling on?" he asked.

"I don't know," I answered.

"Well, then, Comrade, how should I know?" he replied, releasing a full mouth of smoke and laughter. "Go look for a needle in a haystack."

I did what he asked and, despite reason and common sense, I went to look for a needle in a haystack, ignoring all rules and orders. I followed the chaos of revolution and civil war. I hitched rides on the roofs of trains, hung off their buffers, hid away in train cars full of coal. Once, a young officer who was conveying horses for the army took me in and let me ride among his horses for a while. In return, I taught him some German words that he was eager to learn but that his Russian tongue could not begin to pronounce. Another time, my train stopped in the middle of a field near Sinelnikov station. I don't exactly remember if this was near the first or second Sinelnikov station, but I do remember that there was a blackout and we spent an entire night in that darkened field. We weren't even allowed to light a cigarette. All sorts of awful noises echoed in the field. People said that the rails had been sabotaged and that lawless bands from the village of Gulyai-Polye were going to descend on us and that Marusye, the band's leader who was called "Marusye, the Vagabond,"[65] was coming with others on horseback.

I spent several weeks wandering through Ukraine, never spending

---

65 Marusye was the *nom de guerre* of Maria Grigorevna Nikoforova, an anarchist partisan leader.

a day where I had spent the night. In Kharkov, I stumbled upon people who had traveled with the train from Kiev. They told me I could probably find my family in the town of Sumy, but I didn't find them there and so I went off to Poltava, where I was told they might be. And there I was advised to look in other places. I finally found my family near Poltava, in a small town with the long name of Stantinograd.

The town was quiet, and its abandoned earth was covered with straw and dung left by horses and oxen. Sluggish peasants dragged themselves along on their ox-drawn wagons, smoking their pipes and prodding their lethargic animals with equally lethargic commands. The Russian signs on the shops were smeared and badly painted over with Ukrainian words so that the peasants could read them. But the peasants couldn't get anything in those shops—no oil or salt or tobacco or even axle grease. The shops were locked, and hanging from their rusty locks were signs that said all private businesses had been confiscated by the Soviet powers and were closed until further notice. The peasants' dull eyes stared at the pictures of pointy-bearded Trotsky, the anti-Christ under whose regime there was neither God nor commerce.

Only at the stalls in the large, circular marketplace could any kind of trade be found. No one would take paper money, but for a patched shirt you could buy a sack of potatoes, for a pair of worn pants, a *pood*[66] of cornmeal; for a needle you could get a dozen pumpkins. I had never in my whole life seen such large, tasty pumpkins as they had in that town.

I had absolutely nothing to do in that miserable place, but we had nowhere else to go and no way to leave. I took all but the clothes on my back, carried it off to the market and traded it for potatoes and pumpkins. We had small portions of bread that my wife received for her work in the military hospital set up in the town. We lived in one room of a house that belonged to someone who had deserted from the Revolutionary Army. We had no idea what this man who had to save himself from the Soviets was: a police chief? a priest? But whatever

---

66 About thirty-six pounds.

else he was, he was definitely a religious, true-believing Christian. Icons of all sizes hung in every single room of his large house. Small, medium, large, huge, they hung in old heavy black frames, in carved cabinets, even in the entryway. My neighbor, a thin, blond Ukrainian, took down a different holy picture every day, broke it into pieces and used it to cook his scanty meals. When his pots were done, he let me put a few potatoes on the holy fire. But mostly I made do with pumpkins.

The days were long and there was sunlight until midnight. The sun set so late because, in order to conserve oil and light, the Soviet powers had set the clocks four hours ahead. The sun rose equally late in those summer months, never before eight o'clock. People got up with the first sight of dawn and the long, hot days stretched out until nightfall. No newspapers reached the town and I had no idea what was going on in the wider world beyond this godforsaken place. Only the military funerals broke the monotony. Day after day, like clockwork, one soldier after another was carried out of the hospital. They had succumbed to their wounds or to typhus. The hospital chief, a Christianized Jew with a calf-like face and a Russian name— Kozyulin—had the soldiers accompany the dead with great fanfare, complete with a wagon draped in a red flag, several soldiers in full military gear and even three medics playing trumpets. My neighbor, a military commissar, made the same speech over the fresh grave of every soldier: the fallen one had sacrificed his life for the revolution and he assured the corpse that the world proletariat would inscribe him among its heroes. Other than these funerals, absolutely nothing happened in this desolate town.

Out of great boredom, I decided to try to write something. But I had neither pen and ink nor paper, and you couldn't buy them because these things weren't even available at the market. I went off to an official who had taken over the confiscated shops to ask if I could have some writing materials. An elderly Ukrainian, wearing wide trousers and enormous whiskers that made him look like a Cossack out of one of Gogol's stories, told me to write a request and to write it in the language of the land. I couldn't write a single word of

Ukrainian, but I tried to follow his request, thinking what Jews had always thought in such situations: write bad Russian and it will look like good Ukrainian.

"Give me ink and a pen and I'll write a request," I said in a Russian mixed with Polish words in order to please the staunch Ukrainian.

"In order to get writing materials to write a request, you must write a request," Gogol's hero answered with great solemnity.

"But how can I write a request without writing materials?"

"So don't write one," Gogol's Cossack advised.

"But I really do need writing materials."

"So write a request!"

It was an enchanted circle from which there was no escape.

My neighbor, the commissar, got a small piece of a pencil for me along with some court records written by a czarist official in elaborate calligraphy. These were old, yellowed court records about a murderer named Mikolyuk, who killed an entire village family because he had wanted to marry a peasant girl whose family wouldn't agree. This romantic murderer Mikolyuk was constantly before my eyes and disturbed my writing. I pictured him, his beloved, and her parents, brothers and sisters who would not permit the match. I saw them so clearly before me—their appearance and clothing and entire being— as though I knew them well. I also heard their voices, their discussions and arguments with the young Mikolyuk whom they did not want in their family. These people from this dreadful town crept into my bones even though they had been dead for decades, as Mikolyuk most likely was too. They made it impossible for me to collect my thoughts and write the story that I had set out to write. I just kept on erasing and crossing out my closely written Yiddish words that were crowded in between the lines of the calligraphic Russian transcript.

I probably would have remained the entire summer and maybe even the winter too in that awful town where pumpkins were cheap, but the revolution caught up with me even there.

One morning I heard loud, constant shooting from somewhere in town. My neighbor, the commissar, left his pots boiling on the icon fire in order to sound the alarm for the few soldiers still in town.

Although no one had seen who was shooting, we knew that it had to be Batko Makhno's gang.[67] They were all over southern Ukraine and they popped up where they were least expected. Even the hospital orderlies and the three trumpeters were taken from their jobs and given weapons with which to fight the enemy. The tall, blond commissar was in the lead, the rifle on his limber back looking like a part of his body. He was one large weapon. When, after a hard day of fighting, he had been unable to defeat the attackers, he dispatched a horseman to a neighboring garrison for reinforcements from the regiment of international soldiers stationed there.

The foreign fighters—Hungarian Hussars, Germans, Latvians, Chinese, and even some Galician Jewish boys, prisoners from Kaiser Franz-Josef's Austrian army—marched confidently through the town to fight the enemy of the revolution. But they returned dejectedly. They had fallen into a trap, with enemies on all sides. The victors had not even shot them, but had used their swords to hack them up like cabbage. The next day, scores of ox carts driven by peasant women brought the slashed men from the battlefield.

Later my neighbor the commissar returned from the field where he had managed to push back the attackers. His long body was even thinner than usual, bowed down, dark. This time, his speech over the common grave of the slaughtered foreigners burned as brightly as the flame he would make out of the icons. Afterwards, he spent hours in front of the house, oiling and polishing his rifle.

"It needs a good cleaning," he muttered. "With my own hands I stood thirty of them against the wall and sent them off to General Dukhonin's[68] headquarters. (The staff at General Dukhonin's headquarters had long since been sent to the Next World.)

---

67 Nestor Ivanovych Makhno (1888–1934) was an anarchist called Batko (Father) Makhno. He commanded the Revolutionary Insurrectionary Army of Ukraine, which fought various factions in order to maintain control of southern Ukraine.

68 Nikolay Dukhonin (1876–1917) was the last commander-in-chief of the Russian Imperial Army. Revolutionary soldiers dragged him from a train and killed him after he was relieved of his duties.

Later the thin commissar chopped up the icons with even greater vehemence. But he didn't manage to cook his meals with the holy pictures of God's son and his mother for long. From the Isthmus of Perekop, connecting the Crimean Peninsula to the Ukrainian mainland, Baron Vrangel's White Russian Army marched through the fertile Ukrainian land.[69] Even though they were still quite a distance away, we anticipated their arrival in Poltava at any moment. I knew that I had every chance of finding a place among the common graves of the foreign soldiers slaughtered on land that was not theirs. I abandoned the court proceedings concerning the murderer Mikolyuk, into which I had squeezed my Yiddish letters, and fled from that southern town so blessed with pumpkins.

My family had to travel with the military hospital that was being evacuated to a safer place, but I was not allowed to go with them. It was impossible to smuggle myself anywhere. All the trains were full of soldiers and evacuated officials. The entire area was at war. All the offices were in the hands of the military. I went to the office that controlled train travel and asked for permission to leave. An ashen-faced man with deep, sharp, dark creases in his stern face sat in a smoke-filled room, full of flies buzzing around the kerosene lamps and the inkwell that sat on a long, coarse table. The man was wearing a pair of soldier's pants and an undershirt, but his overgrown feet were bare. His boots stood near him, as stiff as if they still had legs holding them up. On the table lay slices of bread and a revolver, just as hard and black as the barefoot man, who looked as if he had spent many years as a coal miner or ironworker.

"What do you want?" he asked, addressing me in the familiar.

"I'd like to see the Commander," I said.

"That's me. What do you need?" he answered with a harsh, slow, unnatural voice.

---

69 Baron Pyotr Vrangel (1878–1928) had been in the Russian Imperial Army. He later became the commanding general of the White Army during the Civil War.

I told him how I had come to be there, and that I wanted to go back to Kiev, from which the enemy had already been driven out.

The barefoot man looked at me with dark, wary eyes, full of mistrust. He asked me short, staccato questions:

"Who are you? What are you? Where are you from? What do you do?"

"I'm a writer."

"In which Soviet administrative office do you write?"

I explained that I didn't write in an office, but that I was an author. He didn't understand. I tried to explain in all sorts of ways that I wrote books and published stories. He looked at me with even more mistrust.

"Why do you write all that?" he wanted to know. "Who needs it?"

I didn't actually know why I wrote. I knew even less about who needed it. No one needed my early attempts at writing, certainly not in such times. I didn't know what to answer. The barefoot man looked me up and down with his dark glances.

"Where do you come from?" he asked harshly. "From which country?"

"From Poland."

He gaped in astonishment, showing his large, yellow, tobacco-stained teeth.

"Really? From Poland?" he asked again with a frozen smile on his stiff face.

Poland was then in the midst of a fierce war with Russia.

The barefoot man called someone in from another room. This was apparently his second-in-command. He was as polished and as well put together as my barefoot one was dark and sloppy. He was a tall youth in a uniform worn by men from the Caucasus, covered in knives, daggers, silver hooks, and more. Broad-shouldered, slim, with shapely legs in soft boots and wearing an odd fur hat encircled with golden bands, he looked like some Caucasian operetta beauty. He looked at me with great big black foolish eyes and laughed, showing all his snow white teeth.

"He's a real catch," he said in an odd Russian. "A Polish bird."

He tried to utter a poetic speech about revolution and war, but it was full of errors and street slang and the barefoot one stopped him. Instead of arguing, he brought in a Red Army soldier and told him to go home with me and take everything that I possessed. Other than the court protocols about the murderer Mikolyuk, I had nothing. The barefoot one and the Caucasian thought long and hard about my Yiddish letters and exchanged covert glances.

"The devil only knows what kind of markings these are," the barefoot one said, certain that he had intercepted the most dangerous Polish espionage documents.

The Caucasian "beauty" nodded in agreement. The barefoot one hid the papers.

"Comrade of the Red Army, lock him up until we can clarify this," he said. "And watch him carefully."

I saw that I was in trouble. In these chaotic times of revolution and war, individuals didn't really matter, certainly not ones who came from a country at war with Russia. I wanted to save myself, to prove that my writings were simply innocent stories. The barefoot one didn't want to listen to me.

"Ridiculous!" he said, pulling on his boots. "We'll figure out what you've got in these papers. Move!"

The soldier told me to walk ahead of him and he followed a few steps behind, close enough to reach me with a bayonet or a bullet if I tried to run away. Even though I couldn't see the rifle, I could feel its cold breath on my back.

"It's possible that you're innocent," he said philosophically. "I'm an ignorant man who can't read or write, so I can't tell. As far as I'm concerned, you could go with God and it wouldn't bother me. But I have orders to guard you and I have to obey. That's just the way it is, Comrade."

I walked ahead of him slowly. Suddenly, I saw the military doctor, Kozyulin, who had evacuated the last beds in his hospital. He took a look at me and burst into laughter.

"Hey, Comrade Pushkin," he said jokingly, "which office did you bomb, huh?"

I must have looked too serious for jokes and he stopped laughing.

"Comrade of the Red Army, take him back," he ordered. "I'll go with you and clarify things."

The lazy soldier was quiet for a while, not knowing what to do. After much thought, he told me to turn around.

"Ok. Back means back," he muttered, pleased that he didn't have to put me in prison.

For a full half-hour Dr. Kozyulin harangued the barefoot man about literature, its importance for the masses and its usefulness to the revolution. But the barefoot one remained unmoved, hard as a rock. With great effort, the Christianized doctor recalled the forgotten Yiddish letters he had learned as a child. Smiling, he read one line after another of what I had written in between the lines of the court proceedings. Laughing, he translated it all into Russian.

"I guarantee you he's innocent, Comrade Commissar," he said. "I'm an old Party man."

After much silence, the suspicious comrade finally yielded. "I understand if a person is a worker, a doctor, a secretary," he said. "I've never heard of this kind of writing and I don't understand why anyone needs to ruin paper for it."

He told the soldier to go back to his post and he sat down at the table, slowly picked up the dried-out pen, dunked it in ink and laboriously wrote on a wrinkled piece of paper. With many errors, he wrote that I had permission to take the train and leave the area. Then he spat on the dried-out official seal and added his smeared signature.

"It's hot, Comrades," he muttered, sweating over the hard labor of writing.

I spent another week waiting near the station for a train. Trains went by from time to time, but none of them would let me board, even though I showed them my paper with the seal. The trains were for the military. Many of them carried things from the evacuated areas. Once, a train went by full of cargo and passengers, and I squeezed myself onto the roof of one of the cars. Sitting on the sun-soaked iron roof, I was careful not to get caught by the tunnels and wires that could have left me a head shorter.

The train was a long one, stuffed full of passengers of every kind of appearance and in every kind of dress. There were animals, coals or hay in many of the carriages. No one knew where the train was going. Military trains were everywhere, or else the rails had been ripped up and the tracks destroyed.

"We'll go when and where we can," the train workers answered angrily when passengers kept asking questions.

After a night of sitting on the train, ready to leave at any minute if the line freed up, we were finally able to go. But there was more stopping than going. Either we ran out of coal and the passengers had to chop down trees for fuel, or the train's axles—which had not been oiled for some time—set off sparks that burned the wheels, or something else broke in the old locomotive. That locomotive did it all—whistled, smoked, shot off sparks, gasped, creaked—everything except run. Once, the machinist even left the train on the rails and went off to a village to have a cup of tea with a friend.

He was gone for at least an hour. The way he walked showed that it was no tea that he had been drinking, but rather moonshine brewed by the peasants. That liquor could make you as dead drunk as the machinist obviously was. The train actually started weaving much like the man who drove it. At one point, the train split in two, with one half following the locomotive and the other running backwards. I was in the second half, but fortunately the ground was flat and the carriages stopped once the force of their momentum gave out. We were sure that the drunk machinist was going to leave us there, but he brought the locomotive back, attached it once again with the old, rusty chains, and proceeded as before.

Hours, days, whole nights passed with us stuck in some dump of a station, often in the middle of a field, waiting. We had no idea what we were waiting for, when we would leave or how we would go. My neighbors on the roof, people with lots of bags that they kept unpacking and repacking, talked about the gangs who derail trains, attack them, cut off the noses and ears of Jews and commissars, and more.

My neighbors were odd people. Because they were wearing soldiers' shirts, boots, pants and hats that had no emblems, it was impossible to know whether they were Soviet or enemy soldiers. They could just as well have been deserters still wearing their military clothes or even civilians who, like most men in those times, dressed like soldiers. One of them, a guy who seemed to know all the tricks, all the customs and laws and routes of all the trains—even those that didn't know their own routes—kept on telling angry stories and making jokes about Soviet commissars and officials, all of whom he considered to be Jews. Everyone around him loved his stories. When he got tired of talking, he began to play a guitar and sing war songs. More often than any other, he kept repeating a Russian song with which they seemed to identify:

Hey you, little apple, where are you traveling to and fro?
The military will get you and will not let you go.

My roof companions liked the song about the joyous wedding of Commissar Shneerson even more than this one. It was a song that was spreading across the country like wild grass on untended ground. The song rhymed the names of all the relatives who had come to dance at the marriage of the groom, Shneerson, and his bride, Sara. It included a commissar named Meyer, who confiscated butter and eggs belonging to the laborer; Aunt Yael who worked in the jail; Commissar Vorobeytion who controlled nutrition; Commissar Soloveitchay, who controlled the railway; and Commissar Matty and her daddy. The man with the guitar was obviously making fun of the names of these Jewish relatives, and all the other people on the roof clapped their hands and stamped their feet to the rhythm: "It's oh so noisy at Shneerson's wedding." All the while, they were looking at me threateningly, straight in the eye, and wanted to know why I wasn't singing along.

At night, everyone lay flat on the roof in order to avoid low-hanging wires. They lay in one big pile, smoking hand-rolled cigarettes and telling all sorts of stories about gangs who held up trains and cut off the noses and ears of commissars and Jews.

After one such night, we arrived at a station called Bakhmatsh.

I don't remember if the station was actually on the way to liberated Kiev, where the train was supposed to be going, or if it was forced to run via that station because there was no other way to go. I would no more remember the odd name Bakhmatsh than any of the other stations we passed by with equally odd names if not for a curious incident that happened there.

When we were some distance from the station, near broken, piled-up train tracks and abandoned granaries and carriages, a group of armed men blocked the train and ordered it to stop. The crawling locomotive hardly needed any urging. For a while we didn't know who these men were. Every armed man in those days—whether they served the revolution or its enemies—wore the same torn boots, the same cotton pants, shirts and hats in both summer and winter. They all had the same rifles hanging from straps over their shoulders. The young guitarist put his hands over his eyes and predicted that the men would turn out to be Makhno's soldiers. Meanwhile, his neighbors looked at me angrily. The young man saw the glare of a gold star on one of the officers and became uneasy.

"My brothers in faith, they're looking for smugglers," he announced.

The "faithful brothers" immediately took to their packs, tying and untying them for the hundredth time. The gold star came closer and closer until the entire man was visible. He was dressed in leather from head to toe: his hat, his jacket and the backside of his trousers were all made of the best black leather. The dawn was breaking, and the sun's rays seemed to dance with the gold star on his black leather jacket and with the Mauser pistol sticking out of his belt.

The young man with the guitar took one look at him and motioned to his buddies. "Brothers, it's bad," he said. "The man in leather is a 'Tartar.'"

In those days, that's what they called Jews because of their guttural Russian speech, which, to gentile ears, sounded like they were saying "tartar."

The men once again moved their packs around, opening and closing them. The officer pushed back his hat, showing a whole forest of thick black curls. He measured up the train and its contents with a pair of fiery black eyes and said loudly: "Comrades, out of the train, with all your belongings."

The *r* in his "comrades" sounded exactly like the sounds the young guitarist made when he was mocking the wedding guests in his song. The officer's appearance was as Yiddish-like as his Russian. He had a long, curved nose like that of a crow; his eyebrows were large and thick; his lips, red and full; his fleshy face was brown, burned by the sun and wind. More than anywhere else, you could see his Jewishness in his deep black eyes and in his pronounced eyelashes and eyebrows. But there was absolutely no sign of sadness in these black Jewish eyes; they were laughing eyes, full of joy. The fifty or so soldiers with him were as similar to every other armed Russian peasant as one drop of water is to another: colorless, drab, dull. Their gray clothes were wrinkled and loose, but hand grenades hung from their belts.

The passengers were none too eager to gather their bags and leave the train cars. They kept turning over their things. The least willing to move were the people on my roof.

The commissar urged: "Move it, Comrades. Lift your feet."

I was the first to come down from the roof. I wasn't carrying anything except my cotton pants and jacket, sewn from an old sack. My food consisted of half a pumpkin, a small piece of bread, and the skeleton of a herring. The commissar told me to stand to one side, and he turned to the other passengers and their baggage.

"Red Army Comrades: open everything. Every single bag and pack," he ordered, lighting a fire under his slow soldiers who were haphazardly looking at the bags.

The passengers had no interest in opening their baggage and showing their papers. Some of them had large papers with stamps that served as witnesses to their importance to the Soviet cause. The soldiers, none too quick to understand the papers but still impressed by their size and stamps, didn't dare start up with these important people.

The brown-haired commissar relieved them of their fear. "You can be Comrade Trotsky himself. You still have to show us your things," he answered everyone who declared his own importance. "Take everything out and let's see what you've got there."

His black eyes saw everything. No matter how skillfully someone tried to hide something, he found it out. He wouldn't listen to anyone's excuses. He wasn't impressed by titles or ranks or any kind of explanations, or even by the women who tried to flirt with him.

One blond beauty, tall and wearing a large red cross on her white apron—a sign that she was a nurse in a military hospital—refused to open her valise. She pleaded, cried, fainted.

"Comrade Commissar, I work in a hospital for wounded Red Army soldiers," she argued. "Here are my official papers."

The young man was not impressed by her great beauty or by her papers.

"What have you got there, sister? Salt? Sugar?" he asked, smiling and looking into her pretty, tear-filled gray eyes.

She didn't have salt or sugar, but rather bandages, cotton, and aspirin—all the things that a hospital needed and could rarely find in these times.

Suddenly, the young man cast his black, joyful eyes on the nurse's well-endowed bosom and saw that it looked rather too large even for such a large woman. He told her to take out whatever was hidden there.

She stopped, stunned. "I've got nothing there, by God," she swore.

He looked at her overgrown bosom and advised lightheartedly: "Take out everything that's in there. Or else we'll have to take it out ourselves."

The "nurse" saw that she had no choice, stuck her hand into her bosom behind the red cross and took out a bottle with white powder.

"Take it. Take it all. Take my soul," she shrieked hysterically. "It's your time now."

The commissar took the bottle, opened it, smelled it, and showed everyone what was there. "Really, nurse? Carrying cocaine?" he asked.

She wept loudly. "God," she called, "Holy Mother."

They found more forbidden things in the bags of other passengers: flour, cotton, leather, sugar and, most of all, salt, which was even more expensive than sugar. My neighbors on the roof were carrying large bags of it.

The commissar sent men off to one side to guard the smuggled goods. On the other side he put the smugglers themselves, urging on his lazy soldiers with the guttural *r*'s in "comrades," which he uttered after every few words.

"Quickly, Comrades," he urged them. "Faster, faster. There's no time . . ."

He hurried them as cheerfully and simply as those Jewish coachmen who hustle passengers into their carriages from under the noses of other coachmen before they know what's happening. He must have been a coachman before he became a soldier. It was obvious from his strong body, sunburned face and his wild, curly, dark hair that kept poking out of his hat. He looked like one of those hearty, easygoing young men who have to deal with bad roads, horses, thieves, storms, rain, wind, hungry wolves, and other such dangers. He stood firmly on that desolate bit of Ukrainian earth.

The last carriage he approached was sealed from top to bottom. On its locked doors someone had written in chalk that this carriage contained sailors and entry was forbidden. The young man banged on the door with his fist and yelled, with his Yiddish *r*'s, "Comrades, open up!"

No one answered. From inside the carriage, someone could be heard playing a cheerful tune on a harmonica. The commissar no longer used his fist, but rather the butt of his large, drawn pistol.

"Comrades, open up this minute" he thundered, knocking on the door.

The harmonica grew louder behind the closed carriage door.

The young man pushed his hat still higher on his head as though it were constricting his thoughts. He widened his stance and, planting his feet on the ground as though he were getting ready to plant them there permanently, thundered so loudly that it seemed as if his voice could be heard echoing from miles around.

"Open the door, Comrades, or I'll shoot!"

The harmonica stopped playing and the door screeched open. One sailor stood there, blocking the entire door.

Everyone gaped at him because, even in that land of tall men—and especially of tall sailors—it was astonishing to see such an extraordinarily large person. He looked otherworldly. He was dressed in a blue sailor's suit and everything on him looked ridiculous—hands, feet, shoulders, head. His messy flaxen hair fell into his cold eyes. On his hairy chest one could see a tattoo of the head of a gypsy girl. On his shoulder he carried a belt made of machine-gun bullets. And there were two guns and a dagger sticking out of his belt. His pale, unmoving face seemed frozen. It was impossible to tell if he was young or old. On his face, with its incredibly large cheeks and strong chin, there was a comically small, stubby nose that looked like it consisted of just two little nostrils. The door of the train car was too small for him so he had to bend his head out of the door to see anything, and that made him seem even less like a normal human being. He looked like one of those pictures of pirates that were on the covers of adventure stories for boys. He spoke as coarsely as he looked. "What d'ya want?" he said with a voice that sounded as if it came out of an empty barrel.

In the eyes of all the onlookers the young commissar seemed to lose half his height next to this giant in the carriage door. My roof mates, who were now under guard, exchanged looks that predicted bad things for the brown-haired young man in leather. But the commissar stood as sure of himself and as cheerful as before.

"Comrade sailor," he said, with those Yiddish *r*'s, "you and all your mates have to get out of the carriage so we can search it."

The sailor was quiet for some time, as though he were trying to decide if it was worth his while to speak to this young man in leather. After some time, his low bass voice could be heard saying, "Comrade Commissar. We are sailors of the Soviet fleet and no one searches us. Understood?"

The commissar looked up at him and said calmly, "Comrade sailor, I also serve the Soviets and I have orders to search everyone without exception, Comrade."

The huge sailor stretched his head out still further and with icicles that should have been eyes measured the young man from top to bottom. He didn't look angry, but scornful, mocking him the way a lion would look at a goat that stood in its way. "Young man," he said familiarly, omitting the honorific title, Comrade Commissar. "Young man, I already told you that we are sailors, the pride of the revolution, and no one will search us."

"Comrade sailor, I have orders to search," the young man in leather answered. "Don't obstruct the functions of a commissar of the Soviets." He said it proudly, clearly pleased with himself for using such impressive words.

All the passengers paid close attention, waiting for what would happen next. The armed soldiers looked back and forth between the sailor and their commander. It was hard to know whose side they were on. The locomotive personnel stood there curiously. "It's gonna be something!" they predicted, rolling tobacco into pieces of newspaper. "Yup, it's going to be," some of the passengers added.

For the entire duration of the trip in that long and slow train, people had talked about the carriage that had been locked and seemed as though it didn't even belong to the rest of the train. The only time its passengers had been seen was at station stops, when one of them went to stretch his legs. Some young, disheveled girls could also be seen with the sailors. They wore makeup, colorful clothes, and high-heeled shoes that were all too citified and strange in these revolutionary times. The girls giggled each time the sailors had to carry them down from the carriage because it was too high off the ground for them. They ran back to the carriage just as quickly as they had left it. In their rushing, one could see that they were still unaccustomed to their sinful lives.

Even though neither the sailors nor their girls had spoken to anyone else, all the passengers in the other carriages and on the roof knew that in that locked carriage people were having a good time. It was clear from the songs played on the harmonica, and from the bass voices of the men accompanied by the girls' sopranos, and from the laughter and shouting, and even more from the secretive silences that followed the boisterous noises. No one dared go in, but everyone knew that the sailors were living it up. They were cooking whole sides of beef, guzzling prewar cognac and wine. They had a machine gun and prevented other passengers or the conductor or even a military patrol unit from entering the carriage. In the boring hours waiting at train stations or in fields, the bad times were made a little sweeter by telling stories about the life those sailors were leading.

"They're living high on the hog," people said jealously, but also with the kind of pleasure people have when describing the sins of others. "They can give everyone the finger because no one dares start up with them."

Even though they were envied, they were also liked for their care-free attitude, joyful life and, more than anything else, for not letting a representative of the Soviet powers walk all over them. They espe-cially found favor in the eyes of people whose papers and bags were not entirely in order, or those who were unhappy with the new people in power. It was clear to everyone that the brown-haired commissar had started up with people he had better have left alone, and that he wouldn't look good in the end. The passengers took pleasure in the young man's inevitable defeat, knowing that he would have to leave the carriage like a beaten dog forced to leave the meat on a butcher's block. And yet, the young man didn't leave the carriage, even though the sailor had not let him enter.

"Comrade sailor, I'm warning you. You should get down from the carriage yourself," he said cheerily. "Otherwise we'll have to do it for you."

This was too much for the overgrown sailor, still standing in the door of the carriage. He didn't say a word, he just laughed. Laughed so loud and long that his whole body shook with laughter.

"Comrades," he called to his fellow passengers on the train. "Come see who thinks he's going to take our carriage. Just look at him, this leather-wearing rabbit."

The carriage door opened wider. Some two dozen sailors stood there, unbuttoned, unkempt, dissolute, and carrying revolvers. They looked at the commissar and laughed. Only one of them—an older, stooped man with the pale, sickly face and large, expressionless fish-eyes of an alcoholic or cocaine addict—wasn't laughing. Instead he spat through his teeth, many of which were missing.

"Meow," he said, looking at the young commissar, as if to say that the young man was a mouse who shouldn't move closer to the sailors unless he wanted trouble.

The sailors laughed louder and even some of the soldiers laughed, to the delight of the other passengers. The commissar looked daggers at his laughing men, letting them know that their laughter could mean danger for the entire company. He restored order. "Attention! Present arms!" he commanded loudly.

The soldiers obeyed immediately. The commissar removed his Mauser from its holster, placed his finger on the trigger and stood in front of his soldiers.

"Sailors," he yelled, omitting the title "Comrade." "Get out of the carriage or we'll shoot."

The giant among the sailors ordered his men to raise their pistols and took his own pistols out of their holsters.

There was strained silence for a while as both sides sized each other up, like roosters at a cockfight. Suddenly, the giant of a sailor with the expressionless eyes started yelling hoarsely: "Comrades of the Red Army, don't listen to this damned Jew. They drink our blood. These Jew commissars drink the revolutionary blood of Russia's sons." He pointed to his own bared neck as if to show how they were drinking his blood.

Everyone stood frozen in their places. The Jewish passengers looked down when they heard the horrible words that no one expected to hear there. The other passengers exchanged silent glances. The blond beauty began to make the sign of the cross, as if hoping for a miracle. Everyone looked at the soldiers to whom the sailor had spoken. Their faces showed nothing. They anticipated the moment when they would put their weapons away, but the young man in leather, pale with rage, didn't give them a moment to think. He worked quickly, firmly.

"Comrades, surround the door!" he ordered. "Present arms."

Like automatons, the soldiers immediately obeyed. In the rising sun, their bayonets shone red, as if covered in blood. The giant sailor made a gesture and suddenly a small thing, wrapped in oil cloth, materialized. When the tarp was taken off, it revealed a machine gun.

"Fire!" commanded the commissar, and the sound of rifles could be heard.

"Fire!" the sailor's bass echoed, followed by the crackling sound of the machine gun. It was as if the thing that had been under the tarp was choking on something too big for its throat.

All the passengers threw themselves on the ground. I could hear the blasts of gunfire and machine guns and the screams of men on both sides. Soon, we heard the commissar's voice, recognizable because of his Yiddish *r*'s.

"Comrades, throw your hand grenades!"

I held my breath as I burrowed my face deeper into the dirt, listening hard for the grenades that would surely come next. But suddenly, the machine-gun fire stopped and all was quiet. It was a heavy silence, worse than all the previous noise.

When I got up from the ground, everything was over. Yellow smoke could be seen through the dawn's light. The smell of gunpowder was everywhere. Sailors jumped down from the open train car, with hands raised above their heads. The commissar, with his Mauser in hand, searched every one of them and threw down each pistol, rifle, and bullet belt he found.

"Take it away and guard it" he said to one of his soldiers, who was dragging the machine gun.

With his pistol butt, he counted the sailors. "Don't move!" he warned. "If you budge, you'll get a bullet in the head."

The sailors stood motionless and pale. The giant's cheeks were shaking, going up and down as if they belonged to a bulldog. Only the older, stooped sailor with the pale, tired face swayed in his long, wide sailor pants that looked empty, as if there were no legs in them. He kept on tearing at his throat, yelling, "They're drinking our blood! Look!"

"We'll look in the stockade," the young commissar said lightly, as if nothing at all had happened.

He jumped up into the conquered carriage quickly, along with some dozen soldiers, and began to empty it. "Faster, Comrades," he thundered.

The soldiers started throwing out all sorts of smuggled goods: a bag of salt and a screeching girl; a pack of leather and a crying girl; some cotton and a fainting girl. With every new piece of contraband, the young man laughed louder.

"Look at what they're carrying, the pride of the revolution!" he said loudly, staring at the sailors who stood squeezed next to one another, still with their hands raised and surrounded by pointed bayonets.

The passengers were silent, looking with wide eyes at the numerous bags and sacks that had been thrown onto the ground. My neighbors on the roof avoided looking at anyone.

The locomotive began to whistle, creak, smoke. The commissar told the arrested men to put their baggage on their backs and encircled them with his armed soldiers. With his revolver in hand, he counted and recounted the prisoners several times and loudly ordered, with his Yiddish *r*'s:

"Walk in a straight line. Don't turn around. March!"

The bright sun reflected off the bayonets of the armed men. The locomotive suddenly whistled frightfully, as if warning the remaining passengers that it was getting ready to leave.

David Zaritski

1914–1978

D AVID ZARITSKI WAS unusual among *Forward* contributors in
that he was an Orthodox rabbi, writer, and journalist who was
active primarily in Israel's Orthodox Jewish press.

Born in Pinsk, in what is now Belarus, Zaritski studied in the local
branch of the Novaredok yeshiva, a network of rabbinical seminaries
that focused on ethical and spiritual development. He later went to
study in the yeshiva of Rabbi Israel Meir Kagan, better known as the
Chofetz Chaim, in Radin, Poland.

During the Second World War, Zaritski fled to Siberia and after
the war moved to France, where he worked with young Holocaust
survivors and published a collection of poetry titled *Oysgetrinkte oygn*
(*Dried-Out Eyes*).

In 1949 he immigrated to the newly founded State of Israel and
settled in the religious Tel Aviv suburb of Bnei Brak. In Israel, Zaritski
became one of the founders of the Orthodox newspaper *Hamodia* (*The
Informer*), and served as a contributor to the Yiddish magazine *Di
Yidishe heym* (*The Jewish Home*), a publication of the Chabad Hasidic
movement.

Zaritski was a prolific journalist throughout his life, although his
most influential work was a novel for young readers published in 1952.
Translated from Yiddish to Hebrew under the title *Shimke: Yeladim
be-maskhet ha-gvurah shel ha-dor* (*Shimke: Children in the Heroic Chapter of the Generation*), the novel tells the story of an eight-year-old boy
who fights as a partisan in the forests of Poland.

"The Edge of Death" appeared in the *Forward* on June 20, 1948, just after the founding of the State of Israel, during a trip by Zaritski to the United States. A prefatory note to the piece describes the author as a frequent contributor to the newspaper who has "dedicated his life to Jewish migration to Israel" and whose story is based on his own experience during the war.

The Edge of Death

(JUNE 20, 1948)

Translated by Chana Pollack

I AM THE GRAVEDIGGER.

Small and large, deep and flat, wide and narrow graves. It all depends on who died and when. For instance, during the typhus epidemic, I had no time to dig proper graves of one meter's depth, as is necessary. I was only able to burrow down far enough so that the straw mat shrouds didn't peek out. The deceased waited patiently, their feet curled up into a smile at the tiny slats beneath them, at the tall mountains, and at the high chimneys of the brick factory. In the evening's darkness their faces mix together with the alabaster lime, and I've got to take care not to sling an extra corpse in as I dig another grave.

Raging dysentery demands narrow graves. The dead are then as lean as the wooden planks that serve as tombstones, which sit in waiting alongside. Placed in the earth, the dead make a flimsy sound. Corpses tall or short resemble birch twigs that have drifted for a while through the barren forest and will splinter with any movement. Not to mention the children. The first time I dug a child's grave I recalled having once scooped out a similar hollow in our orchard for our little kitten. But then I cried and now I wait impatiently for the bitty grave to be filled in already, so I can get my couple of rubles.

I only dig graves at dusk. I labor all day long at the local brick factory, pushing wheelbarrows full of raw bricks to the oven. Behind me is the constant bellowing of the tall Uzbeki named Albakov:

"You, *Padla*[70] *Nu!* Get to it, you stiff!"

Padla meant me. What difference was there, between me and the white horse grazing all night long, not wanting to drag the lime, while I dawdle, neither eating nor sleeping, and still having to lug the wheelbarrow along.

Another thing I'll always remember about pounding the burning ground barefoot—the carrion.

A horse can't by any means be a counterrevolutionary nor be sentenced to such labors.

When, at the end of the month, I received my wages in the amount of thirty-eight rubles cash, there was no way I could have known what to do with that money. I might have purchased quite a few things—a couple pounds of bread or a bit less than a liter of milk, four cups of dried black sunflower seeds, a kilo of potatoes.

Yes indeed, I could have gorged on a meal with that money. I wouldn't have been too sated afterwards, but at least I'd have savored the pleasurable taste of bread in my mouth.

And what about the remaining thirty days? God didn't abandon me. People were dying like flies. Each one dying as it was willed—some from typhus, some from dysentery, from hunger, from lice and filth, and there were those who simply dropped dead in the street. A burial society was formed, and once that was in place, a burial specialist was needed—not to supervise the cemetery, but to dig the graves. So in the evening, after my factory work, I dug graves, charging sixty rubles each, and by the time they'd finished saying the mourner's prayer I was already at the market buying bread with my money.

Understand? Bread!

And when three days passed and nobody died, I didn't eat for three days.

---

70 A Russian curse.

On the fourth day I was informed that there was a grave to dig. A large grave, they told me, and deep—meaning it's a regular corpse. He died the usual way, an elderly man in his bed.

Evening was descending and could be seen through the mountain gaps, creeping higher up their peaks. Cemeteries surrounded the area. To the left was a Polish one. A memorial for Anders's Army,[71] three long rows of graves with little white crosses looking like dead solders standing at attention. The graves leaned on each other as though they were about to topple over. On the right, pouring out like a wave, were the Uzbeki graves, wide and small with large mounds of earth. They seemed to be looking on mutely and severely at the clay huts built into the mountains. Higher even, where one mountain split into two, the Russian cemetery scrambled over it. There the Communists weren't the majority. Nearly all the graves had crosses crafted simply from two thin slivers glued together, gnarled and wretched. They'd fall off daily only to be raised back up. Fewer boasted a lonely, defiant red marker, carved out of stone or sticks of wood. Communist leaders lay beneath them.

Right to their side on the descent of a small mountain was the Jewish cemetery. When I first took up my post, there were only a few graves of the older Bukharan Jewish settlers. Now the cemetery covered the mountain and tumbled down into the neighboring valley. These were dismal graves, caved in, as thin and gangly as their owners. Those who had erected wooden headstones would find them stolen by morning. There was neither brick nor cement available and frequently, over time, your foot would get tangled up in the straw mat shroud of a nameless corpse.

It made no difference to me who lay there. I had to dig the grave, a large one, measuring one meter eighty in length, eighty centimeters wide, and one meter twenty deep. Since the deceased had a family, he wasn't wrapped in a straw shroud but in white shrouds. People wept.

---

71 The informal name for the Polish Armed Forces in the East, led by commander Wladyslaw Anders.

Yes, people cried, and I was astonished and terrified. They didn't drag him by the shoulder like an old chunk of wood they'd filched, but honorably. It was impressed upon me that I'd receive eighty and not sixty rubles this time. This was my third day without bread. With no bread it was impossible to work—and so it would go.

The route wasn't long but it was uphill. It wasn't my feet but the eighty rubles that dragged me onward—the three pounds of bread I'd have in my hands in an hour or two. The food would sate my eyes for a bit and then I'd bite into the cushy, supple bread with my chattering teeth. Each scrap down my throat would cause tremors through my body.

That very same hunk of bread rolled ahead of me, coaxing me uphill. The evening air cooled my clammy face, and even the lice had sympathy and let me be.

I collapsed at the site where I was to dig the grave and felt my heart about to burst from my chest. I was trembling from exertion. I lay on the hard, cold ground. The evening dew, like white ocean foam, covered me delicately. It made the mountains seem close together, and it seemed that soon the crosses would roll down like boulders from the mountain streams and cover me over.

Somewhere a goat bleated and the echo resounded a thousandfold. It made a strange barking sound that rippled as it crashed over each stone and as it rolled between tombstones and crosses, until in the end it clung to the earthen mounds. The sun had long since lain down on the other side of the mountain, and the scorched grass seemed to undulate before ceasing its whispering as it was veiled by dew.

All I saw was the breathtaking vision of a huge, three-pound lump of bread wheeling before my eyes. The life that tried to roll away from my weakened heart hung before me. All I needed was one hour, only one hour's toil, and then—

B-R-R-R-R-E-A-D!!!

After that I'd lie on the ground in my hutch, sleeping peacefully, stuffed.

My mood picked up. A bit wobbly, I gritted my teeth and began to carve up the dense, clay earth with my pickaxe. Beneath that first layer the earth was much softer and I could already work with a shovel. Minutes passed. Hacking at it increased my circulation, my muscles twitched, I was drenched in sweat and yet dehydrated. The earthen pile grew high. The ditch got deeper, taking on the shape of a grave.

Suddenly, I felt an enormous raindrop on my face. That was a hideous jolt; it never rained there in the summertime. And now, suddenly, rain.

The drops got larger, sticking to my cotton cap and weighing it down. The rain got heavier until it was no longer a shower but a storm. Like most rainstorms there, it was torrential, and I was completely soaked. That wouldn't have been so terrible had it not completely soaked the clay beds. The earth stuck to the shovel. I'd dig and try to throw dirt off, and couldn't. Every shovelful was so heavy I couldn't hoist it, and had to unpack each one by hand.

I felt my hands getting heavier. Perhaps it wasn't my hands but the shovel. It gradually drew me towards the ground, hunched over. My feet dragged through the grave's clay bottom until I could no longer move. My God! How heavy the human foot can be! The grave narrowed. I felt the walls pressing in on me, creeping along, coming apart and then cleaving back together again. They seemed sticky and horrifyingly cold to my watery eyes—and silent.

The shovel drops out of my hand. It falls and splashes mud on my face. Only now do I feel water trickling in on all sides of the grave, covering my toes.

I leaned against the walls of the grave and felt the clay saturate my shirt and penetrate my body, slithering over it like long, cold worms. I felt the ground tugging at me. She reached out to me on all sides, beckoning me with her sopping clay hands. From the mountains came the muted sounds of footsteps in the distance. The fog shifted, becoming bitter and menacing. Suddenly thousands of dark eyes lit up the rain-drenched darkness. Peering into my woozy eyes, they laughed provocatively. The water in the grave had now reached my knees and I sunk slowly deeper. My feet froze, like two wooden slabs mired in the clay. I was finally left sitting and weeping in the brackish water.

What would be?

I wasn't thinking any longer. All I wanted was to eat. I felt death's slow approach from high atop those mountains and from lower down. It was coming from underneath, crawling upwards like a snake from my feet to my heart, my chest, my mouth . . .

I had dug myself a grave. I couldn't stop the thought from burrowing into me. I ruminated on it as peacefully as I used to consider my dinner plans.

The grave was exactly my size; there would be no need to dig either longer or wider. I was as spindly as the spade handle that was drifting aimlessly in the water and that couldn't be hoisted out. And when the moment came and they arrived with the deceased, folks would search for me, cursing me out, saying that I'd abandoned my post mid-job. When they approached the graveside to relinquish him, they would trample on me.

I reflected on this very calmly. Just then all my fear of death was lifted. In its place was the incessant craving for relief; to stretch out on a soft, warm bed, sipping a cup of tea with raspberry preserves, drifting into sleep. Most important—my feet would no longer be stuck here. Marooned in the brackish gray water, they tormented me dreadfully. I tried to move, but my energy had gone under. My hat lay askew over my eyes and I couldn't straighten it out.

Through numb lips I recited the confessional prayer. The rain cascaded into my mouth and I heard myself rasp. The words surfaced and were cast out into the rain and fog.

I felt the water rise. My arms were partially submerged by the time I'd recited my confession and it was a truncated version:

"God! Thank you for the effortless death, as for my ghastly life. The graves were my subsistence, and now they're clawing it all back."

I bowed weakly and felt something so heavy crushing my cumbersome head that I could no longer hold it up. The burden moved deeper within me, and my hungry heart swiftly and firmly snapped shut, stunning me . . .

The folks arriving later on with the corpse found me. It was exactly as I'd imagined it, before I lost consciousness. They were angry with me and meant to finish digging the grave on their own, when they leaped into the half-dug grave and fell right on top of me.

They told me that they spent a long time trying to revive me, and thought the grave would be mine. It seems I was fated to go on living, in order to tell you how it is to be on the edge of death.

Wolf Karmiol

1910–1987

W OLF KARMIOL WAS a writer, teacher, journalist, and survivor of the Lodz Ghetto. In his fiction he often depicted his own experiences, both during and after the Holocaust.

A native of Lodz, Karmiol graduated from the city's Jewish-Polish high school and went on to study literature at Warsaw University, where he received a master's degree. In the mid-1930s he moved to Palestine, where he pursued graduate studies at the Hebrew University in Jerusalem.

Upon the death of his father in 1937, Karmiol returned to Poland, and was imprisoned in the Lodz Ghetto from 1939 to 1945. While in the ghetto, Karmiol worked as a teacher, wrote plays and short stories, and married his wife, Sabina. He survived the Holocaust by hiding in the ghetto after its liquidation in August 1944.

After the war Karmiol remained in Lodz, where he worked as a journalist for a Polish newspaper and published stories in the Yiddish newspaper *Dos naye lebn* (*This New Life*). After learning that his wife had also survived the war and was living in Sweden, he bribed the captain of a fishing boat to smuggle him into the country.

In 1947, Karmiol and his wife immigrated to the United States, where he taught in Jewish schools in Philadelphia and Detroit, and worked for Israel's General Federation of Labour—known in Hebrew as the Histadrut—in New York.

Throughout this time Karmiol continued publishing fiction in Yiddish newspapers and literary journals. "After Liberation," which appeared in the *Forward* on May 12, 1968, reflects Karmiol's experience as a journalist in the immediate aftermath of the Holocaust, and describes the narrator's attempt to report on an incident similar to the infamous Kielce pogrom in 1946, in which some forty-two Jewish refugees and Holocaust survivors were murdered in the presence of Polish Communist forces.

In 1970, following the death of his wife, Karmiol immigrated to Israel, where he published several collections of short stories, including *Hersh and Miriam and Other Stories*, which appeared in English in 1973.

———

After Liberation

(MAY 12, 1968)

Translated by Chana Pollack

HUGE RUSSIAN TANKS making grating sounds rolled through the snow-covered streets. Trucks filled with soldiers sped down the road towards Berlin. The clanging of metal, the clamor of engines, the sound of soldiers' voices, carried through the frigid air over the evacuated streets of Lodz, its boarded-up shops, its shuttered homes.

Battered and solitary, only a few days out of the ghetto, Yosef stood on the sidewalk and contemplated the Red Army marching through.

Here they are then, the liberators . . . too late though to save the tens of thousands of Jews in the ghetto.

The row of tanks came to a halt. A tall man with a long gaunt face called out from a truck: "Comrade!"

Yosef came closer. The man wearing a gray officer's uniform bent down towards him. "Were you in the ghetto?" He said it in Yiddish, hiding his mouth by cupping his palm over it as if blowing through a tube, so that soldiers in a nearby truck wouldn't overhear him.

"Yes!" Yosef's face lit up and he reached a hand out to him.

"Are there many Jews left?" The Russian Jew bent down to Yosef.

"Very few, very few."

The tanks moved on with a clattering din. The officer bellowed. "So long!" And he waved his hand.

The surviving Jew followed him with his eyes until he disappeared at the bend in the road.

Yosef ambled slowly along. He found himself on Piotrkowska Street. Shop windows were broken, doors torn off.

House walls were darkened with graffiti reading LONG LIVE THE POLISH ARMY! LONG LIVE WLADYSLAW GOMULKA![72] Half a dozen Poles in sheepskin coats stood in the shadows of a little restaurant. A late-arriving Red Army soldier, submachine gun in hand, rushed to meet his unit. A woman, wrapped up in a shawl, lurched by him. A cocky youth sold homemade cigarettes. Two ragged children stood outside the grocery store pulling their faces back from the cold windowpane where a loaf of bread lay.

Yosef lingered at the entrance to the editorial offices of *Lodz*, where a small group read the Polish newspaper's freshly published headlines from the front pages.

He went upstairs into the hubbub of people, the chatter of typewriters and the smell of machinery.

The editor, outfitted in a chartreuse uniform, raised a pair of sharp blue eyes at him, and grumbled:

"What do you have to say? Are you trained in Polish language and literature? Sure you are! Get to work, you'll be our copy editor and try writing some yourself as well. The secretary will get you a map to the station and we'll find you an old uniform and a pair of boots."

So began the journalistic career of Yosef Pravidla.

Before long his name was a frequent byline in the Polish press. The young journalist reported news and wrote features articles.

More of the liberated Jews arrived in Lodz. The community center resounded with the racket of nervous feet; anxious, worry-filled eyes;

---

72 Wladyslaw Gomulka (1905–1982) was a postwar Polish Communist leader.

the odor of sweat and cheap tobacco; the rancid air of ditches and barns; neglected men in German military jackets; women in found clothing with straw-strewn disheveled hair and faces covered in sores; rumpled young women restraining themselves from scratching—and everyone talking at once, arguing and babbling, like orphans who feel the warmth of their new home and smell the aroma of cooking.

Yosef used to run up the stairs to the community center breathlessly, asking the vocal women whether they had encountered his wife, who had been deported from the ghetto. They eyed him scornfully.

"Were we once individuals? Numbers, merely numbers!"

In the factories where Yosef went to gather material for his reporting, the workers besieged him with questions and complaints.

Yosef had just left the government-appointed factory director's office, which used to belong to the Zeibert Brothers. He was surrounded by the women weavers and cutters.

"We have to stand all day long in dust and dirt, and we don't receive even one drop of milk."

"And the Jewish children do receive milk."

"Yes, that's true, they do receive milk and all kinds of provisions."

"How do you know this? And how many children, on the other hand, survived?"

Yosef was furious.

The workers surrounded him.

Yosef was jerked about in place but remained upright—he wanted to chase after them, screaming until their eardrums burst: "You see and know it all—except the diamond ring on the director's hand. He's permitted to steal from you being that he's Polish! And whose factory was it originally, if not the 'kikes'?"

With the arrival of the refugees from Siberia, Jews from the camps, and folks who had hidden in villages and forests, pale Lodz took on the redness of their sunken cheeks.

The city buzzed with weddings, balls and dances. The former nightclub Tabarin was packed with Russian artists, acrobats and illusionists. The orchestra played "Warsaw, My Warsaw" and drunken Poles and tipsy Jews lamented the destroyed Polish capital. The Jew-

ish newspaper that had begun publication brought news of a wedding in a Jewish town near Warsaw where local farmers and gentile
townsfolk had entertained the bride and groom with song and dance.

One night Pravidla's grim, elderly landlady, steeped in worry and
fear, entered his room.

"Did you know that in Rojek, near Lublin, they murdered two
Jews?"

Yosef headed to the editorial offices only to find that no one had
yet reported news of any murders.

At the community center it was confirmed. For a while unrest
in the provinces was discussed. The rabble claimed that ever since
'46 the kikes had grabbed the reins of power in Poland. Who knew
what the Poles were planning?

The writer went over to the editor's office.

"I'm heading to Rojek," he informed him urgently. "I've got to
find out who's to blame for the death of the refugees."

The head of *Lodz* nodded his head.

"Comrade, you are brave, but the road there is dangerous. The
area is teeming with the Home Army [73] fascist guerillas who are fighting the government. You'd best arm yourself."

The journalist missed the bus and had to take a truck carrying
passengers through the towns and villages on the way to Lublin.

Aside from Yosef, the "luxury vehicle" carried a couple of farm
wives and their husbands, who agitated themselves the entire way
as they loudly discussed how the Russians were shipping coal out of
Poland and ransacking its best and finest.

By evening the vehicle was jerking along, causing Yosef to recall
grim memories. The peasants lay outstretched on the bench, snoring.

"Up! Get up and get out!"

---

73 The dominant Polish underground movement during World War II.
Although the Home Army was disbanded after the war, individual militias loyal
to the Polish government in exile continued to operate against the Soviet army
and the Polish Communist government.

The passengers were blinded by electric lanterns cutting through the darkness.

The driver was ordered to halt the trip until further notice.

The soldiers vacated. The driver cursed harshly. People stood on the sidewalk beside the immobilized truck.

An ominous hand suddenly tore off the raw black cover of night. A pinkish glow lit up the sky, as if day was breaking. Spilling across the horizon was a sea of flickering red.

"Jesus Christ! The Home Army lads are burning through the forest!" The gentiles crossed themselves fearfully. When would the Poles cease shooting each other?

Bloody tongues wrapped in gun smoke licked the dismal sky. From the distance came the windswept aroma of scorched pine trees, shrubbery and gold-hued grasses.

It was midday by the time Yosef reached town. The only member of the ruling militia the journalist encountered grumbled that the Home Army lads had murdered the two Jews.

Yosef meandered between the wooden houses, observing the peacefulness emanating from glowing sun-streaked windows bordered by white curtains and decorated with milk pails full of flowers.

Grandmothers' peeled potatoes sat on porch settees, warming themselves in the sun.

An elderly Polish woman swayed in her rocking chair in front of a red brick house at the end of town.

"Peace be with you," she greeted the journalist.

"I'm from the city and I'm looking for a nice piece of bacon, perhaps you have some?"

"For our own, always. But not for the Muscovites or the kikes."

"I see, you hate the kikes as I do."

"Oh, I know them well. We just rid ourselves of those last two a few days ago."

"Tell me more about that, I'm curious."

"They came to town, having returned thinking we'd welcome them with bread and salt—the creeps were searching for family and friends the Germans had wiped out long ago. They started brawling and Polish townsfolk ran over, as did the local farmers, and dragged the two kikes to the orchard with pitchforks, knives and iron cudgels. They beat them, wounded them, and stabbed them to pieces."

Yosef lost the strength to stand upright. He dropped onto the stairs leading up to the house.

"Where's the grave they tossed them into?" He asked the elderly woman.

"The militia knows."

The government-appointed representative dozed with his head on the desk. When the journalist shook him awake, he jumped up and angrily demanded:

"What's wrong with you? Where are you from?"

"Come along then!" Pravidla drew a revolver from his bag. "Come show me the Jews' grave or I'll shoot you on the spot. You and this entire town will be locked up in prison! It's just too bad, if I could only hang each of you here in the marketplace!"

The deathly-pale envoy lowered his head and walked on wobbly feet.

The cemetery was studded with broken tombstones. Chickens and ducks dawdled amidst graves. The victims' grave lay next to a fence—an earthen mound trod over and marked by footsteps.

"On your knees!" Yosef ordered the gentile. "And kiss the sacred ground!"

The gentile lowered to his knees and placed his lips on the grave.

"Now leave, and wait to be summoned by the court!"

The militant left. Pravidla quietly spoke to the hallowed ones:

"We won't forget you, and the Christians won't forget me either."

Yosef gathered up a handful of earth from the long grave.

"I take this with me, on my way out into the world!"

SECTION FOUR

The Old Country

THE *FORWARD* WAS a forward-thinking newspaper. Alongside its progressive political outlook it encouraged its readers to make a home for themselves in the United States. Instead of isolating themselves in a social and cultural ghetto, it urged them to learn about American culture. Rather than dwell in the past, it looked to the future.

This open-armed embrace of the new world wasn't always well received. Socialists disliked the paper's preference for populism over ideological rigor. Intellectuals objected to its broad sensationalism, both in its news reporting and in its literary output. And those committed to the furtherance of the Yiddish language condemned the *Forward*'s seeming indifference to that cause. By wholeheartedly encouraging its readers to learn English, it could even be said that the *Forward* sowed the seeds of its own decline.

But together with the optimistic spirit that carried the *Forward* through the first decades of the twentieth century, it always had at least one eye looking backwards. Even after mass immigration to America, cities like Warsaw and Vilna remained major centers of Jewish life, and the Yiddish press served as a vital link between those communities and the growing Jewish population in the United States. Nearly all *Forward* readers had family in Europe, and in the *Forward* they could read news of the places where parents and siblings—even spouses and children—still lived.

News of home quickly took on a nostalgic flavor as well. The towns and cities of Eastern Europe represented not just a different place, but also an older way of life. The Jewish market towns of the Russian Empire, with their synagogues and schools, markets and craftsmen, formed a common background for first-generation immigrants, and a vividly pictured heritage for their children and grandchildren. Even prior to the Holocaust—and certainly after it—Yiddish fiction took an elegiac tone, looking back at a world that was vanishing even before it was brutally wiped out.

Thus readers of the *Forward* relished Zalman Schneour's vignettes about his upbringing in Shklov, which appeared in the paper for decades. Many of the stories by Isaac Bashevis Singer, who published regularly in the *Forward* from the time of his immigration in 1935, took place in a mythologized version of the old country, full of spirits and demons and magical forces. And starting in the 1970s the *Forward* began publishing the renowned Yiddish novelist Chaim Grade, who wrote numerous stories about his own hometown of Vilna, as it had existed before the war.

To be sure, such work was not strictly an exercise in nostalgia. In these stories the complexities and contradictions of Jewish life in Eastern Europe were examined in detail, from the injustices inflicted on women by a patriarchal society to the religious, economic, and social fissures that had been appearing at least since the nineteenth century. And following the Holocaust, the *Forward* became a powerful repository of Jewish memory for the people, communities, and institutions that had been lost. This was the world that the *Forward* and its readers had come from, and which had now all but disappeared.

Yona Rozenfeld

1880–1944

Y ONA ROZENFELD, ONE of the more obscure masters of modern
Yiddish prose, was a regular literary contributor to the *Forward*
until the mid-1930s, when a creative dispute with editor Abraham
Cahan caused him to leave the newspaper.

Born in Tshartorisk, in what is now Ukraine, Rozenfeld received
a traditional religious education until the age of thirteen, when both
of his parents died of cholera. With the help of an older brother he
moved to Odessa, where he worked as a lathe operator for ten years,
an experience he later described in his 1940 autobiographical novel
Eyner aleyn (*One Alone*).

Rozenfeld began writing in his early twenties and showed his work
to I. L. Peretz when the latter visited Odessa in 1902. His first publication came two years later in the newspaper *Fraynd* (*Friend*), and
he continued to publish stories in both the European and American
Yiddish press.

In 1921, Rozenfeld immigrated to America, where he became a
regular contributor to the *Forward*. He also wrote for the Yiddish
stage and became best known for a dramatic adaptation of his early
short story, "Competitors." Several collections of his work appeared
in the 1920s, and a posthumous volume of selected works was published in 1955 under the editorship of novelist Chaim Grade and the
critic Shmuel Niger.

"A Holiday," which appeared on October 8 and 9, 1922, is set in
an unnamed European city and illustrates the unspoken tensions
between Jews and Christians in this commercial metropolis.

In the mid-1930s the *Forward* stopped publishing Rozenfeld's work on the insistence of Cahan, who felt that Rozenfeld's focus on character psychology and his discursive style had become too difficult for readers. Rozenfeld died in New York in 1944.

A Holiday

(OCTOBER 8–9, 1922)

Translated by Rachel Mines

SAYING GOODBYE FOR the eight days, Elya, the worker, shook hands with his boss and the boss's two daughters, wished them a happy holiday, and left.

The workshop had already been swept and cleaned when they parted. The apprentice boy had gathered the last few shavings into a sack, flung it over his shoulder and taken it away. The house too had been cleaned and tidied, and the family prepared to wash themselves. The boss went off to the baths, but his daughters had to bathe at home in a tub, a large wooden vessel in which they washed laundry. And the girls smiled at the thought of stripping naked and bathing.

Elya said goodbye and left. The girls didn't invite him to visit, thinking that if he wanted to see them he'd do so on his own, uninvited. But each in turn smiled into his eyes to show him they'd be pleased to welcome him back as a guest. It was their father who said, "Drop by!"

Half an hour after the worker left, the apprentice also left, and his departure was a rather strange event. He had room and board in the family home; he ate and drank there, slept there every night of the week, and suddenly . . .

"Drop by over the holiday!" both girls said, and smiled.

The first two days of the holiday went by. They passed with eating and resting in Passover peace and cleanliness. The workbenches stood covered with bedsheets and old tablecloths, giving off an air of unhappy boredom.

Left to themselves, the family members felt detached from one another, with the melancholy of close kinship. Leyzer, the head of the household and the girls' father, yawned repeatedly, accompanying each yawn with an "ekkkhh" or "kha-kha-kha." He seemed to exhale the two-thousand-year exile with each yawn. He'd worked hard before Passover and, recovering quickly, was soon bored with resting. His limbs, used to decades of hard work, ached and longed for movement, and his spirit took no pleasure in idleness. But there was no enjoyment to be had except to relax and eat a good meal. Leyzer was not yet old; he was only fifty-two, and during the holiday he found his mind longingly drawn to the bodies of strange women. His own daughters felt distant and extraneous to him, and he no longer understood what was clear to him on every other night of the year: the sacrifice he had made for his children by not remarrying.

The holiday was already beginning to wear. Having rested and eaten well, the family started to long for regular workdays, for the clamor and banging and new faces of an ordinary day. After lifelong familiarity with the ever-present racket of trade and the workshop, it seemed that something had been silenced, and instead of the peace and stillness of the holiday, they felt only a lull in the workweek. The week had fallen silent. They'd covered it up with bedsheets and tablecloths, and the workbenches were rendered mute and paralyzed.

The girls looked forward to seeing the worker. True, they hadn't invited him, but they expected him anyway. They were certain he'd come, though they didn't know the time or day. So they watched for him from morning to night, and waiting made them tense, nervous, and impatient.

On the fourth day of the holiday, two guests arrived: the apprentice and his father. Out of respect for his father, the boy was invited in and seated at the table with his employer and his daughters, which the girls found amusing. They smiled at each other and at the boy, amused to be treating him like a respectable person. On looking him over, they observed quite a change in him. He was wearing a new outfit; his hair was cut and trimmed, his sideburns cut aslant above his ears, and below his sideburns you could see a razor had gone over his cheeks and shaved off all the fuzz. His young shaved cheeks made him look older than his years. Before the shave, you could see he'd had peach fuzz. But now, afterwards, you could see he'd been shaved, and that made him seem older and more masculine.

"If I'd seen him in the street, I'd never have recognized him," one daughter said.

"Me neither!" said the other.

Surprisingly, they did in fact think something of him; he drew and held their girlish attention, and their vague, unconscious attraction kept them smiling.

The girls set up the samovar. This was the first time the apprentice had been in the house when the girls, and not he, had done the job. He was given the honor of carrying it in, however, and was pleased to have his old job back, since it made him feel more at home. He carried the samovar carefully, at arm's length from himself and his new suit, and it looked like the samovar wasn't being carried at all, but that it floated through the air ahead of him, tugging after it the young man: a fresh, new youth in a new outfit. Drawing him to the table, the samovar placed itself in a brass tray, and releasing the young man, it showed itself off: its shape, its boiling and hissing, and the fire and coals beneath.

The girls poured tea and set large and small nuts on the table. The boy perched on his chair, unable to sit still. This was the first time in his life he'd been given the chance to sit at a table and crack as many nuts as he pleased. And because he wanted all of them, not just to eat but also to put in his pockets, he couldn't take even one. He was as pink as a newborn baby, and his eyes shone as though he'd suddenly entered into a new kind of existence. He felt he was in that house and seeing those girls for the first time in his life. He pondered the fact that he'd seen them many times in their undershirts, with bare arms and breasts, and now they were acting like his presence embarrassed them.

And though he thought it more pleasant to see them that way, without blouses, he now felt himself more manly, someone before whom they'd be ashamed to display themselves. That both were now dressed up for the holiday excited him even more, and his whole body, from head to foot, became aroused. Not knowing whether this made him more manly or, on the other hand, more boyish, his self-possession deserted him. Poor thing: he melted like a candle among others, which melts in its own flame and in the heat of those around it. He melted in his own fire and in the girls' presence.

"Eat, don't be embarrassed," said Ettele, the younger daughter, and smiled.

"Is there still a little wine?" Leyzer asked Beylke, the elder.

Yes there was; there were still good things in the buffet, which Beylke hadn't set on the table. She wasn't being stingy with the things she hadn't offered, but she didn't know what sort of guests the visitors were, so she treated them as she always treated informal visitors, people who dropped in during the holidays and must be given something. And for them, she thought, a glass of tea and a few nuts would do.

Apart from that, Beylke was on edge, annoyed that it was the apprentice who'd come by, not someone else. Despite her displeasure, however, she welcomed the boy as someone who was better than no one. Her situation was like that of a hungry infant, who, instead of a nipple, has a finger put in its mouth. The finger doesn't soothe the baby's hunger, but it stimulates the digestion, and sucking on it makes the baby happy. It was like that for Beylke. In some way, the boyish figure represented a man. When he'd appeared on the doorstep, her first thought was that he'd somehow been directed there to make fun of her: that instead of an adult man, this fifteen-year-old boy had showed up in her home, as if the wide, unknown, masculine world had sent him to convey a masculine greeting. Really, though, if she hadn't already been older than a young girl by five, six, seven, or eight years, she wouldn't have been offended.

The two men, Leyzer and the boy's father, sat there with nothing to say. In fact, the boy's father wanted to talk; he wasn't there just to exchange holiday greetings, but to get something out of Leyzer for his son. There was no time during the week, so he'd put off the discussion until the holiday. But now he sat silently. He couldn't just come straight out with his reason for being there, especially on a holiday when he'd been welcomed as a guest.

Leyzer, of course, knew the boy's father had come to make demands on him; there was nothing new in that, he knew it from the fathers of other apprentices in the past. So Leyzer waited for the other man to speak so he could talk him out of whatever he wanted and be done with it, and then they'd feel more free, and Leyzer would be able to pass time with him as he would with a member of the family. But as long at the boy's father had something to say, a barrier stood between them. They sat at the same table, Leyzer's table, like strangers, even worse than strangers, and were silent.

"The holiday's flying by," said Leyzer.

"Time flies," the other man replied, and combed his hairy fingers through his thick rounded beard, trimmed in honor of the holiday.

"Have some nuts," said Leyzer, "they're good with tea. And you," he asked the apprentice, "why are you sitting there like you're waiting for a handout?"

Ettele scooped a double handful of nuts from the triangular glass bowl, went over to the boy, told him to hold open his jacket pockets, and dropped every last nut inside.

"He's grown up," Leyzer said to the father.

Like all bosses, Leyzer knew that the matter of wages was at the heart of it all. Simply put, during the last year or two, the young man had grown up, become more mature and adult.

"Yes . . . but what will come of it?"

The apprentice's father stopped cracking nuts. Breaking the empty shells with his fingers, he got down to business. To the girls, this was even more cheerless than before, and each in turn slipped out of the room. The boy quietly left the table and stood by the window. He stood there the whole time his father and his boss were discussing him and arguing over him, cracking nuts one at a time with bare hands and eating them. Ten minutes later, Beylke came back in. Attracting her attention with a quick smile and a wink, the boy put a nut on the windowsill and cracked it with his forehead. The nut smashed to pieces, and they could see its innermost heart, which looked like a shattered brain.

THE JEWISH PASSOVER ended with the beginning of Easter, and the young Jews who had just been through their own holiday slipped unnoticed into a foreign one. Two worlds and two peoples mixed together, and those who poured outdoors to welcome their holiday had no doubt that that they were the ruling nation. They flooded into the streets with complete freedom and the authority of their beliefs, expressed in religious ceremonies with lanterns and candles. Free and powerful, the Christian crowds dominated the streets with their numbers, and they attracted and absorbed the Jewish "children of freedom" (as it says in the Passover ritual) who, temporarily assimilated and willing to follow, were swept along. Setting aside their own desires and identities as Jews, they mingled with the Christians in their religious celebration, with foreign people in a foreign world.

Among the hundreds of young Jews who mingled with the thousands of Christians were Beylke and Ettele. They'd left home that evening and gone into the street, where they fell in with the stream of Christians—Christians carrying candles which lit each face and the necks of each person to each side, which also seemed, in the light of the candles, to be faces. Like the other young Jews who'd been drawn into the Christian stream, the sisters walked without candles, and they sensed they were exposing their Jewish origins. They carried their Jewish feelings hidden deep within themselves: outwardly they mixed with the thick crowd, but inwardly they felt entirely separate, as if the crowd was not composed of the same kind of human beings as themselves. They were uneasy, but glad to be out of the house; their discomfort masked the tiresome life they led at home, which felt especially tiresome during the holiday and more so now, at its end.

The silence of the now-hushed church bells seemed deliberate. At twelve o'clock, the deepest hour of the night, they would ring out wildly and urgently, impressing upon the gathered devotees that the most important hour of the holy festival had arrived. Now, in the provisional silence, people were quietly filling the length and breadth of the cobbled sidewalks, gravitating to the streets and squares where the churches were located. Near and far, among the streets and houses, stood the churches with their high stone walls, crowned with pediments and crosses. The peaks towered above in the vast, dark air. Beneath them, tall, narrow windows were illuminated with so much light that they didn't even look like windows, but rather like sheets of bright, living, transparent color, marked into squares by black iron grates. The windows looked like transparent doors with iron grates, forged into a tall, many-storied prison.

Beylke and Ettele were drawn along into one of the churches. It seemed to them both that they'd fallen into an alien, multicolored world: there was so much brightness, so many candles, and so many people. Everything together and each thing separately drew their attention with its frightening strangeness. They wanted to extricate themselves, but there was no opportunity. They were walled in on all sides by a compressed, breathing, and motionless crowd. Everything around them was foreign; even the air was different, Christian: too strange and heavy to breathe.

From some distant place of honor the babbling of the priest could be heard, accompanied now and again by a shrill, shrieking choir. With difficulty, the people surrounding them tried to extend their arms but were unable to cross themselves because they were packed so tightly together; so they piously made the sign of the cross on the foreheads of those standing next to them, almost as if they were crossing their own foreheads.

The two sisters stood pressed tightly against each other, breast to breast. They looked at each other and smiled, finding comfort and familiarity in the other that they'd never felt in their own home: an honest, Jewish comfort.

They got home very late. Their father opened the door for them and lit their way with a candle.

In the house, Passover still lingered. Pieces of matzo and a few Passover dishes lay on the table, stirring sadness and longing, as though an old grandmother had just died. You'd gotten nothing from her during her lifetime and nobody needed her, and yet, now that she's dead, you're a bit sorry. The family hadn't enjoyed Passover at all, aside from lazing about and being bored, but they felt some regret that it was over.

Each sister took a small piece of matzo and bit into it. They didn't particularly feel like eating, but they ate unthinkingly for comfort and for the love of their own holiday.

The church bells rang, informing the households of Jewish tradesmen that they were surrounded by a widespread Christian world with its Christian life and its hundreds of bells that ring and call, inspiring joy and devotion in Christian hearts. And the Jewish tradesmen felt all the lonelier, even more isolated from the outside world during the Christian holiday: more distant from gentiles than during regular working days, and at the same time more separate from other Jews, especially those who ran their own shops, got their business from the streets, and closed their doors in observance of the Christian holiday.

Under the clang of the church bells, Leyzer arose well before his usual time either on holidays or workdays. He got up early, rested and tired, exhausted and lazy after eight days of rest, too lazy for more rest, and far too lazy to work. He got up for work earlier than usual to give himself an hour's free time on a regular workday.

Going into the workroom, he stood by the glass door that led to the courtyard. Jaws wide open, he yawned into the rising sun. Its morning light was stirring the workroom and everything in it to life. It shone into Leyzer's gaping yawn, illuminating a mouthful of neglected teeth, rotted before their time. His eyes, damp from yawning, glittered like glass lenses.

The church bells rang continuously, awakening longing, loneliness, and sadness in his Jewish heart. He looked at the covered workbenches and fleetingly recalled the thirty-five years he'd known them. He'd wanted to leave them at least five times in the past, but couldn't manage it. One by one, he uncovered the three workbenches and the week was unveiled. Three dirty, blackened workbenches. In uncovering them after this time of separation, it seemed like he'd rejoined something of his own, a piece of his own life. Turning one wheel and then another, he felt as though he were touching a part of himself, a part of himself not much loved but intimate nevertheless. And it seemed to him that the holiday, which had come for eight days and was then gone, was also one of his own, but it was . . . yes, it was like an aristocrat who occasionally condescends to drop in on his poor relatives. After his departure a kind of unhappiness lingers; and when everything returns to normal, the relatives start to resent both his arrival and his departure. That's how Leyzer felt after the holiday; something both good and bad had come with it, and now, when it was over, everything was the same again, and he felt a longing for both the good and the bad.

Going into the house, Leyzer got ready to pray. He was neither a fanatic nor a freethinker. He prayed because his father had prayed and because he himself had prayed all his life; and also because it seemed that not praying would be the behavior of either an aristocrat or a lout; and also because things weren't going so well for him that he shouldn't pray; and finally because he was already getting on in years and, in his old age, it was too late to stop.

Touching the *tefillin*,[74] which he hadn't held in his hands for eight days,[75] it seemed that he was touching the workweek: the week that just then seemed holier than the holiday, holier and more intimate. Laying the cold *tefillin* on his bare arm, he felt a biting chill go through his whole body, and tightening the leather strap, in the early morning stillness, in the early morning workday after the holiday, among the Passover dishes and other remnants of the holiday which had not yet been cleared out of the room, he began the weekday blessing for laying *tefillin*:

"Blessed are You, Lord our God, King of the universe, who has

---

74 Phylacteries.
75 *Tefillin* are worn only on weekdays, and not on the Sabbath or holidays.

sanctified us with his commandments and has instructed us regarding the commandment of *tefillin*."

In the room where the Passover things still lay, Leyzer stood in his *tallis*[76] and *tefillin* and prayed the weekday prayer in the weekday style, muttering the words rapidly, mechanically, often forgetting he was praying, not paying attention to his own prayer. In the unceasing ring and clang of the church bells, a Jewish unhappiness woke in his heart, and the bells' clamor inspired him from time to time to pray more earnestly and piously.

The apprentice arrived later. His boss could scarcely recognize him, the boy had changed so much during the eight-day holiday. His lips were plumper, his cheeks redder, and in his old, torn garments, he looked like a living piece of Passover wearing everyday work clothes. He glowed like a bit of early morning, like a bit of spring. Young life and freshness radiated from him. Made shy by the eight-day separation from the household, he lowered his eyes and said, "Good morning."

Leyzer said nothing about his being so late. He understood, in an indistinct sort of way, that after eight days' rest, the boy had to be late on the ninth. His very coming to work was a novelty in and of itself, because every other day of the year he didn't arrive at all; he was a member of the household. Now he was like a worker arriving at work, and that made Leyzer smile.

Throwing off his jacket and cap, the boy laid the belt over the wheel, dampened and oiled it, gave the wheel a turn with the foot-pedal and asked the boss what to do. The boss told him that for now, he should go set up the samovar.

THE GIRLS GOT up very late, and because their own holiday was over and it was the first day of the Christian holiday, they arose in a depressed mood, bone lazy and disinclined to start working, though

---

76 Prayer shawl.

there was a lot to do. They had to wash all the Passover dishes and store them away for the year in their proper places, and they had to bring the everyday dishes out of storage and do the same with them: wash and dry each piece.

It was a regular weekday; but because it was the first day after the Jewish holiday and the first day of the gentile holiday, it seemed more difficult than a usual weekday, and a heavy sadness depressed the girls' hearts.

One washed, the other not yet washed, both in their slips, hair in tangles, the girls entered the wide, sun-drenched corridor. With dazzled eyes, they stood by the glass door and gazed out into the courtyard. They could see people coming and going. Gentile children ran around and stuffed big pieces of yellow Easter bread into their mouths. It was just like the day before, when the Jewish children had run about clutching their pieces of matzo.

"Did you get enough sleep?" their father asked. "The samovar must be cold by now."

Each in turn, the girls went back into the house and surveyed the mess. Neither lifted a hand to do anything. They were not so much sleepy as despondent. They yawned, and each drank a glass of lukewarm tea from the Passover samovar in a Passover glass at a Passover table, and it seemed to them that the Jewish Passover had fallen asleep there and was sleeping into the workweek and into the gentile holiday. Or perhaps Passover was dead, lying like a corpse, and until the corpse is removed from the house, it's both there and not there at the same time.

In the workroom, the week was already underway, busy as usual, though Elya, the worker, hadn't arrived yet. His workbench stood between Leyzer's and the apprentice's in idiotic, paralyzed immobility, and shavings from the two other workbenches showered onto it like hail on a dead horse.

"For everyone else, Passover's eight days long, but when it comes to me, it's nine," Leyzer grumbled.

He'd nursed a hidden grudge for some time because the worker held himself apart from the household and particularly from the girls.

Leyzer wasn't as annoyed by his absence on the ninth day as by his not having shown his face during the eight-day holiday.

He recalled his daughters' late return on the previous night. Maybe they'd met up with the worker somewhere? Looking through the window into the house, he caught sight of them and said:

"He's not here yet, eh? So late! He must have been living it up until all hours last night."

They didn't answer, and Leyzer went on, "And you two, where were you so late last night?"

After eight days' leisure, Leyzer felt too sluggish to work. He got up from the workbench, shook the shavings from his beard and clothing, went into the house, and seated himself as he usually did after a day's work. He watched the girls, who were finally busy clearing away the holiday things. He watched the workweek taking shape in the house and felt sick at heart. From every direction, far and near, he could hear the unceasing clanging and clamor of the church bells. It was no longer the deeply religious tone he'd heard at midnight, but a completely different sound. Now the ringing was happy, impetuous, without order, sequence, or rhythm: a sound to rouse the hearts of believers to belief. Now it awoke courage and joy; it summoned the Christian world to life and pleasure in the holiday.

And here, in Leyzer's house (as in the homes of hundreds of other Jewish tradesmen), with the clanging of the holiday bells people ushered out the Jewish holiday and ushered in the week; but under the subconscious pressure to assimilate, they dimly felt the workweek was neither a workweek nor a holiday. This foreign holiday, like a current flooding into a poor Jewish house, sapped the will and hands of the strength to work, and people sat enervated, in a state of suspension. Though idle, they took no pleasure in their idleness. They felt an apathetic discontent with their own holiday which had just ended, with the gentile one which was just beginning, and with their own workweek, which had just arrived to be greeted with the joyous sounds of a foreign holiday and a foreign, Christian life.

Zalman Shneour
1886–1959

ZALMAN SHNEOUR IS best known as a writer of Hebrew poetry and of Yiddish prose, although he wrote poetry and prose in both languages.

A scion of a Hasidic rabbinical family, Shneour was born in the city of Shklov, in what is now Belarus. He received both a traditional and a modern education, and began writing Hebrew and Yiddish literature at a young age.

At the turn of the century Shneour visited Odessa and became friendly with the city's Jewish writers, including the "grandfather" of modern Yiddish literature, Mendele Moykher-Sforim (Sholem Yankev Abramovitsch), and the great Hebrew poet Haim Nahman Bialik. Shneour later lived in Warsaw, where he became close to the city's Yiddish literary eminence, I. L. Peretz.

Shneour continued to live a peripatetic life for most of his adulthood. Between 1904 and 1906 he lived in Vilna, before moving to Geneva and Paris, where he studied literature, philosophy, and the sciences, and then to Berlin, where he studied medicine. During the First World War, Shneour was held in Berlin as a civil detainee because of his Russian citizenship. Between 1924 and 1941 he lived in Paris, before escaping German-occupied France for the United States.

Shneour started writing for the *Forward* in 1927 at the invitation of editor Abraham Cahan, who met with him in Paris. According to Hillel Rogoff, who was the managing editor, and later the editor, of the *Forward*, Cahan was congratulated by his staff upon his return for having recruited a writer of Shneour's reputation and prestige.

For more than two decades Shneour published both short stories and serialized novels in the *Forward*. "That Which Is Forbidden," which appeared on April 25 and 26, 1929, was part of a series titled *Shklover Yidn* (*Shklov Jews*), which was published as a book the same year. Here Shneour offers psychological insight into the mind of a child while vividly depicting the relations between Jews and non-Jews in a relatively traditional Eastern European context. As literary critic Dan Miron writes, the book "seethes with the bitter alienation of a boyhood in a restrictive society, with rebellious critique of the Jewish traditional family, with vicissitudes of a difficult puberty, and with a welter of negative emotions and childish libido gone wild."

That Which Is Forbidden

(APRIL 25–26, 1929)

Translated by Sarah Ponichtera

I

BEFORE URI'S ADOPTED son Velvel was even seven years old, a hidden desire for the forbidden awoke within him.

The evil impulse arose like an early morning mist, and every time this fog clouded his young mind, his innocent heart would tremble, sensing danger. Yet, in this quiet trembling there was also something of an illicit pleasure, a sweet pain rooted in unacknowledged desire.

The thoughts were still indistinct. However, Velvel knew it would not be long before he would sin. He feared the terrifying but somehow alluring temptation coming closer and closer to him, and longed for it at the same time.

If Velvel could not understand the adults, with their beards and hairy hands, at the very least he tried hard to understand. Fat papa Uri said that according to the Torah one was not permitted to do certain things, and Velvel was afraid of him, and of committing a sin. He tried to convince himself that his father was right, and refrained from doing those things. For example, papa Uri said that on the Sabbath you aren't allowed to tear paper, even if you were just playing. Velvel dreaded the "Fiery Knight" he was told would punish such sins in the World to Come. Even more, he feared his father's leather belt. So he didn't tear any paper. But deep in his heart he harbored a profound, burning suspicion of the adults around him. He suspected that behind all these things that weren't allowed there was a great and wonderful secret that could soothe the soul, like cold water on a hot day. But the adults didn't take him into account, since he was still little, and just tried to frighten him and hide the great secret from him. And Velvel longed to know. The secret of that which was forbidden teased his imagination, floating before his eyes in unnameable colors and wondrous tastes.

One Sabbath the impulse overtook him to tear a piece of paper, even a small piece. It had to be on the Sabbath, of all times! Any other day, it would have been fine. For a long while, he wandered around confused, fighting a battle within himself. In the end— his heart pounding, his breath short and hot, and his tiny fingers trembling—he tore the paper, slowly and carefully, so that no one would hear. But his little brother Fayvke, the wretched brat, saw and heard, and immediately told their father, who was just waking up from his Sabbath nap, testy and yawning.

"He tore paper, Papa! Him, him, Papa! The newspaper, look, look there!"

Papa Uri loosened his yellow leather belt, and shouted, "Come here, you good for nothing kid!"

It did no good. The secret of the forbidden drew him in more and more.

He was drawn to the sound of the Catholic church, where the bells rang down the street from the gardens behind Uri's house. What was happening inside? How did they pray? What kind of prayer books did they have? What were those soft and sad songs that he heard? His friends said that the songs could steal you away from the synagogue. Was that true?

One day, on a Christian holiday, when throngs of people were filing into the church—the men in their new hats, and the girls with their colorful ribbons—he found himself going inside along with them, almost inadvertently. Frightened by so many unfamiliar sights, he was swept in with a wave of celebrants. Thrown off-balance, he even forgot to remove his hat.

Candles were burning, there on the foreign altar. A strange darkness prevailed in spite of their light. Someone was singing a peculiar song, and a suffocating sweet scent filled the air. It must be the incense he had heard about! Crucified figures made from marble stood in every corner. "Do not make for yourself a graven image . . . "[77] How did they pray in such darkness? Everyone around Velvel was kneeling, kissing the pierced stony feet of the statues . . . He was left standing alone, staring fixedly, his mouth half-open. Suddenly his heart clutched, and he was overcome with the frightening and compelling desire to kneel along with them, to pray and say the *Shema*[78] with great concentration, while kneeling . . .

Velvel went pale, and his father's bearded, pious face swam before him in the mystical darkness and then disappeared. An aged, hunched Christian woman dressed in black appeared in the shadows. She stood for some time, watching him with cold eyes. After a while, Velvel heard a soft, almost imperceptible voice, a voice without teeth. "Why do you stand there, dear? Go pray, speak with God!"

At first he didn't understand her words, since she was speaking to him in Polish, but her meaning was clear enough. When she repeated her words, a cold sweat ran down his neck, and a sudden urge to flee this place, and this scary old woman, came over him. "Pray to God,"

---

77 Exodus 20:4.
78 A prayer deriving from Deuteronomy 6:4, "Hear O Israel the Lord our God the Lord is One."

she said. The thought of saying the *Shema* in this place, kneeling here
. . . what was wrong with him?

A few months later, when he had completely forgotten about it,
he ran into the old Christian woman on his way home from school.
He was sure it was the same old woman who had told him to pray in
church. He was terrified, and fled from her as if from a great danger.
He could never have explained why.

II

IT WAS NOT long before the evil impulse came over him once
again.

In Papa Uri's kitchen there were a couple of old boards in the floor
that bent down, off kilter from the rest of the floor. One day, Fayvke,
Velvel's younger brother, got his foot caught in the gap, and fell down
hard, screaming to high heaven. Mama Feyge pulled on her headscarf
and made an arrangement with Trochim, the Polish carpenter. The
next day at six in the morning, the deafening sound of a saw woke
Velvel from his child-like slumber.

Velvel knew: Trochim must have arrived. Quickly he pulled on
some clothes. He wanted to see for himself how a floor was fixed, how
they fitted the smooth, fresh-smelling new boards to the old ones, to
see the shiny long nails flying into the white wood.

"Up so early, my good man?" Mama Feyge asked him sardonically.
"On your way to synagogue for morning prayers?"

"If it's impossible to sleep anyway . . . if they're sawing away like
that . . ." Velvel mumbled, washing his hands. Leaving her, he slowly
snuck over to where Trochim was working and touched his tool kit,
which sent him into a paroxysm of excitement: "Look, Mama, how it
shines, how it sparkles!" But Mama Feyge just shot him an irritated
look. He was excited by everything he saw: how the sawdust showered
down from the saw, how the boards smelled of pitch. Velvel heard the
sound of Trochim diligently sawing and hacking behind him, sighing rhythmically as he worked. A sigh and a saw, a sigh and a hack. A

minute later he was fulminating over a wayward nail. Velvel took his time, stretching out his breakfast as long as he could before he had to go to school.

The carpenter cursed him in his own language: "Little boy, stop stuffing yourself and get to school!"

On the side table his mother used for nonkosher food, Velvel saw Trochim's dirty bag. He peeked into that too and got excited again, running over and grabbing his mother's apron. "Mama, look at the strange food he brought! Is this the kind of thing our neighbors eat, Mama? Look, Mama, do you see?"

"That's his, that's his! What's wrong with you? What do you care what he eats? Get away from there!"

God, he was so curious. He was practically dying of curiosity and his mother was yelling at him! He pulled himself together and moved away from the bag, so that no one would suspect him. But in truth his mind never left it . . . What could possibly be inside? What sort of thing would someone like Trochim eat? What did Polish food taste like?

At eight o'clock Trochim put down his saw, untied his satchel and sat down to eat. Velvel was still standing there, and he watched closely, like a cat, as the peasant brought each bite of food to his lips.

The Pole had brought out of his sack half a loaf of rough soldiers' bread, a rude knife with a sharp tip that seemed as suited for stabbing people as for slicing food, a small paper packet of salt, and finally— a square of some pale meat threaded with red veins that Trochim regarded intently.

"Mama, Mama, look! Is that pork?" His heart was pounding with excitement and longing.

"So what if it is? Get away from there. How many times do I have to tell you not to stare at people while they're eating?"

Velvel walked away but continued watching out of the corner of his eye. Trochim had cut his bread and pork into neat squares, flat and inviting. The bread was black and opaque—the meat, white and glistening. One color brought out the other. The tip of Trochim's nose, his fingers, his teeth, and his knife were smeared with the fat of the forbidden meat that he was eating. He dipped every piece in the coarse salt, grinding like a millstone, and the sound of his chewing filled the house. Velvel imagined they could even hear it outside on the street. Velvel looked at his mother, who stood with her back to the warm oven, hands folded over her belly. She was watching Trochim obliquely and with a little pity, a little disgust, a little mockery, as though she wanted to say:

"Poor fool, poor fool, what a meal you have for yourself here, poor thing . . ." Lost in thought, she turned aside and spat quietly.

"I understand," Velvel thought angrily, upset that he had been driven away not once, but twice. "I understand!" He suspected that even such a pious woman as his mother longed to savor the unknown taste of the forbidden Polish food, just as he did. Her spitting was an act of contrition to God.

Trochim got to work putting his food away. He ate with great single-mindedness, engrossed in the act and pleasure of eating, like a healthy animal or simple villager.

Velvel could no longer contain himself. "Mama, I want to eat! Bread with . . . cheese, mama. No, with butter . . ."

"And what about saying your prayers?" Mama Feyge replied angrily. "Obviously you're not going to make it to school in time to participate, so you might as well do it here. Pretty soon your father will be back from synagogue, and you better have it done by then!"

Velvel went into the dining room to say his morning prayers. They had never seemed so long and boring, especially the parts blessing God and thanking God for having made him a Jew, thereby giving him the opportunity to serve Him through observing Jewish law. It seemed to go on forever.

Meanwhile, Trochim kept eating lustily.

"Blessed are you O God, ruler of the universe, who did not make me a gentile . . ." Velvel murmured the Hebrew words that he said every morning fluently, while his head was spinning with thoughts of the incredible forbidden taste . . . a flavor that would inspire and invigorate . . . Trochim was so lucky. He could do anything he wanted! He knew all the forbidden secrets. Gentiles had it so good!

His prayers were interrupted by the sound of Mama Feyge suddenly throwing a fit, yelling at Trochim in a voice fit to wake the dead. Running back into the kitchen, Velvel saw what had happened. Mama Feyge had taken a set of fresh loaves of bread out of the oven, and Trochim, who was used to eating coarse black soldier's bread, got excited and picked up a fresh brown loaf, sprinkled with caraway seeds, asking Mama Feyge how much it would cost to buy it, smearing pork fat from his hand all over it. Disaster! Now the loaf was completely unkosher—ruined.

Mama Feyge explained as best she could in her broken Polish that as soon as he touched it with his pork-covered hand, it was forbidden to eat it. Nonkosher! *Feh!* She could not understand how it occurred to him to just grab a loaf of bread that wasn't his. In Yiddish she cursed him that his hands should fall off.

Trochim, meanwhile, could not understand what he had done wrong. It made no sense to him. Confused and concerned, he scratched his ear. He made a mournful face and asked in Polish, "What's wrong? Why are you yelling, Miss? Did I hit you? Did I steal your goat?"

With great curiosity, Velvel regarded the poor innocent loaf of bread that was now forbidden. He tried to see what made it nonkosher, but could find nothing. It was a warm loaf of bread, brown and glossy, sprinkled with fragrant caraway seeds, just like all the other loaves. But nevertheless . . . when Trochim had touched it, he had divulged to it the secret of the forbidden. The secret loomed over it. His mother must be afraid of it. If not, why would she have yelled at Trochim so much?

"Mama, Mama, there's nothing wrong with it! Look, nothing got on the bread!"

"Do you want to be excommunicated? Dear God in heaven! As if the bread wasn't enough to deal with. Who asked you to weigh in? Just wait until your father gets home . . ."

In the end, Mama Feyge worked out a deal with Trochim: he would buy the bread from her for half off. Bread, that had cost her thirty groschen to make, she would sell to him for twenty . . . no, fifteen!

Okay? She placed the loaf on Trochim's side table (the one meant for nonkosher food), silently wishing he would choke on it, and left in a huff. Trochim followed her, still arguing. Velvel grew nervous. He looked around—no one was there. Quietly and with great delicacy, he crept towards the nonkosher bread, which beckoned to him with a forbidden, secretive smile, crackling quietly as it cooled. In a flash, he bent over the table and licked the bread's browned crust, his heart pounding. See? He knew it! If he wasn't mistaken, the bread had no particular unfamiliar taste. Where was the taste of the forbidden? Why had his mother been so frightened?

He took one more lick, but still could detect nothing out of the ordinary . . .

He heard footsteps. Someone was coming! Velvel spun around and crept out of the kitchen.

III

VELVEL COULD NOT erase the image of those neat squares of pale meat from his stubborn head.

A year later, a new baby was born in Papa Uri's house. They named him Yerachemielke. Mama hired an elderly Polish woman to help care for him. This seventy-odd-year-old woman, who had light gray eyes in a large head, was always wrapped in a red shawl—a complicated one, with tassels and folds, like you see in Belorussia. This lady was very familiar and casual with everyone, even Papa Uri. She would stuff baby Yerachemielke with porridge and milk until he could barely move. She kissed him and hugged him as though he were her own baby, all the while cursing her daughter-in-law, who had driven her out of her own house, forcing to her leave her own village, her own garden, where she had planted onions and cucumbers as a child. And now . . . now she was forced to serve in a stranger's house, among Jews.

This old lady would secretly buy Velvel sour apples whenever she went to the market. But at the same time, she would always tell on him to his mother and father whenever she knew that he was up to something. And Velvel, who was now becoming a teenager, would pay her back in kind. He would steal whiskey and bread for her from the cupboard, but also lose his temper from time to time and throw her tattered boots at her, calling her an old witch as she fled.

Frequently she and Velvel would find themselves in deep philosophical discussion about the differences between their religions. She showed Velvel her old brass cross—a strange bauble, decorated with blue glass beads. She said she had inherited it from her great-great-grandmother, who had walked on foot to Kiev on pilgrimage. Tremendously impressed, Velvel touched it tremblingly with a pinky finger, then went to show her his father's *tefillin*.[79] He showed her how Jews wore them in prayer. This was how they wrapped the straps, did she see? This was how they wore the one that goes on the head. Did she understand? Afterwards, they would roll up their left sleeve. Look! The old woman nodded her bushy head, not understanding a word, regarding Velvel with wonder and suspicion, like one would an underage magician.

"Aha! Aha!" she would answer him in the provincial manner, open-mouthed, after every word, indicating that she understood very well.

"Aha! Aha!"

In the end, she permitted herself to touch, with great respect, the letter *shin* that adorned the box that was worn on the head. Clicking with her tongue, she asked quietly, "So this is your cross?"

Almost every Sunday her son Mikita would visit her. Mikita was tall and thin. His cheekbones were sharp and shiny, his nose fleshy and haughty. When he turned to you, the first thing you noticed was his large nostrils, and after that—his small, pale blue eyes.

Every time Mikita arrived with his coarse shoes and his broad hello, he brought with him an unfamiliar scent, peculiar to gentiles, into Papa Uri's house. It was the scent of barns, and leather, and cheap Russian tobacco, and tilled fields. Mama Feyge would get cross, and Papa Uri would smoke a cigarette right away. But it didn't bother

---

79 Phylacteries.

Velvel. Something about Mikita attracted him, and he waited impatiently to see him on Sundays, arriving in his sheepskin coat. Velvel was strangely drawn to this coat, which was a dark red in the front, with a yellow patch on the back. He liked touching the leather outside, which had hardened from rain and snow. He liked touching the soft sheepskin inside.

And Mikita did what he came to do. Dear "Matka" would lovingly call his elderly mother "nonna," and use every trick in the book to wheedle her out of her meagre earnings. He would cross himself and swear to pay her back, beating his chest in self-reproach at his past failures in this regard, going on and on to such a degree that in the end his mother, silent and defeated, would hand over her few pennies. As soon as he was out the door, his mother would start cursing a blue streak, damning her deadbeat son and wretched daughter-in-law to the seven hells.

When they served Mikita tea, he would pour it into the china cup little by little, gripping the saucer with both hands, as though afraid someone was going to take it away from him. Without lifting it from the table, he would slurp the tea with deep sighs of contentment. Holding a cube of sugar in his teeth, he would exhale a cloud of hot steam, while wiping sweat from his brow with his coarse linen sleeve. He would take such huge bites of bread that each one sent a shiver down Velvel's back.

After drinking tea with sugar and eating a good bit of bread, Mikita would grow lighthearted. He would take out his copper pipe, stuff it slowly with Russian tobacco, call over Fayvke, Velvel's five-year-old brother, and ask him in Polish for a match. The little one would stand silently, abashed and afraid, put his little finger in his mouth, sneak out quietly and run to his mother, crying his heart out. From the other room, Mikita would try to make up with him, saying in broken Yiddish, "Aw, little boy! What, you scared? I want only . . . you good . . . just . . . give match!" He laughed, rattling off a nonsensical string of Yiddish words, trying to soothe the boy.

But with an older child, like nine-year-old Velvel, he spoke very intelligently. "Among your people," he would say meaningfully, "everyone eats challah, challah and more challah. You could eat fifteen challahs and still not be satisfied! Maybe even more!" At this point, Mikita would show Velvel a tiny pinch of bread with his dirty fingernails. "With us, in Makorovke (this was the name of his village), after this much, you hear, 'Enough brother, you've had your piece, it's enough.'" And he would wave his hand dismissively in front of his nose, so Velvel would understand exactly how he felt.

Sometimes he would tell them a tale about one of his best pigs, who had gotten sick. He had started dragging his hind legs, poor thing. He told him (Mikita told the nonkosher animal, that is), "Do you really want to die like this, and waste my money? Cursed beast!" One blow with a wooden cudgel and it was over. He salted the meat to save it for the holidays. It was good meat. But after they ate it, they all got sick, dragging their limbs, just as the pig had. Everyone had it. What a sickness it was! This "listeria" was a terrible thing. His little daughter Marina had gotten sick from it, and wasn't able to eat a thing, not bread with herring, not cabbage, not blintzes with sour cream. He had gone to town and bought her a pastry with raisins, and even that she wouldn't touch. "So," he said, "She died." Just like that!

Before he left, Velvel wrapped up a big piece of challah for him, and Mikita would thank him with a clap on the shoulder from his great paw.

"Visit us in Makorovke sometime, little one! We'll serve you potatoes with fresh dill and sour cream!"

Of course, Velvel could have the same potatoes with sour cream at home. But still . . . Why did some part of him faint with desire to visit Mikita in Makorovke? Why did he long for Mikita's potatoes, for fresh sour cream?

If only his father was nicer! Then he would let him go and visit!

But his father was not nice, and did not let him go.

One day Velvel overheard Mikita telling his mother, Yerachmielke's nanny, that he would bring her some pork next Sunday. Unconsciously, a shudder went through him, and he kept it in mind, and waited impatiently . . . What did Mikita's pork really have to do with him, who would be a yeshiva student soon? And yet, he waited . . .

IV

THE NEXT SUNDAY, when Velvel came home from school for lunch, he found the nanny a little tipsy. In a tremulous voice, she lovingly related that her son Mikita had only just left. He had shared a bottle of whiskey with her, told her how much he missed her, said he wanted her to come back home to Makorovke soon, and brought her a present of roast pork. A lovely piece, too! It was right over there, under the sofa in the nursery, in a pot. What a son he was, after all! It was just that wife of his, the wretched woman, may she rot in a pit, and so on, and so forth.

The boy ate his lunch without tasting it. He kept finding reasons to go into the nursery, and stole glances at the package under the couch each time, before slipping back out. Finally, Mama Feyge got tired of his running back and forth, and shouted, "Don't you have to get back to school?"

When Velvel came home in the evening, the house was quiet. His father was still at synagogue, his mother was at the market, the nanny and the baby were sleeping, and his little brother was playing quietly by himself in the kitchen. He snuck into the nursery, crept under the sofa and quietly lifted the pot lid. He looked inside the pot and caught a glimpse of a glistening piece of meat, wrapped in a simple linen cloth. Suddenly frightened, he replaced the lid and left.

In the middle of the night, when everyone was asleep, and the nanny was snoring in the nursery, Velvel suddenly awoke, as though someone had shaken him. He tried to get back to sleep, but could not. "The pot . . . the pot . . ." Slowly, Velvel slunk out of bed, went back to the sofa, went down on all fours, and looked into the pot with terror and trembling, as though he were leaning precariously, staring into a terrifying black abyss. Under the sofa it was black as pitch. It was so dark he could not see the pot, yet he felt it there in the secretive blackness. Sensed it, like a cat sensing a mouse. His white shirt glowed palely in the darkness. He didn't dare to actually touch the pot. He couldn't say why not.

Several days passed, but the thought of the pot still tormented him. The pot, and the secret that lay inside it . . . The secret! Velvel tried to form a clear image in his mind of what was inside the pot. He thought maybe it was like a kind of honeyed pastry, a taste that was out of this world. They said that eating pork made people healthy, healthy as a horse . . . That was what they said. Perhaps it would give him a healthy red glow like he had seen among the Polish children. Healthy!

Velvel woke early in the morning and tried to concentrate on thoughts of his teacher, of prayer, of studying Talmud . . . but he quickly grew bored, and yawned. But as soon as he thought about the pot and its mystery, suddenly he grew limber and lithe, and sprung out of bed to get dressed, quick as could be.

Velvel began making preparations for his "sin." The devil alone knew how a nine-year-old boy could suddenly become so clever and calculating, so cold-blooded that no one in the house suspected him of a thing. He understood right away, for example, that it would be difficult for him to take a piece from the large roast in the pot. To sneak over to the sofa, take off the lid, unwrap the linen that protected it, take out the whole roast and cut off a small slice with a knife that he would need to have hidden in his pocket—all that would not be easy. Someone might interrupt him, or the old crone might notice that something was missing. What a present Mikita had sent! Now he had to be sharp and clever, lest his adventure be exposed.

He summoned all his patience and began to wait for the old woman to break into the pot on her own. It seemed she was worried that it would not be enough for her, so she cut the roast into smaller and smaller pieces, to pace herself. This was her nature, and she did this with everything: bread, meat, pickles. Very likely there would be some left over, and he could just take a tiny bit—she wouldn't notice a thing! He found a paper bag in which to store his future treasure, and took to keeping it in his pocket. Velvel had always been a very neat person, so no one wondered why he might have a little bag with him to store something.

Another day passed. Now it was Thursday. When Velvel came home from school for lunch, he saw that the old Polish woman had taken her gleaming white roast out of the pot. She cut off eight small slices for her lunch, wrapped up the rest in its linen, put the pot back in its place, and sat down to eat. She chewed slowly, absorbed in her food. Her wrinkled cheeks and creased temples moved in tandem, jumping and bending like the parts of a machine. Her chewing was driving Velvel crazy. She didn't care that any moment his mother would order him back to school. But Velvel kept his composure. He leafed mindlessly through an ornamented book, stealing glances all the while at the pieces on her plate. He was afraid she would ruin this for him by eating everything up. He knew her, after all. What if she cleaned her plate, the old crone? May she rot. His mother was always saying, after all, that she was eating them out of house and home. Velvel had heard her say that not too long ago. But wait! She was crossing herself. She untied the strings of her apron and hiccuped. Three whole pieces of pork were left over from her lunch! She stood up and sighed. Looking piously up at the ceiling, she put the three leftover pieces back in the pot, not even bothering to wrap them back up in the linen.

Velvel grew hot with anticipation. Soon he would achieve his goal. Part of him still didn't want to, but nevertheless he would. But his mother ruined it. She arrived in the nursery, her sleeves rolled up, with a broom in her hands, breathing heavily. It looked like she had just been in a fight with someone. As soon as she saw Velvel, she unleashed all her pent-up rage, screaming at him and waving her broom. "Get to school! Why are you hanging around here, driving me crazy! You should be in school!"

Velvel sprang to his feet and rushed to school. His face was still flushed and his heart contracted with desire. The afternoon dragged on interminably—the same dour teacher with his quick ruler, the same afternoon prayers, after that the evening prayers, a typical dinner, and then bedtime with the same snoring coming from the nursery. Velvel was afraid to approach the pot at night. Under the sofa a tiny black, clever, demon awaited him, licking the pot with its sharp tongue, and staring up at him with shrewd eyes.

V

THE NEXT DAY, Friday, Velvel had only a half-day at school. He was freed at two o'clock and came home to a light pre-Sabbath lunch. He ate without appetite, and then wandered around the house aimlessly. He kept taking naps in his nicely made bed, or playing listlessly with his little brother. In his agitation, the repetitive tunes of the Torah verses they were learning in school echoed in his head like a drill.

"Mama! Do you know how they make a *shalsheles?*"[80] he asked suddenly.

"A *shal-* whatsit?"

"*Shaallshellles,*" he dragged the word out for emphasis.

"Go bother your brother!"

Velvel walked away, not feeling a shred of guilt. His head was foggy, and he felt flushed. He was waiting for the nursery to be empty. Every so often, he would peek into the kitchen, where the enticing smells of peppered fish and baked apples were beginning to fill the air. There he practiced quietly lifting a lid so that no one would hear. But his mother heard, and gave him a push out the door along with a curse and a threat that his father would hear all about what he was up to. Velvel was never left alone in the nursery even for one second. The bastards! As soon as the nanny would leave, his mother would rush in. When his mother left, Fayvke would roll his little wooden wagon in. "Voom! Voom!" Now, of all times, he had to play wagon driver! When Velvel tried to drive him away, he responded with hysterical cries, as though Velvel had pinched him. His cries brought the nanny and his mother rushing back in. The springtime sun was already setting into the distant woods. Late afternoon rays poured red light over the village's shingled roofs. As if in spite, someone asked Velvel to clean his father's boots. After that he had to quickly get ready, wash his hair with steaming hot water, put on his nice pants for the Sab-

---

80 Hebrew for "chain."

bath and run out and buy candles, which his mother had forgotten to buy, as she always did.

When he returned, he found himself once again in the nursery.

Shhhh! This time, no one was there. The baby slept, moving his lips silently. Little soul! The only thing he knew to dream about was a bottle of milk. A cow mooed, somewhere far off. Hush, cow!

Quickly, Velvel dropped to his knees next to the couch, still in his nice Sabbath clothes. His mother would see! He grabbed the paper sack out of his pocket and adroitly removed the lid from the pot. Soon he felt one of the small squares of meat touch his hand. As though it were dangerous, Velvel flung it into his paper bag, careful and swift, barely touching it. The bag went back into his pocket. It was done!

Velvel looked around—nothing. The clay pot stood in its place like an idol. It was silent. Could it be that nothing had happened? But his heart was pounding hard. He could hardly swallow.

The cow mooed loudly. It was closer, it had wandered into the street. It lectured him in its language, "It's a sin!"

Velvel grew ashamed of himself and walked out of the room slowly, with a studied air of dignity. He still had to cross the kitchen before he would be safe. They were drinking tea in there, waiting for his father to return from afternoon prayers. His father must be praying now, whispering solemnly, facing the wall . . .

"Where were you hiding out, while we all were drinking tea?" Mama Feyge's voice called out from the other room.

"I'll be right there," he answered out of the corner of his mouth, spinning around. A second later, he was climbing up a ladder, nimble as a cat, heading for the attic, which connected the ceiling of the house to the roof of the adjacent barn. This little attic was always full of hay and straw. From here, they could throw the cow's food down to her stall without leaving the house. The dry, fragrant straw crackled strangely under his cautious steps. In a distant corner of the attic, he found the hollow he had made for himself a day or two ago, where he could commit his "sin" in peace.

The large cracks in the rotten shingles seeded the small attic with a gray, thoughtful light. Through them you could almost make out unfamiliar roofs, the gilded spire of the church, tiny shadows of people . . . And not far from Papa Uri's house, a Polish horse, its face hidden up to its ears in a feeding sack, its head moving back and forth. It seemed to Velvel that the horse was deliberately nodding to him. And the cracks in the shingles were looking at him, like laughing, thievish, half-closed eyes which see everything that people try to hide.

But Velvel gathered his courage and moved deeper into his hollow, focusing on the straw, looking for a darker place, so dark he would not even be able to see himself, and then took out his hidden treasure.

His hands trembled. At last he would know the true taste of forbidden food. He had wanted this for so long, so badly, and had waited so patiently. Nevertheless, he had to force the first bit into his mouth and make himself chew. It was difficult to take the first bite of the unfamiliar, taboo food.

Salty. Fatty. Unpleasant. This was what was so exciting about eating pig? Where was the wonderful taste he had imagined? The amazing secret? Where was the secret that the Polish people knew?

Velvel tried to talk himself into believing that the nonkosher food was delicious, good and healthy. He bit into the fat with his front teeth, making contact with its veins. He wanted to see clearly how it thickened, how it was formed.

He chewed . . . did he have a choice? But oh, how he wanted to stop. No, on the other hand, it was good. Very good! But this, this was pig flesh? What about the secret? The secret . . .

"Velvel!" a voice rang out. "Where did he disappear to? It's time to welcome the Sabbath!" It was his father's voice.

He sat for a moment, trembling. But even so, his fear pushed him to take the piece of pork, bury it deep, deep in the straw, and spit out its forbidden taste. He trembled, and spit.

"Velvel! Just wait, I'll show you to keep me waiting . . . !"

"There's no sign of him in the garden!" The guilty boy heard his mother's voice from his lair in the straw. He heard people walking around, looking for him. But did they know what he had done? Suddenly he heard a terrifying suggestion: "Maybe he is up in the attic?"

It was the nanny's voice. That old witch! Right after that, he heard his little brother Fayvke's carefree voice: "There! There! Yesterday he was there! And the day before that too!"

Right away Velvel heard heavy footsteps on the ladder. It was father, it was father! Oh, he had to swallow the last piece of pork! Otherwise it would betray him. His father was coming!

The boy crouched in his dark hole and waited. They might think that he had disappeared entirely. Father's footsteps came closer. He could hear how he was breathing, furiously. The straw crackled and whispered around him. Velvel felt as though a terrifying wild beast were stalking him, hoping to devour him.

And choked, wild words, "Hm? Where? Wait, wait wait . . ."

The hands, which were feeling between the bales of hay, were coming closer and closer. He could almost see a head! A terrifying bearded head with pieces of straw stuck in its dusty hair. It was him! He was finished!

Velvel had rolled up his nice Sabbath pants when he burrowed into the straw, and now the bright white of his socks gleamed in the darkness. His father grabbed him. "Aha!"

Velvel felt strong hands dragging him out of his hiding place in the straw. Falling on his back, he felt a horrible slap on his face as though it came from Heaven. Velvel kept quiet.

"What are you doing here?" A slap. "Why would you be crawling around in the attic right before the Sabbath?" Another slap. "Were you born in a barn?" Another slap. "You don't answer your father's call?" Slap. "I'm asking you, why are you up here?" Slap. "Don't you have any respect for the holy Sabbath?" Slap.

Velvel absorbed the blows, laying stretched out on his back, with clenched teeth. He felt like boiling hot water was being poured on his face.

Papa Uri grew disturbed by his young son's stubborn silence. He suddenly pulled Velvel up from the straw. With both hands, he held his shoulders, and looked deeply into his round eyes. In the pale evening light, which filtered through the cracks in the roof, he saw a round, child-like face, a cold and stubborn stare—and trembled. He let go of Velvel's shoulders, leaned against a nearby heap of straw, dazed, and stammered out, full of regret, "So, tell me . . . what is this? Well . . . what is going on with you? What will happen to you? Will you be all right, in the end?"

For the first time, the boy burst into tears.

Miriam Karpilove
1888–1956

MIRIAM KARPILOVE, ONE of the most prominent women Yiddish writers of the early twentieth century, worked in nearly every literary form, including short stories, belles-lettres, plays, and novels.

Born in Minsk to a family of nine children, Karpilove received a Jewish and secular education, as well as vocational training as a photographer and photo retoucher.

In 1905 she immigrated to America, where she settled in Bridgeport, Connecticut. An ideological Zionist, she joined the Labor Zionist movement and lived in Palestine in the late 1920s.

Karpilove began writing for the *Forward* shortly after her arrival in America. In the 1930s she was hired as a staff writer for the newspaper, and became well known for serialized novels that focused on women and the challenges they faced in a society with shifting romantic and sexual mores. Between 1920 and 1937 Karpilove published seven novels in the *Forward*, along with shorter works.

"In a Friendly Hamlet" appeared in the newspaper on June 14, 1934, and portrays a young woman trying to resist an unwanted marriage against the backdrop of a patriarchal society.

In a Friendly Hamlet

(JUNE 14, 1934)

Translated by Myra Mniewski

I T'S DISGRACEFUL; THE indignity of it is just too much. The country Jew's daughter, the bride, ran away from the groom, the in-laws
and all of the guests who had come to celebrate her wedding, and fled
the house in a panic.

Out of the house and straight into the barn. She could not feel at
peace, so she abandoned everyone and made straight for the livestock!

She went to the cows to unburden herself, feeling as though the
speechless creatures might possibly be able to help her. But, regret-
tably, the animals turned away from her. Only one, her Hadoylia, the
spotted cow that she had welcomed into her arms when it was calved,
the one she had hand-fed, using her finger to place the gruel into the
calf's mouth so that it would think it was her mother nursing her—it
was this beast, with her sorrowful eyes, that consoled her. This animal was the one who felt the bride's condition, understood the injus-
tice perpetrated on her.

So the bride cuddled up to her cow and talked to her.

"You have no idea how good you have it to be a beast. If you were
in my shoes, they'd be trying to find you in order to marry you off to
some lowlife with big boots covered in muck. That's the kind of bull
my dear father has brought me from the market! If my mother, may
she rest in peace, were still alive, he would let me remain in the stall.
He wouldn't be looking to entrap me, just to free himself to marry
more quickly. It is bitter to be an orphan. Bitter as gall!"

As if showing her agreement, the spotted bovine lowered her head, making it easier for the bride to snuggle her.

"Don't let them take me away from you. Kick them, knock their teeth out if they try to come near us. I'd rather stay here with you than go under the wedding canopy with such a bull, such a horse."

Presently, the bride's father came into the stall from the house.

"Listen here, girl!" he yelled out menacingly. "Don't ruin my life—get in the house now!"

"I won't go!" The bride clung tighter to the animal.

"Oh you won't, won't you?" her father retorted angrily. "Do you want me to smack your face to bits?"

"Skin me alive and send me right to my mother's grave." The bride burst out in tears.

Her father kicked the dung with his foot. "Stop howling and shut your big mouth. You should be glad that someone is willing to have you, my haughty one. The nerve of her protesting like this. It's not to her liking!"

"I'd rather die!" The bride sobbed. "I'd rather fall down dead!"

Her father softened up a bit: "Chava-Tsire, don't be a fool, listen to your father, I want the best for you, for your sake. He's a good groom for you. After the wedding he'll turn into a *mentsch*.[81] He likes you, he wants you, he's eager to talk to you. He was itching to follow you into the stall. We were barely able to hold him back. It's improper for a groom to run into a stall in pursuit of his bride. It's unfitting, he'll be laughed at."

The old man had barely gotten his words out when the groom appeared, whip in hand. "Father-in-law!" He sounded as if his mouth were full. "Let me talk to the bride myself for a minute. I have a tongue in my mouth, I can speak."

The bride's father looked at his future son-in-law for a minute and nodded his head. "Okay, talk! Maybe she'll listen to you more than to her father. I'll be right here on the other side of the door listening," the elder said, and stepped away from the couple.

---

81 Literally, "person."

The groom approached the bride swishing his whip, and then, as if ashamed, produced a slight smile. "An ox has a long tongue but cannot speak . . . eh, it's not good to kick and scream . . . uh . . . I mean hesitate. It's been preordained. Get a load of this beast—does she produce a full share of milk? My horse eats a full portion of feed—a full pail with no cover. He's a noble steed. He steps lively and tows his load. I would never sell him even if you covered me with gold. I've known him since he was a colt."

Getting closer to the cow, he began to pet her. She, with her big eyes, looked mournfully and in wonderment at the groom.

"She likes me," the groom brayed at the bride—ha, ha, hee-hee. She's not kicking or agitated—she's a good animal. I have a good match for her. God willing, after our providential wedding, I'll arrange hers."

The bride blurted out irately, "I don't want to. I'm not going to marry you!"

"You're not! Why? Every girl wants to get married!"

"I don't want to!" The bride maintained.

"This is not good!" the groom stamped his foot in his big boot on a pile of dung. "What will people say? They'll laugh and say all sorts of horrible things. It will be ugly. They'll call me a castoff, a waif who loafs about at strangers' homes. They'll make me out to be a farmhand. I'll be a good husband. I won't do anything to hurt my wife. I'll listen to everything she says—may I die if I don't. I'll treat her as if she were heavenly. I'm good at pleasing. I'll polish up with time. I'll be respectable. On my own I'm a simpleton. That's why I want someone who is above me. I will bow down to you."

Looking down, the groom kept on talking and talking while leveling the dung pile with those huge boots of his, until the bride's father came in.

"*Nu,*" the father eyed them, "how long is this going to go on? People are waiting. Who ever heard of such a thing—a groom and bride in a stall. This is a place for horses, for animals!"

"It's okay, father-in-law, it doesn't matter," the groom said. "It's not important where we speak, what's important is what we're saying. I'm speaking to the point here and directly to the bride: I will not leave this spot until I can show my face to decent folks. I'd rather be struck by lightning and not live to see tomorrow as my name is Moyshe."

"Enough already, enough," the bride's father motioned with his hand. "Out of the stall. Go! *Nu, nu!*"

Like creatures being driven out to the field, the bride and groom lumbered out of the stall and made their way to the house, the country Jew in the lead with the two of them in single file behind him.

When they got to the door, the country Jew detained his daughter to have a few words with her.

"Look here, be a *mentsch*, do what you're told. If you don't, your groom will shake himself loose of you. After the ceremony you'll climb all over him as much as you want, but not now. *Nu*, go, lead with your right foot! And may it be with good fortune!"

With her head bowed, the bride trudged from the stall into the big house. Women and girls, her friends, clustered around her. They took her into a side room and danced around her. They brushed her hair, primped and groomed her, and the whole time they were petting and gussying her up, they wished her good luck and happiness.

In the house the men fussed over the groom. They were advising him as to what to do when the time came to veil the bride, to go to the canopy, and later. The groom, fidgeting, didn't know where to rest his big hands, as he didn't have his whip at hand. The derby they'd put on his head kept sliding down over his eyes. He was hot. Gentiles from the area began gathering at the house and leaned on the walls.

The bride's relatives brought over glasses of brandy and snacks. The peasants, especially the women, sipped their drinks and grimaced while covering their mouths with their hands. They stole looks at the groom and whispered to each other, then burst out in laughter. The musicians took out their instruments. The younger women, in their colorful dresses, gathered to dance a quadrille. Girls danced with girls, and men with men.

The bride's father squabbled with the matchmaker, the wedding jester and the groom's spokesman, all of them set on taking a piece of him. They wanted him to pay up now, before the ceremony; they wanted to be paid what he had agreed to. He kept putting them off, saying he'd pay them after.

"What do you want from me?" the father of the bride insisted, spreading his hands. "Why are you all on top of me? What do you think, that I'll run away? If I said I'd give the speckled cow, I'll give it! And I'm giving the bride's trousseau too. I'm also making the wedding, providing room and board, and throwing in a bit of cash as well. What more do you want of me? Wait until the wedding gifts are distributed. There will be enough for everyone. Don't ruin the party. The groom has agreed to everything, let's just hope the bride goes along with it too."

"The bride is seated!"—came the call from the room where the women were. "Seat the bride!"

The two opposing sides lined up to make way for the bride. The entertainer cleared his throat and quietly tutored the groom, informing him how to conduct himself during the seating: "You'll very slowly take hold of the bridal veil and cover her face with it. When I give you the signal, that's when you'll do it."

The groom nodded his shaggy head and pulled at the buttons of his vest with the fat fingers of his huge hands. He was nervous and impatient. He wanted the wedding to be over already so that he could be alone with the bride. She pleased him; she was sweet. Not such a thick imbecile like that other girl they wanted to fix him up with last year. The only trouble with this one was that she was kicking and screaming and running away. But that's nothing, he'd break her in. It would be like it is with a new horse, it takes some time before it gets used to whoever is holding the reins. He'd have to break her in . . .

Kadya Molodowsky

1894–1974

KADYA MOLODWSKY WAS a writer, teacher, editor, and one of the great Yiddish poets of the twentieth century.

Born the second of four children in Byaroza, a town in what is now Belarus, Molodowsky received a Jewish education from her father, a religious school teacher and proponent of Zionism, and received secular instruction from private tutors. Her mother ran a dry-goods shop and later managed a kvass factory. After passing her high school exams, Molodowsky received a teaching certificate, and from 1911 to 1913 taught in the cities of Sherpetz and Bialystok. She then moved to Warsaw, where she studied pedagogy until 1914.

During the First World War, Molodowsky worked in homes for refugee children in Ukraine before moving to Odessa and then to Kiev, where she began to write and publish. In 1921, Molodowsky married and moved back to Warsaw, where she would live until 1935. In Warsaw she taught in both Yiddish- and Hebrew-language schools, and published in the literary journal *Literarishe bleter* (*Literary Pages*) and edited the literary page of the newspaper *Fraynd* (*Friend*). In Warsaw she also published four books of poetry to critical acclaim, including the 1935 volume *Freydke*, a sixteen-part narrative poem about a heroic working-class woman.

In 1935, Molodowsky traveled to the United States with the intention of visiting relatives in Philadelphia, Washington, D.C., and Boston. Instead, she wound up settling in New York, where she was later joined by her husband. In New York, Molodowsky began writing for the *Forward*, where she remained a contributor until her death.

Her first contribution to the paper was a series about great Jewish women written under the pseudonym Rivke Zilberg, although she soon began publishing poetry and fiction under her own name. A collection of her stories, *A shtub mit zibn fenster* (*A House with Seven Windows*) was published in New York in 1957.

"A House on the Hill," published in the *Forward* on March 4, 1962, sees Molodowsky taking a look back from her American vantage point to the small-town Jewish life of her youth.

———

A House on the Hill

(MARCH 4, 1962)

Translated by Kathryn Hellerstein

ARKE WAS THE only male in the narrow market where fish were sold. The other fish sellers, all women, made fun of him: he might as well have been wearing a dress. He lived on the hill, there where all the poor people lived, and he would have remained a poor man to the end of his days if his three grown daughters, Golde, Gitele, and Gishe, had not pushed him aside and begun to work at earning a living themselves. Gitele threw out the old braided baskets and bought a large white basin for tench. The little fishes, the gudgeons and the crucian carp, she left completely out of her business. Let "them" deal with those, she said about the other vendor-women, and set out pike, carp and tench on her table in the market.

Gitele wore high, shiny galoshes and on her head a bonnet with a dangling pendant, as if she were the nobleman's granddaughter and not Arke's daughter at the fish market.

On Thursdays, she herself traveled to the lake to bring the fish, and everyone in town knew that Gitele's fish were fresh from the water. All the wealthy housewives in the city flocked to her as customers, and she even supplied fish to Adamke's tavern, where the gentile noblemen went to drink beer.

Behind her back, the women vendors in the market heaped abuse on Gitele. "On Thursday, may she break her arms and legs." But to her face they praised her and said that she had made her father, that *shlimazel*,[82] into a respectable person.

Arke began to go to the synagogue to study with all the well-to-do men, and they even started calling him Reb[83] Areh. Although they all still lived on the hill, his family rose to genteel standing. No one was surprised anymore when, on the Sabbath, Gitele and both her sisters would stroll down Church Street in straw hats, like the pharmacist's daughter, and Reb Areh donated a whole ruble as a contribution to provide the poor with Passover necessities.

But Areh's wife, Feyge-Tsipe, prayed to the Lord that no one, God forbid, should give her daughters the evil eye, and on the Sabbath, when her daughters would gaze into the tiny mirror that stood on the corner table and put on their straw hats before taking a walk, Feyge-Tsipe pleaded with them: "You don't need those straw hats! Why do you need to show off in the city? Why do I need people to be envious of me? Mendel the Miller's daughter walks here without a hat, and your father is still not Mendel the Miller, who has a house in the middle of the market."

The table had already grown too small for their business, and so they rented a wooden stall. In the market it was said that they'd hit the jackpot. The daughters wanted to leave the squalid hill, and Gitele proposed to pay installments on a house that was for sale in the market. Areh nodded his head and said, "*Nu*, when you come up in the world, God forbid, you don't sink again. Why not?"

But Feyge-Tsipe pointed at the ceiling with her hand and said, "This roof has been lucky for me. My daughters were born here, and they grew up here, and thanks be to God, now we're the equals of

---

82 An inept or bungling person.
83 Yiddish for "Mr."

respectable people. I'm not going to leave here. People will be jealous of us if we puff ourselves up and move to a house in the market. And in a city, when the tongues start wagging, God protect us from what can happen."

When she saw that Shimen the broker was coming to speak with Areh about the house in the market, she grabbed the doorframe and shouted: "I'm not leaving here! They'll have to drag me out!"

Shimen the broker was intimidated by such talk and fled. Areh ran after him and replied: "*Nu*, so now you see what kind of a woman she is, my Feyge-Tsipe, she's attached herself to the house."

Returning, Areh tried to persuade Feyge-Tsipe. "For the sake of making matches for our daughters, you need to do this. What kind of a matchmaker will come to you up here on the hill? And what better kinds of bridegrooms will be brought to you down there!"

But Feyge-Tsipe held her own. "If a good match is meant to be, it will come here too."

All the neighbors on the hill knew the story and rejoiced. "Feyge-Tsipe doesn't want to leave the hill. Never mind that the hill is not really the social scene."

And everyone wished Feyge-Tsipe all the best.

It was a Friday. This was between Yom Kippur and Sukes,[84] when Berezovski traveled up to the market in his open carriage, pulled to a stop near Gitele's wooden stall and wanted to buy a tench. Berezovski was a rich Jew who lived on a large farm near the city, maintained other fields and dealt in lumber. And whenever he used to travel to the city, everyone would make money: dry-goods merchants and tailors, cobblers and butchers. The women fish sellers looked at this customer from a distance and were envious: "*Nu*, what then? To whom will Berezovski travel for fish? To Gitele with her shiny galoshes. One rich man is drawn to another."

Berezovski was a man with an open hand and never haggled with anyone. When he sensed that the price was being raised a bit, he used to say, "In Berditshev it's more expensive."

---

84 The Feast of Tabernacles.

Why he said "In Berditshev" no one ever knew. But that was his saying. Gitele had already placed the tench on a piece of paper when Berezovski's son approached the table, grabbed the tench and took a look under the gills.

Gitele became enraged. She grabbed the tench from his hand, threw it back into the white basin and exclaimed: "Get out of here! No one looks under the gills of my tench."

Father and son stood stock still as if in shock. The young man wiped the fingers of his hand with his handkerchief, as if he wanted to wipe away the shame, and the older Berezovski became suddenly disturbed—this was the first time in his life that someone hadn't want to sell him a piece of merchandise.

"What kind of a business is this?" he said, and stared at Gitele, astonished and curious.

Gitlele stood, her hands on her cheeks. The pendant on her head rocked back and forth and she answered him provocatively: "This kind of business is what it is!" Her lips pressed together angrily, and she looked like an empress who does not want to sign a treaty.

Her older sister, Golde, interjected. "*Nu, nu*, Gitele, what kind of a game are you playing?"

But Gitele grew more stubborn, jiggled the pendant back and forth and, with an angry little smile, said: "No one looks under the gills of my tench." And as if she were seized from within by spitefulness, she refused to sell them the fish. Even the tench in the bowl seemed angry.

Old Berezovski murmured: "In Berditshev, you can actually get fish." And both men, Berezovski and his son, returned to their carriage empty-handed, as if they'd lost a large bet.

Old Berezovski went first and did not look back, but his son stopped, turned his head around and saw Gitele still standing there with her hands on her cheeks, watching them. He gave her a smile and wagged his finger at her. His smile touched Gitele to the quick, and she looked after them until they drove away in their carriage.

Even before the girls came home from the fish market, Feyge-Tsipe already knew the whole story with the Berezovskis, that Gitele hadn't sold them the tench. All the fish sellers had gossiped about it, and they had brought this news up the hill.

Feyge-Tsipe paced through the house, agitated. She met her daughters with a shake of the head. "You're driving me crazy! Gitele, the genius! She wouldn't sell a tench to *Berezovski*! All the gentiles at the lake work for him in the forests and the fields. They cut down the trees for him, they transport the lumber for him! All he has to do is say a word, and you'll be minding a dried-up fish stall, you won't even have a tench tail to sell!"

Feye-Tsipe's face darkened, as if a calamity were advancing upon her. The older sister, Golde, cried: "I told her! What kind of a game is this? But when Gitele is stubborn . . ." And Golde wiped her eyes with the hem of her dress.

When Areh came home from prayers, he found all three girls quiet, as if they'd been slapped. They hadn't even washed their hair, as they did every Friday before blessing the Sabbath candles.

Feyge-Tsipe told him the tale of the tench and voiced all the bitterness in her heart. "A house in the market they want! Turned into aristocrats! Fine folks! To Berezovski they wouldn't sell a tench! Who knows what will come of this . . ."

The sorrow of all the poor people of the hill fell upon Feyge-Tsipe and spread across the whole house.

Areh paced back and forth near the set table, and before he began to make *Kiddush*,[85] he cheered up and shouted to his wife: "What are you moaning about here? Berezovski is a Jew. He won't be in a hurry to betray Gitele to the gentiles! To ruin a Jewish woman!"

Gitele took her time and answered her mother, "*Nu*, why get all worked up about the fish? I will open a shop selling dairy products, and on Passover, I will apply for a license to bake matzo!" She remembered the young Berezovski's smiling eyes and, in the middle of everything, burst out laughing.

"The girl is crazy," Feyge-Tsipe said, and, fortified by her husband's words and her daughter's confidence, proceeded to set out the

---

85 The ceremonial blessing on wine made on the Sabbath and holidays.

Friday evening dinner on the Sabbath table. They ate in silence. After the meal ended, the little flames of the Sabbath candles began to leap and then to go out, and the darkness threw sadness across the table.

On Thursday, as usual, Gitele traveled to the lake to buy the biggest tench, pike, and carp. She had hidden her fear from her sisters that her mother might have been right and that she would return home with an empty wagon. Into her mind came the image of the poorest family on the hill, Henye the feather-plucker, who came all the time to borrow the two groschen she needed to buy Sabbath candles. Gitele sat in the wagon, engrossed in her thoughts, and was silent. Petrukhe, the gentile who drove with her every Thursday for the fish, asked her a question:

"What's with you, Gitele, are you sick? You don't seem like yourself."

"No, Petrukhe. I just had a dream. A dream . . . that I had fallen into a pit." At that very moment, Gitele dreamed up a dream for Petrukhe.

"Yeah, yeah," the gentile said. "A bad dream will bring life to an end."

Her wagon full of fish, Gitele returned to the fish market on Friday before dawn, and all her fears had vanished. With her shiny galoshes and her bonnet with the pendant dangling on top, she stood as usual near the white bowls and looked like a noblewoman among the neighboring fish sellers. She didn't notice with her eyes, yet she sensed that Berezovski's carriage was approaching. This time, the young Berezovski came alone, without his father. Gitele's heart pounded. She didn't know whether it was with joy or fear. Just as on the other day, he wagged his finger at her. He approached her stand. He stood there quietly, didn't say a word and smiled. Gitele was fire red. She summoned all her strength and took a look at him.

"*Nu*," he said. "Will you sell me a tench?" His eyes sparkled gleefully, and Gitele lost all of her strength. Even the pendant on her head didn't stir from its place. Without saying a word, she selected the prettiest fish from the bowl, weighed it, wrapped it in paper, and handed it to him. The young Berezovski followed all of her movements with his gaze. He said to her, almost complaining: "No one's looking under the gills of your tench, but how much does it cost?"

"A sleepless night," she answered him simply, as if she were giving him a price, and she called to her sister, "Golde, go make the change." And she fled behind the stall, where the barrels stood.

Through the cracks in the stall Gitele watched as the young Berezovski stood for a while near the carriage; then he quickly jumped up, pulled at the reins and drove away.

Fairly often he drove his carriage to Gitele's stall, and the women merchants in the narrow market murmured: "This is fishy—they're testing their luck." But her mother used to say when her daughters would mention young Berezovski, "I hate what's too good to be true."

A pain smacked Feyge-Tsipe in the temples when, surprisingly, young Berezovski did not come to see Gitele at the stall in the fish market, but at their house on the hill. Gitele, who was cutting "wide noodles" at the table, raised the knife up high, as if to take a photograph. The young man approached her and said, "Put down the knife! In your hands, it could ruin a man!"

Gitele put away the knife, and they both laughed. This was the happiest laughter that was ever heard on the hill. When the young man left, Feyge-Tsipe walked around with a damp handkerchief on her temples and complained: "I am afraid of what's too good to be true."

For the residents on the hill, it was like a dream, or a miraculous tale, when Gitele became the bride of young Berezovski. The wedding was held in a big city. And on the hill, it was told that Gitele went to the wedding canopy in golden slippers that the bridegroom bought her as a gift.

But even Gitele's golden union could not budge Feyge-Tsipe out from under her roof. And she did not want to ascend to a house in the marketplace.

"Here," she said, "I bore my daughters, here I raised them. Here luck shone on us. Why should I leave my house on the hill?"

Isaac Bashevis Singer

1902–1991

ISAAC BASHEVIS SINGER is perhaps the best-known Yiddish writer in history, thanks to the widespread publication of his work in English and his 1978 win of the Nobel Prize for Literature. But Singer's affiliation with the *Forward* went back decades before that.

Born in the village of Leoncin, near Warsaw, he was encouraged in his literary ambitions by his older brother, Israel Joshua Singer, and decided at a young age to become a writer. For ten years he was employed as a proofreader for the Warsaw literary journal *Literarishe bleter* (*Literary Pages*), while also working on his own writing and translation projects.

While still in Warsaw, Singer began sending contributions to the New York-based *Forward* and, after immigrating to the United States in 1935, became a staff writer for the newspaper. Over the following decades he contributed hundreds of pieces, including serialized novels and short stories, book reviews and literary essays, and many columns of news reports and commentary. For his literary work, Singer used the name Isaac Bashevis, which derived from his mother's first name, Batsheva, while his other writings appeared under the pseudonyms Yitzkhok Varshavski and D. Segal.

Although Singer translated much of his own work into English with the help of younger collaborators, many of his articles and stories never appeared anywhere but in the pages of the newspaper.

"The Hotel" (not to be confused with another story titled "The Hotel," which appeared in the 1988 collection *The Death of Methuselah and Other Stories*), appeared in two instalments, on January 15 and 21, 1972. The story is Singer's rendition of the "King Incognito" trope common to many works of world literature and folklore. Here, Singer provides a winking, postmodern acknowledgment of his predecessors while also exploiting the theme to its fullest.

————

The Hotel

(JANUARY 15–21, 1972)

Translated by Ezra Glinter

SUCCESS CAN BE a blessing or a blight, Reb[86] Meyer Marshinover used to say. It all depends on what you do with it. When you start telling yourself "My strength and the power of my hand created this wealth for me,"[87] you're just one step from slipping up.

The story happened to us in our town. We had one hotel and it belonged to a Pan[88] Pavlovski. There was a railway junction, where many merchants and noblemen used to arrive, but Pavlovski didn't allow for any competition. I can see him now: a short little gentile with curled whiskers; a dark-complexioned man who considered himself a big shot.

The hotel had three stories and it was always full. A few times the Jews tried to build another hotel, but Pan Pavlovski always managed to bring their plans to naught. He would send an informant to the governor. He would collude with the city authorities and with the police superintendant. He was buddy-buddy with all of the bureaucrats, and no doubt bribed them all. Since he had no competitors,

---

86 Yiddish for "Mr."
87 Deuteronomy 8:17
88 Polish for "Mr."

there were always more guests than rooms, and he made out like a bandit.

There was a Jew in town named Reb Berish Srotzker. He was a Kozhnitzer Hasid[89] and had a bit of an inn where simple Jews used to stay: a preacher, a matchmaker, sometimes in-laws in town for a wedding, Hasidim. Pavlovski didn't let Jews in, aside from rich ones. He had become so wealthy that he had bought an estate from a nobleman. He was a partner in the water mill. He set up a brewery and had hundreds of acres planted with hops to use for making beer. He had two daughters and he sent them to study in the big cities. He would drive around by himself in a coach, like a count. He lent money for mortgages and half of the houses in town were signed over to him. Talk about success!

Usually, when noblemen came to town, they would first send a letter: Reserve a room for so and so, the son of so and so, who will be arriving on such and such a day. Pavlovski could read Russian and Polish well, and he had people who helped him. A few times a year a lot of visitors would come, and there wouldn't be enough room. Pavlovski knew who was important, and who was not. For the bigwigs everything was prepared, but a poor gentleman without money would be sent to spend the night at Berish Srotzker's place. There everyone slept in one big room, like in a poorhouse. It would happen that a gentile wouldn't want to go along, and would start screaming and cursing, but Pan Pavlovski, though a small man, had a pair of strong hands and knew how to land a blow. He also used to carry around a revolver. In short, he was a power to be reckoned with.

Now listen to what can happen. Someone told the governor of Lublin that in our town and district improper dealings were taking place. Someone, seemingly, had informed on the chief bureaucrats. So the governor prepared himself to come to town dressed like a normal Russian and under a different name, so no one would know who he was, and investigate the matter. He didn't come alone, but

---

89 An adherent of the Hasidic movement originating in the town of Kozienice, or in Yiddish, Kozhnitz.

with another official who was also disguised. Before they arrived, they sent a letter to the hotel saying that so and so, with such and such names, were traveling from Lublin and that rooms should be prepared for them. Pan Pavlovski read the names, saw that they were unknown people with no pedigree, and as though he preferred not to have any guests at all, put the letter aside and forgot about it entirely.

Late at night the governor arrived with his companion. Coming into the hotel, they told Pan Pavlovski to prepare rooms for them, but Pavlovski said:

"All the rooms are occupied."

"How could that be? We wrote that we were coming a month ago," argued the governor.

"First of all, I don't remember that you wrote," Pan Pavlovski replied. "And even if you did, I don't owe you anything. It's my hotel and I can give a room to whomever I please."

"What should I do?" asked the governor, and Pan Pavlovski answered:

"There's a Jew over there who has an inn full of bedbugs—go to him." And he added: "If it doesn't suit you, you can sleep in the street."

The governor wasn't accustomed to such language. "This isn't right," he protested. A scuffle broke out and Pan Pavlovski grabbed the governor by the collar and prepared to throw him out. The assistant took up for the governor, and there was a fight. Pan Pavlovski struck them both. He pulled his revolver on them. Had the governor said who he was, Pan Pavloski would have fallen at his feet and kissed his boots. But his arrival had to remain a secret.

After much bickering the governor and his companion decided to go to the Jew, Reb Berish Srotzker, and spend the night there, whatever it might be like. Reb Berish Strotzker's place was also full. Hasidim were traveling to Kozhenitz and were staying with him. But a Jew doesn't think himself a big deal. Reb Berish took the Russians in with friendship.

"It's full of guests here," he said, "but I will give you mine and my wife's beds."

"Why would you do that, Jew?" asked the governor. "Are you that greedy for money?" And Reb Berish answered:

"I wouldn't offer our beds for any amount of money, but we Jews are in exile and we must bow our heads. This world belongs to the gentiles."

The governor's assistant laughed, and the governor said: "The other world also belongs to us, because you Jews don't believe in Jesus."

"What is in the other world and who is considered important there, that we will know later," Berish answered.

"In the meantime we are here and we are hungry and thirsty," the assistant said. "Do you have any liquor?"

"I have everything," Reb Berish said. He brought the gentiles a flask of whiskey and broth and meat left over from supper. The maid woke up along with Reb Berish's wife, Yente Beyle. The governor and the assistant stuffed themselves with food and drink. Jews must not drink wine with gentiles,[90] but they can have a bit of liquor. Reb Berish had a brandy and became expansive. He asked the guests:

"How does it happen that you aren't at Pavlovski's hotel?"

"We are too insignificant for him," the governor said. "He only has room for noble people."

"How does he know who you are? You could be the most important dignitaries," Reb Berish asked, and he told them a story about an emperor who dressed himself like a shoemaker and went to mix with the populace.[91]

The two gentiles laughed so hard they could hardly sit still. "You can be sure that we are no emperors," the governor said. "We wouldn't even be worthy to heat the oven of an emperor."

"And what's so great about an emperor?" asked Reb Berish. "He is also flesh and blood."

---

90 According to Jewish law, wine handled by gentiles becomes nonkosher, for fear that it has been consecrated for idol worship.

91 A reference to *One Thousand and One Nights*, among many other literary and folkloric sources.

A conversation ensued, and the gentiles forgot about sleep. The assistant asked:

"How is it that there's only one hotel in town, when there are so many guests?"

"Pavolvski doesn't let anyone build another one," Reb Berish answered.

"Why not?" asked the governor. "Does the town belong to him?"

"We've already tried to build one, but he won't allow it," Reb Berish said. "He bribes anyone he needs to, and as they say, 'when you grease, you go.' He's mixed up with the entire government."

"Whom does he pay off?" The governor asked.

"Whom not?" Reb Berish answered. "They all take."

"All?" asked the governor, and Reb Berish said:

"Yes. All."

"Do you believe that the governor in Lublin also lets himself be bribed?" The governor asked.

"He is presumably so rich that he doesn't need it," Reb Berish said, "but the temptation of money is great. The small-fry can be bought for a pittance, but the big ones get a lot."

"That is to say, Jew, you don't believe that there are honest people?" The governor asked. And Reb Berish answered:

"There are, but how many? The takers and grabbers are the majority, and the majority run the show."

The governor had in fact come because he heard that bribes were being taken and laws were being broken. He himself was a count and an important person to the czar. He said: "When the dirty dogs who take and give bribes hang, we will have cleaned the dirt out of this land."

"It wouldn't help," Reb Berish said. "To hang someone you need testimony, and the corrupt ones don't do it with witnesses. These bureaucrats don't take anything themselves, but use their wives. Sometimes people send them presents on the festivals. Others play cards and for the sake of appearances each one plays the bribe money. How can all this be investigated?"

"Does this mean there is no solution?" asked the governor. And Reb Berish said:

"No."

"Have you also given bribes?" asked the governor.

"At Christmas and Easter I send them a few rubles," Reb Berish said. "If not, they would find me guilty of a thousand sins."

"What kind of sins?" asked the governor.

"Maybe the place is not as clean as it should be. Maybe so many people shouldn't be sleeping in one room. They have a thousand prerogatives and the judge can, if it pleases him, interpret them as he likes. They could, God forbid, ambush me in a dark alley and beat me, or burn down my house. I might know who the arsonist was, but because there were no witnesses, I dare not even complain. Even if there were witnesses, they would be afraid to testify."

"If you speak the truth, Jew, Russia is lost," the governor said. And Reb Berish replied:

"So it has been and so it will remain. The greatest protectors of the robbers and thieves are the judges and the laws. But what is the world? Just a corridor. The one who follows God's commandments and does good deeds in the corridor will enter the palace."

There followed a discussion about Judaism, rabbis, and because Reb Berish was a little drunk, he began telling the gentiles about the Kozhnitzer Rebbe:[92] what a saint he was, the wonders he performed, and how he spoke words of Torah full of the deepest secrets.

"Could one bribe him?" asked the governor. And Reb Berish said:

"He receives petitions and donations,[93] but if you offered him all the treasures in the world to do the most meager sin, he would laugh at you." The governor spoke up:

"Jew, your speech has disrupted all of my plans. But since you are correct, I cannot punish you. I ask one thing: take me to your Rebbe.

92 Spiritual leader of the Kozhnitzer Hasidic movement. Here a reference to Moshe Elyokim Bri'o Hopsztajn (c. 1757–1828).

93 In Hasidic practice a rebbe is typically presented with a written question or request from one of his followers, which is accompanied by a monetary donation.

Since the world is full of thieves, I would like to know an honest man." And he added: "You should know, Jew, that I am the governor."

Reb Berish thought at first that the nobleman was making a fool of him. But the governor showed him a piece of paper. He said: Keep quite, Jew, or else I will have you hanged. Swear on your *tzitzis*[94] that you will stay silent as long as I live. Reb Berish swore. He only told the story later, after the others man's death.

WHEN REB BERISH heard that the governor was his guest at the inn, and that he wanted to be taken to the Rebbe in Kozhnitz, Reb Berish was overcome by fear. What would the governor see in Kozhnitz? Neither the Rebbe nor any of his intimates spoke a word of Russian. Reb Berish himself had learned only a bit from the guests who stayed with him when there was no room at Pavlovski's. That night he didn't sleep a wink.

The governor and his adjutant had come without a coach, so no one would know that they were important people. Reb Berish had to travel with them on a wagon full of Hasidim. When the Hasidim saw that Reb Berish was bringing two Ivans[95] to Kozhnitz, they were amazed. But Hasidim are Hasidim. On the wagon they made toasts, sang Kozhnitzer melodies and refreshed themselves with little cakes. The Ivans were also honored with a drink. The adjutant asked the governor, "What kind of wild animals are these?" But the governor answered:

"They're doing no one any harm."

In Kozhnitz it was just then a memorial day, perhaps the anniversary of the Maggid's[96] death, or that of another holy man. Hasidim were drinking liquor and dancing. Reb Berish let the attendants know

---

94 Ritual fringes worn on a four-cornered garment.
95 Yiddish colloquialism for Russians.
96 Lit. "preacher," a reference to Yisroel Hopsztajn (c. 1733–1814), also known as the Kozhnitzer Maggid, and the founder of the Kozhnitz Hasidic dynasty.

that the two Russians wanted to be taken to the Rebbe, and the Rebbe called them to come in. In Kozhnitz there was a corner lawyer who used to be a Misnaged,[97] but later became a devoted follower of the Rebbe. He served as the translator. The governor gave the Rebbe a petition and a donation, and the Rebbe spoke to the translator: "Tell him that a righteous man wants to be good himself, while a wicked man wants only that others should be good."

When the translator repeated these words to the governor, he went red in the face. The governor of Lublin had worried only that the people in his province were not behaving as they should. The Rebbe had put his finger on the spot.

"What should I do?" the governor instructed the interpreter to ask the Rebbe, and the Rebbe instructed the interpreter to answer:

"First, yourself do no wrong."

I don't remember the entire conversation, but the governor later told Reb Berish that the Rebbe pierced him with every word. He even performed a miracle. The governor had a daughter who was six months pregnant. The Rebbe repeated her name and said: "She will have a male child."

The Rebbe couldn't have known from the note that she was pregnant—the copyist had written only her name. In fact, she gave birth to a boy.

Why should I ramble on here? The governor and his companion stayed in Kozhnitz over the Sabbath. They danced with the Hasidim, and treated them to whiskey. In the town of Kotzk[98] this would never happen. The Kotzker Hasidim are grumps and scoffers. Their Rebbe,[99] moreover, never let anyone see him. But in Kozhnitz there was so much brotherly love that there was even some left over for gentiles.

The governor told Reb Berish: "I go to our balls, and there's a

---

97 Literally, "opponent," a reference to the Jewish adversaries of the Hasidic movement.
98 Kock in Polish, home to the Kotzker Hasidic sect.
99 Menachem Mendel Morgensztern (1787–1859). For the last twenty years of his life, Morgensztern lived in seclusion and refused contact with his followers.

black cloud. The music plays, but no one is happy. I dance with some noblewoman and right away she asks me for a favor: I should make her husband a marshal or a notary public. These Jews with their torn frock coats and crushed fur hats are really happy. They are not drunk. One glass and they become self-assured." The gentile spoke the truth. Kozhnitz had a joy not of this world. When you went to see the Rebbe in the study house, all of your worries and cares fell away.

The governor and his attendant went to the Rebbe's table. It wasn't possible to seat them, because of the wine. But the Rebbe gave orders to pass them his leftovers.[100] The governor of Lublin took a little piece of fish that had passed through ten pairs of hands and ate it. Reb Berish's hat trembled on his head. What would he do if the governor lost his temper? He could throw the entire group in jail.

After the Sabbath, before the two gentiles took off, they went to the Rebbe with the translator and stayed there for over an hour. Just like his father, the Maggid, Reb Moshele was as small as a six-year-old child. He had a white beard that grew from his ears to his shoulders. He was so weak that he had to put a fur under his feet because the floorboards were too hard. But when the Rebbe cried out, "Amen, may his great name be blessed!"[101] the study house trembled.

The governor offered to give the Rebbe money to renovate the study house, the ritual bath, and the house where the Rebbe lived. But the Rebbe answered: "The walls are infused with holiness. We dare not tear them down."

And the study house remained as it was. Misnagdim require a beautiful synagogue, a cantor with a melodious voice, a choir and who knows what else. Hasidim laugh at all that. Why is a new table better than an old one? Foolishness. When you learn Torah on the table it becomes a vessel of holiness.

On the way back to Marshinov the governor said to Reb Berish: "Jew, I will send you a permit to build a new hotel."

---

100 According to Hasidic tradition, the Rebbe's leftovers, or *shirayim*, are distributed among the Hasidim at communal gatherings as a source of blessing.
101 Part of the common *Kaddish* prayer.

"Sir, I don't have that much money, and I don't want to start up with Pavlovski," argued Reb Berish. But the governor said:

"I would stop here on the road each time I want to travel to Kozhnitz to your holy man, and I don't want to stay with that blockhead. I could have put him in chains, but your Rebbe stopped me."

The governor took revenge in a different way. When the wagon arrived in town, he went with Reb Berish to the inn. The attendant went out to announce that the governor was in Marshinov. The gentiles were in an uproar.

"Where is he staying?" they asked. The attendant said:

"With the Jew, Berish."

"Why not with Pavlovski in the hotel?" they asked, and the attendant said:

"You'll know why later."

In Marshinov there was a fuss and a furor. The police superintendent immediately ordered that the streets be swept. Jews shut their stores. The bureaucrats put on their uniforms with their medals and everyone ran to Reb Berish at the inn.

When Pan Pavlovski heard that the governor was in town and that he was staying at Reb Berish's place, he was struck dumb. He put on the fancy suit that he saved for important noblemen and for authorities from Lublin and Warsaw. Other guests were occupying the rooms, but Pavlovski instructed them to pack up their things right away and make room for the governor. Just the fact that he, Pan Pavlovski, had to go to the Jew Reb Berish at the inn was already a slap in the face.

He arrived at the inn and found it full of bureaucrats and soldiers. The guard didn't want to let him in. "Who are you, exactly?" the Cossack asked, spreading out his hands to show that it was forbidden to enter. Pavlovski managed to sneak in nonetheless.

Pavlovski went in to see Reb Berish. At the table sat the two Russians that he, Pavlovski, had thrown out. Around them stood officials, officers, and the chief of police. Pavlovski just about died on the spot. He threw himself on the ground and begged for forgiveness. "I didn't know who you were!" he howled. And the governor repeated to him a teaching from the Rebbe, as the interpreter had translated it for him. In heaven, the Rebbe said, it's no great trick to serve the Most High. There, everyone sees the glory of God. The trick is to serve Him on Earth, where his countenance is hidden and one must have faith.

Pavlovski's entreaties didn't help—the governor didn't want to go with him. They had made a ball and a feast at Reb Berish's, and they sent Pavlovksi straight home. Noblemen mixed with Hasidim. Noblewomen sat with Yente-Beyle in the kitchen and ate grits from tin dishes.

Before the governor traveled back to Lublin, he took out of his pocket a suede wallet full of gold coins, and gave them to Reb Berish. Reb Berish didn't want to take them, but the attendant shouted: "Take, Jew! Or we'll send you to Siberia!"

A few weeks later, Reb Berish had acquired a location, partners, and had begun digging the foundation of a hotel. He had the permit in his pocket, and didn't have to bribe anyone.

Now, listen to this: When Pavlovski returned home, he started thinking about what had happened to him—how he had not let the governor into the hotel, and had even struck him. And from all of his brooding he fell into a depression. If the governor had him beaten or had put him in prison, he could have endured his punishment and gone on as before. But because the governor had met him with kindness and he, Pavlovski, had not received any punishment, he took the matter to heart. He became quiet and wouldn't speak to his wife. He stopped coming to the hotel and left it entirely to his managers. He no longer lent anyone money for interest and didn't even try to collect his debts. The governor's stay at Reb Berish's had shamed him and he lost the will to live.

Pavlovski called for Reb Berish. When Reb Berish arrived, Pavlovski said to him: "Why do you have to build a hotel? I want to sell you my hotel."

"What will Pan Pavlovski do?" asked Reb Berish, and Pavlovski answered:

"I will go away from here, to wherever my eyes take me."

Pavlovski sent for a notary and sold Reb Berish the hotel for next to nothing. He wanted to sell him his house also, and even began looking for buyers for the brewery and for his half of the mill. He wanted to die of sorrow. But when the governor heard that Pavlovski was dangerously ill, he forgot all of his calculations and wrote Pavlovski a letter, saying that he should travel to the Rebbe in Kozhnitz and the Rebbe would help him.

Pavlovski did as the governor said. What wouldn't a person do to save his own life? The Rebbe called him in and the same interpreter translated what the Rebbe said. It seems that the Rebbe even gave him an amulet.

Pavlovski stayed alive and became a friend to the Jews. They tell me that every Passover he used to send charity to the Rebbe. He sent him a gift on Purim also. Repentance helps everyone. It's even taught that Nebuzadran[102] did repentance and his repentance was accepted. Each year both the governor and Pavlovski sent petitions to Kozhnitz with donations. Because the truth is with the Jews, the gentiles must come to us. The truth is stronger than anything. But when the truth is no longer on our side, it won't be long until no remainder or remnant is left.

---

102 The Babylonian general who, according to the Bible, laid siege to Jerusalem prior to the destruction of the First Temple. According to the Talmud (Gittin 57b) he later repented and converted to Judaism.

Chaim Grade
1910–1982

CHAIM GRADE, a native of Vilna, Lithuania, is best known today for his rich novelistic descriptions of the city's prewar Jewish life and of its historic rabbinical culture. In his prose and poetry he depicts Vilna residents young and old, rich and poor, religious and secular, learned and ignorant, and makes the city itself into one of his central characters.

Born into an educated family, Grade suffered the loss of his father at a young age and was raised in poverty by his mother, an apple seller who lived in the basement of a blacksmith's shop. At thirteen he left home to study in the network of Novaredok rabbinical seminaries, which focused on ethical instruction and self-improvement. Later he became a student of Avraham Yesha'yahu Karelits, also known as the Hazon Ish, one of the preeminent rabbinical authorities of the first half of the twentieth century.

At age twenty-two Grade abandoned his religious studies in favor of secular literature and became associated with the literary and political movement *Yung Vilne* (Young Vilna). His first volume of poetry, *Yo* (*Yes*), was published in 1936, followed by the epic poem *Musarnikes* (*Musarists*), whose title refers to the proponents of Jewish piety and ethical development he had encountered in his religious training.

Upon the German invasion of Vilna in 1941, Grade fled to the interior of the Soviet Union, leaving behind his mother and his wife, Frume-Libe, thinking that the Germans would not harm women. Only after the war did he learn that they had been murdered by the Nazis.

In 1948, Grade immigrated to the United States with his second wife, Inna Hecker-Grade, where he began writing prose works in addition to poetry. These included the 1951 philosophical story "My Quarrel with Hersh Rasseyner," about the possibility of faith after the Holocaust; the autobiographical novel *My Mother's Sabbath Days*; and the epic two-volume *Tsemakh Atlas*, translated by Curt Leviant as *The Yeshiva*, which also dealt with Grade's formative religious experiences.

For most of Grade's postwar career in the United States, his main journalistic outlet was the *Tog-Morgn Zhurnal*, a liberal daily newspaper. When the paper closed in 1971, Grade began contributing to the *Forward*, usually publishing once a week in its Sunday literary section. In the decade before his death he published novellas, short stories, and two serialized novels, one of them left unfinished. "Grandfathers and Grandchildren" appeared from December 17, 1972, to January 21, 1973, and was republished in 1974 in a book titled *Di kloyz un di gas* (*Synagogue and Street*) along with three other novellas. While those works later appeared in English translation by Harold Rabinowitz and Inna Hecker-Grade in the collection *Rabbis and Wives* (Alfred A. Knopf, 1982), which was a finalist for the Pulitzer Prize, "Grandfathers and Grandchildren" remained untranslated until now.

Like much of Grade's late work, "Grandfathers and Grandchildren" can be read as an elegy for the Vilna of his youth. But even within this lost world Grade presents the growing fissures between its young and old, religious and secular, inhabitants. While Grade presents the story from the perspective of the grandfathers, his own life split the difference between the young Talmud scholars Shloymele and Hirshele, on whom the grandfathers dote, and the grandfathers' irreligious offspring, from whom they have become tragically estranged.

Grandfathers and Grandchildren

(DECEMBER 17, 1972–JANUARY 21, 1973)

Translated by Curt Leviant

I

UNDER THE COLD stone arches of the Old Shul[103] old men sit by oaken prayer stands. The tips of their beards, woven of silken threads, touch, stroke and caress the pages of yellowed sacred books. On their wrinkled, parchment-colored faces, full of tiny cross-hatched lines, their smiling, good-natured eyes squint in the sun. The attempt of the sun's rays to melt the snow of their white beards and earlocks is in vain. The rays tickle the tufts of overgrown hair in the grandfathers' nostrils and ears, just like the grandfathers love to tickle their grandsons. Oh, those grandsons! As long as the little demons are young and play with grandpa's beard and earlocks, pluck prickly hairs from his nose and tug his ears, the grandfathers can hoodwink them into reciting a blessing over a sugar cookie. But when they are a couple of years older, the grandsons quickly sense that they don't have to obey their grandfather; it's the housemaid they have to obey. And if the daughter-in-law notices that her father-in-law is fussing over her youngest son, trying to get her little treasure to put on a yarmulke and *tzitzis*,[104] the daughter-in-law exclaims:

"Father-in-law, don't torment the kid! He's not going to be a rabbi!"

---

103 Yiddish for "synagogue" or "school."
104 Ritual fringes worn on the corners of a four-cornered garment.

Foolish women! And if not a rabbi, does a Jewish child have to be raised a gentile? The old men hide behind the prayer stands, and the sun too hides behind a cloud, commiserating with these graybeards and their gloomy thoughts. When, with God's help, the youngest grandson approaches bar mitzvah age, the parents will hire a tutor for him, one of the modern, enlightened fellows, to teach him to read his Torah portion and deliver a sermon. After the speech, the festive meal, and the celebration, the bar mitzvah lad will perhaps put on his *tefillin*[105] a couple of times—and that's it! By then the grandfather will surely be lying under a mound of earth—but he will have no repose there, for even in the True World he will know that his grandson is not putting on *tefillin*.

And are their sons any better? The elders grumble to themselves and stir behind their prayer stands like thin, wind-shaken twigs of withered shrubs. Some sons! When they were young boys in *kheyder*,[106] their studies went fairly well. During their youth too and right after their weddings, when they went into business, they still put on *tefillin* every morning and went to synagogue every Sabbath. But the more successful they became, the more they shook off the yoke of ritual observance. Right after the wedding, the daughters-in-law too covered their hair for a while with a kerchief, out of respect for the master of the house and owner of the shop. But from the time all the earnings were gradually transferred to the children—and they too already had grown children—the now-fat daughters-in-law sought to outdo one another in beautiful apartments, clothing, and jewelry. And their husbands followed them like colts. After all, they even take their wives to the circus, where animals prance about on two legs like men, and men crawl around on all fours and leap and tumble like wild beasts. It's an upside-down world.

Now why do they need one credenza after another and so much gold- and silverware? The laden shelves display big and small hand-cut crystal glasses that sparkle and gleam; they glint with a cold pierc-

---

105 Phylacteries.
106 Religious elementary school.

ing light, glitter with an artificial luster. When guests sit in the house and the glasses are set on the table, only then does one first notice that the long-stemmed goblet with the wide base can hold only a couple of drops of whiskey. So why then is so much glass wasted on this? They fool everyone and play like children. During meals the masters of the house show off more with the dinnerware than with the food itself. The guests tap their knuckles on the plates and listen to the tone like to the movement of a clock. There's no end to their cries of amazement at the hand-painted teacups. Does it make a difference what you eat or drink from? Even the Sabbath candlesticks adorned with flowers and candle-rings, and the Hanukkah menorahs with their little pitchers for oil, are for the young people more for display and decoration than for fulfilling the *mitzvah*[107] of lighting Sabbath candles and kindling the Hanukkah lights. And the old parents are also there for the sake of show and not for observing the *mitzvah* of honoring one's father and mother.

The sun reappears from behind the clouds and finds the old men still hidden behind their prayer stands, just like it seeks and finds rabbits in bushes. There is hope for the People of Israel, the sun consoles them. Jews are eternal, and the Torah is as eternal as the heavens above the Earth. About this the old folk have no doubt; of this they are absolutely certain. No trifle—God, the Glory of Israel! These men have no concerns about the Master of the Universe, but they are sad, immeasurably grieved at heart, at not having a bit of joy from their children and grandchildren. So the old ones run away from their homes to the Old Shul. But here too it's dreary. In this holy place there are no young shoots, no young Torah scholars. Here no fresh young voice rings out like a little bell, no sweet melody resounds as if from a violin. Even men who have to say *Kaddish*[108] or observe a *yortsayt*[109] do not set foot here. The mourners know that the one *min-*

---

107 Commandment.
108 The mourner's prayer
109 Anniversary of a death.

yan[110] in the Old Shul starts precisely on time and that here they don't rush through the prayers. If a guest strays in accidentally, as soon as he sees the old men with their white beards perusing sacred books, the newcomer retreats at once, as if he had peeked over the fence at the World to Come.

And so the days and weeks of the summer months drag on. The longer sunlight streams through the windows, and the brighter it shines, the more profound is the stillness that hovers in the Old Shul. The graybeards do not talk to one another. They are done with talking. But in the sunny silence they clearly hear the Torahs sighing in the Holy Ark, longing for young hands to open them, to hold their wooden handles and roll the parchment forward; to hear a young man sing out the weekly Torah portion with the traditional melody and for the chanted words to reverberate cheerfully out through the open windows. The old men also hear the morose silence of the Talmuds in the bookcases. It is fair to say that these volumes now have to study with one another, because no one else uses them for learning. The Jews of the Old Shul are the sorts who prefer dipping into the stories of *Eyn Yaakov*[111] and reading a chapter of *Mishna*.[112] Their intellect, now in their old age, doesn't appreciate the convoluted Talmudic passages. The big sets of Vilna Talmuds and the editions of Maimonides' works have been on the bookshelves from days gone by, when the study house[113] was full of scholars. Exhausted by these gloomy thoughts, the old-timers doze off. From all sides the mute and loyal sentinels regard the men: the gleaming copper washstand, the big silver Hanukkah menorah, the small brass balls on the four corners of the iron balustrade around the *bimah*,[114] the decorated Holy Ark, the chandeliers, the bookcases.

---

110 Prayer quorum.

111 A sixteenth-century compilation of Talmudic tales and legends.

112 The first major work of rabbinic literature, redacted in the third century C.E. and included as a component of the Talmud.

113 Synagogues often served as centers of both prayer and religious study.

114 The small platform in the center of the synagogue from which the Torah is read.

A silence, otherworldly and mysterious, reigns in the study house until the old men wake up, happy and frightened, as if an angel had touched them. They notice that sunlight is still shining through the windows of the Old Shul. Compared to the age difference between them and their grandsons, the sun is much older. Oh, how much older is the sun than they and their grandsons combined. Nevertheless, it reappears every day as though newborn, as in the words of the prayer, "God in his beneficence renews daily His deeds of Creation." The sun is always replete with radiance; yet its radiance is always different. When it appears mist-covered with thin gray clouds, its light is silver-white. At times it looks like brass, pouring out a blinding heat that stings one's eyes. Occasionally, it sparkles like the dark red copper washstand. Before dusk the setting sun resembles a gigantic golden wheel, as if fallen off Elijah the Prophet's fiery chariot. The wonders of the Creator! The sun illumines many millions of stones, trees, living creatures and human faces. The Creator of the World can surely see and hear everything at once, as it is written: "He who fashions all their hearts and discerns all their works." [115] But alas, these modern grandsons who know everything ask: How can God be everywhere at the same time? They really know it all, these grandsons! And their silly parents swell with pride at their clever remarks.

The grandfathers wipe the gathered moisture from the corners of their mouths and attempt to immerse themselves in their sacred books. But in their old brains, overflowing thoughts chafe against one another. These modern grandsons of theirs don't even believe in angels. "We haven't seen them," they say. What fools they are! A man born on a ship in the middle of the ocean who lives his entire life on water would be incredulous too if you told him that there is such a thing as land, where trees grow tall and each tree develops hands called branches with countless fingers called leaves. That a tree is not a person, a fish or a bird, but still lives its own sort of life, unlike wood or stone, which has no life at all. So, then, would a person who has spent all his life at sea believe that? Exactly the same thing is true

---

115 Psalms 33:15.

about angels. How can someone born of woman in this World of Falsehood see an angel, a seraph, a cherub from the World of Truth? Only the great saintly souls whose thoughts are more engaged with the World to Come than with This World, only they can see angels. These grandsons of ours are really first-rate researchers, the grandfathers giggle to themselves—and then suddenly notice a little bird perched on the rim of a window.

Some of the graybeards with keen eyesight clearly see the bird turn its head and tail, jump with its long legs, raise and lower its wings, and chirp and peep merrily, as if wanting to call to its kin. And indeed, another half-dozen winged rascals soon join him at the window, hopping about seeking seeds. They tweet and twitter, open and close their pointy beaks and roll their round little eyes—until one of the old men coughs and suddenly all the birds lift up from the window, flutter, tremble like sparks and disappear. The other old men cast angry glances at the cougher, and he too feels vexed with himself at his lack of restraint. On the other hand, he reconsiders, the sparrows didn't necessarily flee because he scared them off. Maybe they weren't frightened at all, but since sparrows have wings, they want to fly. The elders gaze for a while at the window and, even more dejected now, lower their eyes to their books. Of course, it's nice to see and hear birds singing and hopping about. But it's much nicer to see and hear Jewish children studying Torah. Birds will chance upon the Old Shul again, but young learners never chance upon this place.

Nevertheless, the old men of the Old Shul will not go to pray and study in a livelier study house. They know full well that their synagogue is even older than the Vilna Great Synagogue. They have prayed here all their lives, shed a sea full of tears and reveled in joy. As long as their feeble legs can still drag them up the steps to the Old Shul, they will not seek out any other holy place. During the summer their children plead with their fathers to spend a Sabbath in the woods, where the family has a dacha. But they decline and smile scornfully into their beards: as if they have nothing better to do than yawn in the woods and watch their children desecrate the Sabbath!

They wouldn't even go to the Chief Rabbi of Vilna's dacha and leave the Old Shul without a *minyan* for the Sabbath.

All summer long the sunlight coming in through the synagogue's windows shines into all the corners to see if maybe one of the elders who awaits its refreshing warmth is missing. Gradually, the sun begins to rise later and sets earlier, until the day comes when one of the old men climbs up on a bench to close the windows before the onset of the first autumn winds. With the daily blowing of the *shofar*[116] starting the first day of the month of Elul,[117] a cold wind also begins to blow in the graybeards' wizened bones, and one's heart shudders at the coming Day of Judgment.[118] The wrinkled faces become even more wrinkled and furrowed, replete with hard roots and prickles, like mown fields. Their silken beards, each of whose hairs shone individually in the summer, now become matted and ashen gray like cobwebs in the fall. Raindrops roll down the windowpanes and tears stream down hairy cheeks. All their lives they have hustled and bustled, turned the world upside down for their children, everything for the children, and now these grandfathers are superfluous to them. The elderly father is considered senile because he wants his children to be a bit more observant before the approaching Days of Awe.[119] What fools they are! If it's inevitable that an old man becomes senile, then the same thing will befall you too. But judging by their laughter and self-confidence, it's perfectly obvious that they either don't think of man's ultimate destiny or assume it's not applicable to them. There is a dyers' club and there is a diers' club, but it doesn't occur to them that every human being is a member of the latter group. Man is the sort of creature who doesn't believe that fire burns until he gets

116 The ram's horn, which is blown after morning services starting a month before the new year.
117 The twelfth and last month of the Jewish year.
118 Rosh Hashanah, the Jewish new year, is considered to be the day on which God passes judgment on the world for the year to come.
119 The ten days between Rosh Hashanah and Yom Kippur, the Day of Atonement.

singed. Oh, Master of the Universe! Cast us not into old age; do not forsake us when our strength is ebbing![120]

II

DURING THE WINTER the old men do not sit in their corners. They gather around the big white-tiled stove. Some sit on the nearby benches, their faces towards the small, open door of the stove, where the wood has already burned up and only the embers glow. Their shimmer plays on the yellow skin of the elders' lined foreheads, mossy eyebrows and white beards. Reflected too on their faces is the light of the bulb in the big flat lamp hanging over the table and the flames of the melting candles on the prayer stands. For a while their beards and earlocks take on a greenish cast, like the old bronze of the chandelier and the mold on the books. Soon the wrinkled faces start to look like the yellow parchment of old scrolls. Three old men sit huddled together warming themselves, but each one is seemingly enchanted by a different light. The skin of one man's face is furrowed like the hard brown bark of a tree in the woods at sunset. Another man's face gleams with the reddish blight of moss soaked with autumnal dampness. In the beard of a third man burns a hellish fire that gradually darkens until it is filled with the mysterious glitter of a golden treasure. Outside of this illuminated circle the entire study house sinks into darkness. The heavy candelabras that hang on iron chains from the ceiling, the round stone pillars under the arches, the tall Holy Ark, and the east-facing part of the *bimah* all hover in a deep otherworldly blackness. The bluish snow from the nearby roofs and the distant frosty, star-filled sky shines through the darkened windows. In the snow-glow and the greenish twinkle of far-off stars, the front of this holy place, mute and still and engulfed in gloom, looks like a frozen ship in the Sea of Ice.

During the summer, when each of the graybeards sits in his own

---

120 Paraphrase of Psalms 71:9.

corner, days can pass without a word being exchanged. But when winter comes, they sit together with their backs to the stove or facing the glowing coals and talk about their wives: they've spent a lifetime with them—and still don't know them! Whatever their children do is well and good, and all the nonsense the grandchildren prattle is pure wisdom. Ah, that these old mothers and grandmothers in wigs,[121] who have cried their eyes out over holiday prayer books and Yiddish supplications, should become so foolish in their old age! Some stroke of good fortune! What ridiculous joy! They've lived to see children's children. Well, whose footsteps are they following, these children's children? A cat can have grandchildren too, but a Jewish woman of valor[122] shouldn't have a cat's brains. The grand-sons don't even come to their grandfathers and grandmothers any more for a blessing. They are already blessed with knowledge; they know it all and understand everything. The chicks are now teach-ing the hens. But you, silly hen, why are you running after them? Chickee, why are you clucking in rapture? The men laugh and look at the closed and sealed double window, half of which is covered with frost, while the other half is clear, like a person with a cataract in one eye and clear vision in the other. The old men remember the birds' merry chirping by the window during the summer. Swallows still stray into the Old Shul during the spring, but kids who are just learning the alphabet—never!

And it just so happened that on such a wintry night, forged in frost and darkness, a young boy came into the synagogue. He wore a big hat with flaps over his ears, big shoes, and a long, broad, cotton-lined little overcoat. He squeezed in among the old men by the stove with his hands behind his back like an elderly scholar and pressed his little back against a couple of the heated tiles. The white-bearded old-timers moved aside to give the honored guest more room. They regarded him for a long while, then asked him:

---

121 Married women traditionally cover their hair according to Jewish law, although that covering can be a wig.
122 A reference to Proverbs 31:10.

"Whose father are you?"

The little boy's black eyes flashed; he sniffed with his frozen red-dish little nose and laughed:

"I'm not a father yet. My father's name is Avrohom and he's called Avromke the Old Clothes Man because that's what he sells in the courtyard. My mother has her own shop down the street where she sells clay pots and tin pails."

"So what's your name?" they asked him. "Do you have any little brothers? And where do you go to school?"

He replied to each question separately, like an adult.

"My name is Itsikl. And I don't have any little brothers. I have little sisters. And I study at the Dvora Kuperstein School.[123] But right now I'm not going to school. It's too cold."

The old men wrinkled their brows; they wracked their brains but couldn't recall hearing about such a school.

"We know of a study house named after the saintly Dvora Esther,"[124] they told Itsikl, "but we've never heard of the saintly Dvora Kuperstein, nor of a *shul* named after her."

Once again Itsikl burst out laughing.

"It's not a *shul* where you go to pray. It's a school where you learn how to write Yiddish and do arithmetic and draw with a pencil and sing too."

"And do you know how to pray? Do you wear *tzitzis*?" the men asked him.

"I don't know how to pray and I don't wear *tzitzis*," he answered.

Did you ever hear of such a thing? The old men shook their heads sadly at one another. All along they had been under the impression that only the grandsons of well-to-do families grow up like gentiles. Now they see that today the children of the poor can too.

The men found a prayer book with large letters to enable Itsikl to

---

123 A Yiddish-language school in Vilna, founded by the teacher Dvora Kuper-stein in 1912.

124 Dvora Esther Gelfer (1817–1907), a philanthropist and founder of a chari-table foundation that provided interest-free loans.

learn the alphabet. It's a topsy-turvy world, the old men muse. When they went to school one teacher taught ten boys; now a *minyan* of bearded men surround one little Jewish boy, and the ten grandfathers tell him:

"Read, Itsikl, read!"

But it's like talking to the wall. The lad is seven or eight years old and he can barely crawl through a page of Hebrew—no doubt when it comes to crawling over a fence the little rascal can do that with ease. He even brags that he can sail through a Yiddish text but he doesn't know the morning prayer "I give thanks to You," nor can he recite a blessing. Just listen to what Itsikl says! In the Yiddish school he is taught to sing little ditties. Sure! Can you imagine them teaching him the Psalms for the morning service? So it turns out that the workers who once rebelled against the Russian czar and sang songs in the streets have heirs. Itsikl told them that his teacher had taken the class for a walk in the fields and shown them flowers. Itsikl seems to be a smart boy, but he talks like a fool. Why does he need field flowers? Is he about to become a village peasant?

The next evening Itsikl came back; now the men welcomed him as one of their own and left him a spot right by the middle of the stove. One of the grandfathers offered him a piece of dark honey cake, his reward for saying a blessing. Another grandfather took a couple of copper coins and a silver ten-kopek coin out of a little chamois purse with nickel buttons and presented it as Hanukkah money to a grandson not his own.

"True, it's already two weeks after Hanukkah—but it's never too late to pay a debt," the donor said, and sat down to teach Itsikl to read from the prayer book.

But the man who had given Itsikl the dark honey cake was peeved at his neighbor for snatching away his pupil. When the lesson was over, the cake giver whispered into Itsikl's ear:

"Do you perhaps have a friend? Bring him here with you and he'll also get a piece of cake."

Itsikl brought his little sister, Sarah, who was one year younger, a tiny girl with a moist face and small as a fish. She was all bundled up, wrapped in a little woolen shawl and wearing big knitted mittens like an old lady. As Sarah's older brother helped her remove her mother's wraps, her damp black silken hair glistened. The cake man smiled and said:

"So it's a girl after all?"

But the grandfather was so eager to have a pupil he turned his reasoning on its head. A girl has to know how to light candles and be able to read the Yiddish supplications. Moreover, she's named after our matriarch, Sarah.

"Soreleh,[125] do you see this little critter with a bent back and with a little head on the top and on the bottom? Do you know what letter this is?"

"It's an *alef*," she answered with the hard dry voice of a woman shopkeeper who can't stand a customer vexing her for naught.

"But you see, Soreleh, you didn't know that when under the *alef* there's this tiny sign that looks like a little step, then the *alef* is pronounced 'aw.'"

With his back bent over almost in half and with a walking stick in hand, one of the old men looked like the letter *hey*. This man now approached Itsikl with a practical suggestion.

"Bring over some of your friends from the street. Tu B'Shvat[126] is coming soon and everyone will get carob.[127] They can warm up by the stove and fool around as much as they like, as long as they're willing to learn how to become Jews."

For this Itsikl found eager customers much more quickly than he could find buttons to play with. Half a dozen boys appeared in the Old Shul. One of them was a tall boy with sunken cheeks and protruding ears red from cold. He had big teeth and whinnied like a horse: ho-ho-ho! When he talked he kept his hands in his pockets to show he wasn't afraid of anyone. His nickname was Leybke Ox,

---

125 Diminutive of Sarah.

126 The fifteenth day of the Hebrew month of Shvat, a holiday celebrating the "New Year of the Trees."

127 It is traditional on Tu B'Shvat to eat fruits from the Land of Israel, such as carob.

because when he fought, he kicked and butted his head, starting low and aiming up just like an ox with its horns. Nevertheless, for him too a teacher was found, a man who compared to Leybke looked like a kitten next to a gigantic mouse.

But the fighter had a thick head, and his teacher recalled in amazement that in days gone by great scholars emerged from sons of poor families. Nowadays, it turns out, one can stem from a poor family and still be a boor. Never mind, Leybke's teacher consoled himself, with me that cabbage head will end up learning how to read Hebrew. By now the young voices of boys studying the Five Books of Moses already rang out in the study house. Next to each one sat an old man, swaying back and forth.

"Say it, little boy, say it. *Bereyshis*, in the beginning. *Boro*, created. *Elokim*, God . . ."

In the wintry outdoors, the wind blew the snow from the roofs to the streets and from the streets onto the roofs. The icy cold crept under fingernails and sliced into foreheads. A blizzard whirled before the men's eyes, but the graybeards of the Old Shul proceeded slowly through the storm. Wearing fur caps pushed down over their ears and thick woolen scarves pulled up over their noses, the old men groped their way forward with their walking sticks to keep from sinking into the snowy void.

Awaiting them in the study house were their pupils, whose voices tinkled like little silver bells—and for their young charges the teachers were ready to risk their lives.

In vain the old men's children cried out, "Where are you heading to, Papa? It's a danger to life and limb out there."

"You think you're still a youngster, father-in-law? They've even closed the schools because of the severe frost, and yet you still insist on going out."

Their own wives yelled even louder. "He's become a tutor in his old age! You've got your own sons and grandchildren, may they live and be well."

The graybeards did not answer. They just stared wide-eyed at their wives, seething in silence, as though they were in the middle of the Grace After Meals and were not allowed to interrupt their prayer. But once he was outside and on his way, one of the old men laughed into the woolen scarf that squeezed his beard and covered his mouth.

"What a cow she is! Can you call what she has sons and grandchildren? All she has is a houseful of gentiles and boors. And to them she kowtows, as if to a pagan god. Foolish woman! Doesn't she realize that students are one's true children?"

III

THE OLDSTERS KEPT their promise and did not stop the boys from running around the *bimah* and playing hide-and-seek between the benches and prayer stands. While the students were fooling around, the teachers sat by the stove, their heads lowered into their shoulders, and slowly rocked back and forth over their holy books, seemingly oblivious. Still, they couldn't pretend they didn't see a thing when the little scamps discovered the trapdoor to the little storeroom under the *bimah* from which they dragged tattered prayer books, Bibles and ethical tracts. These books containing God's name had long been waiting to be laid to rest in a coffin and buried like a dead person in a cemetery, accompanied by eulogies.[128] But these torn holy books and loose pages never expected little rascals to rummage through them looking for lost treasures.

The grandfathers pushed their brass-rimmed glasses up onto their wrinkled foreheads, regarded the mess the little brats had made, and laughed. Because of advanced age their arms dangled down to their knees, and as they walked, their hands shook like empty pails on a yoke. Yet they took the trouble to bend down to the ground to pick up the stacks of scattered, torn-out pages, while softly and calmly teaching their pupils that treading upon holy books is a great sin.

---

128 According to Jewish law, texts bearing God's name cannot be thrown out but must be buried in a cemetery.

"If you boys have so much fun tearing up prayer books and Bibles, here's what you can do. Pray and study every day, and then the books will fall apart of their own accord."

So either because the rascals feared the distress of having to pray and study so much, or because they realized that the old men were crawling about on all fours, they suddenly swooped down to the floor to gather up the torn pages containing God's name and quickly stuff them back into the little storeroom under the *bimah*.

But with grownups the old men were not as good-natured and patient as with the little pranksters.

One day a man in a fur coat with a broad sparse beard and gold-rimmed glasses wandered into the Old Shul for the afternoon service. Seen through the beard, his chin was as naked and visible as a stone in a field. During the Silent Devotion the elders swayed, deep in morose contemplation, like a row of bent willows whose branches hang down to the water's edge. The guest stood straight, rooted like an oak. His frock coat with a vent in the back was brand new, unlike the old men's threadbare and rumpled caftans. The stranger heard something going on in the study house: a commotion and scampering of feet, as though demons were dancing overhead. He turned from the wall where he was reciting the Silent Devotion and saw a group of urchins playing tag amid the benches and knocking over prayer stands that crashed to the floor with a bang. Two of the urchins were going wild on the *bimah*, leaping at each other like goats and dragging the coverlet off the reading table. But what most astounded the guest was the old timers' attitude. They swayed back and forth calmly as if they didn't hear the tumult, or as if it didn't bother them. In that case, the guest decided, he wouldn't interrupt his prayers at a point where it was forbidden to do so, and he turned back a second time to face the wall, swaying piously. Suddenly, behind his back he heard whispers and soft laughter, and at once remembered the fur coat that he had draped over the *bimah* railing before beginning to pray. Now he turned again and saw that what he had intuited had come to pass: the little devils were gathered around his fur coat, plucking hairs from the collar and tying together the edges of the pelts that were sewn in as a lining. But as soon as the scamps saw the enraged man striding towards them, flailing his hands without a word, they scattered.

After prayers the guest asked the old men if there was a school for little boys in the Old Shul, and who was the teacher.

"Yes, we have a school here in the Old Shul and all of us are the teachers," said one of the beaming and happy grandfathers.

"Can't you stop these bathhouse bums from going wild? I would drag these little bandits out of the synagogue by their hair," the guest said, his face flushed with anger.

But the old men became angry too—so incensed that their hands began to shake.

"So pick yourself up and leave. Go in good health but don't tell us what to do. You think we're back in the old days? Nowadays you can't utter a word of rebuke to students. You have to deal kindly with them, with complete tenderness."

The man in the fur coat left, shrugging his shoulders: if you can no longer lift a leather strap to these bandits, why it's the end of the world!

On Tu B'Shvat, the teachers fed their pupils carob, just like, during that same week, boys fed crumbs to little birds on the Sabbath of Song.[129] Since Soreleh had weak teeth, full of tiny black holes, and was unable to eat the hard, dry carob, Leybke with his big horsey teeth ate up Soreleh's portion and even mocked her brother.

"Here, Itsikl, take these seeds and plant them in a flowerpot and then they'll grow into your own carob trees."

Itsikl did not take the carob seeds, but he was afraid to call Leybke "Ox" lest he butt or kick him. Now Soreleh was crying and her teacher, the man with the cake, consoled her:

"Tomorrow I'm going to bring you a whole piece of cake. And today I have another present for you. Since you're a girl, I brought

---

129 The Sabbath in which Exodus 15:1–18, the Song of the Sea, is read in the synagogue, which often falls close to Tu B'Shvat. In Ashkenazi Jewish communities it is customary to feed wild birds on that Sabbath.

you a little blackboard and chalk, and I'm going to teach you how to write."

But it was of no use that the old man also became a teacher of writing, for soon Soreleh stopped coming.

"She has to stay at home and take care of our youngest sister," Itsikl told Soreleh's teacher, "because my mother has to be in the shop with her clay pots and tin pails."

The cake man felt heavy at heart, for he had gotten to like Soreleh so much. But the other teachers were not overly concerned that a similar problem might also befall them.

"It's just a girl after all. She's not obliged to have any know-how in the tiny letters."

Right after this, however, Lebyke too stopped coming to the synagogue and Itsikl reported that since the snow had frozen, the Ox spent days on end sliding on his little sled. Since no one had derived much pleasure from Leybke anyway, the teachers compared him to the raven that Noah sent forth from the ark.[130] The raven did not come back, even though the flood still covered the earth.

"When the waters receded, the little dove too did not return," the old men sighed. Ah, woe, they had to pray for freezing weather and blizzards to keep their students from running away.

In order to hold onto the boys when freezing weather would no longer drive them into the study house for warmth, the old men made moralizing comments like:

"The Torah, Itsikl, is like water. Without Torah the world would be like a desert."

"The Torah, Meirke, is like fire. Without Torah the world would be as dark as a cellar where you keep potatoes."

The little boys liked to hear their teachers' comments for several reasons. First of all, it was a break from studying. Secondly, they were spoken to like grownups. And thirdly, the teacher's white beard looked like an entire wintry forest. But the forest is full of winter frost, while the teacher's beard is warm and so dense one could hide

---

130 Genesis 8:7.

in it. And besides, the teacher doesn't pinch like a father or yell like a mother. The teacher speaks softly—so softly you can barely hear him. He strokes your head and his beard strokes your cheeks. Sometimes he cries, but not loudly like a child. The teacher cries inwardly. One can hardly hear his sobbing, but tears stream from his eyes until his beard becomes as wet as a washcloth. But if you ask him why he's crying, he gives you a very strange answer.

"I'm crying because my grandsons don't need a grandfather."

And he falls into a fit of coughing and coughs so hard he can't catch his breath.

Besides words of wisdom and piety, the students also wanted to hear nice stories and of these the teachers had an endless trove, like an orchard strewn with apples and pears. But all these nice tales ended the same way: that one must study Torah. There was one story about a man from long ago who climbed up to the glass roof of a study house in order to hear and see the men studying down below. He was so engrossed in trying to follow and understand the scholars' remarks that he didn't realize he had been covered with snow.[131] Then there was a tale about a very saintly man who studied with his feet in a bucket of cold water to stay awake.[132] And another one about a good, devout but thickheaded boy who wept so bitterly about his inability to learn anything that Elijah the Prophet came to him and studied with the lad every night until he grew up to become a great scholar.

Itsikl's teacher, the one who had given him Hanukkah money, promised his pupil that during Sukes[133] he would let him carry his *lulav*[134] and *esrog*.[135] And on Simchas Torah,[136] when the men dance

---

131 Babylonian Talmud, tractate Yoma 35b.

132 A story often told about Rabbi Elijah ben Shlomo Zalman, better known as the Vilna Gaon (1720–1797).

133 The Feast of Tabernacles.

134 A palm branch that is shaken together with a citron and the branches of myrtle and willow plants on the holiday of Sukes, per Leviticus 23:40.

135 Citron.

136 A holiday immediately following Sukes, during which the cycle of weekly Torah readings is completed and begun anew. Literally "The Rejoicing of the Torah."

around the *bimah* with the Torah scrolls, Itsikl would get a glass of wine and a piece of honey cake just like a grownup. Seeing that the boy wrinkled his brow, displeased that he would have to wait so many months until Sukes, the teacher rushed to make him happy.

"Soon Purim[137] is coming and I'm going to give you a Purim treat—a homentash[138] filled with poppy seeds and a packet of raisins too."

Another man, who was teaching Meirke, bragged to his student that the Old Shul was the oldest in Vilna, even older than the Great Synagogue.

"Here we have a community register; it's a sort of book in which all kinds of wonderful stories have been recorded. So it's easy to see what a great honor and privilege it is to sit and study in the Old Shul."

But when Meirke wanted to look at this book called the "community register," his teacher didn't know where it was. Instead, he showed Meirke a silver Torah pointer shaped like a little hand with an outstretched index finger. Meirke ran his rosy little fingers over the heavy pointer and exclaimed:

"Leibke Ox has a pair of brass knuckles. When he puts those brass knuckles on his hand and gives someone a good smack in the face, his face becomes mush. That's what Leibke says, that show-off."

Hearing this, the teacher shuddered.

"At least say, 'forgive the comparison,' for yoking together this Torah pointer and the brass knuckles. This silver hand I'm showing you is not made to hurt anyone. With this silver hand the *gabbai*[139] points out the words on the parchment to show the Torah reader where to read."

The carved animals and birds above the Holy Ark, the Stars of David hand-cut into the windowpanes, even the hammered flowers in the big Hanukkah menorah, were no longer a novelty for the

---

137 A holiday celebrating the salvation of the Jews from the genocidal plans of the Persian vizier Haman, as described in the biblical Book of Esther.

138 A triangular stuffed pastry supposedly in the shape of Haman's purse, traditionally eaten on Purim.

139 The beadle or sexton of a synagogue.

little students. So the teachers came up with the clever idea of showing them the treasures in the drawer under the reading table on the *bimah* and in the little cabinet beneath the Holy Ark. There lay a *shofar*, yellow and transparent as honey; a silver *esrog* box with four thin legs, and a spice holder shaped like a little tower used on Saturday night for the *Havdalah* prayer;[140] this little tower had tiny doors, a roof and a flag on top.

Nevertheless, all these beautiful things could not compare to the crowns and the silver pomegranates—also used as crowns—that were placed on the two wooden rollers of the Torahs. Moreover, the Pure Ones, as the Torahs were called, were adorned with belts and silken shawls, and covered with either dark red or deep blue velvet mantles. And placed over all these coverings were engraved silver breastplates.

"You see, little boys, what a beautiful Torah we have," the elders said triumphantly.

The lads gaped with amazement into the open dark Holy Ark, their heads pressed together like lambs around a well.

IV

THE BLIZZARDS ABATED. The snow piled up on the roofs was higher than the low-slung little houses. The women peddlers with their baskets sat on low stools, their limbs stiff as they dozed. When one woke up and stirred, a mound of snow fell from her head scarf right into her baskets. Seeing that she had woken up from her sleep in vain—there were no customers in sight—the woman started praising her frozen apples in a loud voice.

"Bottles of wine! Bottles of wine! Who's buying Malaga grapes?"

Hearing no response the woman dozed off again and sat there benumbed, like the pointer on the scale that hung over her head, an

---

140 The prayer marking the end of the Sabbath and the beginning of a new week.

iron witness for the World to Come that she had given honest weights and measures.

During the day the snow dazzled one's eyes on the broad streets, and at night it reflected, mirror-like, the twinkling green stars. But in the narrow little lanes around the Old Shul, during the day the snow lay yellow like a corpse. Even before dusk it had already turned gray-black, trodden by the feet of passersby. When night fell and the smoky kerosene lamps were kindled in the little shops, the narrow lanes were webbed in a mysterious play of light and shadow.

The toil-worn faces of the shopkeepers gleamed a hot deep red, as if the little stores with the wooden herring barrels had been magically transformed into wine casks made of glass. The women peddlers by their baskets took the half-extinguished firepots from under their aprons and kept blowing into the embers until the coals began to glow anew like great copper sunsets opposite their soot-covered faces and their kerchiefs capped with snow. Porters wearing cotton-wadded furs and beggars in long raggedy coats warmed themselves around a little tin stove in the middle of the lane. They looked like a secret band of exiled sons of prophets around a burnt-out bonfire in a dark dense forest. All were silent, their faces hidden in the blackness of the night; only their heavy hands with outspread crooked fingers were lit up by the little stove that crackled and sprayed sparks.

As soon as daylight reached the narrow little lanes, it already looked like twilight. On one such day a short man wearing a high winter hat and big felt boots stopped in front of a windowless little shop with only a door opening to the street. Inside sat the woman shopkeeper, wearing a long dress and a half-coat covered with a short fur. Her head was wrapped in a shawl and her feet swathed in layers of cloth over her felt boots. But since she was still cold, she sat with her back pressed to the wall so the wind wouldn't blow at her from front or back. The old man stuck his head into the shop and asked the saleswoman:

"Do you have a teapot? In the Old Shul we have a tin pail to bring hot water from the tearoom. We also have plenty of glasses and saucers for the entire *minyan*. But what we do need is a porcelain teapot to brew tea."

"I don't have any porcelain or glass dishes. I just have tin teapots," the woman answered, and then added: "If you pray in the Old Shul, then you surely know my Itsikl, who studies there with a teacher every evening."

"Indeed, it's me who is your Itsikl's teacher," the old man cried out, delighted with the supposed coincidence. "Ay, ay, ay, what a boy your Itsikl is!" he enthused, smacking his soft lips over his toothless gums. "Itsikl has some smart head on his shoulders. Good heavens! He's amazing! May no evil eye befall him! He's got a voice like a boy who sings with the chief cantor's choir of the Great Synagogue, and he's got a zest for learning like the Gaon of Vilna when he was a little boy and gave a sermon in a big synagogue packed with Jews. A Jew once met the Vilna Gaon but didn't know he was the Vilna Gaon. He asked him, 'Where does the Gaon of Vilna live?' And the Vilna Gaon replied, 'If you want to, you too can be a gaon.'[141] And that's exactly how it also is with your Itsikl. With a little son like that, with an heir like Itsikl to say *Kaddish* for you, you will earn a place in the World to Come."

"I don't know about the World to Come. With my husband having to sell old clothes in the courtyard and me having to freeze here by my clay pots, we don't concern ourselves with the World to Come," the woman answered with surprising rancor. "But me and my husband are pleased," she continued, "that our little boy has somewhere to go and get warm in this freezing weather and learn at the same time . . . knowledge never hurts."

The short man in the high winter hat become confused and stammered something through his toothless gums that couldn't be heard or understood. Then he found his tongue again and said softly:

"Since you are Itsikl's mother and I'm his teacher, I'm going to buy a tin teapot from you. It will come in handy. Your Itsikl is some boy! An absolute gem!"

---

141 Great scholar or genius.

Later the buyer of the teapot told the men of the Old Shul, "I've paid my tuition," and his listeners shook their heads sadly. When they were little schoolboys, their impoverished parents worked their fingers to the bone to pay for their education. And nowadays the teachers have to pay for their pupils. Nevertheless, it's worth it, as long as they are not left without young successors. After this the other old men went out into the little lanes to look for the mothers of their students.

Meirke's mother sat in Ramayles Courtyard in a dug out cellar filled with black coal that she sold by the bucketful. She also sold bundles of split wood bound up with twisted straw. The teacher didn't know what to do. The freezing cold had doubled the weight of the wood bundles and the hard straw knot was covered with ice. How could an old man like him summon the strength to carry such a load up to the study house? But since the saleswoman, out of deep respect for the teacher who was studying with her young orphan, had crept out of the little cellar pit, her coal dust streaked face beaming with joy, Meirke's teacher bought two bundles of cut wood.

"My only request is," he told her, "that the bundles remain here with you until I can find someone to carry them up to the Old Shul."

"I'll bring it over for you. It's not beneath my dignity," the woman replied, then added: "and by going there I can also see the synagogue where my little boy sits and studies . . . But how can I leave my business unattended?"

"I'll watch your shop. So go, but don't dilly-dally," the old man urged the woman as she mulled over the propriety of leaving the teacher as a watchman. Only after Meirke's mother had obeyed and gone off carrying the bundles of wood to the study house did the elder begin to examine the wall facing him.

Half-buried in the ground and the snow, two little windows from a cellar apartment stared out at him. And high up on the roof was a crowded jumble of crooked attic windows and long, narrow, soot-blackened chimneys. For its entire height and width the wall itself did not have a single window and appeared deaf, mute and blind. Bare bricks, black as night. Why is this wall here fencing off Ramayles

Courtyard from the rest of the world? the old man wondered, standing there with his wrinkled little beard, hunched over like a big sparrow freezing on a telegraph wire.

Some of the graybeards also stood by the women fruit peddlers on the street, holding little paper bags of frozen apples they had just bought.

"True no one envies you now," the men consoled the women, "but because of the Torah your sons are studying, you will be warm in the World to Come."

The short and squat fur-covered fruit peddlers stood with their legs spread over the firepots and listened with a pious look on their faces, just as they did on Rosh Hashanah and Yom Kippur to the woman who read out the prayers in the women's gallery.

From an unearthly hiding place in the frozen distance the snow kept on falling without letup and the residents of the narrow twisted little lanes sank even deeper into the snow, like tree stumps in a rotting forest.

V

ON PURIM, WHEN the *Megillah* [142] was read, the Old Shul was inundated with smoke and powder, the smell of sulphur, shooting and wild drumming. Every time the Megillah reader chanted the names of the evil Haman and his wife, Zeresh, one group of youngsters banged their sticks on the railing of the *bimah*, while an even larger group fired off their homemade "guns"—big hollowed-out iron keys filled with gunpowder. [143] These "guns" were hurled at the wall or at one of the stone pillars around the *bimah*. A reddish green flame flashed, followed by a deafening explosion. These bursts in all corners, simul-

---

142 Literally "scroll," but in the context of Purim a reference to the Book of Esther.
143 During the reading of the Book of Esther in synagogue it is customary to symbolically drown out the names of Haman and his family with noisemakers.

taneously and then successively, resounded loudly in the study house. The Megillah reader, one of the old men, waited patiently until the firing had ended, and then continued calmly.

A big crowd of people had come to the Old Shul to hear the *Megillah*. Some were men who came to pray regularly on Sabbaths and holidays. Others were people who happened to chance by. Seeing the inferno that the boys had let loose, these newcomers were ready to throw them out by the scruffs of their necks. But the old men lashed out at the regulars and the strangers with a wild rage:

"Enough! You come once in a blue moon and these boys come here every day."

These men, who came to pray only on Sabbaths and holidays, knew very well that in the middle of the week a tenth man was occasionally lacking for a *minyan*.

"But these Haman-beaters are not yet bar mitzvah," they countered. "And a boy under bar mitzvah cannot be included in a *minyan*."

"Yes they can!" the oldsters cried out. "In an emergency a little boy holding a Pentateuch can be counted as a tenth for a *minyan*, even if he's years away from his bar mitzvah."

The next day the old teachers gave their students big poppy-seed-filled homentashen as Purim treats and also told them nice stories from the *Targum Sheni*, the Aramaic translation and elaboration of the Book of Esther. But when the graybeards returned to their own homes for the Purim feast, they vented their anger at their children and grandchildren for thinking only about stuffing their guts and not the miracle and joy of Purim.

After Purim, however, when the deep freeze abated, the students gradually returned to the noisy little lanes. The brighter the sun shone through the scattered gray clouds, the more restless and dejected the old men became. They sat by the hot glossy white tiles of the heated stove, looked outside, and marveled at how quickly the chunks of ice were melting, even quicker than the wax melting on a *Havdalah* candle. How it dribbles, drips and trickles on the windowpanes. See the flash and the sparkle. Drops of water are illumined in the rays of the sun, and the rays, in turn, are reflected in the drops of water. Every once in a while a crackling sound was heard up on high and a heap of snow slid down noisily and merrily past the windows, as though the snow could hardly wait to descend. Full of sparks, the light and transparent smoke of the chimneys surged impatiently upwards. But for the old men the first sign of spring was not a happy occasion. They became even more sensitive to the inner pain in their desiccated bones and sad at heart at now having fewer and fewer students.

When Meirke stopped coming, Itsikl still held on, but his remarks didn't cheer his teacher. Itsikl had declared that in his Yiddish school where he studied daily until three in the afternoon all the children made fun of him for wearing *tzitzis*. And his father said he wasn't overly fond of religious Jews. When they haggle with his father over a coat or a jacket, they tell him to rip open the lining to see if wool and linen are intermingled there.

"Why should it bother the religious Jews if wool and linen are sewn together under the lining?" Itsikl asked.

"Because it's *shatnez*,"[144] the teacher answered. "And the Torah forbids wearing *shatnez*."[145]

"Why does the Torah say this?" Itsikl continued.

The teacher groaned out his reply:

"No one really knows for sure why it's forbidden to wear a garment made of wool and linen."

"So you see my father is right," Itsikl cried out, and he too stopped coming to the Old Shul.

Then the grandfathers went out once more to the mothers of their students. They trudged through the snow in high galoshes, even though they no longer wore the heavy winter fur caps and now donned the Jewish-style cloth hats with a stiff brim and a cloth visor. The old men made their way forward carefully, taking little steps over the mud-splattered cobblestones and on the

---

144 A mixture of wool and linen, or other mixtures prohibited by the Torah.
145 Leviticus 19:19, Deuteronomy 22:9–11.

puddle-filled sidewalks, and thought they heard the shouts of their runaway pupils all around them. They stopped and turned their heads slowly but saw nothing in the blinding sun. The gray peeling façades and unplastered walls of plain bricks, suffused with a bright luster, dazzled the old men's weak eyes. Sounds of lively voices echoed from near and far, like in a fog on the other side of the river. The elders dragged themselves further, looking for the mothers of their students in the shops, in the cellars, and by the baskets of the fruit peddlers on the street.

"Is your Itsikl sick, God forbid?" the teacher said craftily to the woman who sold teapots, as though nothing untoward had happened. One is permitted to play the fool in order not to embarrass a person and help him repent.

"Why sick all of a sudden? Let my enemies get sick!" the woman answered with a burst of anger.

Just as in winter, clay pots and tin pails were all about and hanging on the wall. But Itsikl's mother no longer wore a heavy woolen shawl. She wasn't even ashamed to sit with her hair uncovered in the presence of the teacher; moreover, she gave vent to her sour mood by saying:

"My little boy can't go to both the Yiddish school and the Old Shul. My husband says that both at the same time are not a good match. 'Either an angel or a priest,' says my husband. I hope to God my little Itsikl won't be a priest. But he also won't be a rabbi. It's not within a poor family's means."

Meirke's mother, out of respect for her son's teacher, crept out of her little basement shop full of coal and exculpated herself by saying:

"I'm a widow, always busy with trying to make a living and my 'Kaddish'[146] is growing up without a father's supervision. So he's doing what his little friends are doing out on the street. They've stopped going to the Old Shul, so he stopped too. And besides, I need him

---

146 That is, the one who will say the mourner's prayer for her after her death.

to deliver a bundle of wood or half a bucket of coal for my women customers who don't want to carry the merchandise by themselves."

The woman did not stop thanking the free tutor for the good deed of teaching her "*Kaddish*" a page of Hebrew. But she concluded exactly the same way as Itsikl's mother:

"Meirke will not grow up to be a rabbi. A poor widow like me can't afford that."

No longer dressed in their winter furs and woolen shawls, the fruit peddlers looked younger; their reanimated faces had a rosy bloom. They sold a pre-spring item—oversized soured apples soaking in full buckets of water.

"Kvass apples, kvass apples," they called out sprightly, and around them gathered a crush of customers, mostly men. They savored the delicious winey flavor even before they bit into the soured apples. Their tongues cleaved to the roofs of their mouths; they relished the taste, sucked in their lips and pointed a finger, as though at a washtub full of live fish:

"No, no. Not this apple. That's the one I want."

The peddlers quickly pulled the kvass apples out of the bucket and at the same time spoke to the graybeards from the Old Shul, who humbly waited for an answer, like poor people waiting for a handout.

"We thank you grandfathers for letting our boys come in to the shul during the winter to warm up. But now that spring is coming and the weather is mild, we can't tell our kids not to run around and have fun. Poor children don't have any other bit of joy, so let them play as long as they're young.

"And furthermore," the fruit peddlers concluded, "you grandfathers have your own grandsons and children too who are also rich and well provided for, as folks here on the street say. So why don't you study Torah with your own grandsons and then you'll earn as much World to Come as you want?"

What do you say to that? That's precisely what the prophet complained about—that our grandsons don't want to study Torah, the grandfathers thought, and just nodded pleasantly and absentmindedly without saying a word. When they returned to the Old Shul, they no longer sat around the stove and no longer spoke to one another as they did during that wonderful period when little students had sat next to them. Every one of the old men crept back to his little corner by the cold wall where he would sit during the summer. They sat silently behind their big oaken prayer stands, looked out the windows, and tried hard to focus on something else—like, for instance, that barely three weeks remained until Passover. In that case, it was high time to think about a bakery to bake *shmura* matzo[147] and about ordering wine from the Hasid for the Seder.

VI

THE ELDERS OF the Old Shul were destined to have another kind of experience with students—this time grown-up Torah scholars, young masters of Talmud. One morning, around the time the little boys stopped coming in the evening, a seventeen-year-old youth stormed into the synagogue. He had a pair of healthy ruddy cheeks and a wrinkled, scholarly forehead under a little hat that was pushed back on his head.

"Do you have *Kreysee Ufleysee*[148] in your study house?" he asked one of the men with an impetuous tone in his voice.

The old man either hadn't heard or hadn't understood. So the preoccupied young scholar spoke even more impatiently.

"I mean the book *Kreysee Ufleysee* by Rabbi Jonathan Eybeschutz, the Rabbi of Prague.[149] Do you have that text? I have to look something up."

One graybeard found a bundle of keys and opened the bookcase

---

147 Matzo, or unleavened bread, which has been supervised from the time the wheat is harvested, to ensure that it has never had a chance to leaven.
148 A commentary by Rabbi Jonathan Eybeschutz (1690–1764) on the *Code of Jewish Law* by Rabbi Yosef Karo (1488–1575).
149 Eybeschutz was a rabbinical judge in Prague from 1736 to 1741 before becoming the rabbi of Metz and then of the three communities of Altona, Hamburg, and Wandsbek.

cabinet. The other old men also drew near and looked up at the young scholar, who stood on the little ladder and rummaged through one shelf of books after another.

"You have a great collection of sacred texts here by the early and later rabbinical authorities, but you don't have *Kreysee Ufleysee*," he said, jumping down, and ordered the men to open another cabinet. There stood a large edition of the Vilna Talmud, bound in black leather and green linen, a complete set of the *Code of Jewish Law* with covers hard as stone, and a four-volume set of Maimonides' works with gilt spines. The young Talmud scholar did find something, but not the book he sought. The books he chose he handed down to one of the grandfathers, who stretched his hands up to the scholar just like Moses our Teacher when he received the Torah at Mount Sinai. At the third cabinet the young scholar remained up on the little ladder, deeply immersed in a text with torn covers and yellowed pages. He swallowed page after page with his eyes and nodded enthusiastically. "Amazing," he said to himself, and the elders around the little ladder looked up at him as if at an angel of God who stands between heaven and earth.

"So it's true what everyone says, that great scholars used to sit and study here in the Old Shul. There's a treasure here," the young scholar said, and finally leaped down with several holy books—responsa from leading rabbinic authorities of former times. His words delighted the old men immensely, as if he had brought news that this was the year that the Jews would finally be redeemed from exile.

But when the youth posed a difficult question—how come the Jews here are totally unaware of the precious rare volumes in their own study house?—the old men's joy dissipated and they began sighing: "Ah, woe unto us, the heirs of the Old Shul. We can still manage to study a chapter of *Mishna* and peruse a bit of *Eyn Yaakov*, but *our* heirs don't even know that and want no part of a holy text. Only God in heaven knows what will happen to the treasures of the Old Shul."

"And whose son are you, young tree?" one of the oldsters asked, and then realized that one shouldn't use the familiar form when addressing a scholar. "Would you mind if I asked what family you come from?"

The men in the synagogue learned that the young man's name was Shloymele and he was a grandson of the old rabbinic judge, Reb[150] Shloymele Cohen. He studied at the Kletsk yeshiva and had come home for Passover earlier than the other Torah scholars because his mother missed him so much. The old men now ceased to be amazed: since the youth was a grandson of the late Reb Shloymele Cohen, Vilna's rabbinic legal authority, it's no wonder that he was so ripe with knowledge. Even though the graybeards weren't scholars, they did know the Talmudic aphorism: the Torah returns to its old abode. And they had heard that the great sage, the Chofetz Chaim,[151] long life to him, had said that indeed the Torah does come back to its old home, but when it is denied entry, it departs humiliated. That's why it can happen that nowadays children of rabbis don't take after their fathers and grandfathers.

While the men stood huddled together, murmuring like Jews who gather in a knot outside the synagogue to recite the blessing on the new moon[152] and speak to their own shadows, Shloymele lay half stretched out on the table amid the books he had dragged down. He was turning pages, skimming, looking here and there, perfectly at home and with such confidence, like the old men looking for a prayer in worn-out yellow prayer books. When he stood up he noticed that the men were still standing around him.

"Would it be possible for you to do your studying here at the Old Shul while you're home for Passover?" the elders asked him humbly. "We don't want to encroach on the Gaon's Shul, God forbid, where you probably do your studying. But the Gaon's Shul has a *minyan* of recluses, thank God, while in the Old Shul we don't have a single scholar who sits and studies here."

---

150 Yiddish for "Mr."

151 Rabbi Israel Meir Kagan (1839–1933), known as the Chofetz Chaim (literally, "the one who desires life") after the title of one of his works.

152 The blessing on the new moon is traditionally said outside the synagogue on the first Saturday night after its appearance.

"I don't study in the Gaon's Shul. I study at home, but I'm lacking holy books," Shloymele replied and wrinkled his scholarly brow. "With pleasure! It'll be much more convenient for me to sit and study in a study house where there's no lack of sacred texts. I'll also talk it over with my friend from the yeshiva to have our regular study sessions here. My friend Hirshel is the grandson of Vilna's town preacher, Reb Hirshele, and he also came home before the end of the term at the yeshiva because his mother is sick."

Hearing who Shloymele's friend was, the old men swayed and rocked back and forth like a group of white birches in a field.

"Of course we knew the old Vilna town preacher, Reb Hirshele! What a speaker he was, the Vilna town preacher! He was a master scholar, a saintly man, and the words he spoke were sweet as honey. And the rabbinic judge, Reb Shloymele." The elders stopped. Perhaps they hadn't sufficiently showered praise on the grandfather in the presence of his grandson. "Oh, what a man Reb Shloymele was! It's no wonder that grandfathers like that have such extraordinary grandsons."

"My grandfather wrote annotations on the Talmud and called his book *Kheyshek Shloyme*.[153] But I dispute my grandfather's *novellae*. His opinions are nothing special and rather simplistic. He doesn't penetrate the heart of the matter. I also dispute the Maharam,[154] he sounds like a grandma," Shloymele said, narrowing his wise eyes and then storming out of the study house in the same fashion he had come in.

When both youths sat themselves down in the eastern corner of the synagogue to study together, the old men saw at once that the town preacher Reb Hirshele's grandson was a totally different creature. Hirshele was one year older than Shloymele. He was eighteen, tall and thin and pale-faced. His decency and sagacity were seen in his tranquil eyes, his calm manner of speaking and the fine way he debated. Shloymele, on the other hand, studied with a loud and angry voice, as though he were constantly refuting his grandfather's com-

---

153 Literally, "The Desire of Shloyme."
154 Rabbi Meir of Rothenberg (1220–1293).

ments on the Talmud. Hirshele swayed slowly and hummed sweetly to himself like his grandfather, the town preacher Reb Hirshele would do years ago while delivering a sermon. If the two friends couldn't agree on an issue, Shloymele would talk quickly and incessantly, waving both hands and gesticulating with his thumb. During all this Hirshele listened with a smile on his pale face, pulling at a lone blond hair on his chin, or gazing at his long, elegant fingers. Finally, his turn came and he expressed his view softly, calmly, briefly—and then he continued to smile, no matter how much Shloymele gestured, shifted about, seethed and negated the commentators upon whose remarks his friend had based his argument. "He says absolutely nothing. What he says there is of no consequence whatsoever."

The elders slowly stood up from where they sat and came to watch and listen with delight. It's a miracle from heaven! Two strong broadwinged young eagles had flown into the Old Shul. One could see at once that Shloymele was sharp, a fiery interpreter of texts. And the fact that he didn't even spare his own grandfather, Reb Shloymele, and faulted the *novellae* of this former rabbinic judge, well, may such dishonor befall every grandfather! And Hirshele surely was wise, proficient and level-headed. Just see how meticulously he wears his little hat and drapes his neatly folded coat on the railing of the *bimah*; apparently, that's the way everything he has learned is stored in his brain. And the way he conducts himself with people—he's velvet and silk. The old men now went back to their seats, hid behind their prayer stands, and sighed:

"Would it have been so bad if we had grandsons like these? Of course it wouldn't have been so bad, but one has to earn it from God."

But the delight the Old Shul regulars had with someone else's grandsons was marred whenever they recalled that after Passover the two young eagles would fly back to the yeshiva. And so among themselves the old men deliberated behind the *bimah* and devised a plan. The next morning the two brilliant young scholars hadn't even had a chance to open their Talmuds when before them stood three elders with three beards, looking like a snow white Yom Kippur curtain for the Holy Ark. From both sides of the *bimah* other old men slowly drew near, as though waiting for the Torah scrolls to be brought down after the reading, whereupon they would touch the mantles with two fingers.

The three old men stammered and sighed at length before these two young scholars, until it became clear that they desperately needed a teacher.

"So why don't two well-known young scholars like you do a *minyan* of old Jews a favor and study with us? We're not asking you to do this for free, God forbid. We will pay you."

For a while the two youths stood there confused and embarrassed. Graybeards were offering to become their students. Then Shloymele burst out laughing.

"And what will I study with you? *Aggadah?*[155] I skim over such matter in the Talmud with a glance."

"*Aggadah* is just fine for us," the grandfathers replied. "We're dying to hear some nice, pious tales from the Talmud. And without a teacher, the Aramaic of *Eyn Yaakov* is a bit hard for us to penetrate. The truth is that studying the laws of Passover in the *Mishna Berura*[156] is absolutely crucial for us right now. The holiday is fast approaching and we have to bake *shmura* matzo and get rid of the *chometz*.[157] And so we have to know the applicable laws and act accordingly. It's no small matter, *chometz* on Passover!"

"And the laws pertaining to the Counting of the Omer?[158] Moreover, the customs of how to conduct oneself up to Lag B'Omer[159] and after Lag B'Omer are very complicated, especially if one is elderly and one's memory isn't so good. Then before one turns around it's already the eve of Shavues.[160] Certainly one can't be an ignoramus

---

155 The parts of rabbinic literature consisting of stories and legends.

156 A commentary on the first section of the *Code of Jewish Law* by Rabbi Israel Meir Kagan (1838–1933), otherwise known as the Chofetz Chaim.

157 Leavened bread or other baked goods, which are forbidden on Passover.

158 The counting of days between Passover and Pentecost, as per Leviticus 23:15–16.

159 The thirty-third day of the Counting of the Omer, traditionally a day of celebration.

160 The holiday of Pentecost, celebrating the giving of the Torah on Mount Sinai.

regarding a law about the holy days of the giving of the Torah," said another old man, listing the most important things he had to know. He wanted to make sure he had secured for himself a teacher in time for the whole summer.

"All right, I'll study *Aggadah* with you and Shloymele will study *Halacha*,"[161] Hirshele concluded with a clever little smile, as though he understood very well that besides studying Torah the old-timers had something else in mind.

During the evening, Hirshel, the town preacher's grandson, studied *Eyn Yaakov* with his students. When a stranger happened to come into the Old Shul for an evening service, he must have been transfixed with amazement. Sitting around a table was a group of Jews with beards and earlocks of finest silver, and the lamp above the table cast added beams of pure silver. The graybeards sat huddled together like schoolboys and teaching them was a pale youth. Besides doing the old men a kindness and having the good deed of spreading Torah learning, Hirshele also wanted to test his ability to explain texts well, as if he was already thinking of becoming the head of a yeshiva or assuming a rabbinic post. He took a statement of the sages and interpreted it according to the views of the various commentators; then he added his own comment which, even though it wasn't apparent in the remarks of the sages, nevertheless lay deep in their words, like a pearl in the sea. The old students were delighted with their young teacher and mused that he had inherited his way of speaking and the sweetness of his words from his grandfather the town preacher. If only he wouldn't rush back to his yeshiva. Recalling this, the old men's beaming faces clouded over, and behind their hunched backs the shadows stretched out as long as the years of their lives.

With these same men Shloymele studied *Mishna Berura* at twelve noon; in no way did he indulge in casuistic arguments, nor did he shout as he had done while studying with his friend. First he quoted the law as stated in the *Code of Jewish Law* in Hebrew and followed it

---

161 Legal subjects.

with an explanation in Yiddish. Then he stopped and waited patiently for the students to slog their way through the just-reviewed passage. And while they were inching along, Shloymele quickly scanned the commentaries, just like a grandson would give a quick glance up at a flying bird while waiting for his grandfather. Finally, the oldsters finished and Shloymele clearly and crisply summarized the law. Only occasionally did the keen scholar in him burst forth and he would mutter to himself, "What in heaven's name is he babbling about?" Or he would shrug his strong young shoulders and say, "He deserves to be put into a baby carriage along with his new interpretations."

The Old Shul regulars would overhear this and take delight in this too. Their young teacher had no qualms about disputing the commentators and not even the *Mishna Berura* itself. "Ay, ay, ay, what a grandson the old rabbinic judge, Reb Shloymele, has left us!" And once again the graybeards fell into rapture and the four gigantic stone pillars around the *bimah* also joined in their delight. "What a grandson! He's helping us keep the Old Shul alive."

Just as the two young Torah scholars differed in their interpretations, they also differed in manners and civility. Their elderly students rose in respect each time Shloymele and Hirshele passed them. Both youths knew that a person must stand up even for a young Torah scholar, tender in years but wise, especially since they were teaching the old-timers *Halacha* and *Aggadah*. But between themselves there was a constant dispute as to how a scholar must comport himself. Shloymele's view was that a great scholar shouldn't even turn around. It didn't matter if people stood up or not, if they praised or rebuked him—he had to make his way to his place by the synagogue's eastern wall. And he acted accordingly. Apparently, Shloymele had already rehearsed how he would behave when he became a great rabbi. Whenever he entered or left the study house, if he had to consult a sacred text in the bookcase by the western wall or if he simply wanted to walk back and forth in the Old Shul to stretch his young limbs, he did not even look at the graybeards who rose in respect for him. But Hirshele's attitude was different, totally different. When he entered or left the study house, he twisted his way through the benches where no one was sitting to avoid having anyone stand up for him. His view was that a truly great scholar scrupulously avoids troubling another person, especially the elderly.

One day before Passover the students gave their teachers their wages. The old men made an honest assessment: they had studied with them for almost two weeks. They would continue to study with them during the intermediary days of Passover,[162] and right after the holiday they would again resume their studies. So they wanted to pay the scholars in time, for older people should not be debtors. Neither of the two yeshiva students had in mind to accept tuition money, but each one reacted in his own fashion. Shloymele burst out with a cheerful laugh and stuck out his hand. Holding a handful of bills and coins—he didn't even glance at the sum—he at once strode over to the charity boxes by the door and put the money into all the boxes. Shloyme, the teacher of *Halacha*, acted according to the law. Instead of discovering astounding new insights in the Talmud, he had torn himself away from his own studies and taught Jews the *Code of Law*, from which he would not derive any new interpretations. So he was due compensation for loss of time from learning. But what he did with that money was nobody's business. But when Hirshele, the teacher of *Aggadah*, was offered money for tuition, a shudder ran through him. God forbid! He was not a synagogue trustee, nor would he be any-one's *gabbai* for distributing charity money. If a Jew wants to give to charity he has to do it himself.

VII

ALL YEAR LONG an old father is a burden. But when it comes to the Passover Seder he's at the seat of honor. The invited guests like to look at the old man wearing a white linen robe, leaning on white pillows. The silver of his beard blends with the silver candlesticks

---

162 The third to fifth days of Passover, which are still part of the holiday but when most kinds of work may be performed.

and the dishes on the table. The wine in the goblets is reflected in his eyes. As much as the Seder guests would laud the lady of the house for the delicious food, they will later remember the essence of the evening: the old man sitting at the head of the table.

"He's a jewel in the house. A precious ornament."

But now one couldn't recognize these elders. Instead of reciting the *Haggada*[163] with a beautiful melody and expressing joy that their children were making a Seder, the old men complained that nothing was done according to *Halacha*, and looked suspiciously at every dish that was served. Even the previous night at the ceremony of searching for *chometz*, the old men's children noticed that their fathers had undergone a change. Police in the bright light of day do not search so diligently if illegal sales are being made through a shop's back door or if merchandise is being sold without the state tax stamp as their fathers did in searching every little corner for a stray piece of *chometz*. And the children felt even worse during the Seder, when their elderly fathers took out their *shmura* matzo. The guests could not contain their smiles seeing the burnt *shmura* matzo,[164] black as earth—pieces of crumbled coal. And later, when their children reproached them: "You embarrassed us in front of our guests," the old men replied with barely audible rage:

"A father is not your Elijah the Prophet's cup of wine that's placed on the table once a year.[165] Do you really believe that when we open the door and say 'Pour out Thy wrath,' that Elijah the Prophet enters?"

The grandsons too couldn't fathom this biting attack by enfeebled old men who already stood with both feet on the Other Side. The entire week of Passover the graybeards looked at their grandsons with derision and bitterness.

"The rabbinic judge, Reb Shloymele, and the Vilna town

---

163 The rabbinic text detailing the biblical Exodus from Egypt, which is read at the table on the first and second nights of Passover.
164 In addition to being specially supervised, *shmura* matzo is also often baked by hand rather than by machine.
165 An additional cup of wine is traditionally poured at the Seder for Elijah the Prophet.

preacher, Reb Hirshele, have left grandsons—and we too are leaving grandsons!"

During the intermediary days of Passover and after the holiday, both yeshiva students continued studying with the old men, who glowed with even greater pleasure. As much as they loved learning *Halacha* and *Aggadah*, they knew that they would never develop into scholars. What pleased them most was that the two yeshiva students were using the sacred books of the Old Shul and that the study house resounded with young singing voices. But just as the old-timers of the Old Shul had been afraid during the winter that the little boys would run away when the frosts subsided—a fear that was justified—now the old men were afraid of summer, and now too their fear was not gratuitous.

Shloymele, the teacher of *Halacha*, was complaining to his white-bearded students that he wanted to return to the yeshiva but his mother had asked him to stay at home and join the family on vacation.

"Going on vacation is time lost from Torah study, and according to the law, honoring one's mother is not obligatory when it involves lost Torah study time. Nevertheless, I'm trying to persuade my mother in a nice way to let me go back." Even though the old students were overjoyed with this, they didn't show their delight and answered slyly:

"Excuse us for saying this, teacher, but your mother isn't wrong. She just wants you to rest up a bit."

Hirshele, the Vilna town preacher's grandson, also complained to the old men: "My mother still isn't well and I can't return to the yeshiva."

Knowing that the genteel and sedate teacher of *Aggadah* would not get angry, the grandfathers spoke to him openly and forthrightly:

"With God's help your mother will get well soon, so why don't you remain at home and study with us in the Old Shul? This way we will have a teacher and the bookcases won't remain forlorn. In the Kletsk yeshiva there is no lack of famous scholars, may their numbers increase, while in our holy place we don't hear the bell-like voice of a youngster studying Torah. There used to be a time when all the benches in the Old Shul were filled with the old, young and the very

youngest learners. Now we are left, old folk who are not truly scholars. So stay with us and the merit of the Old Shul will help you be
successful in your Torah studies. When one studies in the Old Shul,
one is also rewarded by getting a good match."

This long explanation exhausted the grandfathers and they stood
before their young teacher with pleading eyes, open mouths, and lowered beards. Hirshel stared down at his pale and long elegant fingers
and looked up at the old men with a smile in his tranquil eyes.

"I'm still a student myself and indeed not one of the excellent ones.
So how will I be able to improve in learning if I don't hear lectures
by the head of the yeshiva and if I don't have friends with whom I can
review the topic under discussion? My parents won't agree to this
either."

The old-timers saw that they were wrong. Nevertheless, their passionate wish that a couple of scholars would sit and study in the Old
Shul had so fired them up that they still sought a way of holding onto
these two grandsons. All the little golden bells on the Torah crowns
did not tinkle as sweetly and merrily as the singing voices of these
young Torah scholars. Perhaps it would be a good idea to go to their
mothers and make their case to them. Your sons, may they live and be
well, they would tell the mothers, your sons are grandsons of the Vilna
rabbinic judge, Reb Shloymele, of blessed memory, and of the Vilna
town preacher, Reb Hershele, of blessed memory. So, then, the oldest
synagogue in our city has a greater claim to students than a yeshiva in
the small town of Kletsk.

But the oldsters realized at once that the mothers of these children
of rabbinic descent would most certainly answer: Even though we're
mothers, we let our sons live away from home so they can develop
into distinguished scholars. And now you come along and want our
children to stay with you in your study house to keep you from feeling gloomy. Would that be right? That's what the mothers would ask
and to that the old men would have no response.

"But the truth of the matter is that the mothers wouldn't speak that
way if we had proper brides for their sons. But if our own grandsons
are out-and-out gentiles, what sort of impression would our grand-

daughters make, girls who haven't even been taught how to light the Sabbath candles? Fine brides they would make for the future Vilna rabbinic judge, Reb Shloymele, and the future Vilna town preacher, Reb Hirshele!"

Thus the graybeards said to one another and laughed bitterly until they decided that it would be better not to go to the mothers at all and thus avoid subjecting themselves to disgrace and humiliation.

The two youths returned to their yeshiva right after Lag B'Omer. As they bid goodbye to the Old Shul regulars they wished them long life and hoped they would remember the Torah precepts they had studied together. Both scholars realized that they could not wish the old men joy from their children for they had lost hope that their children would return to the strict observance of Judaism in their lifetimes. So wishing the old folk such joy would seem like they were making fun of them. The young master of Talmud, Shloymele, begged the old men's pardon for his impetuousness if, while teaching, he seemed to be strict. Hirshele too apologized.

"Please don't take it amiss, gentlemen, that we're not remaining here with you. We ourselves still need a teacher."

The elders murmured something but their lips trembled visibly and one could not hear what they were stammering. With great effort they just barely managed to stifle their sobs, for it would have been a terrible shame to see these young scholars off with tears, while their own mothers saw them off with joy. So they stroked their backs and arms silently, but their beards shook like torn spider webs. Even after the youths were gone, the old men stood by the door and remained silent together, like weak, abandoned birds in a meadow near a river in gloomy autumn, when the fit birds fly high in the sky to warmer lands. Later the graybeards crept back to their corners and hid behind the big prayer stands.

The voices of the young scholars at their Talmuds echoed for a long while in the grandfathers' hairy ears. The sun once more moved from the northeast past the windows of the southern wall and headed northwest, radiant and delighted that in the meantime everything in the Old Shul was still the same. The engraved plaque with the Psalmist's words, "I have set the Lord always before me,"[166] standing on the marble-topped reading desk shone along with the sparkling brass balls on the railing around the *bimah*. The stove's glossy white enamel tiles glistened brightly by the western wall. The copper washstand at the entrance glimmered dark red like a sunset. The big Hanukkah menorah shed a cold silver light like a mist-wrapped moon. Only the old men behind their prayer stands sat there with lightless eyes. They became even more bent over, their beards even grayer and sparser, their faces even more wrinkled. The sacred texts that the two young masters of Talmud had used lay scattered on the tables. In the four big round stone pillars around the *bimah*, one could see the holes made by the shots from the "guns" fired by the street urchins during the *Megillah* reading on Purim—the abandoned elementary school of the Old Shul.

The old men flitter from dreams to daydreams. Itsikl's former teacher suddenly jolts awake, frightened, and feels his beard. Into his sleepy brain a foolish thought had strayed and buzzed like a fly. While Itsikl was studying with him, he forgot to tell the boy that if he would come to the study house on Tisha B'Av,[167] when little boys have a custom of throwing thorn balls and wild pine cones into men's beards, he'd let him do that too.

"What am I dreaming about, and what am I thinking of? I'm dreaming about pine cones and already thinking of Tisha B'Av, when it's still less than three weeks to Shavues," the old man rebuked himself, groaned, and dozed off again, his wrinkled beard at the edge of the prayer stand.

Another old man daydreams that he sees the stone huts built over the graves of the Vilna rabbinic judge, Reb Shloymele, and the Vilna town preacher, Reb Hirshele. Over the moss-covered roofs of these little gravesite huts, tall trees grow and their leaves sparkle and shine; they tremble with religious ecstasy and joy that they have the privi-

---

166 Psalms 16:8.
167 The ninth of the month of Av, a day of mourning commemorating the destruction of the two temples in Jerusalem.

lege of growing over the graves of such saintly men. The old man consoles himself that he too will be laid to rest in this same cemetery where these two profound scholars are buried and they will be a shield over him, for he had sat in the same study house where their grandsons had studied and had enjoyed their words of Torah.

A third old man isn't sleeping at all. He sits with tightly knitted brows and thinks: "It's high time to carry out what I promised myself long ago. I will pay a recluse in the Gaon's Shul in advance to say *Kaddish* for me three times a day for an entire year and study a chapter of *Mishna* every morning on behalf of my soul. Better to have the hired *Kaddish* of an honest stranger than the *Kaddish* of a son who does not keep the Sabbath."

Meirke's teacher also dozed off, but when he woke, he did not remain absorbed in morose thoughts. By nature he was a man with a happy heart. He went to the wash basin to wash his hands and had in mind to review everything he had learned in *Halacha* and *Aggadah* from the two brilliant young scholars. While so doing he thought that the study house did a great deed by bringing in those frozen street urchins to warm up and study with them. Indeed, spring came and the little rascals ran off, but they did learn how to read Hebrew. Even if these students forget their teachers for the present, in later years they will remember, and they will long for the old men of the Old Shul.

SECTION FIVE

New Horizons

I N THE LATE nineteenth and early twentieth centuries, the Yiddish press was the most popular outlet for literary publishing. This was not unique to Yiddish, of course—authors from Charles Dickens to Harriet Beecher Stowe published most of their works in serialization. While books were expensive to produce and buy, a newspaper paid for itself in advertising and could be bought by readers for just a few cents.

Today few newspapers continue to publish fiction. The same is not true of the *Forward*, however. Under Boris Sandler, who was editor-in-chief of the Yiddish *Forward* from 1998 until 2016 and is himself an accomplished writer of fiction, drama, and poetry, the newspaper continued to publish the most talented contemporary writers in the language. And as Yiddish publishing has shrunk, the *Forward* has become an even more vital outlet than before.

Like everything regarding Yiddish—as well as journalism, literature, and publishing—much has changed in the century since the *Forward* topped a circulation of some 250,000 daily readers. Today the *Forward*'s audience is no longer a mass public, but a specialized readership that looks to the newspaper to uphold the best Yiddish literary traditions, in every possible medium. Thus, the *Forward* not only continues to publish fiction in its biweekly print edition, but has a special section of its website devoted specifically to literary writing, a rarity for any newspaper today.

As much as things have changed, however, certain things have stayed the same. The Yiddish fiction found in the *Forward* is as much an international endeavor as it ever was, with writers hailing from Israel, Europe, the former Soviet Union, and elsewhere. And it continues to represent an immense diversity of both style and subject matter. Just as their predecessors did before them, today's contributors to the *Forward* are constantly expanding the boundaries of what Yiddish fiction is, and what it might yet be.

Blume Lempel

1907–1999

O NE OF THE most experimental authors of modern Yiddish prose, Blume Lempel often dealt with erotic themes and subject matter, and made use of free-associative and stream of consciousness literary techniques.

Born in Khorostov, in what is now Ukraine, Lempel lost her mother when she was twelve years old, and received little formal education. In 1929 she decided to immigrate to Palestine, but after stopping in Paris to visit an older brother, wound up living there for nine years. In Paris she attended night school and married a furrier, Lemel Lempel, with whom she had two children. In 1939, Lempel moved to the United States with her family. They settled in New York, where Lempel attended classes at the New School for Social Research.

Lempel's first published writing was in 1943 in the newspaper *Der tog* (The Day), where she wrote under the pseudonym Rokhl Halperin. In 1947 she serialized a novel titled *Tsvishn tsvey veltn* (*Between Two Worlds*) in the Communist newspaper *Morgn-frayhayt* (*Morning-Freedom*), while writing other pieces for Yiddish newspapers and literary journals.

Lempel published two collections during her lifetime, although much of her work remained uncollected. In 1950 she moved to Long Beach, Long Island, where she lived until her death in 1999.

"A Journey Back in Time" was included in Lempel's 1986 collection *Balade fun a kholem* (*Ballad of a Dream*) and was published by the *Forward* on November 5, 1999, to commemorate its author's death.

Its phantasmagorical style and sexual subject matter are typical of Lempel's experimental and introspective tendencies, making it a fitting tribute to one of the most innovative writers of recent Yiddish fiction.

———

A Journey Back in Time

(NOVEMBER 5, 1999)

Translated by Ellen Cassedy and Yermiyahu Ahron Taub

I DON'T KNOW WHAT draws me to the mountains. According to the *Encyclopaedia Britannica*, I'm actually more closely related to the sea. The sea is closer geographically too. Nonetheless, whenever I have a day off, I leave the city and make the five-hour bus trip to the mountains—my mountains.

We pass by other mountains on the trip up, some wild and overgrown, some bare and stony, some impassable, like the source of my own beginnings.

Throughout the journey I keep my eyes closed, blindly holding onto the thread leading me to a connection—but with what or with whom I don't know. I don't want to know. According to my mysterious nameless guide, it's best to save my energy: through an unexpected twist of fate, what is now totally unimaginable might well come true.

My longing for the mountains is mysterious even to me. I feel as if I'm obeying an attraction stronger than reason. Visions that first awakened in the cradle come back to life with the full, magical force of childhood imagination. As I sit looking at a cloud-covered peak whose snowy crown ascends into the mists, I too climb into the heavens. I follow footpaths that lead nowhere. I come to the mountains as if to a long-forgotten graveyard, yet I recite no prayers of supplication. I have nothing to ask for. I have a home, a husband, successful children. I do nothing but sit, thinking about everything and nothing, until the birds take me for an inanimate object and alight on my head to peck at the buzzing flies inside.

Suddenly a snake springs out of the tall grass, interrupting my reverie. As soon as it detects my scent, it goes still, gazing at me with its haughty eyes, as if reminded of something. I stare at it and it stares back, its snake eyes full of hatred, mine full of regret. Suddenly it stretches itself out, spits, and slithers away.

The snake's bitterness lingers on my tongue for a long time. I wonder why the snake itself did not take a bite of the apple from the Tree of Knowledge. Why did it so generously give away such a fateful secret?

The mountains possess a reality all their own. And so I sit and weave one thought into another, leaving the outside world far behind. Metaphors flow feverishly through my mind. Dream-images glide like underwater ships, with fairy-tale ogres clambering up their masts to wait for the maidens to descend from the world above—maidens who will tame the beasts with their siren songs and instruct them in the ways of earthly passion.

I sit there until just before nightfall. And if the keeper of the forest happens by, I sometimes spend the night with him. We make no appointment beforehand, both of us believing that you never know what mood you'll be in tomorrow or next week or even an hour from now. This applies especially to those who dwell in the mountains. They can never predict what will arrive from the other side. The sky might be bright blue, the sun shining on the silken lake, when all at once the mountains prick up their ears: A thunderclap erupts. Trees bend to the ground. The river roars with waves chasing waves. A mighty cloud like a rebel god overpowers the sun. Waters pour from the sky, and the waters below rise up to meet them.

Once, as day faded into night, I followed the dirt road into the forest. The storm was still raging. Lightning had set the trees afire, but rain was extinguishing the blaze. In the dark of night I stood in water up to my knees. Leaning against a tree, I lifted my arms and waited for a miracle. I could make out the hoot of an owl, the laughter of a lizard. Unafraid, I raised my voice and cried out. My cry was like a song, the song sung by the biblical shepherd girls at the well when distant footsteps set the mountains to trembling.

Rising above all other voices, my song drew the watchman to me and my tree. I could see the beam of his flashlight from far away as it danced through the trees and scoured the bushes. Finally it stopped at my feet, touched my body and played over my face, blinding me. Asking no questions, the woodsman picked me up and threw me over his shoulder as if I were a wild animal he'd shot and killed.

Inside his cottage it was dark. He dropped me onto a bed covered with furs. I could hear his heavy tread, and by the shine of a lightning flash I saw him bend over the fireplace. As the flame caught, I made out the stuffed head of a deer on the wall. Its broad antlers gave proof of a noble pedigree. Golden eyes looked out at the room as if the deer were wondering what it had done to cause some wrathful god to exile it to this alien place.

My eyes on the shadows leaping on the walls, I didn't notice the keeper of mountain and forest approaching my bed. His hand on my heart was at once tender and heavy. "Not from around here," he whispered as if to himself. "Who doesn't know that trees attract lightning?"

I wanted to say that not only trees attract lightning; people do too.

His shadow on the wall assumed bizarre forms, sometimes a billy goat, sometimes a pagan god with singed wings. I felt his tongue slowly drawing lines on my brow. "Don't wipe off the sign," he said. "I'll be back."

He returned with a cup of black coffee mixed with something spicy. On the old-fashioned gramophone, Barbra Streisand was crooning a torch song. He said little, I even less. Silently he removed my shoes, my wet clothing. Without a word, he covered my body with his own.

Deep in a psychic state, I pursued every possible path, looked for every possible key. I saw the deer on the wall take off for the spring where all manner of living things were drinking clear water. On the bank, a naked man stood on all fours like the other animals to drink his fill from the plenteous source. When the deer caught the scent of a two-footed creature, it pricked up its ears and ran back to its spot on the wall.

The man who watches over mountain and forest presses his ear to my heart. His lips move slowly as if in prayer. I wonder to whom and for what he's praying, but I dare not ask. As always, I look for the knot in every tangle, paying attention to each thread along the way. Some threads break off to form other tangles. I feel the tension roiling in my blood. To hide the trembling inside me, I begin to stammer, calling him names that have caused mountains to quake, locusts to fall to the ground.

Rain drums with fat fingers, muffling my words. Windowpanes rattle in the whistling wind. In the fireplace, wood yields without resistance to devouring flame.

The hair on his chest is stiff and prickly. A smell of mint rises from his body.

Half-awake, all in a dream, I give myself to him. I've been ready since yesterday, since last year, since centuries ago. I recognize him by the Adam's apple stuck in his throat, destined to be neither spat out nor swallowed. We meet on the virgin prairie, the meadow of times past. I know his ways, his desires. I am the I of today and the she of yesterday. I am the wife of long breasts and ripe hips, low brow and wide mouth. She is naked and knows not to cover her shame. Civilization has not yet touched her wildness. She frolics in his arms. Passion responds to passion, strength flowing from him to her and back again. A shift here, a new rhythm there, all separation put aside. She is both he and she, all sexes together, black as the devil and white as an angel. Not knowing what she is, where she's going, or what she'll become, she ties a knot in the umbilical cord stretching from the days of our ancestors over all the hard ground, so that I will remember— or perhaps forget—that what once was will never be again. Listening to the howl of the wolf and the cry of the hyena, she nestles closer to his side. No more prey or predator tonight. The lion and the lioness lie down together in each other's arms. Time stands still. Not time, but this moment is what counts. This moment is all.

There were other encounters to come, but they were only facsimiles, corruptions. The stuffed deer over the fireplace looked pathetic, more theatrical than suggestive. The fire had gone out. The linden trees no longer gave off their rainy scent. Instead, there was only the metallic smell of central heating. Overnight, he too had changed. No longer one of a kind, he now wore dark glasses, tight pants, and a fashionable haircut, as if posing for a picture. The mystery was over. Armed with a new passport, he had switched his identity. The former woodsman sold his land and went off to the big city. Civilization knocked down the cottage, filled in the lake, blew up the mountain. In their place, the god of surplus value built a twelve-story luxury palace with glass walls, its steel roof topped with a gilded rooster, like the golden calf at the foot of Mount Sinai.

Yes, I still make excursions, if not always in the same direction. Even when I'm not sure what the question is, I keep trying to find the answer. I search the mountains, looking high and low for question and answer alike. I know the exact time of year when the sun stays its course and exactly when it turns around. I know when the morning star becomes an evening star and when the three sister stars in the Orion constellation suffer their legendary beating. I do not look at the Milky Way.

A lunatic once said to me: Don't be seduced by a seductive word like "truth." As we both know, the truth is this: aside from you and me, nothing exists.

Yente Mash

1922–2013

Y ENTA MASH, ONE of the preeminent Yiddish writers of the late
twentieth and early twenty-first centuries, was born in Zguritse,
a small town in what is now Moldova. She received both a Jewish and
a secular education and was trained as a teacher.

In 1941, when Mash was nineteen years old, she and her parents
were exiled to the Siberian gulag by Soviet forces along with other
"bourgeois elements." There her parents died, and Mash endured
seven years of hard labor under extreme conditions of privation and
terror.

After the war Mash married and made her way to Kishinev, which
was then the capital of the Moldavian Soviet Socialist Republic. For
years she worked as a bookkeeper while struggling to recover from
the physical and psychological scars of her experiences in Siberia.

In 1977, Mash immigrated to Israel and settled in Haifa, where,
in her fifties, she began to write and publish. Her first publication
appeared in the journal *Di goldene keyt* (*The Golden Chain*), edited by
poet Avrom Sutzkever, and won praise for its startling, vivid depic-
tions of the twentieth century's cataclysms and upheavals.

As Mash's career developed, her work plumbed her life experiences
across both decades and continents. Her short stories and memoiris-
tic essays were published in Yiddish-language journals on both sides
of the Atlantic, including the *Forward*. Mash was honored with Israel's Itsik Manger Prize in 1999 and with the Dovid Hofshteyn literary
prize in 2002.

"Mona Bubbe" appeared in Mash's 1986 collection *Meshane mokem*

(*A Change of Place*), and was published by the *Forward* on March 16, 2012, in honor of Mash's ninetieth birthday. It takes place in the Jewish community of Kishinev, just as its members were leaving for Israel in the 1970s and 1980s.

Mona Bubbe

(MARCH 16, 2012)

Translated by Ellen Cassedy

EVERYONE IN THE city knew her, but none of us knew her real name. No one knew where she came from or who she really was—Jewish? Christian?—but we accepted her anyway, along with her peculiar name. Someone had dubbed her "Mona Bubbe" behind her back, and everyone called her that as if there was nothing strange about it, because . . . well, because in truth she didn't matter much to any of us.

IN THE FIRST years after the war, Jews began returning from the evacuation. First we wept over the ashes of our ruined towns, and then we moved to the cities and looked around for a place to live—a corner, a room under a leaky roof, anywhere we could settle down and unpack our troubles. New to the big city, we were hungry for something familiar to nourish our souls, something to call our own. We were overjoyed when we ran into Zeke, the gaunt, towering prophet who'd apparently been sent straight from heaven to lift our spirits and relieve our loneliness. Zeke was delighted with us too. So long as we gathered around and kept on listening, he didn't care who we

were. Often enough he forgot we were there and addressed himself
directly to the Lord of the Universe. Day and night, he went around
in a shapeless overcoat three sizes too big, clasping an open book to
his chest like the Ten Commandments. We started thinking of him
as a kind of Moses, even though, unlike Moses, he didn't stutter—in
fact, his tongue was as sharp as a knife.

Zeke always orated in Hebrew, and never in a side street but always
right in the center of town, or sometimes in the park where we used to
stroll in the evenings on the trail of the latest gossip. A crowd would
form, some admiring, others shaking their heads over the crazy fool.
Some worried that the man's recklessness was going to get him into
big trouble. They begged him to watch his step, stop his flapping and
jabbering. But reasoning with him was tough. He believed he was
God's messenger. It was up to him to create peace and unity in the
world, to persuade the lost flock to stop following the false messiah—
that is, the Soviet regime. Yes, he went that far. Fortunately, even
among us Jews, hardly anyone could understand what he was talking
about. Most of us considered him a harmless lunatic. But the secret
police had people who specialized in such types. They concluded that
this Zeke with the baggy coat was only pretending to be a madman.
He might look like a disturbed person, but that was only a mask. In
fact, he was an American agent, an anti-Soviet propagandist. In short
order he was whisked away, and no trace remained of the prophet
with his giant coat and holy book. Now the streets were deserted,
especially in the evenings.

It took a while for Mona Bubbe to show up. Why "Mona Bubbe"?
Well, why not? First of all, she was a woman, so she needed a woman's
name. And, whenever she thought someone was making fun of her,
she'd flash her eyes and gnash her teeth like a *baba*, a witch. Your
blood would curdle. But at the same time you'd see a curious smile
on her lips, just like Mona Lisa's. So some joker came up with the
name Mona Baba, a combination of beauty and hag that was about
as bizarre as she was. Since people were pretty sure she was a Jew, it
didn't take long for her to become Mona Bubbe. The Jewish word
for "grandma" gave her a kind of protection, as if our community

was watching over her. In fact, she was a minor character who would never take the place of Zeke the prophet in our hearts—but still, better than nothing.

AFTER THE COMPLETION of "Komsomol Lake" and the splendid tree-lined path that surrounded it, another site on the south side was designated for an impressive stairway with columns, fountains and a garden. The whole area was called the Summer Park, just like in Leningrad. There were halls where various games were played, a movie theater, and an open-air stage. All in all, it was a magnificent city project, which provided the starving population with cultural activities to consume along with our miserable crusts of postwar bread.

At first people went down to the park in droves to breathe the fresh air and enjoy performances by the philharmonic. Later, when we had a little butter or sausage to go with our bread, we went less often, especially on weekdays, and we skipped the free concerts. Most of the benches in front of the stage just sat there empty, in spite of the hardworking musicians all dressed up in their tuxedos with flowers in their lapels. They were required to play, whether or not anyone was listening. The whole thing was painful for them—artists don't like sawing away for no applause. But eventually they got used to it and even came to find the situation somewhat amusing, especially since not all the benches were actually unoccupied. Every day, their devoted listener, the one and only Mona Bubbe, took her place in the front row.

Who knows? Maybe the concerts became part of her daily routine for no particular reason, or maybe she was a classical music fan. In any event, she never missed a concert. Every day the musicians put a white flower on her seat, just like the ones in their buttonholes, and waited for her before starting to play.

As befitted a lady entering a concert hall, Mona Bubbe arrived dressed to the nines, every detail reflecting her personal sense of style. Over a white blouse she wore a checkered jacket adorned with tucks and pleats. She had a round black hat perched on top of her head, with a checkered ribbon tangled up in her long, loose hair—very fetching. Her white gloves were cheap but spotless, and she carried a black purse with the kind of fringe that was fashionable about fifty years ago.

What stood out most, though, wasn't her clothing. The poor woman really went to town with her makeup. She covered her moon face with a thick layer of powder, outlined her eyes with coal-black pencil, and smeared cheap red lipstick like a clown's all over her lips. People couldn't stop staring at her, but none of us said anything. No one wanted to get involved—not that she would have paid attention anyway.

On the bandstand, none of it mattered. When the musicians saw her coming, they'd strike up a march. She'd lower her eyes coquettishly, and the corners of her painted lips would turn up with pleasure. She'd sniff at her flower, take her seat, and gracefully signal that she was ready to listen.

Then the concert would begin. Fool or not, Mona Bubbe knew exactly how to behave when she felt accepted rather than pushed away. What an honor it was to be entertained by such renowned virtuosos! When it came time to applaud, she pulled off her gloves and made as much noise as she could in the empty space. Which side got more out of the encounter—she or the ensemble—was an open question.

So a year passed, then another. As the violinists grew older, they were not replaced. Most of the players were Jews, though some Moldovans, onetime wedding musicians, could also be found among the basses, the big horns, and maybe the cymbals and the kettledrums.

Our Mona Bubbe wasn't getting any younger either. A distinct web of wrinkles could be seen around her mouth, even under the thick layer of powder.

ONE DAY WHEN Mona Bubbe arrived in the garden, a violinist and a cellist were missing. She noticed right away but didn't feel she had the right to ask, so she said nothing. After the concert she lingered by the gate but still couldn't bring herself to approach anyone. She went home upset and on edge. Not long after, two more cellists and the principal clarinetist disappeared. Mona Bubbe nearly fell ill. She stopped going to the garden. Let them manage without her. By the time she learned the whole story, it was too late. Now, in the evenings, the bandstand in the Summer Park stood empty, except for the boys who fooled around on stage before going to the cinema.

Mona Bubbe had lost her anchor. All of her beloved musicians were leaving the country. She couldn't begin to understand why. It felt like a personal blow. How could they abandon her after all her years of devotion? She took to snarling and spouting profanities in the streets again, then went back to the Summer Park, hoping for news. It was unbelievable to her that they would just run off without even saying goodbye. She ached, she agonized, and then she made up her mind.

On a Wednesday, Mona Bubbe screwed up her courage and set off for the train station. The platform was jammed—so many traitors all in one place! Trembling, she kept close to the wall. She knew that when people were in a festive mood they tended to pay more attention to her. Best to stay safely out of sight.

Everything was in such an uproar that no one even noticed the train pulling in on platform one. Then the real crush began. People screamed and hollered and climbed on top of one another to toss their luggage through the windows. Why such a rush? Mona Bubbe wondered sourly. Was life here so unbearable—even with the philharmonic and the summer park? What was the matter with them all? Then, suddenly, three violinists caught her eye. They were already on the train, standing at the window and saying goodbye to their companions. Mona Bubbe felt faint. She lowered her eyes. Better not to look, not to see the loathsome world that had forgotten her so easily, abandoned her so casually to the likes of drunken Vaska, wobbling and tottering with the cymbals in his hands. Who now would welcome her to the park with a march? Where now would she find refuge? Choking back tears, she turned her face to the wall. It was then that they recognized her by the ribbon in her long hair. Mona Bubbe—here, for them! Deeply moved, they waved and smiled, but she wasn't looking.

"What's her name?" one of them asked the others.

"You know—Mona Bubbe!"

"Not that—what's her real name?"

No one knew.

"Try it—maybe she'll answer."

"Mona Bubbe!" Their voices rang out on the platform.

She didn't turn. And when a young man nearby tapped her on the shoulder, she only bared her teeth and shoved him away.

"You crazy thing, what are you hitting me for? Can't you hear them?" He pointed at the train. She turned then and saw the three violinists beaming and waving goodbye.

Everyone on the platform was gawking at her. Mona Bubbe lifted her head and seemed about to speak, but instead her face twisted. The tears that were caught in her throat spilled out over her cheeks, mingling together the moon-white of her face, her coal-black eyes, and the wine-dark red of her lips.

Mikhoel Felsenbaum

1951–

MIKHOEL FELSENBAUM IS among the most prominent contemporary Yiddish writers.

Born in Vasylkiv, in Soviet Ukraine, he grew up and spent most of his life in the Moldovan city of Floresti. In the 1960s he studied stage directing, theater, and art history in Leningrad, and worked as a theater director in the Moldovan city of Balti (known in Yiddish as Belts) between 1969 and 1973.

Felsenbaum began publishing his work in Yiddish in the 1980s, in the journal *Sovetish heymland* (*Soviet Homeland*). In 1988 he founded the Jewish theater of Balti, where he staged his works in Yiddish.

Since 1991, Felsenbaum has lived in Israel, where he has published numerous poetry collections, plays, and short stories, and became a regular contributor to the *Forward*. His 2001 novel, *Shabesdike shvebelekh*, has been translated into Russian and German, and an English translation, *The Sabbath Lights*, is in progress.

"Hallo" appeared in the *Forward* from October 24 to November 13, 2008. With its irreverent style, dissolute narrator, and contemporary setting, the story illustrates the continued development of Yiddish fiction in the twenty-first century.

Hallo

(OCTOBER 24–NOVEMBER 13, 2008)

Translated by Eitan Kensky

I

HER DAILY EARLY morning "hallo" makes me crazy. And even before she moves on to her usual "Good morning. How did you sleep?" I'm a mess and more than mystified about where to start my answer. To say that I slept like I was lying on top of a sack filled with sharp stones is really not that important. But how do I tell her what *does* matter, that every night I get to sleep with her is like a holiday? One that only falls, unfortunately, as the saying goes, once in a Purim. So it is that during these regular days of our lives, really every single morning, the voice in the receiver wakes me from somewhere faraway: "Hallo. Good morning. How did you sleep?" I mean, the time will come when I finally answer her: "May my enemies live through such a year!"

In short, we met completely by accident, in Basel, at the annual Book Fair, one fine, warm spring. Truth be told, a different representative of our publishing house was supposed to attend the fair. I myself am an expert in advertising and have nothing to do with publishing books. But my colleague was laid up in the hospital with two broken legs, plastered over with casts to his belly button. No one was eager to schlep all that way with hundreds of books and booklets, then shmooze fair attendees nonstop for three days—no such eager people existed. And, in general, our collective is very small, almost everyone who works there is a retiree, and they can't lift their behinds off the chair without aching. My usual excuse—that I don't have any-one to watch my sheepdog, Melekh—didn't help this time. Each one of my coworkers was ready to take Melekh in, as long as he didn't have to schlep to Basel. I never had much work at the publisher's, that is true. So it was determined that I would travel to Basel and my dog Melekh would stay with my boss's children, a guest in their village.

Faced with no other choice, my dog traveled to the village and I traveled to Basel, though my head was preoccupied with completely different things, none of them any good at all. First, about a month before this all took place, my wife packed her suitcases and went to her mother's. She didn't, God forbid, divorce me. She simply gave me an ultimatum: her or wine; they won't go together anymore. And when I kept drinking, she just left for her mama's. "I'll come back," she said, "but only if you stop drinking." I can't say that I was happy with her "and-there-I-go." On the contrary: my heart almost exploded, my soul cried, but my hand was still drawn to the glass. What can you do? I love to drink, and I can't turn down the pleasure I feel that extraordinary moment when liquor enters my veins and I carry myself into another world.

The children and the Mrs. called me almost every day, because, lately, I felt god-awful—I couldn't sleep or eat and I suffered ter-rible stomach pains. Finally, I went to the doctor. The test results were bad, very bad. They discovered that I had "the good disease," and they demanded that I stop drinking right away: the sooner I could have an operation, the better chance I had to stay alive. The first few days I went around dazed and had no clue what to do. Meanwhile, I hadn't told my wife and kids anything. Who knows how anyone's going to react to the "good news?" So I was truly happy when my colleague shattered his legs and I had to take his place at the book fair in Basel.

There really wasn't much work to do at the fair. You have to stand around the publisher's display all day long. Occasionally you have to tell some salivating, cloying yuppie about postmodern Yiddish litera-ture. Even more boring were the meet-and-greets with well-known authors—especially the presentations of their idiotic books. But the banquets were extraordinary, with fine wines and tasty hors d'oeuvres. At one of these severe "à la fourchettes"[168] I stood off to the side and chatted with Thomas Weizner, a really great writer from Geneva, when suddenly my eyes fell on a middle-aged woman approaching us: she was a tall, picture-perfect aristocrat with green-blue eyes, dressed with impeccable taste, simple and elegant, with expensive diamonds on her finger, neck and ears.

"Herr Lazar, allow me to introduce my friend from Germany, Frau Maria Koenig. Frau Koenig, allow me to introduce my comrade from Israel, Herr Jan Lazar."

My hands and feet grew cold. For a while I stood there motionless, like clay. What can I tell you? My tongue stuck to the roof of my mouth; I felt like I was choking and going to lose myself. I'm not a kid anymore. I've seen and known many women in my lifetime. But I'd never met a woman like that before. And besides, a kind of thump in my heart let me know—that's her, your one and only, your fate, your life and death.

"A pleasure, Frau Koenig," I said quietly after an idiotic pause, and suddenly I gave her a peck on the cheek.

"Jan, don't be so formal. Call me Maria," she said peacefully, exactly as if we'd already kissed before.

"Oh, I didn't know that you knew each other!" Thomas Weizner said, astounded.

"*Doch.* I've read Jan's love poems in a couple of anthologies, in French and German translations," Maria answered with a peculiar womanly smile. "I believe that I can feel Jan's soul inside of me, even from far away."

I stood there with my mouth wide open and I felt my head start to spin.

Thomas Weizner perceived the delicateness of the situation, kissed Maria's hand, tapped me on the shoulder and said goodbye. "My dear Maria, forgive me, but I have to go to my readers. I leave you in good

---

168 A light meal. Literally, "with a fork" (French).

company. We'll see each other later." And Thomas left and joined a group of idlers on the other side of the hall.

I stood near Maria, caressed her hand, and kept caressing her hand. I forgot everything in the world, my problems and disease. I had simply fallen in love with this woman, whoever she was, she who stood by me, and let me caress her hand.

"Jan," Maria said ever so quickly, caressing me with her slightly crossed eyes. "I know an excellent Greek restaurant not far from here. I am inviting you. There is nothing more to do here."

II

IT WAS A magnificent night. We sat in a small restaurant, ate a Greek salad with salty cheese and loads of olives, drank a crisp village wine and talked. To tell the truth, *I* talked and drank. Maria didn't speak or drink; she just ate and stuck in a short "aha," or "*ja, doch*" every now and then. But with only that, she still managed to tell me that she was a journalist and, as far as writing goes, she writes about the relationships between different ethnic groups in Europe, and also about the relationships between Jews and non-Jews after the Holocaust. Her still and peaceful voice matched the murmurs of the Rhine at night, which flowed somewhere near the restaurant's half-open window.

It was almost midnight when we left the restaurant. It was drizzling, and Maria invited me over to her room. The second she opened the door to her hotel suite, her cat—male, hairy, red, and as big as a dog—pounced on me.

"That's my Basilio. And this, Basilio, is Jan," Maria said, petting the cat on its head. "He is my beloved and he always accompanies me on my travels."

"I have a beloved at home; a sheep dog."

"What's his name?"

"You're going to laugh, Frau Koenig, but my dog is named Melekh, 'king,' the same as your German name, 'Koenig.'"

"Oh, is that so? Though I've never seen him, do tell him that I love him like a member of my 'Koenig family.'"

We sat at the small table, drank juice and made out like ravenous high school students. Maria's lips became hard and hot, her breasts heaved under her blouse and her fingers kneaded my shoulders. It was like we'd gone crazy.

In bed it was cold. Maria was inflamed, I was drenched in hot sweat and whispered nonstop:

"Maria, I love you, I really love you."

"I also love you. Your smell makes me crazy . . ."

The last thing I remember: a beastly scream tore out of me and Maria, half-faint, tightly pressed her palm to my mouth and hushed the words, "Quieter, my love; the neighbors are going to call the police."

III

STRANGE NOISES WOKE me in the middle of the night. At first I didn't understand where I was, and what kind of beast was lying on my chest, snoring like a healthy peasant.

"Don't be afraid," I made out Maria's calming voice. "It's Basilio. You're lying in his spot. Don't wake me so early, I am tired and happy."

"Very interesting," I tried to joke, "I've never slept with a male cat before."

Maria didn't answer, but she petted Basilio on his head and went back to sleep.

"Thank God she doesn't travel with an ox," I thought, and moved the pasturing cat to the side, lying half-awake, half-asleep until the early morning. We left the hotel in the late morning and took breakfast at a small coffee house in the old city. It was the last day of the fair, and the next morning I had to travel to Zurich since my flight to Tel Aviv was from there. I sensed that I had to tell Maria about the "happiness" waiting for me in Israel.

"Maria, I have to tell you two very important things."

"*Ja*, tell."

"First, I love you very much and you are very dear to me."

"I too love you and you are dear to me."

"And second, I am not healthy. I have to undergo an operation, the sooner the better. I'm giving you my word: if I stay alive, I'm going to come to you as soon as I can."

"I will wait for you. I'm in need of you."

"I'll come visit you tonight. Tomorrow morning I'm leaving."

"No, I have a lot of work today. You are going to sleep at your place, and I will sleep at mine. But tomorrow morning I will come to the station and I will accompany you. Don't be angry. Believe me, on my word: you are very dear to me, I felt it right away, from the first moment I saw you. And that's enough for me. For today, that's enough."

Maria gave me her calling card and we said goodbye. I spent the whole day packing up books and, between you and me, calling Maria, but her cell phone was silent, all day, evening and night. The thought came to me: this bright aristocratic woman had played with me like a doll and thrown me away like something she no longer needed. It was a kind of accidental intrigue heavy on feelings and passion, nothing more. All night I tossed in bed and I sought out my beloved in every corner of my visions. She was right there in front of my eyes, but I couldn't reach her. I didn't fall asleep until it was morning and I almost missed the train.

I saw her from the distance. Tall, in a light pelerine, she stood on the platform near the Zurich-bound train and waited for me.

"Hallo. Good morning. How did you sleep?

"Maria, I really love you."

"I love you too."

"You aren't going to leave me?"

"No. How can you ask that?"

"Because I'm afraid that you're going to abandon me."

"I won't abandon you, but you have to stop drinking. I saw it holds you back. And it may further disrupt our relations."

"Yes, I'll do it, because I really love you."

"I will wait for you."

"But how can I find you. I don't even know where you live. The only thing on your calling card is your cell-phone number. I called you maybe twenty times, yet you didn't answer my calls."

"Don't be afraid, I will find you."

We said goodbye. I got into the train car and stood by the window. I couldn't take my eyes off her face, her hands, her long black hair and the short pelerine, which hung from her like a part of her body.

"Maria, my darling," I whispered nonstop, "I love you, I really love you . . ."

The train jerked and departed the platform.

IV

IN ISRAEL ONLY my precious Melekh awaited me. When he saw me, he almost went out of his mind with joy. I spent whole days running around from one doctor to another—here tests, there consultations. My wife helped me a great deal, but she didn't want to hear any talk about coming back home because I hadn't stopped drinking.

This time my dog Melekh was sent to visit my eldest daughter. The operation was long and difficult, but the surgeon said that in about six months, with God's help, I would forget that I ever had the good disease. I was laid up in the hospital a few weeks, then I went home again. Traveling every day to Tel Aviv for work was impossible, so I began to work from home. I didn't have that much work, only a few booklets to prepare for publication.

One fine early morning the telephone woke me. I lifted the receiver and heard Maria's voice.

"Hallo. Good morning, Jan. How did you sleep?"

We talked away an hour, about half of which we spent talking about Basilio and Koenig, as Maria took to calling Melekh.

A few months drew out that way. Every morning: "Hallo. Good morning. How did you sleep? What's Koenig doing?" And at the end: "Maria, I love you very much."—"I also love you very much." When one day she didn't call me, simply because she didn't have the opportunity, I almost went out of my mind, I didn't know what to think, I called her every ten minutes, but her cell phone was silent.

The next morning everything cleared up and Maria's early morning "Hallo" brought me back to life. By then I knew that my lover lived in Leipzig, that she had four grown children, all of whom were married, that she herself was a divorcée, and that she had to work hard and often in order to support herself and to help the kids. Even Basilio demanded a lot of time and love.

Four months after the operation I felt like a kid again. I gamboled with Melekh in the field, began writing more and more and drinking little by little. I wrote love poems for my Maria and drank a good, white Bordeaux, but no more than two glasses a day, as if my doctor had prescribed it. I was able to sit at home and do what I wanted. It only took me a few hours to make a booklet, but I was always able to drag it out for a few weeks. I had plenty of time to think about my Maria. For the first time in my life, I had become an almost free man. In short, I could be me, Jan Lazar, a free, happy man in love with a beautiful, picture-perfect woman, Maria Koenig. She hadn't forgotten me, hadn't flung me away. Instead, she woke me every morning with a faintly melodic "Hallo." And were it not for the sorrow of not sleeping with her, I would have said that I was the happiest person in the world. And if not the absolute happiest person, then definitely the number-two person on the list, right after the pope in Rome.

V

AT THE VERY beginning of fall my boss suddenly called me on the phone and asked me to come to the publishing house for an important conversation. What kind of conversation, he didn't say. I didn't know what to think. Various idiotic thoughts swirled around in my head.

When I got to the office, the boss was seated in a deep armchair by a tea table. It was covered with a small bottle of my beloved Martell and a dish of toast points, red roe and juicy lemon slices.

"So, what're you up to, Jan?" the boss asked without any hello or a shake of the hand.

"What's that's supposed to mean? You know quite well that I'm working; every week I prepare a new booklet."

"That's not what I'm talking about. I'm asking, how do you feel?"

"Thanks. I feel good."

"Well! If so, let's make a toast and drink to your success." Without another word, the boss slowly poured the cognac into two thin glasses.

We drank the glasses, tasted the roe and toast, and the boss continued.

"I received excellent evaluations of your participation in the Basel book fair. Thanks to you, we earned some pretty pennies."

I could tell that the boss was playing some sort of sick game and that he had his own pocket—and not me—in mind, but I said something else.

"Well, if so, Mr. Bossman, then let's drink to the success of your publishing venture. I understand that you intend to give me a bonus. Say, a couple hundred?"

The boss almost choked on my question.

"If there were a bonus—I would take it. Besides, who's talking about money? Listen to me—and use your common sense this time."

"Good, I hear you."

We drank, snacked, and the boss continued:

"Obviously you come from Europe. You know the mentality of the Europeans, you speak a lot of languages, and, to tell the truth, you really don't have that much work here, do you? I didn't bother you when you weren't healthy, but now, since you are healthy again, I am officially requesting that you represent our firm at the Leipzig book fair."

When I heard the word "Leipzig," my heart went cold. But at that very moment, I began my own game.

"Forgive me, what fair?"

"Leipzig," the boss answered. "What, you've never heard of the fair? It only takes place every year."

"Of course I've heard of it. But that is one of the biggest and most lucrative book fairs in the world, and do you know how long it is? Not three days, like the Basel fair, but a couple of weeks."

"And your point is? We have *things* to display. And besides, I'm thinking about *your health*. The summer heat is starting here in Israel, and you've only just had an operation. It wouldn't hurt you to cool down in Europe for a while."

"No, I can't go away for such a long time. I have to visit doctors every week. And what will I do with my dog, with Melekh? No, I'm sorry, I can't travel."

The boss considered this for a while, poured some more Martell into our glasses, and offered me his hand:

"Good, we'll pay for your health insurance and your dog will go back to my kids, to the village. They've come to love him. So, agreed?"

"When do I have to give you my answer?"

"What do you mean, when? Right here, right now."

I thought about it, scratched behind my ear, and barely said out loud:

"Well, if your kids love my Melekh, then I agree."

The second the bus stopped in front of my house, I ran to the telephone, but Maria's cell and its typical "Sorry, the desired telephone-partner is out of area. *Bitte*, try telephoning later," doused me in cold water.

Half the night I tossed and turned and couldn't fall asleep. It felt like Maria was here somewhere, near me. I heard her voice, saw her marble shoulders, her ripe, firm breasts and long lithe legs; I felt her hot lips and quiet breath. But whenever I opened my eyes, looked out into the darkness and listened to the night sounds, I saw that the space next to me was empty and heard only Melekh's muted, heavy breathing.

That night Maria came no more.

VI

"HALLO. GOOD MORNING. How did you sleep? What's Koenig up to?"

"Good morning. The King is sleeping, but I am coming to Leipzig."

"Very good. That makes me happy. When are you coming?"

"The day after tomorrow."

"Good, we'll meet at the train station. Have a good day and give Koenig a pet for me."

"And me?"

"*Doch.*"

"Regards to Basilio."

"I'll pass them along. *Tschüss.*"

My boss was no warmhearted man; he was a stingy pig. Always. Listen to this: because he bought me health insurance and solved the Melekh question, he immediately regretted his generosity and decided to "be economical" with the ticket. He actually did his research and found me a seat on a Saturday tourist charter for an attractive price. When I got to Leipzig, after eighteen hours bumbling around the skies and shaking in trains, I, well, you can imagine what kind of troubles I wore on my face.

I was truly terrified of leaving the train, but the second I did so, I saw my little treasure facing me—tall, shapely, refined, elegantly dressed . . . and facing her was me—exhausted, useless, in a wrinkled suit with black bags under my eyes. I was even scared of kissing her because I knew that I would never again hear her passionate, "My darling, how I love your scent, your smell just drives me wild."

But an aristocrat remains always an aristocrat. Maria gave me a kiss on the cheek and immediately suggested, "Hallo, if you want, we can go straight to my friend's. She's off traveling for a few weeks, and she left me the keys to her apartment. You will bathe and then we'll go eat. Your fair won't run away from you."

It was almost noon when I woke the next day. There was no Maria near me, and instead of her cat Basilio, there was a note on my chest this time. "Hallo, my darling. That was a wonderful night. You can find the keys for the apartment and a light breakfast in the kitchen. I love you very much. Until later. Yours, Maria."

The whole day was spent dealing with the displays and books from our publisher, but by nighttime everything was ready for the opening ceremonies—and I ran to the apartment to wait for Maria because her cell didn't answer my calls.

Maria came about a half-hour later and immediately "rejoiced" me with the news that we had been invited to a dinner at the Chinese consulate.

"Therefore, my darling, go, wash, dress and let's go. I had a hard day and I'm very hungry."

At the dinner I sat like my seat was made of nails. Eating with chopsticks wasn't something I could do, and it was impossible to make out any of the Noodle-German the Chinese spoke. That whole night I didn't feel any better than I did after my trip from Tel Aviv to Leipzig via Istanbul, Prague, Munich, and Fulda. The dinner was important to Maria because she was gathering materials for a big article about the Chinese diaspora in Germany. At about midnight we left the consulate and drove to the apartment. But Maria didn't come inside.

"My darling, I'm tired. I must get some sleep. I've had a hard day. We'll see each other tomorrow. Sleep well."

And she drove away. I was left alone in a foreign city, in a foreign apartment, in the middle of a foreign night.

The same thing repeated itself the next day, only this time we were invited by a group of students from Kosovo. I spent four days in Leipzig getting to know all the local diasporas—except the Jewish one. I didn't go to a dinner at the Russian-Jewish community center. I simply refused.

"Maria, I don't cook any worse than any of these Greek restaurants, Spanish restaurants, and cultural societies. Tomorrow, God willing, let's eat here, in your friend's apartment."

"Good, my love. Until tomorrow. Sleep well."

The next day I ran away from the book fair the second the clock struck noon. I shopped for ingredients, ground up breadcrumbs and cooked. I toiled into the night, but in the end I set an authentic Jewish table—four types of appetizers, four salads, chicken soup with egg noodles, chopped liver in sweet and sour broth and, for dessert, a cold compote of Israeli fruits. I did not set any wine on the table.

We had a beautiful evening and an extraordinary night. In the morning I lay in bed near Maria and thought, "My God, I've been in Leipzig over a week and I've barely been with my beloved. Always in the company of immigrants. Everything's going kosher at the fair. The publisher's book displays interest no one; not one person has stopped to ask, 'Where do you come from and what are you selling?' So, why do I need to stand there like a golem?"

"Maria," I said to my beloved, "Maria, it's Friday now, the weekend. You are tired and I am tired, so let's go somewhere, get out of town."

"Yes."

VII

"THAT IS A good idea. I have good friends who live in a village not far from Leipzig. They have a small restaurant and a couple of rooms for close friends."

"So let's travel to them."

"Yes, my love, tomorrow we'll travel to them."

In Israel, when someone tells you that it isn't far, it's really not far, a couple of minutes by foot. But in Germany . . . well . . . it took a good couple of hours to get to the village that Maria said wasn't far, but I didn't have any regrets. We were alone, and that made it a holiday. It was a whole twenty-four hours of rest and godly love. We strolled in the forest, ate tasty meals, slept in a giant country bed, and whispered nonstop:

"I love you."

"I love you too, very much."

By noon the next day we were back in Leipzig. Maria went straight to some sort of important meeting, and I hung out in the pavilion of the book fair counting flies.

I could barely wait any longer. At the lunch break I beat it straight to the nearest beer cellar and drank a few steins of cold beer. Only then did things start to feel easier.

I didn't go back to the fair. I simply didn't have the strength or desire. Besides, tomorrow was the closing ceremony and that night I had to travel to Munich. I bought a bottle of brandy, wine, hard cheese, and some fruits, and came home to wait for my lover Maria. By the time Maria got there, I was more than a little "tired." Maria, on the contrary, looked more beautiful and happy than she ever had before. She was dressed in a white blouse with a long Spanish collar and in an elegant black troika. What can I tell you? . . . She immediately smelled the cheap stinking alcohol but behaved like a true aristocrat. I said foolish things; she was silent and ate fruit. Then she was finished with the fruit and she got up and wanted to go. I stopped her:

"Maria, stay, today is my last night. I beg you, stay."

"No, I'm going home."

"Why?"

"Because I don't recognize my beloved Jan. Today, you're foreign to me. Take your hands away. Sleep well. Tomorrow I'll call you."

And Maria left. I was left alone. With a half-bottle of brandywine, but without my love, Maria. Half the night I moaned like a crazy person. My head was clouded, but I felt like I was losing the best thing I had ever had in my life, that I was losing the love of a woman, the kind who appears in this world maybe once in a thousand years. I wailed and drank until I fell into the void of black sleep.

VIII

I CAME BACK to Israel a broken man, drunk as Lot. A week later I left work and spent whole days searching for my Maria, but her cell was silent and none of my European journalist friends had ever heard the name Maria Koenig. Most likely, she signed her articles under different noms-de-plume. I didn't fit in anywhere. Israel grew too cramped; maybe also the world at large.

I stopped drinking, came to my senses and found several of my old friends. They helped me get interesting work as a translator in a small transport firm. My life was back on the rails.

On the rare nights when I slept in a hotel room, I slept with my cell phone in hand. I swear to you, not once did I get to see my magical dream through to the end. The same thing every time:

"Herr Lazar, *bitte*, in an hour people will be waiting for you in this place or that."

"Herr Lazar, there is a vehicle waiting for you by the entrance to the hotel."

Herr Lazar come here, Herr Lazar go there. And suddenly, one fine early morning, the end:

"Hallo. Good morning. How did you sleep?"

"Oh, my God, Maria. Where are you?"

"I am in Kosovo."

"What are you doing there?"

"I'm gathering material on the refugees. And where are you?"

"I am in Transnistria."

"Where is that?"

"It is between Ukraine and Moldova. Maria, I love you very much."

"And I love you, and I want to tell you, that in about three months you are going to be a father and I will become a mother to our son."

The air was trapped in my throat. I broke out in tears into the receiver.

"Hallo, Jan . . . Jan, hallo . . . hallo . . ."

Boris Sandler

1950–

BORIS SANDLER, THE editor-in-chief of the *Yiddish Forward* from 1998 until 2016, is an award-winning writer of Yiddish drama, poetry, and prose.

Born in Balti—known in Yiddish as Belts—in what is now Moldova, he attended the Music Conservatory in Kishinev where, following graduation in 1975, he played violin in the Moldovan Symphony Orchestra. In 1983 he received a graduate degree from the Maxim Gorky Literature Institute in Moscow.

In the 1980s Sandler began writing in Yiddish for the Moscow-based journal *Sovetish heymland* (*Soviet Homeland*) and later joined the editorial board of the publication. In 1989 he created a Yiddish-language program on Moldovan State Television titled *On the Jewish Street*. From 1989 to 1992, Sandler was president of the Yiddish Cultural Organization of Moldova and the Yiddish editor of the bilingual journal *Undzer kol* (*Our Voice*) in Kishinev.

In 1992, Sandler immigrated to Israel, and in 1998 to the United States, where he became editor of the *Yiddish Forward*. He is the author of fourteen books of poetry and fiction, and his works have been translated into Russian, English, French, German, Hebrew, and Rumanian.

"Studies in Solfège" appeared in a collection published by Sandler in 2008 and tells the story of a young music student who undergoes a sexual awakening. It was published on the website of the *Yiddish Forward* on December 16, 2015, in *Penshaft* (*Pencraft*), a section dedicated to the publication of contemporary Yiddish literature.

Studies in Solfège

(DECEMBER 16, 2015)

Translated by Barnett Zumoff

THAT SUMMER, I finished the seventh grade of music school and prepared to take exams to study further at a music institute. At that age, when I was not quite fourteen years old, I could hardly have known that by making that decision I was taking a serious step in my life, or, as my mother used to say: "Once and for all!"

On the other hand, I don't know whose part in the decision was bigger, my mother's or my own. She had been dreaming about my musical career, it seemed, even before I was born. In the very delivery room, the first time they put me to her breast, my mother stuffed her nipple into my mouth and immediately took my little hand out of the swaddling clothes to look at my little fingers. She told me the story more than once; I began to clearly picture her doing it, and I even remembered her joyous cry at that moment: "Pianist!" I think I shuddered then and shunned my natural milk source. After that, my mother says, I didn't want to take her breast, and I nursed only from a bottle with a nipple.

I had never played so much as I did that summer. Neither my mother nor my father made me; they didn't stand over me and pester me, "Go, play a bit now; I've forgotten what the piano sounds like; the poor piano is standing there all alone," or other variations on the same theme.

I used to sit at the instrument for three or four hours and repeat the program my teacher had taught me in the seventh grade, and which I had played for my final exam. I had been especially successful with Mozart's fifth sonata; I played it at our music school's final concert, which was held in the building of the municipal drama theater. It's possible that it was at that moment, after the last chord, when the hall, packed with happy parents, grandparents, relatives, and friends of the young talents, erupted with heated "bravos," that I felt the first taste of real success.

My teacher, who continued to keep an eye on me and met with me once, sometimes twice, a week in his house, was satisfied with me. Nevertheless, after one such lesson, he remarked regretfully: "It's a shame, Lyove, that over the past seven years you didn't devote yourself to your playing as much as you do now . . . but you have good potential." And yet, he would sigh, something was missing from my playing, especially in Chopin's nocturne. "There are nuances," he would say, "that I can't teach you. You have to feel them yourself, find them and pull them out of yourself." At the same time, his free hand would fall artfully on the white keyboard with his fingers splayed, each touching a key and burying itself in it. "Like this, like this," the teacher would virtually sing, as if at that moment he were actually pulling those darn "nuances," which I was supposed to feel, out of himself. "Like this, like this," his lips would whisper, and he would quietly, *pianissimo*, confirm it with a chord from the nocturne. I would return home flattened out like a mashed potato. What does he want from me, my teacher? What further "nuances"? "He's tearing at my heart," as my mother would say.

But there was another thing that was tearing the heart out of me back then. On the entrance exams for the music institute, there was a subject called "solfège." To sing and conduct a line of notes from sheet music with one hand is to "sol-fa," or "solfège," in musical terminology. It presented no difficulty for me whatsoever. But there was another thing: intervals and dictations; there I needed help. Not, God forbid, because I'm tone-deaf—it was because learning to determine intervals and transcribe dictations requires that someone play them for you. In music school, it had been the solfège teacher, but I didn't want to go to her house to have her prepare me for the exams. Truth be told, I hated her—I don't even know why. Maybe it was because she always had a cold, and she used to constantly blow her reddened nose in front of the whole class. They said she had once been an opera singer but had lost her voice and was forced to come out to us in the sticks to teach solfège. She was also the director of our chorus, in which I sang and which I greatly disliked. More than once she chased me out of rehearsal because of my mischief.

As had often happened before with other problems, my mother also solved the problem of solfège. My mother was a nurse in a hospital, but her dream had always been to be a concert pianist. "If not for the war," my mother would sigh, "I would surely have become a pianist. The war robbed us of everything: our youth, our hope, our dreams." So my mother had worked hard to instill in me, her only son, all her so-called "cheese." My father used to laugh at her: "You're putting all of your cheese in one dumpling!" By "dumpling," of course, he meant me. "See to it that the 'dumpling' doesn't burst!" he would say.

My mother used to come home from work exhausted, especially from night shifts. This time, however, her face radiated joy. Why? A guest had come from Czernowitz to Doctor Tsipkin, with whom she worked—his niece, who was a student in the music institute there. She had finished the third grade and was going into the fourth.

"What does she play?" I asked, still not understanding the relationship between my mother's glow and Doctor Tsipkin's niece.

"She doesn't play, she sings," my mother answered with a special kind of pride. "So I asked Doctor Tsipkin to ask her whether she would spend some time with you on solfège."

When she mentioned that Doctor Tsipkin's niece sang, I immediately pictured my former solfège teacher.

"She probably has a red, stuffy nose," I said, thinking out loud.

"What are you muttering there?" asked my mother, not understanding my far-fetched assumption. "Doctor Tsipkin thinks highly of you. He immediately called home and spoke with his niece."

Doctor Tsipkin was a surgeon, and fortunately I had not yet needed his "golden hands." I had already heard that he was a great music lover and had a magnificent collection of records. My mother thought the world of him, but all her talk about him ended with a sigh: "And that a man like him should suffer such a misfortune!"

The misfortune was his son, Nyuntshik. One could see the young man walking in the street, with his father holding his hand the way you would lead a little child, though he was the same age as I was. Just from his appearance you could tell that all was not right with Nyuntshik: fat, with a big head that blended into his short neck and reminded one of a block of wood, he moved clumsily, with short steps and with his fat thighs rubbing against one another. Occasionally when I was strolling in the park with my parents, we would encounter Doctor Tsipkin with his son alongside him; I never saw his wife with them. Doctor Tsipkin would immediately begin to praise me: how good I looked, what a good student I was, and what a capable child I was in general. When he finished with my general virtues, he would turn to my special talents and would ask me what I was playing currently and whom I liked better—Gilels[169] or Richter.[170] At the same time, he would keep turning towards his son as if he were looking for confirmation as he explained my clumsy answers. "Lyove plays the piano and is graduating from music school this year." Or, "We've heard Emil Gilels play the sonata—remember?" Nyuntshik, as was his custom, would look towards me in a dignified manner, not moving his block-like head. His little eyes, which were round as buttons, would rest their gaze on my face, and he would push out his little mouth with its plump lips towards me, as if he wanted to give me a kiss or was waiting for someone to stuff a pacifier into it. I could barely restrain myself—because I didn't want to insult him—from shouting the provocative word "Fool!" Nyuntshik had Down syndrome, and often the remainder of our stroll would revolve around him, poor thing. My mother took it very much to heart, because she pitied Doctor Tsipkin and his unfortunate son.

"After all, in the delivery room your crib was right next to his," my mother would sigh.

---

169 Pianist Emil Gilels (1916–1985).
170 Pianist Sviatoslav Teofilovich Richter (1915–1997).

That "great good fortune" didn't particularly please me, and once, after such an encounter, I even asked my mother whether Down syndrome was contagious.

Now Doctor Tsipkin's niece, like a snowflake on a hot summer day, had fallen onto my head to teach me solfège. Even more: I had to drag myself to the doctor's house. How else?

Our lessons began immediately, the next day. The niece herself opened the door for me. I learned right away that the mistress of the house, that is, Doctor Tsipkin's wife, had gone to a sanatorium, and that Nyuntshik was at a special dormitory. I listened to the entire introduction while following my teacher down a long, dark corridor. I was able to see her face only after we went into the upstairs room. She turned to me and ended with, "So no one will disturb us." After a short pause, she added, "My name is Miradora."

Her name—two intervals of augmented seconds—made such a sound in the room, which was flooded with the morning sunshine, that I felt compelled to immediately transcribe the sounds as notes, as my first musical dictation: "Mi-ra—Do-ra."

I even transferred my cardboard folder, with my notebook, a pencil, and an eraser—everything I needed for my class—from my right hand to my left, as if I wanted to free the right hand to give the folder to Miradora and then announce my own name. But I remained standing there with my mouth open, like her cousin Nyuntshik. For a brief instant, perhaps for the first time in my life, I felt how insignificant my own name, Lyove, was. It didn't have a drop of musicality—it sounded like the mooing of a cow: "Lyo-o-ve-e!" On the other hand, my formal name is Lyev, which means "lion" in Russian, but since I was short and skinny, to call myself Lyev . . . Just look at how a name can play games with you!

Nevertheless, I said, not loudly but firmly, "Lyev." For a moment I saw before my eyes a whirling hoop surrounded by flames, through which the real Lyev sprang—practically a circus. Miradora was apparently not surprised by the burning hoop with the beast jumping through it. On the contrary—she simply asked me:

"Is it all right if I call you Lyove? It's more intimate that way."

As I recall it, Miradora was no beauty. My mother would never have said about her: "What a girl! A beauty! Blood and milk!" She was indeed plump, but her cheeks did not have the healthy pink color that could get my mother to award her highest rating: "blood and milk!" Her nose, which was rather long, with a charming bump in the middle that struck my curious gaze, showed no signs of a constant cold, thank God! What in truth fascinated and seduced me was hidden in her eyes, but I became aware of that only later.

On the first day our lesson went very productively, as my father would have said. I transcribed two dictations and trained my ear to correctly appreciate intervals: the sounds of two different pitches played together. Miradora sent them to me from the piano, like signals, and waited for me to call out: "Second, fourth, seventh . . ."

"Correct, but which second, minor or major?" My teacher didn't let up: "Which fourth, perfect or augmented?"

Miradora didn't spare me; she shot intervals at me, such that within ten or fifteen minutes they began to ring in my ears. Did she want to demonstrate her fluency or point out my helplessness in this part of solfège? Try to understand girls, especially from big cities!

She closed the lid of the piano and exclaimed: "For a beginning—not bad!"

She actually spoke that summary, with her full lips, like the niece of a doctor; it was supposed to mean, "The patient is ill, but he'll live."

I began to put my meager possessions back into my folder—the notebook, the pencil, and the eraser. I was eager to see the other side of the door.

"Can you come tomorrow?" my teacher asked.

"Tomorrow? No!" I firmly replied.

In my head, I was already chasing the words, stringing together one word with another: not tomorrow, not the day after tomorrow, not the day after the day after tomorrow . . . Out loud, however, I said: "Tomorrow I'm going to my piano teacher." And that was absolutely true.

"In that case, come the day after tomorrow, at eleven thirty-five."

I stopped puttering around with the ribbons on my folder, and raised my eyes to Miradora.

"Eleven thirty-five!" she confirmed the time. She knew how to ask for what she wanted. "Come, I'll let you out."

That evening, when she came home from work, my mother came to my room immediately.

"Well—what happened? Are you satisfied? Doctor Tsipkin praised her highly."

At that moment, I was reading some book, and I simply didn't have an appetite for satisfying my mother's curiosity. It would have been different if it had been in the afternoon, when I first came home from my strict solfège teacher. Her words, uttered quietly in her lyrical soprano voice, scraped at my brain like the claws of a hundred cats. "Come, I'll let you out," as if I were a puppy—a poodle or a pinscher. Inside me, everything was simmering and boiling, and above all I was angry with my mother—why had she gotten so enthusiastic about Doctor Tsipkin's niece? But by evening, my anger had receded. Furthermore, every time I looked at Miradora's face (in my imagination, of course), it was as if I were watching an old silent film—as if people were moving fast on the screen, waving their hands, moving their lips; you didn't hear a word but everything could be understood. On the screen of my boyish imagination, now she would raise an eyebrow when I didn't guess a diminished fifth, now the bump on her nose would twitch when she confirmed with satisfaction, "Correct!" And now her lips would shape words in a silent language that echoed warmly within me: "Lyove—it's more intimate."

For that reason, I answered my mother with telegraphic brevity:

"The day after tomorrow—eleven thirty-five."

"What does that mean?" asked my mother, already used to my strange speech.

"We're meeting again."

I arrived at the door of Doctor Tsipkin's apartment precisely on time and rang the doorbell. Miradora led me, as before, to her uncle's office, where there was a concert piano against one wall. Over the instrument hung two portraits of young women—Doctor Tsipkin's two sisters. As Miradora explained to me, both of them had been killed in the ghetto, together with their parents. Only the doctor and his brother, Miradora's father, survived, because they were able to flee and join the partisans.

"One was named Mira and the other was called Dora," Miradora explained to me. "That's why my name is Miradora."

She sat down on the round piano stool and began to play the dictation. It was a familiar melody, and I quickly transcribed the notes. I could, of course, have said that I had finished it, but something held me back. In addition, my eraser, which I was rolling between my fingers, slipped out of them and fell to the floor.

That trick with the eraser was very common among the students in our grade, especially during solfège classes. We would ostensibly lose the eraser on the floor, and after getting permission from the teacher we would bend down to look for it. From under our desks, we could see the skinny legs of the former opera singer. Her long, brown stockings were held up with rubber bands above the knee. She would be sitting at her desk, looking around at the class so the young talents would work "conscientiously," as she loved to repeat, and not look into each other's notebooks. Didn't it occur to her that during a dictation we could look at something other than our neighbor's notebook? After class, we whispered about what we had seen from under the desks during those few short moments, and again our boyhood fantasies played out fully.

Did my eraser slip out of my fingers accidentally this time, or did the thought of playing the foolish boys' trick nudge my elbow? But I remained seated there for a moment, looking at Miradora's face, which had turned towards me. The doctor's desk where I was sitting was the kind of old office desk that takes up a lot of space and is intended to elicit respect for its owner. I, on the other hand, felt even smaller and more insignificant at that desk. My father had once said about a certain person that he looked like a flea on a platter. That's probably what I looked like at the doctor's desk.

With one motion I was under the desk. Crawling on all fours, I felt around on the floor like a blind man. After the bright sunshine that had been falling on the surface of the desk from the tall window, I saw only blackness. At that moment, I thought that now I really looked like a yard-dog in a dark doghouse; I lacked only a chain. I could barely restrain myself from looking in the direction of where my current solfège teacher was sitting, but a mischievous sunbeam sprang under the table after me and landed precisely next to my eraser. I immediately grabbed the eraser as if it would run away, but the audacious sunbeam started trembling, and in the blink of an eye it climbed up onto Miradora's legs. My gaze followed the sunbeam and encountered two naked, girlish knees. A dark patch of shadow separated one knee from the other; they quickly pulled back as if they were frightened. At the same moment, I felt a blow to the head. My temporary doghouse was apparently too small for a big hound like me.

"Are you trying to break my uncle's desk?" I heard her ask.

I crawled out from under the desk, rubbing the spot where I had been hit with one hand. In the palm of the other hand lay the eraser, a witness to my dog-like search. Miradora apparently understood my trick; at least the smile in her eyes indicated that she did.

"You know what?" she suddenly proposed. "Let's do an *entre-acte*, a sort of musical intermezzo."

She turned around on the round stool, as if the stage setting had been shifted, and began to perform. After a brief introduction, I could hear her soft, somewhat tremulous voice.

I knew the piece immediately; it was "Solveig's Song," by Edvard Grieg:

Winter will disappear, and Spring will go away,
and Spring will go away;
flowers will fade, covered with clear snow,
with clear snow covered.
You'll return to me—my heart promises me,
my heart promises me.
I'll remain true to you—a little flower from your wreath,
a little flower from your wreath.

Of course the music grabbed me, as it always did when I let myself be lulled by the sounds that intertwined like vines swaying back and forth, and I with them . . . no time, no space, no hustle-bustle. That's the way it had been when I had the occasion to sit in a concert hall or listen to a record. Here Miradora was playing and singing just for me, and the tender, sad melody slowly led my gaze to her uncovered, rounded shoulders and the downy bundle of black hair on her neck. I squeezed into my armchair, as if any movement on my part could disrupt the scene.

The song finished, but my dream, woven from silence and air and entwined with sunbeams, still persisted for a few moments before my eyes, and then also dissipated.

I was apparently supposed to say something, as is the custom when one finishes listening to a piece, or at least to show some sign that I was still there—that I hadn't run away or fallen asleep. But it was Miradora who spoke. I heard a word that I had never heard before in my life and didn't know the meaning of.

"*Kama Sutra*—do you know what that means?"

I felt as if my brain, until now saturated and overrun by the beautiful music, had suddenly frozen, had been transformed into a block of ice—as if someone had laid a cold compress on the spot where I had just recently received a blow. I felt that I mustn't let myself be diminished in the eyes of this big-city girl, so I said whatever occurred to me at that moment:

"Of course—*Kama Sutra* is a type of Japanese wrestling."

I was astonished at how easily and with what certainty that foolishness slipped out of me.

But Miradora seemed to know in advance that I simply couldn't know the answer. The explanation for the strange word was already on the tip of her tongue.

"*Kama Sutra* is a sort of poetic book about the art of love. It was written in India, hundreds of years ago. *Kama* was the name of their god of love."

My knowledge about love, at that time, had been nourished only by occasional boys' stories, told furtively by someone in a corner of the courtyard or on a bench tucked away in the dense bushes of the municipal garden. Sometimes there was a bit of gossip about a neighbor's daughter who strayed from the straight and narrow path, who went dancing at the officers' house and hung around with soldiers—in a word, acted like a whore. There were stories about "pinching" and "touching" girls from the next class while sitting in the movies; there was even a fascinating story, told with all the details, about how someone spied on his older sister rolling around in bed with her fiancé, both of them naked, before they were married. Once someone pulled from his pocket a packet of wrinkled photographs that looked like playing cards but were actually cheap pornographic pictures, with little marks of the four suits in the corners.

The titillating chatter and nonsense didn't last long in our over-stimulated circles; we quickly switched to other talk and fantasies, which were certainly not lacking. But they used to return at night in our beautiful dreams, and there, without fear or shame, they would flare up and seize all our senses and limbs with burning heat.

Miradora got up from her stool next to the piano, and with several soft steps came over to the armchair in which I was still sitting, sunken into the depression in the cushions that Doctor Tsipkin had made with his fat back and heavy behind. She sat down on the soft arm and was quiet for a moment, casting her eyes down at my hands. I was resting them on my legs, covering my bare knees with my palms. I had worn shorts almost all summer; my mother used to sew them for me herself, or, more accurately, re-sew them from pants that had gotten too short.

Now, when Miradora was sitting so close to me, I suddenly felt how short my shorts actually were, and I was ashamed of my naked thighs.

"You have beautiful hands," I heard her quiet words, "long, thin fingers like my singing teacher's."

Miradora took my hand and laid it on her own knee, the way she might have carried a kitten from a basket of rags to her lap. And just like a helpless little animal, I obeyed her wishes. My shorts had suddenly gotten tighter and were cutting into my flesh. Miradora bent down to me and touched my forehead with her lips . . .

One time I had wanted to test whether my flashlight's dead battery was good for anything else. Following my friend's advice, I touched the tip of my tongue to the narrow little strips of tin that stuck out of both sides of the battery, a short one and a long one. The moment I did so, I felt as if a bolt of lightning had cut through my whole body, from the top of my head down to my toenails. Until I tore my tongue away from the two little strips of tin, it seemed to me that my eyes were themselves burning like two electric lights. I felt just such a lightning bolt now, after Miradora's lips touched my forehead. But my eyes were closed, as if a short circuit had occurred; I didn't see anything. Her hands had freed me from the oppressive tightness of my shorts. The heat from her mouth spread across my knees, and when I tried to cover them with my hands, my fingers touched the downy bundle of hair on her neck . . .

That night I dreamed, not about just anyone but about the Indian god of love—*Kama*. He and the well-known movie star Raj Kapoor, who acted in all the Indian films that were shown in our city, were alike as two drops of water. My mother used to come home from those films with red, weepy eyes but satisfied, because there was always a happy ending. And appropriately for an Indian film, a few of which I also had the occasion to see, *Kama*-Kapoor was dancing and singing in my dream; he danced to Mozart's "Turkish March" and sang "Solveig's Song" in a light, feminine voice.

In the morning, I woke up late, so I grabbed something to eat from what my mother had prepared for me before leaving for work and then I ran to my teacher. On the way, I realized that in my haste I had forgotten to take my folder, with all the paraphernalia I needed for my solfège lesson. I stopped and stood there, torn by doubt. "What will you do there without the folder?" one part pulled me to go back. "Don't you already have better things to do there without the darn folder?" the other part teased me. Pulling up my pants, which had slipped down to my hips, I continued to run. I found a compromise: "Miradora will decide herself what to do."

Miradora did indeed find a solution. She proposed that we spend more of our time on intervals; that, she said, was a weak point in my preparation. After the two previous classes, I felt more at home in Doctor Tsipkin's office. As evidence of that, I immediately sat down on the floor, which was covered with a soft Persian rug, and tucked my legs beneath me. Miradora just shrugged and sat down at her instrument.

Was I only thinking then about intervals? The previous night I had unexpectedly sampled a taste of *Kama*, and a worm of curiosity was gnawing at the pit of my stomach, just like when I had a craving for sweets. My mother always recognized it from my beggarly appearance and searching eyes. She had a certain nook, as she used to call it, where she hid various candies, cookies, and a handful of pistachios or raisins—not only for herself, of course, though my father had crowned her with the nickname "*nasher*."[171]

Apparently, as I was guessing the intervals, my face also showed signs of searching for a little "*nash*," similar to last night's taste. Finally my teacher exclaimed: "OK, that's enough solfège for today." She went over to the bookcase, opened the glass door and pulled out a thick book. I was astonished—did she want to start reading with me? Probably poetry, yet. That was all I needed!

She sat down on the floor next to me and laid the book on her knees. She kept it there for a few moments, as if deliberately, so I could look at it and remember the beautiful red cover, on which artfully entwined letters were stamped in gold. She did that later too, at our subsequent meetings, as if it were part of some sort of ritual whose consummation would come later. My gaze clung to the long, curlicued inscription, and I mouthed each letter, with a quiet, drawn-out K-*a-m-a* S-*u-t-r-a*.

Miradora maintained her poise. After leafing through several pages, she quietly but clearly read a passage: "Each person who lives for about a hundred years must at various times practice *Dharma* and *Kama*. He must do so in such a way that they will harmonize with one

---

171 Yiddish for "snacker."

another, and must not misuse them. He must master *Artha*, under-standing the world, in his childhood; in his youth and mature years, he must follow the teachings of *Dharma* and *Kama*."

Understanding very little of what I heard, I asked hurriedly: "Why only 'a hundred years'? My mother always says 'until a hundred and twenty years.'"[172] Miradora apparently took my question seriously. She rubbed the bump on her nose with two fingers and tried to answer: "Perhaps the early Indians didn't live as long as the Jews . . ."

She quickly returned to her reading: "*Kama* is the art of receiv-ing pleasure, with the help of all five senses, led by wisdom and the soul . . ."

Cuddling with one another, we were not lacking then in any of the five senses about which the *Kama Sutra* preached, but our curiosity led us to follow its teachings. We hungrily turned the pages of the old book, discovering colorful pictures of men and women resem-bling the dancing couples in Indian films. They were wrapped in airy, transparent garments, and were surrounded by dozens of beautifully embroidered pillows. They held our gaze, infecting our imagination and our bodies with a previously unknown feeling of pleasure. Even more shameful: throwing off our skimpy summer clothes, we clum-sily followed the wise advice of the great *Kama*.

I started to run to my solfège classes the way our tomcat ran to catch mice in our attic, and like the tomcat, I would come back home tired, exhausted and happy. Eating quickly, I was eager to lie down on our couch. My mother was astonished: "He's never slept in the afternoon—the preparations aren't easy for him, poor thing."

Almost two weeks passed that way. I was probably not a bad student—both with respect to solfège and with respect to the teachings of *Kama*. I was already cracking the intervals like nuts and transcribing the dicta-tions accurately on the five lines of my notebook. After playing them twice, I would hand the transcribed melodies to the teacher to grade.

---

172 In Jewish tradition 120 years is considered to be the ideal life span, based on the age of Moses.

And, as we had up until now, after the musical introduction we would lie down on the soft rug.

At that time I didn't yet have any idea about yoga or meditation, but the old book *Kama Sutra*—a bargain for any dealer in secondhand books—apparently possessed hidden strength that embraced us and carried us away the minute Miradora opened it. That strength flung us way up to the high heavens and then let us fall like two full vessels bound together. That's the way it happened more than once in my dreams, and when it seemed to me that at any moment I would crash into the thick crust of the Earth, I would wake up in a cold sweat.

We didn't want to wake up and separate from one another, and if we did have to, it was only to catch our breath and then again let ourselves be carried along by the magical power of *Kama*.

We never once kissed each other on the lips, like lovers, or touched a lip to a cheek, nose, forehead, as happens when playing the piano and one's finger strikes the wrong key. We were both studying a new, unknown work, written hundreds of years ago so it could now be revealed to us. We were playing the revived song, and we were inspired by the sounds to an overwhelming rapture.

But the eventual end of my lessons had been haunting me since my first encounter with Miradora. I didn't know how long she would be visiting her uncle, and I didn't dare to ask her. It was like a game: you know it will come to an end someday, but you don't want to think about it. That day caught up with me.

The door was opened, as always, by Miradora. I didn't get to open my mouth before she indicated, by putting her finger to her lips, that I should remain silent. Once we were in Doctor Tsipkin's office, she explained that late the night before her uncle had brought Nyuntshik back from the dormitory and that he was now sleeping in his room.

"Unfortunately, it won't be possible for us to have our solfège lesson today," Miradora said in explanation, and added even more quietly: "Tomorrow Nyuntshik's mother too is coming home from the sanatorium."

I felt a lump in my throat that tried to find a way out through my tears. I tried hard to swallow it. Miradora was now standing facing me, so close that we both had to cast our eyes down. For the first time our lips touched and locked.

We now had no need for the *Kama Sutra*'s advice. The rug seized us and, as in that Oriental story, carried away our young, entwined bodies to the heavenly regions. The flight was so fast that my every limb burned with a fever and my sweat, mixed with tears, couldn't cool it down. I heard the sounds of a Chopin nocturne, indeed from the same piece I had played. The music penetrated me so deeply and substantially that I felt the coolness and softness of the keys . . . Suddenly the music was disrupted by strange, false sounds, as if a string had snapped. I trembled, but Miradora's hot breath in my ear didn't stop. I heard the familiar whisper "Shh!"—how every mother quiets a suddenly upset baby. Nevertheless, I managed to turn my head and saw the sleepy face of Nyuntshik. He was next to us, on his knees, with his underpants down, masturbating. Miradora's hand was moving across his fleshy, black-haired thighs like a white, lost snake. And in my ears I again heard "Shh!"

Miradora went home the next day. I found out from my mother, who greatly regretted it, poor thing: "I never got to thank the girl . . . I bought a big box of chocolate candies for nothing." Perhaps that's a good thing, I thought—Miradora wouldn't have touched the candy anyway; she had once told me that chocolate is poison for a singer. But the box of candy, even though my mother hid it in her "nook," was quickly emptied.

TRANSLATORS

Ellen Cassedy is the author of *We Are Here: Memories of the Lithuanian Holocaust* (University of Nebraska Press, 2012). In 2015 she was a translation fellow at the Yiddish Book Center.

Kathryn Hellerstein is associate professor of Yiddish at the University of Pennsylvania. She is the author of *A Question of Tradition: Women Poets in Yiddish, 1586–1987* (Stanford University Press, 2014), which won the National Jewish Book Award in Women's Studies, and is coeditor of *Jewish American Literature: A Norton Anthology* (W. W. Norton, 2001), among other books.

Ellen Kellman is an assistant professor of Yiddish at Brandeis University. Her research focuses on the Yiddish periodical press and publishing industry.

Eitan Kensky is the director of collections initiatives at the Yiddish Book Center and chairman of the board of *In geveb: A Journal of Yiddish Studies*. He received his doctorate in Jewish studies from Harvard University.

Jessica Kirzane is a doctoral candidate in Yiddish studies at Columbia University. Her translations have been published in *In geveb*, the *Trinity Journal of Literary Translation*, *Pakn Treger*, and *Jewish Fiction.net*.

Jordan Kutzik is a staff writer and social media coordinator for the *Yiddish Forward* and the editor of its blog for young writers. His journalism, fiction and literary translations have appeared in Yiddish and English in publications in the United States, Europe, and Israel.

Curt Leviant is a translator and novelist. His most recent books are *Kafka's Son* (Dzanc Books, 2016) and *King of Yiddish* (Livingston Press, 2015). His work has been translated into seven European languages and Hebrew.

Seymour Levitan's translations of Yiddish stories, memoirs, and poems are included in numerous anthologies and journals. *Paper Roses*, his collection of poetry by Rachel Korn, was the 1988 winner of the Robert Payne Award of the Translation Center at Columbia University.

Rachel Mines is a native of Vancouver, British Columbia, and the daughter of Yiddish-speaking Holocaust survivors. She holds a doctorate in Old English from King's College London and teaches at Langara College, Vancouver.

Myra Mniewski is a poet, translator, and teacher who lives in New York.

Anita Norich is the Tikva Frymer-Kensky Collegiate Professor of English and Judaic Studies at the University of Michigan. She teaches, lectures on, and writes about Yiddish language and literature, modern Jewish culture, Jewish American literature, and Holocaust literature.

Ross Perlin is a writer, linguist, and translator, and the author of *Intern Nation: How to Earn Nothing and Learn Little in the Brave New Economy* (Verso, 2012). He currently serves as assistant director of the not-for-profit Endangered Language Alliance.

Sarah Ponichtera finished her doctorate in Yiddish language and literature at Columbia University in 2012, and now works at the YIVO Institute for Jewish Research as project manager of the Vilna Collections Digital Initiative. She is currently translating Aaron Zeitlin's spy novel, *Brenendike erd* (*Burning Earth*).

Chana Pollack is the *Forward*'s photo archivist. She frequently researches and translates original *Forward* material for the newspaper's special historical sections.

Yermiyahu Ahron Taub is the author of four books of poetry. He was honored by the Museum of Jewish Heritage as one of New York's best emerging Jewish artists and has been nominated four times for a Pushcart Prize and twice for a Best of the Net award.

Ri J. Turner is a master's student in Yiddish literature at the Hebrew

University in Jerusalem. She is a three-time alumna of the Uriel Weinreich Summer Program at the YIVO Institute in New York, and served as a translation fellow at the Yiddish Book Center in 2014. Her translations and original writing have appeared in the *Forward*, *Afn shvel*, and *Outlook: Canada's Progressive Jewish Magazine*.

Rose Waldman holds a master of fine arts degree in fiction and literary translation from Columbia University. She is currently working on a translation of Chaim Grade's *The Rabbi's House*, which will be published by the Knopf Doubleday Group. Waldman was awarded a translation fellowship from the Yiddish Book Center in 2014 and 2016.

Laura Yaros works as a certified translator and has been an activist in the feminist, lesbian, and progressive Jewish movements for over forty years. She has been a community radio broadcaster for thirty-four years and airs a weekly show called *Matrix* in Montreal, Canada.

Saul Noam Zaritt is an assistant professor of Yiddish literature at Harvard University. He received his doctorate in Jewish literature from the Jewish Theological Seminary, and he is the founding editor of *In geveb: A Journal of Yiddish Studies*.

Barnett Zumoff is a medical doctor, a retired major general in the United States Air Force, former president of the Forward Association, and four-time president of the Workmen's Circle/Arbeter Ring. He has published twenty-one volumes of Yiddish literary translations.